The Cornish Captive

Nicola Pryce trained as a nurse at St Bartholomew's Hospital in London. She has always loved literature and completed an Open University degree in Humanities. She is a qualified adult literacy support volunteer and lives with her husband in the Blackdown Hills in Somerset. Together they sail the south coast of Cornwall in search of adventure.

The Cornish Captive

NICOLA PRYCE

CORVUS

Published in paperback in Great Britain in 2022 by Corvus,
an imprint of Atlantic Books Ltd.

1 3 5 7 9 10 8 6 4 2

A CIP catalogue record for this book is available from the British Library.

Paperback ISBN: 978 1 83895 459 8
E-book ISBN: 978 1 83895 460 4

Printed and bound by CPI Group (UK) Ltd, Croydon, CR0 4YY

Corvus
An imprint of Atlantic Books Ltd
Ormond House
26–27 Boswell Street
London
WC1N 3JZ

www.corvus-books.co.uk

For Clare

Family Tree

BODMIN

PENDRISSICK MADHOUSE

Madeleine Pelligrew	*Former Mistress of Pendenning Hall*
Rowan	*Servant girl*
Marcel Rablais	*French citizen*
Mr and Mrs George Gillis	*Proprietors of Pendrissick Madhouse*

TRAVELLERS ON THE STAGECOACH

Captain Pierre de la Croix	*French naval captain on parole*
Thomas Pearce	*Silk pedlar*

FOSSE

PENDENNING HALL

Previous owner Joshua Pelligrew (1745–1786)

Sir Charles Cavendish MP   m.   Lady April Montville
b.1743   b.1750

Celia	Charity	Georgina	Sarah	Charles
b.1773	b.1774	b.1780	b.1789	b.1791
|m.	|m.			
Edward Pendarvis b.1767	Frederick Carew b.1767			

Hugo Charity   Frederick Alexander
b.1795 b.1797   b.1795   b.1797

Jonathan Troon	*Steward*
Mrs Pumfrey	*Housekeeper*
Ella	*Maid*
Phillip Randall	*Previous steward*

COOMBE HOUSE

Eva Pengelly	*Mother of Rose Polcarrow*
Mrs Munroe	*Housekeeper and cook*
Samuel	*Butler and general servant*
Tamsin	*Housemaid*

Matthew Reith	*Attorney at law*
Alice Reith	*James Polcarrow's stepmother*
Oliver Jenkins	*Butcher*
Thomas Scantlebury	*Shipwright*
Reverend Bloomsdale	*Rector*

THE OLD FORGE

William Cotterell	*Engineer*
Elowyn Cotterell	*Dressmaker*
Eva Cotterell	*Daughter*
Billy Bosco	*Friend*

POLCARROW (Baronetcy created 1590)

Sir Francis m. 1) Elizabeth   2) Alice m. 2) Matthew
Polcarrow   Gorran   Polcarrow   Reith
b.1730 d.1782   b.1749 d.1770   b.1759   b.1755

James m. Rosehannon   Francis
b.1765   Pengelly   b.1781
                   b.1772

Elizabeth   Eloise   Amelia   Edward
b.1794   b.1796   b.1798   b.1799

Henderson   *Butler*

ADMIRAL HOUSE

Sir Alexander Pendarvis m. Marie St Bouchard-Boulay
            b.1743   b.1746

Captain Edward Pendarvis m. Celia Cavendish
            b.1767   b.1773

                Hugo   Charity
              b.1795   b.1797

I am not mad.
I am of sound mind.

I was born Madeleine Eugenia de Bourg
in the Commune of Saint-Malo.
My father is Jean-Baptist de Bourg.
My mother was Marie-Louise Dupont.
My brother is Joseph Emery de Bourg.

I am not mad.
I am of sound mind.

My husband was Joshua William Pelligrew,
Master of Pendenning Hall
in the County of Cornwall.

The King is George III.
William Pitt is First Minister.
The river through London is the Thames.
The river through Paris is La Seine.
Eggs can be made into soufflé,
omelettes and méringue.

I am not mad.
I am of sound mind . . .

Attrapez-les!

'Nothing, Citizen. No papers, names, addresses. I've searched everywhere.'

A heavy hand thumped the oak table. 'Search again.'

The man's voice faltered. 'The bread must be three days old . . . the milk in the jug's sour. There's evidence of hurried packing — wardrobes and drawers left open.'

Jacques Martin swung to face his subordinate, his face livid. 'I said, search again. They always leave something. Find me receipts . . . evidence of who they know. Names and addresses. Where they've been, where they shop.'

Early dawn filtered through the small casement, lighting the jumbled mess of overturned furniture, the drawers emptied of all cutlery and flung across the floor, the glasses smashed against the flagstones. Uplifted rugs lay strewn across the room, the wooden shutters hanging half-open. He had seen all this before. Slipping through his fingers. English spies, like silent snakes in long grass. But not these. He clenched his

3

fingers as if to grip the necks that would soon be his. 'Search the well. *Under* the bucket, not just in it.'

They would have left something. Some trail to follow.

Across the dunes, the sea glinted pink under the rising sun; a desolate, half-deserted farmhouse in a concealed sandy bay. Did they think him so stupid he would not find them? A steady stream of documents and ciphers smuggled to this uninhabited stretch to be secreted to London – organised by a man so elusive he could disappear in plain sight?

Royalist traitors. Snakes, the lot of them.

He watched his companion wind the bucket up from the well. His back hurt, the stiffness in his joints exacerbated by the cold dampness of the empty house. A glance in the mirror reflected his heavy stance, the physique of a sailor; a stocky, dark-haired man known for his ill-temper and ruthless methods of interrogation. First blackmail, then the threat of violence against their wives and children. Then the slow removal of fingers and ears. They always talked. He was not here by chance; evidence had mounted, and if they found nothing he would have the house watched.

Striding to the back door, he stood oblivious to the bird singing in the wind-swept tree. The dripping bucket was turned upside down with a shake of the head. His subordinate was showing fear, glancing anxiously across the courtyard. That was how it should be. All his men should fear him. How else could his network infiltrate every corner of England and Ireland? His methods worked because he instilled fear.

His agents placed in the very heart of London society – innkeepers, lawyers, servants, all passing him a steady stream of intelligence. Coffee shops, printing houses, spies in Edinburgh and Dublin: fishermen, sailors, men posing as *émigrés*; a direct line of communication stretching from Ireland, through Cornwall, to his headquarters in Brittany. Then straight up to Paris.

Three hours they had been searching: everything stripped bare, the floorboards prised up, the wooden panelling tapped for hollow spaces. Anger filled him, the unpalatable taste of being outwitted. Fury made him want to strike out. With no one to hit, his only outlet was the milk churn standing by the back door. Kicking it furiously, he scowled as it clattered across the cobbles. The top burst open and white milk frothed as it rolled towards the well.

His companion bent to dip his finger into the spilt milk. Tasting it without a grimace, he looked surprised. 'It's fresh, Citizen. Not sour. Must have been left this morning – yesterday at the earliest . . . *after* they'd gone.'

Like all good hunters, Jacques Martin remained stock-still, barely breathing, the telltale hairs on the back of his neck beginning to prickle. How many times had he told his men to *make the drop and leave*? Never wait. Never be seen together. Use the secret signs, the top button missing on a jacket, the left-hand tear in the hem of a coat. Never speak. No direct contact. Nothing to incriminate the person who is to pick up the package. He almost laughed it was so obvious – a man with a mule cart delivering milk!

'Search the contents.'

Another churn remained by the door. 'No, wait . . .' Instinctively, he knew it would be hidden in plain sight. He

5

took hold of the handles, shaking the churn vigorously. It was lighter, certainly not full of milk. With a deft flick of his wrist he reached for his knife and prised open the lid, a thrill of joy surging through him. His hand touched leather as he knew it would. 'As I said, they always leave something.'

The bag was hard to retrieve, stuffed firmly through the small opening, and his volley of oaths echoed across the cobbles. He was cursing more with pleasure than annoyance, the pleasure of the chase, the excitement of a find. The bag was of medium size, calf-skin with elaborate brass studs around the base. It would be empty, of course. They were always empty, until you ripped open the inner lining.

It was well stitched and hard to tear, his fingers fumbling as his smile broadened. Visceral gratification accompanied his rising anticipation. He was closing in. He would soon know their names and their contacts – and the traitors who shielded them.

A single letter lay folded behind the satin lining. Flinging down the bag, he held it to a shaft of sun striking the wall behind him. Addressed to *Citoyen Louis Le Blanc*, it was sealed with red wax, the writing neat and easily readable. A smile of contempt curled his thin lips. *Louis Le Blanc*. It was honestly laughable.

He broke the seal, his eyes sharpening at the name on the enclosed letter. *Madame Lefèvre*. His breath came sharp, his heart jolting. *Lefèvre*. So, his fear was justified. The man who once called himself *Arnaud Lefèvre* was still in charge of this den of spies. He had not seen that name for seven years – Arnaud Lefèvre had vanished and never been traced. Yet here was the name, *Lefèvre*. Not addressed to him, but to Madame Lefèvre. She must be his wife.

His pulse quickened, his hunter's instinct sharpening. His gut never lied. Only one man had outwitted him so completely – disappearing into thin air, always one step ahead. But not this time. Sweat covered his brow, his heart hammering. Slipping the point of his knife beneath the seal, he unfolded the letter, gripping it tighter when he saw it was in French.

The postmark was from Bodmin, the letter written in a different hand.

Bodmin Moor

Thursday 22nd May 1800

Dear Madame Lefèvre,

After seven years, I can joyfully inform you that I have found Madeleine Pelligrew. She is alive and is in better health than expected considering where she is, and to what terrible injustice she has been subjected.

As you suspected, she has been moved from madhouse to madhouse. Each time her name is changed and all trace of her captivity wiped from the records. Only by minute examination of the walls of these inhumane and terrible places have I managed to follow her. My search has taken many false turns, across many counties, and there have been times when my despondency convinced me I would never find her. Yet, every new place she entered, she scratched her name and date on the walls and that has been her saving.

Since finding her, I have followed your instructions. I have in my possession two forged doctor's letters certifying her as no longer insane, and I have enough money for a set of new clothes. I would rather spare you the conditions in which this poor woman has been held; suffice to say, I will do everything in my power to keep her safe and bring about her freedom.

I will return her to her brother in Saint-Malo. I need only your instructions.

Your humble servant,
Marcel Rablais

He knew to remain stony-faced. So, Madame Lefèvre was to help a madwoman held captive in a madhouse? He studied the letter again. *Bodmin Moor.* Names of his agents flooded his mind but one stood out from the rest. A smile broke on his lips and he turned away. The perfect agent in exactly the right place; and what was more, he was one of his best. It was so simple, it could have been child's play.

His blood was up, his smile hard to suppress. Madeleine Pelligrew would lead them to Madame Lefèvre, who would lead them straight to Arnaud Lefèvre. The irritating subordinate was staring at him with dog-like expectation, and Jacques Martin's scowl deepened.

'Nothing.' He added a volley of oaths for added realism. 'Nothing but a wasted journey. An *unsigned* letter warning them *they may have visitors.*' He allowed himself a sarcastic smile. 'I've wasted enough time. Get my horse. Remain here and watch the house. Any more milk deliveries and you're to follow *without* being seen. Report only to me. Is that understood?'

The young man nodded, a flicker of fear crossing his face as he stood to attention.

No one must know of this letter — *no one*. This callow insubordinate needed to be silenced. He would send someone tonight — someone whose loyalty he would test. There were plenty of young men lining up to be of service to the Mayor of Saint-Malo.

Mounting his mare, Jacques Martin's mind switched to more favourable pursuits. After sending his instructions to his agent in Bodmin, he would visit Madame Berthe. The thrill of the chase was always pleasurable, but a find like this left him insatiable. Soon, he would know everything about these illusive British spies — their names, the ship they used, their codes, their ciphers, and, most importantly, the people who shielded them.

He spurred on his horse. Royalist traitors. Snakes, the lot of them.

Liberté

Chapter One

'Draw the folly again – up on the hill, with the arches and steps.' Her eyes blinked back at me, far too large for her pale, pinched face. 'That's my favourite of all yer drawings.'

I shook my head. 'No, my love, you must learn to write. Start again . . . An *R*, like this, then *O* . . . then *W* . . . *A* . . . *N*. See how the letters form your name? *Rowan*. Hold the nail steady and start at the top. We've no time for drawing. Drawing is for times long passed.'

Long, long passed.

A shaft of sun squeezed through the gap in the barred window, the straw pallet pushed against the stone wall. Rowan scraped my carefully collected brick dust into a pile, smoothing it flat with her sore hands. Taking the rusty nail, her movements were slow, her fingers clasped, her tongue following every movement as she scratched the dirt. There it was again, the folly. Always the folly, and I rued the day I first drew it for her.

'Were you a *very* grand lady, Elizabeth?'

Tears pooled in my eyes. I hated them all, yet I loved this wisp of a girl. She had been sent to me – this thin, unschooled, dirty-faced, lank-haired, large-eyed, sweet angel – sent straight from heaven. My daughter's age, perhaps a year or two younger.

I knew my baby would be a girl – a true beauty, her father's spoiled darling, my constant and loving companion. She would have sung like a bird, played the harp like an angel.

Darling baby, did you think I'd left you? Hush, my love – crying so piteously. Here . . . let me rock you back to sleep. I clutched my shawl, cradling her in my arms. She must not wake, I must sing to her. My beloved child, warm and safe in my arms. *I'll sing you a lullaby, my darling – one my mother used to sing. It's your favourite – hush, my baby, do not wake. There . . . sleep soundly. You're safe.*

Rowan started backing away, a frightened look in those huge, dark eyes, and I smiled my farewell, hearing the lock turn as I resumed my lullaby. She always left when my daughter needed to sleep, but soon she would come back and we would take tea on the lawn below the terrace. I would order macaroons and wear my best straw bonnet – the one decked with blue ribbons. How Joshua loves that bonnet! I was wearing it when he proposed – so unromantic, as it turned out. He just turned to me and said, *How would you like to be Mistress of Pendenning Hall?* And I had answered, *I'd like that very much, thank you.*

It still makes me laugh. No, I must not laugh; it will wake the baby.

Friday 6th June 1800, 5 a.m.

The crow of the cockerel. By his call, I knew him to be very large, his comb full-blooded and red, wobbling as he stretches out his long neck. He would have a fine plume of glossy tail feathers and a puffed-up chest. He must be perching on the branch, just out of sight.

Half-an-inch gap was more than ever before – a whole slice of the outside world, the straw-strewn backyard, the grey stones of the granite barn opposite. Pressing my eye against the gap, I could see a gate, and a pool of slops glistening black in the moonlight. When the sun struck the pool, it turned murky grey. North facing, because shadows soon fell across the yard, and by midday the light dimmed. There he went again, so proud to herald the dawn.

You didn't wake me, my friend. The terrible itching did.

Half-an-inch's glimpse on the world was so much better than total darkness, far preferable to a cellar or an attic. Cellars bring rats, attics bring bats. Filthy farm outhouses may bring mice and lice, but at least I had Chanticleer.

Of course he's called Chanticleer, dearest husband! Remember the cockerels in Clos-Poulet? Yes, of course you do.

The nail had lost its sharp point but it worked well enough. Another small line added to the others – every day accounted for; every seventh day a line through the others, every fourth week a ring around it. Every twelfth month, an underscore. One year and forty weeks. In twelve weeks' time, they would move me again.

I must pinch away the lice before I scratch myself raw. The shaft of light would last just long enough for me to shake out my bedding and find the lice. Find them and kill them. Lice, both of them.

Charles Cavendish. Phillip Randall. Lice, to be squashed between my fingers.

Footsteps stomped across the yard, a shadow passing my small gap. The lock turned and the door was flung open. Mrs Gillis stood glaring at me, a pair of manacles gripped in her huge hands. 'Ye're to come with us.'

I fell to my knees, backing through the straw. 'Please. I've done nothing wrong. I've been no trouble.'

Rowan slipped silently behind her, tears filling her eyes. Mrs Gillis handed her the chains and shoved her towards me. 'Please . . . Elizabeth, please don't fight me,' Rowan whispered. 'If I don't do this, she'll call fer Mr Gillis . . . an' he's got a terrible fist on him. Please, let me do it.'

I shook her off, pulling away. 'I've done nothing . . . nothing.'

'But it's good, honest it is. There's a man come fer ye . . . he says he knows ye.'

I thought I would be sick. They were too early. I had another twelve weeks. 'He *doesn't* know me – they *never* know me. They just say they do, but they lie – all of them.' I had to make them understand. 'Let me stay, Mrs Gillis. Please, let me stay. I'm no bother. Don't let them take me.'

Her livid hue was visible in the dim light. Her scowl deepened and I cowered, though there was no place to hide. She had a fist on her as fierce as her husband's, her punch flooring me on several occasions, yet the thought of what might lie ahead was unbearable. I had Rowan, I had Chanticleer. I had rays of sunlight and shafts of moonlight.

Rowan reached for my wrists. 'Please, Elizabeth. Please ... it's for the best.'

I could not part from her. Not her. Not my angel from heaven. 'Don't let them take me,' I whispered. 'They keep me chained up ... sometimes they starve me. They beat me and tie my arms behind my back. Sometimes they make me sit all day in a freezing bath. I'm not mad. Tell them I'm of sound mind. Tell them I'm not who they say I am.'

Her voice caught, tears streaming down her cheeks. 'He looks kind ... honest he does. He says ye've been kept wrongly – he has a cart outside.'

'That's what they *all* say. They come all smiles and sweetness and say I'm to go home, but the minute I'm in the carriage they bind me. They chain me. They force fiery drinks down my throat. When I wake up I'm in another cell with another name. I'm *not* Elizabeth Cooper.'

'And her feet,' Mrs Gillis bellowed from the door.

'Here, please let me ...' Rowan clamped my feet.

Hands and feet, the chain heavy, the iron clasps cold against my wrists, the pain excruciating against the open wound on my ankle. I tried to pull back, forcing myself against the damp stone wall. Rather this pigpen than the unknown. Each time, the conditions grew worse. At first I had a bed with linen, a chair and table to dine at; I had tablecloths and goblets, even my own decanter of port. Then the steady decline into filth, each move affording more hardship, my *rescuer* offering the new proprietor less money, exaggerating my madness,

17

laughing at my delusions of grandeur. I was a French parlour maid, a trollop, not a fine lady. I was dangerous, a threat to others. My head was to be shaved, my fingernails kept short. Nothing sharp or I would have their eyes out.

'I heard them talkin',' Rowan whispered. 'The gentleman knows yer brother. He's got letters...'

'They all have letters – they all know my brother. Rowan, *I'm not mad*. Please, promise me... somehow go to the great house in Fosse and tell Lady Polcarrow that Charles Cavendish had my husband *killed*. Tell them the dredging deal was fraudulent... that my husband was *murdered*.'

Mrs Gillis stormed towards me, wrenching my arms as she heaved up the chain, and I stumbled forward. As light as a feather, she had no difficulty dragging me across the courtyard. At the door to the main house she hauled me to my feet, her thin lips pursing. 'Elizabeth Cooper, ye're to do as ye're told.'

'I'm not mad. I'm of sound mind. Please... call me by my correct name.'

A sharp slap stung my cheek. 'That's enough. Ye keep quiet, right? Not a word other than we treated ye well an' ye're grateful for all we've done fer ye.'

I nodded, taking a deep breath, knowing I must give them no grounds to prove insanity. Half-pulling, half-shoving, she led me along a dim passageway. Light filtered through a half-open door and she bent to undo the fetters round my ankles. Straightening with a whinge of pain, her bosom heaved, a wheeze in her cough. 'Not a word against us, ye understand? Not... one... single... word.'

I nodded, biting my lip, waiting to be ushered into the room. Early sunlight streamed through the small lattice window, the huge hunched figure of Mr Gillis sitting at his desk. A stranger was standing by the fireplace, but that was to be expected. They were always strangers, never the same man twice. Mrs Gillis poked me forward, her finger digging painfully into my lower back. The room was thick with tobacco smoke, the carpet and furnishings faded, the air foul. The stranger turned, a look of horror on his face.

'I am *not insane*,' I said, in my calmest manner. 'I am Madeleine Pelligrew, born Madeleine Eugenia de Bourg. My father is Jean-Baptist de Bourg. My mother was Marie-Louise Dupont. My brother is Joseph Emery de Bourg—'

She gagged me then, her shawl cutting off all further speech, squeezing even the chance to breathe. Each time I was more fragile, my strength starved from me. I was as weak as a kitten. A sparrow. They knew I had no strength to fight.

'Unhand her at once.' The stranger sounded furious. 'Draw up a chair. Allow this poor lady some dignity.' In the startled silence, his voice rose. 'Bring her some brandy.'

I could not speak. I could hardly breathe. Inside I was screaming, *No brandy. No brandy . . . the brandy will be drugged.*

Chapter Two

Refusing the drink, I stared back at the stranger. There was kindness in the brown eyes staring so intently back at me. Not the love I saw in Rowan's, but definite compassion. It turned to fury as he confronted Mr Gillis. 'Mrs Pelligrew needs a hot bath before she leaves.'

'Elizabeth Cooper has been placed in my care and will remain so, *until I hear otherwise.*' George Gillis stood up, his heavy frame leaning on his outstretched palms. He glanced at the pile of papers on the desk. 'I've been paid for two years. That's food and lodging and clothes – and funeral expenses *should it be necessary.* She's under doctor's orders to be retained for her own good and for the safety of others.'

'The safety of others? This frail woman who might blow over in a puff of wind! Really, sir, you astonish me.' He had a French accent. A definite French accent.

'Yes, Mr . . . What did you say your name was? Rabbly?'

'Marcel Rablais, at your service, madame.' He was addressing me, his eyes kind again. 'I'm a friend of your brother –

Monsieur Joseph de Bourg. I'm here to release you and take you safely home.'

In his fifties, medium height, he stood with command, his voice full of authority. His wig was brown; his jacket and trousers, once the finest cloth, looked worn. His boots were polished but badly scuffed, his manners formal as he bowed to introduce himself. Respectable, if slightly shabby. They were all respectable, only this time they had chosen to send a Frenchman and had decided to use my real name. Perhaps they thought it would make me go quietly.

'Don't let her size deceive you. A woman like her needs to be locked away from honest folk. She's a danger to society. She may look meek and fragile, but she lashes out.'

'I believe we would all lash out, *under the circumstances*, sir.'

Mr Gillis heaved his great bulk back into his chair, spreading the papers into a fan. 'You know the rules. In my capacity as a registered Keeper of the Insane, I cannot agree to transfer any of my inmates without the necessary authority. Nor can I enter into any discharge arrangements without the sworn statements of two doctors who have visited the person in question and have both, independently, ascertained her sanity. Which is never going to be the case, Mr Rabbly.'

A blackbird was singing on a branch outside the window, white blossom on the trees, the wild expanse of a purple moor in the distance. The air would be fragrant, scented with wild herbs. There would be fresh dew on the grass beneath my feet.

'Mrs Pelligrew, please have this . . .' Marcel Rablais handed me a handkerchief. I had no idea I was crying.

'And crying doesn't help. One minute crying, the next

21

shrieking like a fishwife. Then there's the laughing, and the constant talking to herself – and her demands for tea on the terrace. Or *sorbets*. Like we can just rustle up a *sorbet*.'

'It's not unusual for a lady to order sorbet.' Marcel Rablais bent to open the leather bag at his feet. Drawing out a slim case, he laid several sheets of paper on the desk. They were neatly written, with important-looking seals. They always were. 'I have, here, discharge letters of two eminent physicians who have both examined Elizabeth Cooper and declare her of sound mind. *Both* are on the board of the Commission for Visiting Madhouses, and I believe, sir, that when you've read these letters, you'll agree Elizabeth Cooper can be safely discharged into my care.'

Mr Gillis's eyes sharpened; he gave a nod to his wife to shut the door. Swooping forward, he studied the letters carefully. His voice turned gruff, all pretence of civility vanishing. '*When I visited the lady in question*...?' He stared at Marcel Rablais. 'We both know no doctors have been anywhere near Elizabeth Cooper... on neither April the thirteenth nor April the twenty-fourth.'

The blackbird was singing again, the sun glinting on the white blossom, just as it did in the orchards of my childhood. First the cherry blossom, then the pears and plums, then the apples my father turned into the finest cognac.

Of course I will come, Papa. I love to gather the apples...

They were staring intently. Why stare like that? I had done nothing.

'These letters are meaningless, Mr Rabbly. Once outside, she'll be brought straight back. Talking like that to people

22

who aren't there – cradling her shawl and singing to it as if it were a baby! The woman's clearly insane. You wait . . . she'll start shrieking there's a swarm of mice in her room, or a plague of insects crawling over her. Worse still, her laughter's like the baying of a wolf at full moon. You think I can even *consider* these false testimonials?'

I had no strength to fight; better to go willingly than be drugged and bound. Next, the purse would thump the table, the sovereigns carefully counted out. The seals may be different but the conversation that followed would be exactly the same.

The authority in Marcel Rablais's voice returned. 'I believe, Mr Gillis, that if you open your diary on those dates you *will* find these visits *did occur.*' He reached into his bag and pulled out a heavy purse.

Three guineas, four guineas, a further six shillings, each coin carefully tested and swept into his drawer before Mr Gillis turned back the pages and reached for his quill. Carefully matching the right name of the physician under the correct day, he blotted the ink and flicked the diary pages forward, his pen poised against the day's date. 'Discharged under the care of Mr Marcel Rablais?'

'No.' Marcel leaned forward. 'Discharged into the care of Madame Cécile Lefèvre.'

'Cécile Lefèvre?' A frown accompanied George Gillis's loud grunt. Opening the top drawer, his thick fingers fumbled through a pile of letters. He drew one out. 'We've had a letter from her, asking for the whereabouts of a certain *Madeleine Pelligrew.*'

My heart thumped, an agonising leap of hope.

Marcel Rablais leaned forward, taking the letter, reading it swiftly. 'I'll take this letter . . . In fact, I'll take *everything* you have on Mrs Pelligrew.' At the closing of the top drawer, he reached again for his purse, sliding another guinea across the desk and into Mr Gillis's sweaty palm. A curt nod of his head and the correspondence was in his hands. 'I'll inform Madame Lefèvre that our business is at an end. You'll retain the doctors' testimonies but nothing else. No trace of her must be found. Elizabeth Cooper is now under my care. Unchain her and see to it that she has a hot bath. I've brought clothes and a wig. Be quick. I'm in a hurry to remove her from this foul place.'

The water was tepid, the cloth rough against my chafed skin. Rowan dabbed the bruise developing on my cheek. Already, I could feel the lump where Mrs Gillis's ring had cut my lip. 'There now. 'Tis done. I'm sure it will fade; 'tis not too fearful.'

Tears streamed down my cheeks. I was wrong to hope. Marcel Rablais only knew my brother's name because I had told him when I entered the room. 'He's no different from the rest. Once in the cart, his ropes will appear. I've angered a powerful man, Rowan, and he'll never let me go — Charles Cavendish will never, ever, let me go.' I clutched the towel. 'Dearest love . . . remember that name . . . and remember *Lady Alice Polcarrow*. Promise me you'll get word to them. Somehow, send them word . . . Oh, if only I'd had time to teach you your letters.'

'He called you Madeleine Pelligrew. Is that really yer name?'

My legs were as thin as sticks, my skin scratched raw, my feet still filthy despite Rowan's scrubbing. 'He said I talk out loud . . . that I laugh like a baying wolf . . . that I hold conversations . . . and cradle a baby that isn't there. How can he say that?' I was cold now, beginning to shiver.

Her whisper sounded strained. 'Because ye do, Elizabeth . . . I mean, Madeleine. Not always, but very often . . . and it frightens me. One moment ye're with me, the next ye're far away.'

'In my thoughts, maybe. But do I talk?' She bit her lip. 'What do I say?'

She held up the rough towel, wrapping it round my shoulders. 'Ye talk to yer husband – ye ask him if he'd like to go swimming in the river. I hear ye before I come in. Ye're laughing and coaxing him, saying it's a perfect day for a swim.'

My heart froze. 'You think I'm mad, don't you?'

She dabbed my bald head, taking care not to dislodge my scabs. 'I don't know what to think. Ye're kind and ye're loving, and ye treat me so nice. I don't remember my mamm, nor hardly the woman who took me in. I've had no one treat me like ye do. I've grown to love ye, Elizabeth – I mean, Madeleine – and I'm that sad. That sad . . .'

I held her tightly, or perhaps she was holding me, clinging to each other with the wet towel between us. 'Come with me . . .' I whispered. 'Please, please . . . come with me.'

Her jaw dropped. 'What? Just leave this place? He'd never take me . . . they'd never let me go.'

'I shall insist. There are plenty more coins in that purse. If Marcel Rablais does know my brother . . . then he'll pay for you to come.'

A working woman's gown hung over the chair, rough and worn, with a ruby and cream underskirt, a ruby bodice. Beside it was a cream calico jacket and wig. The brown wig stank of grease, the curls too short. It looked severe, unwholesome, the exact opposite of the golden mane that used to foam around my shoulders.

'Are ye really a fine lady, from a grand house?'

I lifted my chin. 'My father is a wealthy landowner – a wine merchant in Saint-Malo. One summer, I caught the eye of a fine English gentleman with a grand estate. He adored me and I adored him. We were only wed a year. I was expecting his child—' I could no longer speak, my throat constricting as if I were choking, and I clutched her to me, my angel sent straight from heaven. 'Come with me . . . Promise me the moment I start talking to myself you'll stop me? Don't let me laugh . . . don't let me cradle my baby. I've tried so hard – so incredibly hard – to keep myself from madness. But what if they're right? What if I've lost my mind?'

She stood tall, straight backed, wiping her eyes with the corner of her apron. 'I won't let them think that. I'll look after ye. Every day, I'll be there for ye . . . and ye'll get better. Take me to yer beautiful home . . . show me the folly and the river where ye loved to bathe.'

But, my dearest, you love swimming! The sun's so warm and the water's a glorious blue. They've sighted porpoises in the river mouth . . .

She dabbed the towel against my face. 'Ye're doing it now,' she whispered. 'Talking about swimming.'

I stared at her as if a mist was lifting. 'Rowan . . . my husband *loved* swimming. He would never have drowned.'

26

Chapter Three

Bodmin Moor

Marcel Rablais flicked the reins, the cart jolting forward, and I clutched the seat, willing the pony to make haste. *Take us through the gates . . . get us through the gates.*

Rowan's hand gripped mine, both of us rigid, staring ahead. Numerous outbuildings clustered around the ancient granite house, grey, austere, the stench from the stagnant pool almost overwhelming. There were nine of us, she told me; some kept in the house, others in the cottages, three of us in the converted pigpens.

The gown hung from me, the jacket loose, the foul-smelling wig pressing painfully against my sores. I was too scared to breathe; petrified they would race after us and drag us back. In her Sunday clothes, Rowan looked no better than a waif, the sleeves of her blue serge dress too long and badly darned, the hem stained and fraying.

Bartering over Rowan had delayed us. Mr Gillis insisted on a further two guineas, claiming he had paid good money for the girl and was not to be cheated. Marcel Rablais had shaken

27

his head and offered no more than one guinea, but Mr Gillis was adamant and I had stood my ground; I would not leave without her. Marcel Rablais had remained courteous, finally agreeing I needed a maid. It was just that funds were short and we would have to economise.

No, my sweet darling . . . no need to economise. I'm going to spoil you . . .

Rowan slipped her finger to her lips. She shook her head and my stomach twisted. I must have been talking aloud. By the tight stretch of his shoulders, the strength and agility of his movements, Marcel Rabelais looked used to physical labour. The hands that counted out the coins and now held the reins were broad and browned by the sun. The nails were kept short and clean. Charles Cavendish always sent powerful men.

The breeze was fresh, verdant, filled with the scent of herbs and the smell of blossom. So pure, un-foetid, and I breathed deeply, a rush of dizziness making me feel light-headed. The cart was swaying, and I gripped the side. Rutted and steep in places, the path was rising out of the hidden dell. Geese pecked the grass in the orchard, sheep grazing the fields beyond. Once through the gates, I would find a way to escape. Before he reached for the rope to bind me. Before he sent Rowan on her way.

'We'll take the turnpike to Bodmin,' Marcel Rablais shouted as he urged the pony forward. 'It's about four miles once we've passed the lake.'

I began trembling, my skirt shaking. My gown was too hot, the sun beating down on my bonnet, making the lice on my head crawl. I could feel them scurrying around. What if they were cockroaches? They were under my dress, crawling over my legs. He called back, 'See that basket next to you? I've brought a flagon of beer and some strawberries. There's bread and cheese as I thought you'd be hungry. We'll stop at that tree.'

The rope would be hidden in the basket. He would bind me. The beer would be drugged. I must throw it from the cart – without a rope, he could not bind me. I reached over, undoing the leather buckles. *Strawberries.* Plump, juicy red strawberries.

'Madeleine, are you all right?'

I gulped for air, wiping the tears streaming down my cheeks, my sobs so violent they shook my body. No rope. No chain. No fetters, but strawberries. The cart stopped and Marcel Rablais jumped to the ground, holding out his hand to help me down. 'Madeleine . . . are you all right? May I call you Madeleine?'

I could only nod, a fresh burst of tears. 'Please do. I've waited long enough to hear my name.'

His face was stern, no laughter lines, but his eyes filled with compassion. His brow was furrowed, his wig brown, a strong, straight nose, with whiskery eyebrows flecked with grey. His cheeks looked paler in the daylight, deep lines etching the sides of his mouth. He reached for the basket, pointing to the lone tree. 'We'll sit in the shade over there.'

He had his back to me and I lifted my skirt. The cockroaches must be hiding, but the lice under my bonnet were still scurrying. The sheer brightness dazzled me, my eyes watering. Cupping one hand against my forehead, I took his arm and began treading the rough moorland. Fourteen years of no

29

grass. I wanted to fall to my knees and clutch it to me. Feel it, smell it, throw myself down and spread my fingers wide.

The vast purple moor stretched as far as I could see, a handful of trees blown sideways to their roots. Huge granite outcrops pierced the horizon, cattle grazing the rough grass. A blue lake lay glittering in the sunshine, and I stood breathless with wonder. I had forgotten how beautiful the world could be.

And you have robbed me of all this, Charles Cavendish.

Marcel laid out a cloth, pointing to a boulder that could act as our seat. Drawing out two pewter tankards he uncorked the beer. As if knowing I would refuse, he drank freely, wiping his mouth with the back of his hand before offering it to me, and I drank thirstily, greedily, unable to believe how delicious it tasted. Rowan sat beside me, refusing a drink but staring at the strawberries. One nod from me and we both reached for them, the juice running through our fingers and down our chins. Marcel handed me a napkin and I held it sobbing against my face.

'We've been searching for you...following false trails, retracing our steps. They've been meticulous in covering up your whereabouts. I had to force my way into so many hellholes, searching for signs that you were there – finding your name scratched on the walls of increasingly dismal places.'

'We?'

'First with your brother, then just me. At first, your brother believed all was well – that you were comfortably resettled. The rumours were that you'd remarried, but when he didn't hear anything from you, he came searching.'

I gazed across the vast moorland, anger burning my chest. 'How is my brother? Did he marry Emeline?'

'Yes. They have four children – two boys and two girls. The eldest is called Madeleine after you, the youngest, Marie, after your mother. Your father is . . . I'm so sorry to have to tell you . . . but your father died peacefully in his sleep after a short illness.'

I nodded. 'Who is Cécile Lefèvre?'

He glanced at Rowan. 'You can clear away the food now. Take the basket back to the cart and remain there.' His voice dropped, speaking in our mother tongue. 'I've not met Cécile Lefèvre, but I'm in close contact with her. She's a good friend of your brother and . . .' His eyes followed Rowan as she nuzzled the pony. 'You are aware our country is at war with Britain?'

'Rowan told me – but her knowledge is limited.'

'It's been seven years now. As you can imagine, travel between our two countries is severely restricted. I have false papers saying I'm from Guernsey, which is very helpful for those wishing to *leave* or *return* to France.' His eyes pierced mine, alert with hidden meaning.

I had not heard French spoken since my two sisters waved me goodbye at the quayside. Nine months later I heard of their sudden illness. Mother died, too, but Joshua had refused to let me go home, believing it was too great a risk to the baby I was carrying. 'Cécile Lefèvre asked you to find me?'

'No, your brother did. He uses her very efficient services. Cécile Lefèvre will see us safely back to France. I wrote to her, telling her I'd found you and I'm awaiting her instructions.

Until I hear otherwise, we'll go to the address on her letter to George Gillis.'

The beer had fortified me. 'Marcel . . . what if I'm not quite ready to leave England?'

His eyes widened. 'Not ready to leave? Madeleine, are you—'

He was going to say mad. I could see it in his eyes, that sudden flicker of panic. Or was it disappointment, or worse, anger? 'You think me a frail and broken woman who eats no better than an animal, who stinks despite my bath. Whose grip on sanity is slipping . . . but I wouldn't be here today if I had not harboured unfinished business. It's what kept me alive. Monsieur Rablais, I cannot leave England until that business is concluded.'

'Madeleine, I beg you . . .'

His voice had turned stern, his mouth tightening, and I matched it with my own, sounding stronger than I felt. 'I insist you take me to Pendenning Hall.'

'Please reconsider. I believe that to be very dangerous – foolish, even.'

'I'm going to Fosse, Monsieur Rablais, whether you take me or not.'

His frown vanished. For such a stern man, I saw the sudden watering of a tear. 'My dear lady, I *am* taking you to Fosse . . . but please, allow me to dissuade you against Pendenning Hall. It's too dangerous. What if you're recognised?'

I smiled at him, stifling a laugh. Relief, excitement, the sudden granting of all my prayers. He was taking me to Fosse, and he thought they might recognise me? It was too absurd, too funny not to laugh. He looked away and fear shot through me. What had George Gillis said? *Baying like a wolf in the moonlight.*

His arm was strong as he helped me back to the cart. 'We need to hurry if we're to catch the stagecoach from Bodmin.' Too strong. Too powerful, and I pulled myself free. 'Madeleine... please, dear lady. Do not fear me.'

Of course I feared him. I feared and hated all men. They lied, they cheated; not one of them could be trusted. I could trust only Rowan, my own, sweet Rowan.

'Marcel, from now on we will speak only English. I'll have nothing said that Rowan can't understand.' I hoped I sounded convincing. My stomach was churning, painful spasms shooting through me. 'And Rowan's not my maid – she's my adopted daughter... please treat her with more courtesy.'

If he was cross he hid it well, helping me up the crooked wooden step as if I were porcelain. He turned and frowned. Across the moor a man stood silhouetted against the sun. He was leading his mule but had stopped and was staring in our direction.

'We've no time to lose.' His voice was urgent, his lips clamping as he whipped the reins. The pony picked up speed and I fought my fear. He, too, must think Charles Cavendish was having the madhouse watched.

Chapter Four

We wound round rocky outcrops, skirting the reed-fringed lakes with water as blue as the sky. Coaches flew past us, throwing up stones and dust, sounding their horns, making me jump. Everything seemed so fast, everywhere so vast, and I gripped the seat. Rowan's hands remained clasped, her huge brown eyes alert for danger. She kept turning round, expecting the man with the mule to catch us up and drag us back. She had not been out of Pendrissick Madhouse for eight years: a captive like me.

Large black birds flew up as we approached, a bird of prey circling above us, and I closed my eyes, trying to remember their names. Endless days and sleepless nights desperate to keep my wits alive – naming all the birds I knew, the flowers I had planted, the trees in the parkland. Ravens . . . crows . . . no, choughs – and that large bird was a buzzard. My mind felt fragile, like the charred remains of paper rescued from the fire. The edges were curled and blackened, but the centre? The centre was still readable.

Charles Cavendish had not reduced me so low that I could not exact my revenge.

A downhill slope, the road now winding through a verdant valley. Wheat fields rippled beside us, the scent of blossom drifting from the orchards, and I breathed in the sweet memories of my childhood – my sisters chasing me, flowers in their hair, bedraggled posies clutched in their hands.

'That's Bodmin,' Marcel called over his shoulder.

A huge granite building dominated one end of the town, a church with a tall tower the other. Slowing to allow a mule pack to pass, our pony plodded between men and women carrying baskets on their heads. The streets were crowded, vendors shouting their wares. Women were shopping; attorneys from the law court, wearing white wigs and formal gowns, strode along the even pavements. Tradesmen were wheeling trolleys laden with fruit and vegetables, oxen pulling carts. A coach thundered past, and I gripped Rowan's hand.

Everything seemed too loud, too fast, horses foaming at the mouth, drivers cursing. A bugle sounded and I jumped in fear. Our pony shied and Marcel pulled hard on the reins. 'That's the post coach – you'll find a lot has changed.' His scowl deepened. 'Sorry to frighten you like that. They topple carts rather than stop. We're nearly at the inn. I imagine all this is rather overwhelming.'

'Everything's so busy. All these people . . .'

'It'll be a lot busier than you remember. I'll get you settled and return this cart. I'll buy the tickets to Fosse – I won't take long. I'll order us something to eat first.'

'People are staring at me.'

'No. It's just we're blocking the road.' He whipped the reins and the pony walked on.

I did indeed feel overwhelmed, a dull ache building behind my eyes. Malt from the brewery, fresh dung from the stables. A strong smell of varnish – surely that was lilac? The street was narrowing, the buildings crowding over us, but I was grateful for the shade. Freshly baked bread lay stacked in shop windows, the aroma of coffee drifting across the street. Rowan gripped the seat, her eyes widening.

'See all that meat on the block? There's barrows and barrows of vegetables. Look at them ladies' clothes . . . look at them bonnets.'

The dilapidated houses I remembered had been replaced by fine red-brick buildings with large windows, elaborate porticos and iron railings. Pavements had been laid, the dirt and mud now a cobbled marketplace. A bank, a grand hotel, another bank. I remembered it as a long, winding street with houses in poor repair and muddy alleys reaching down to the river, but it seemed so prosperous now, almost double in size.

'I'll pull up behind that coach.'

My heart lurched. The inn looked smarter, certainly, but instantly recognisable as the inn I had stayed at with my beloved husband.

The White Hart, my dearest . . . I stopped at Rowan's shake of the head. 'The White Hart,' I said again. 'My dearest, I've been here before.'

She smiled and a blush burned my cheeks. Marcel helped us from the cart, throwing his leather bag over his shoulder as he opened the heavy door to the inn. The fug of tobacco was instantly unpleasant. Smoke stung my eyes, my head throbbing as if it would burst.

'Through here . . . I'll secure us a private chamber.'

The taproom was crammed to bursting, loud voices pounding in my ears. Bags and portmanteaus were piled next to the unlit fire. Women wearing heavy capes were scolding children, buttoning them up to the neck, pulling down their hats. Men in travelling jackets stood sucking at pipes, holding ale against their chests as they kept one eye on the clock.

The landlord nodded, his bald head gleaming, his sturdy finger pointing to the stairs, and I fought to breathe. Sweat trickled down my back and I stood suddenly rigid. It was not sweat, it was the lice. No, cockroaches. Swarms of them crawling beneath my clothes.

'Get this off.' I started pulling the tight buttons on my jacket, twisting them, tugging them. They were under my wig as well. Hundreds of them crawling up my thighs. My arms were gripped, strong arms forcing me up the stairs.

'In here . . . she'll be all right. It's cooler here. Help her, Rowan. Do everything you can to make her comfortable. I've ordered hot water and something to eat. I'll be back as soon as I can.'

I hardly heard them, but stood ripping off my heavy jacket, fumbling with the drawstring of my bodice. 'They're biting me. Get this off.' At last my gown was off and I stood clawing at my skin, furiously scratching as they swarmed all over me.

'Madeleine, stop. Stop and look . . . *There's nothing there.*' Rowan's urgent voice pierced my panic. 'Ye're itching because ye're sore . . . but there's *no insects* swarming over you. I promise. Ye only *think* there is.'

My head was pounding. I was shivering, my skin bleeding. A knock sounded on the door, a stout woman backing slowly into the room. A towel hung from her arm, a basin of steaming water held in her hands. 'There now. Here's soap an' a towel—' She saw me and froze, backing quickly away. 'I'll bring yer meal when it's ready.'

I stood staring at my reflection – my scabby scalp, the thinness of my legs, the bones jutting out below my neck. Those I knew about, but the hollow, pinched face with such a look of hatred? I stared in horror. Lines radiated from my eyes, a deep furrow in my forehead. A downward clamp to my mouth, my cracked lips smudged with sores. I had no eyebrows, my cheeks pitted with scars and red blotches. I was like one of the hideous gargoyles on my cottage in the garden of Pendenning Hall.

'This water's lovely an' hot. Let me help wash your face . . .' Rowan handed me a warm sponge and I pressed it against my burning cheeks.

'Rowan . . .' I could not to speak for sobbing. 'Would you ask the landlady for some lanolin . . . or balm . . . or goose fat – anything to soothe the rawness. And I need gauze for under my wig . . . and bandages for my ankles.' At the door, I called after her. 'And lace to sew on to my bonnet. Ask the landlady to send for black lace.' She nodded and left and I stared into the mirror once more.

This is what you've brought me to, Sir Charles Cavendish. My lips were moving, my eyes hardening.

Marcel smiled. 'The lace is beautiful and I'm glad you're pleased with it. You deserve so much more than I can give you, but I must speak candidly . . . my funds are limited. Our expenses have already stretched what little I have.' The remains of the cold luncheon lay on the table. Smiling at Rowan, he handed her a cloth. 'We'll take the rest with us.'

I reached for one last slice of Madeira cake. The chicken was finished, the ham and bread demolished. Marcel had held back, watching with pleasure as Rowan and I piled our plates. My fingers were still covered in grease, and a wave of shame reddened my cheeks. I had not even thought to use a fork or cut anything with a knife.

'The coach leaves in half an hour. I've told the landlord my name is Barnard and you're my sister-in-law. That should cover our tracks.'

Cramp gripped my stomach. 'You think we're being followed?'

'Merely a precaution — force of habit.' He opened his bag. 'I have with me a change of clothes — a jacket for me and a travelling cloak for you. We'll not be recognised. Unfortunately, I've nothing for Rowan.'

'Will we stay with Cécile Lefèvre tonight?'

'I'll seek her out the moment we arrive in Fosse. I'll leave you both at an inn.' His voice dropped. 'I must have your promise that you'll say nothing to anyone. Call me Uncle, or François, and *never* speak our real names.' His face softened. 'I don't mean to frighten you. It's just a necessary precaution.'

Through the leaded casement, the town seemed quieter, the steady stream of carts lessening. A leat ran down one side of the road, a stone trough and a pump with an elaborate iron handle on the other. Children were herding geese on the common, a man leading a pig on the end of a strap. Urchin boys sat rolling dice on the street, a crowd gathering outside the inn. Porters were wheeling barrows to carry the luggage. The last time I had stood at this window I had been a beautiful bride of twenty, wearing a sumptuous silk gown and fine jewels, the husband I adored whispering of his urgent need of me.

Pursing my balmed lips, I pulled down the black lace. 'Here's the coach, now.'

Chapter Five

On the stagecoach to Fosse, 4 p.m.

The driver finished checking the horses and signed the
paper the ostler held out.

'My finest horses – they'll give ye no trouble.'

The luggage stowed, the passengers stepped up to take
their seats and Marcel handed me into the coach. Rowan
slipped beside me and Marcel would have squeezed next to
us, but for the guard's sudden shout: 'Sir, place that bag atop,
if you please.'

Marcel shook his head. 'My bag stays with me. There's
plenty of room.'

Placing his bag on the seat, he searched the crowd from
behind the curtain. 'Eleven miles to Fosse and I'm told the
road's clear. They believe we'll make good progress.'

A whistle blew, and the guard pointed to the rear. 'Hurry,
sir. Just one seat on the back.'

With no one else entering the coach, Marcel swung himself
next to Rowan. 'Looks like we're going to be by ourselves,
but with these prices, I'm not surprised. I'll sit next to you,

Rowan, if I may? I prefer to face forward.' His smile turned to a frown, then a grimace. 'Oh, we're to have company, after all.'

Two men stood ready to alight, both tall and carrying bags. The whistle blew again. 'Be quick if ye will. I'll stack those at the back. Hand me yer bags.'

Both men shook their heads. The tallest stepped into the coach, ducking his head to avoid the roof. 'The contents of my bag is too precious. I must cradle it . . .' He took his seat in front of me, his smile apologetic. The younger man's beery breath filled the coach. He smelled of the taproom, of sweat and stale smoke; his hands, with their bitten nails, clasped his huge leather bag.

Marcel shifted his knees and the man fell heavily on to the seat opposite. 'There's little room for that bag . . .'

The man gripped it firmly. 'It's my livelihood, sir. Lose this bag and my family will starve. Can't trust it in any other hands – certainly not badly stowed at the last minute. If it fell off, they wouldn't even notice.' His voice was rough, his accent strange, his eyes drooping beneath heavy lids. An unkempt man in his early thirties, his smile as false as every other man who lied and cheated. He was no doubt calculating our worth, summing up whether he could sell us something we neither wanted nor needed.

'It seems none of us can trust our bags to others.' The first man edged sideways to give him more room. 'Please, put it between us on the seat. It will not inconvenience me . . .'

I watched him through my lace. He was tall, broad-shouldered, with a dignity in his movements. Beneath his broad hat, hints of grey flecked his black hair. He sat upright and correct, the capes of his travelling coat immediately commanding. Yet it was not the sight of him politely not staring at my lace that made my heart jump, nor his instinctive gesture to pull down the blind so that the sun no longer shone in my face. It was the sound of his voice. The very essence of my childhood.

Another whistle, a loud shout to stand clear, and we lurched forward, picking up speed. The houses and shops were soon left behind, the wheels clattering over the cobbles, thundering along the open road. Scattered cottages gave way to cultivated fields, and I could feel my pulse quickening. We were going too fast, we would topple over. The jolting was uncomfortable, the swaying making me ill. I was burning up under the heavy cloak. The yarrow balm had brought relief, but the itching was coming back. *There are no insects.* Rowan had been most insistent, she would never lie.

I tried to fight my sense of suffocation, yet it was taking hold. The coach was too cramped, too enclosed. Like the black cupboard they forced me into after the freezing baths they said would cure me. I could feel the tight jacket binding my arms, the blackness of the cupboard. Hours cramped in pain, refusing to cry out.

There are no insects. I'm not in the cupboard.

A slight nudge and Rowan pointed to her lips. A fierce blush burned my cheeks and I put my fingers against my lace. I must stop myself from speaking. Swaying with the coach, Marcel addressed the gentleman opposite me. 'You are French, sir?'

The man nodded. 'Captain Pierre de la Croix.' He glanced at me. 'At your service.'

'On parole? You're wearing a naval uniform beneath your coat.'

A dignified nod, a slight smile. 'Indeed, sir. One of two hundred on parole in Bodmin.'

'How long have you been here?' I caught the catch in Marcel's voice.

This time a shrug of his broad shoulders. 'Four years. I served my country for twenty years. I was *Capitaine de Vaisseau* . . . my ship, *Espère*, a sixty-four third-rate ship of the line with a complement of five hundred men.' His smile was polite, his eyes returning to the fields rushing past us.

'You were captured?'

'Unfortunately so. Captured off Guadeloupe and taken prisoner. And yes, I do rue the day most terribly. The people of Bodmin are very kind and I have respectable lodgings.' He tapped the bag on his lap. 'My days are fruitfully employed, but my nights are filled with regret. I'd rather be serving my country than mending instruments. And you, sir?'

'A glasswright...a glass blower – from Guernsey. Travelling with my widowed sister-in-law and her daughter. They've a notion to visit the sea.' Hardly concealed animosity had crept into his tone. 'You're allowed to visit a harbour? I thought you were to stay within one mile of your parole town?'

'Blimey, I'm with a coachload of Frenchies!' The young man raised his flagon and drank heavily, wiping his mouth with his grubby sleeve. 'You look harmless enough but you never can tell.' He was heavily bearded, his oily hair spilling over the collar of his dusty jacket. 'Thomas Pearce, vendor to the finest silk merchant in Bristol.' He smiled at Captain de la Croix. '*At your service.*'

Given the swaying of the carriage, Pierre de la Croix bowed as best he could. 'Your servant, sir.'

'Guernsey is *not* France, nor are we French.' Marcel's sharp reply matched his frown. He stared at the mud on Thomas Pearce's damp boots. 'We, too, are at war with France. We've not been conquered – not yet, at least. You're a pedlar? Have you just crossed the moor on a mule?'

Thomas Pearce shrugged his round shoulders. 'I'm not a *pedlar*, I carry sample books...hundreds of swatches of the finest silks from our shop in Bristol. I don't *peddle* silk, I take orders from bespoke tailors and dressmakers. And if I had a mule, I'd not pay through the nose for this journey!' He laughed. 'But there's money to be made in Fosse.'

We were thundering along a road that had no ruts. Everything was different, people's clothes, the lack of men's wigs, the speed at which we were travelling. Thomas Pearce had fallen asleep, slumped against the window with his mouth wide open. *Dirty fingernails like that don't handle silk.* I felt my lips move but no one seemed to hear. Marcel reached for his pipe, sucking furiously until the bowl caught, and sickly sweet fumes filled the air. My stomach twisted, my nausea building. I had eaten like a ravenous dog, yet the chicken had been too rich and lay heavily in my stomach.

Pierre de la Croix must have seen me grip my hands. Standing up, he pulled the window down and a blast of fresh air brought momentary relief. Through my lace, I saw his mouth harden as Marcel blew more smoke towards me. My stomach was cramping, my mouth watering. His pipe finished, Marcel pointed it at the bag Captain de la Croix sat cradling on his knee. 'You mend instruments? You've a clock in there?'

'Not a clock...' A smile curled the corners of his wide mouth. He had a kind face, a small scar on his right cheek, bushy black eyebrows and a strong nose. A handsome man in his prime, yet there was a glimmer of sadness in the blue eyes staring so wistfully at the passing fields.

'A compass, then?'

'A chronometer... one I've mended for Admiral Sir Alexander Pendarvis. I'm bringing it to him.' He smiled, as if he knew what Marcel Rablais would say next.

'A French frigate captain hurtling towards the coast with a chronometer? He trusts you, does he, this admiral?'

Captain de la Croix smiled again, a slight shrug. 'I'm fortunate that he does. Mending such instruments has become my greatest pleasure.' Though he spoke to Marcel, he kept glancing at me. 'Madame, a little more air? With your permission, I could lower the window further?'

My stomach was churning, my nausea increasing. Clasping my mouth, I tried to quell the rising bile. 'Tell the coachman to stop.'

Pierre de la Croix handed his bag to Rowan and pulled down the window. Leaning out as far as he could, he held on to his hat and shouted up at the drivers. 'Stop the coach. STOP. Can you hear me? I said stop. The lady's ill. We need to stop.'

The coach raced on, the answering voice hardly audible above the thundering hooves. 'Never stop... don't stop nowhere...'

'But you must... I implore you. The lady is ill. She's in great discomfort.'

'Next stop Lostwithiel... nothin' we can do about it.'

He pulled back from the window and held out his hand, his grip firm, yet gentle, his strong hands supporting me as I quickly rose. Pulling back my cloak, he helped me reach out of the window as far as I could. The bile was rising, pain churning my stomach. I should have stayed with thin gruel, not eaten great handfuls of greasy chicken.

'I've got you – you can't fall out.'

I hardly heard him. I was groaning, moaning, retching, once, twice, the contents of my stomach flying in the wind. I thought it was over and clutched the window, resting my forehead against my hands. 'I'm so sorry...' But more was coming, the pit of my stomach once again turning inside out. Angry shouts sounded from the back of the coach but I could not help it. I felt as weak as a kitten and sank back on to my seat, my cheeks burning with shame.

He had seen my face when I lifted my lace, yet he was handing me his handkerchief, no sign of disgust in his gentle eyes. I wiped the vomit from my chin, weeping too much to thank him. Marcel stretched his hand towards me. 'Dearest sister... are you recovered?'

I nodded. 'I'm so sorry. The window... and the door...'

Pierre de la Croix took his bag back from Rowan. 'It is of *no* consequence, madame.' He settled back into his seat. 'It happens all the time. I'm afraid it's not like travelling with your own coach and horses.'

I stared at him through my lace, twisting his handkerchief between my fingers. He had spoken with respect, as if he thought I was used to my own coach. Such kindness was almost overwhelming.

He glanced at the splattered window. 'Nothing a few buckets of water won't swill off. If I'm right, we're nearly at Lostwithiel – the Globe Inn is where we stop.'

Chapter Six

The church spire became lost behind the row of town-houses. The horn sounded and we pulled to a hasty stop. Whistles filled the air, shouts echoing across the cobbles. Several passengers alighted, with an equal number scrambling aboard to take their seats. A pie seller held up his tray and was clearly disappointed when Marcel and Thomas Pearce shook their heads.

It was not a change of horses, merely a quick stop. Water swashed against the side of the coach and a boy wiped the window. Beneath the eaves of the stable, the drivers stretched and eased their backs, drinking thirstily from pewter tankards. Captain de la Croix opened his fob watch. 'Six o'clock. We'll be in Fosse before eight.'

The whistle blew and we started forward, crossing the river by way of the arched Tudor bridge.

We should go by river, my dearest love . . . we can float up on the tide and watch the birds.

49

'Yes, we must,' whispered Rowan, her arm slipping through mine.

Every jolt was bringing me closer to Pendenning Hall. Joshua had not drowned: he had been held under the shallow water by powerful hands. I had been inconsolable, screaming and wailing from the shock of finding him. I told them what I had seen, yet no one listened. Not one of them watching as I pointed to the heavy footprints and the signs of struggle. Not one believing I had seen Phillip Randall walk away from the very site just ten minutes before.

The last time I crossed this ancient bridge I had been gagged and bound, the coach heading to Bristol — to Maddison's Madhouse, where I was to be *cured* of my rantings. Cured of the blood pouring from my womb. *Two days* after my husband had drowned. *Two days*. I was to be cured of my writhing and screaming, cured of my wild accusations that Sir Charles Cavendish had falsified a dredging company and murdered my husband to lay claim to our estate. Two eminent physicians had certified me mad from grief, and Sir Charles Cavendish had been *reluctantly persuaded* that medical confinement was in my best interests.

I glimpsed the river through the trees. The water glimmered in the fading light, eerie white branches trailing along the waterline. Driftwood lay on the glistening banks, a rowing boat pulling against its rope. The tide must be going out. Wading birds were picking through the mud, searching the seaweed strewn along the shore. Three miles further and we would reach the ford, the gatehouse and the long drive up to Pendenning Hall.

Every night in captivity, I ventured on silent walks, following the paths round the park, keeping the details alive in my mind – the bend in the road, the cobbled steps, the pole to show the depth of the water. It was almost exactly as I remembered it. Captain de la Croix eased his back. 'Not far now. Are you staying at an inn, or maybe you have family in Fosse?'

Through the fading light, I caught the mistrust in Marcel's glance. He had been polite throughout the journey, but had long since discouraged conversation. 'We'll be staying at an inn – our decision to come was on doctor's orders. My sister-in-law's been ill. He believes sea air will do her good.'

'May I recommend the Ferry Inn? The food is varied and the rooms very comfortable.'

'Thank you.' Marcel's reply cut across the coach.

Thomas Pearce's heavy breathing had accompanied our journey. He woke as we started descending the hill and I watched the narrow road I journeyed every night. The church tower would soon be in sight, the wharfs, the wide river mouth with masts bobbing in the waves. Ships would be lying at anchor, some crowding the harbour, others beached on the tiny fringe on the opposite shore. I would soon breathe the air I had so longed to breathe.

We clattered to a stop. Dogs were barking, whistles sounding. Turning sharply under an arch, a well-lit courtyard opened up, with lanterns burning on either side of the inn door. Stable boys ran to take hold of the horses, the innkeeper rushing out, wiping his hands on his long white apron. 'Ye've made good time. Come this way. There's porters to take yer bags . . . take care now. This way . . .'

He pulled down the steps, opening the door to a blast of wind, and I stood on the cobbles inhaling deeply. I felt giddy, light-headed, the salty air filling my lungs as if they might burst. The air of my childhood, in France maybe; the sea air that had made me strong and courageous. The same coastal breeze that accompanied our childhood walks, the wind I had run against, the sea I had swum in. Already I felt stronger. Marcel came to my side.

'That was a terrible ordeal. Are you all right? I'll soon get you comfortable.' His voice dropped. 'Wait . . . we must make the captain believe we have more luggage.'

Captain de la Croix bowed his farewell. 'A pleasant stay to you. I hope you enjoy your trip up the river – there are some very fine walks to be had. Goodnight, madame . . . Monsieur Barnard . . . mademoiselle. Your servant.'

Marcel watched him go, his voice turning cold. 'We need to stay clear of him.'

His words chilled me. 'Why?'

His brows clamped. 'There's so much I need to explain, but for the moment my only thought is to get you comfortable.' He ushered Rowan closer. 'Remember we're from *Guernsey*. Even then, we may not be safe.'

Rowan's cheeks turned white against her black curls. 'Marcel, are we in danger?' I whispered.

'Not from those who want you silenced, but we are in very great danger from our fellow compatriots. Careful . . . stand back.'

The unharnessed horses were being led to the stable, the grooms scurrying for hay and water. The coach was to be washed, the wheels scrubbed, the stable lads standing ready with buckets and brushes. Most of the travellers had departed, the innkeeper standing by the door waiting to welcome us. Throwing his bag over his shoulder, Marcel shook his head, indicating we were to stay elsewhere.

'How can our compatriots endanger us?' I whispered.

He ushered us forward, his arms firm, his boots making no sound as he crossed to the shadows on the other side. 'Let that silk pedlar get ahead of us – the less we see of him the better. And we won't be staying at the Ferry Inn under the scrutiny of Captain de la Croix. We'll go to the quayside – I need to watch the harbour.'

The muddy banks of the river lay to our left. Everything looked different, yet still achingly familiar. Smart houses lined the road, prosperous-looking red-brick buildings with large windows and lanterns burning on either side of grand doors. The wooden posts along the river were new, a row of boats swinging from iron chains. Yet some things could never change – the freshness of the air, the smell of seaweed, the cockles hanging from the posts, the woodsmoke drifting on the breeze.

'Are your shoes comfortable?'

I shook my head. 'They're too big . . . I'll need to stuff them with more paper.'

The familiar stench of rotting fish made me want to laugh. I felt joyous, like coming back to life, experiencing everything with the same pleasure as I did as a young bride. The same ferry was crossing the river, the same lights shining across the river in Porthruan. In the gathering dusk, a moon hung above the town, its silver light glimmering on the water, and tears flooded my cheeks. I never thought I would see this river again; even in my wildest dreams, I had never expected to come back.

Crowds were gathered on the quayside, sailors standing round braziers, the smell of grilled fish wafting across the stones. The breeze seemed to be blowing away the years of confusion. *Pilchards run in July, mackerel's caught in winter.* The door to the Ship Inn was open and laughter echoed across the street. 'I'll see you settled, then leave you – but only for a short while.'

My confidence was misplaced. Walking among people seemed utterly petrifying. 'Surely you can't think of leaving us in a place like this?'

He reached for his purse. 'I can't stretch to a private room – unless it's absolutely necessary. I'll go to the address I've been given...' He stopped, glancing round. 'It's best you know as little as possible. Just, I very much hope we sleep in more comfortable surroundings tonight.'

A group of sailors lurched past, their stares at Rowan sending shivers through me. 'Please secure us a private room.'

'I need to pay in advance and it's money we don't have. There'll be a room round the back where you'll be safe . . . off the streets and under the watchful eye of the landlord. I need to find Cécile Lefèvre. If I'm unsuccessful, I'll come back and secure a room. I'll be no more than an hour.'

Rowan had never been off the moor. She gripped my hand, close beside me as we entered the crowded taproom. The air was thick with tobacco, the pungent stink of tallow stinging my eyes. Marcel led us into a back room with a heavily beamed ceiling and lamps burning against the wall. The un-curtained window reflected the backs of men huddled round crowded tables. 'There . . . we're in luck. Two chairs at that table.'

He pulled out one of the chairs. 'Don't go anywhere . . . I need to know you're safe. You're Marie Barnard, my sister-in-law, and you, Rowan, are Hélène. You're from St Peter's Port in Guernsey and you're here for your health. Don't speak to anyone – the less interest we excite, the better. I'll get you some wine.'

We watched him weave his way through the tables and return with a flagon of wine and three glasses. Pouring the wine, he finished his without drawing breath. The wine was watered down, mixed with loganberry juice, and I had to stop myself from smiling. Fourteen years of captivity, and I could still recognise adulterated wine. 'Why fear men like Captain de la Croix?' I whispered.

'We must fear everyone – especially officers like Captain de la Croix. I haven't time to explain as I would wish. But while you've been so cruelly held, our country's been rent in two. Those who support the new tyranny grow rich and fat and those of us who hold fast to honour and integrity must hide our true beliefs. It's either that or be slaughtered as a traitor.'

I stared back at him. 'Then what Rowan's told me is true? The King and Queen *have* been beheaded and the aristocrats that support them . . ?' I clasped my hands against my lace. 'What of my brother? We're not the *wealthiest*, but we are aristocrats.'

'Your brother's played his cards well. He's persuaded the

mayor to give him a position of trust. By day he administers the town – handing out fines and petty punishments, imprisoning those who smuggle or cheat. He keeps Saint-Malo under firm order and those who watch him see a man intent on upholding the new regime. But by night he hides and ensures safe passage to those who flee for their lives – helping men and women obtain important documents vital to our friends in London. Do I make myself clear?'

The room was spinning, I felt suddenly faint. 'He helps British spies?'

Marcel had been watching the door, glancing constantly round the tables. He refilled his glass. 'We're part of a secret network – all of us Royalist to our core. We've sworn to serve our country – serve and *save* the country we love. We bring vital communication to and from the British government. Madame Lefèvre is one of us.'

'And Captain de la Croix?'

His face hardened. 'When France declared war on Britain, officers in our navy who remained loyal to the King joined forces with British ships. They fought alongside the British, *against* the new Republic. But they were sought, hounded, stripped of their rank. Many were rounded up, found guilty and guillotined. Most emphatically, not a single one was promoted *Capitaine de Vaisseau*.' He seemed to spit out the words. 'Promotion to such heights is only for those whose loyalty to the Republic remains unquestionable.' He glanced at Rowan. 'Don't be scared, sweet girl. I just need to warn you.'

He lowered his voice. 'We believe a Republican spy is based in Bodmin and we've long suspected him of being an officer

56

on parole. Captain de la Croix has the ear of a British admiral and is well placed to pass on information. That's why we cannot, and must not, trust him.'

Rowan waited until he was through the door. She grasped my hand, her eyes terrified. 'I don't want to go to France...' she whispered.

Chapter Seven

The wine was making my head swim. There were too many people, the tables too full; too much noise, the clatter of forks adding to the raised voices and shouts for ale. There was no air to breathe, the thick tobacco smoke suffocating. Rowan's flushed cheeks deepened to scarlet. 'I'm that uncomfortable. I have to find the privy.'

I nodded. 'We'll go together – I don't feel well. It's the noise – my head is splitting.'

Men were staring at us, their elbows digging into their companions, a corresponding rise of their eyebrows. I had not been incarcerated so long I did not know what we appeared to be. Three hours must have passed. Even the wenches seemed to be losing patience with us – without so much as a farthing, we could not order food. We rose to go and I gripped the table. The heat, my hunger, the wine, the loud voices; everything was confounding my senses and making me dizzy.

Rowan held my elbow. 'I don't like their stares,' she

whispered, helping me navigate the tables. 'I don't think it's safe to stay longer.'

The privy was in a red-brick building, and Rowan hopped from foot to foot while another woman went first. 'Why don't we wait outside the inn?' She glanced up at the moon. 'Where can he be? He said an hour, yet it must be gone eleven. I'm that hungry.'

The privy used, we started pushing our way back through the sailors crowding the taproom. A ship must have docked and orders were being shouted, brimming tankards passing from one hand to another. The crush was unbearable, men knocking against us. One trod on my shoe and pain shot through me.

'Hold my hand, Madeleine. Ye'll be all right.'

I hardly heard her. There were too many people, pain piercing my ears. Clutching my bonnet I forced myself forward, but even more men were crushing through the door, pushing us back. My gown felt like a furnace, sweat dripping down my back. I felt cramped, hot, my heart thumping. Like the black cupboard all over again. Not sweat, but insects. I could feel them crawling under my wig, running up my thighs. I needed to rip my jacket from me, get the hideous clothes off. Cockroaches biting me. The room spinning, blurring.

I felt strong arms around me. I was being lifted up, a voice calling. 'Make room... make room. Excuse me, sir... make room. Landlord, I need your best chamber.' Hurried strides rushed me up the stairs. Marcel had come just in time.

I tore at my jacket. 'Get this off... get this gown off...' I started fumbling with my bonnet strings. 'They're biting me . . . BITING ME . . .' The ribbons undone, I flung off my hat and ripped off my wig. The gauze came away and the itching stopped.

Rowan's voice was urgent. 'There's no insects . . . honest . . . no insects.'

I felt myself lowered gently into a chair. 'I could feel them biting me. Where have you been, Marcel?'

A mirror was on the table and I glanced at my reflection – the broken veins on my cheeks, my wild, bulging eyes. Blood was seeping from the sores on my bald head, weals where I had scratched my neck. A flash of blue at the door caught my attention.

'Who's that?' I could hardly breathe. Someone was talking to Rowan on the other side of the door. She was nodding, smiling, shutting the door, and my stomach wrenched. 'Who was that, Rowan?'

Her voice was strong, her eyes defiant. 'It was Captain de la Croix. He's going to order hot water and a bowl of *nutritious* broth – whatever that is. He's paying fer the room and he won't have ye say no.'

The gargoyle in the mirror was crying, tears streaming down her gaunt face. A hideous mockery of a once beautiful woman. 'He saw me . . . like this?'

She stood behind me, a slight lift to her chin. 'He saw a lady in need.'

'We can't possibly—'

'We can! Honest we can. He's honourable . . . a real gentleman.' A note of steel crept into her voice. 'I don't care what Marcel Rablais says. I know true concern when I see it.'

I held her stare. No man could be trusted. All men lied and cheated. 'We'll make sure Marcel pays him back.'

Rowan shrugged her shoulders. '*If* Marcel comes back. What if they've caught him?'

The room was simply furnished: a heavy counterpane on the bed, two chairs standing against the peeling wallpaper. The washstand held a jug and basin, the table littered with the remains of our meal. The floorboards were scuffed, the rug worn and fraying. The lamp was tallow but glowed brightly, the velvet curtains fringed with heavy gold brocade.

Every part of me ached. My joints felt on fire, my skin burning. With balm on my sores, I sank back in the chair, my feet in a bowl of hot water. Warmth radiated through me. I had not eaten so well in fourteen years. Captain de la Croix had ordered chicken broth and egg custard for me; a pie, bread and cheese, and a large plate of apple dumplings for Rowan. Tiredness was creeping over me, a sense of absolute exhaustion. The church bell chimed – eleven thirty, and still no sign of Marcel Rablais.

I must have fallen asleep. A knock woke me, Rowan rushing to open the door.

The landlady bustled past her. 'That's good – ye've eaten everything. That's what I like to see.' She stood back, hands on her hips, smiling at my feet still in the water. 'If ye're not done with that, I'll come back fer it.'

'No . . . I'm finished. Thank you so much . . . and the broth was delicious . . . everything is perfect.'

Her wispy hair seemed determined to escape her mobcap. Her sleeves were rolled to the elbow, the laces on her bodice on the point of bursting. Even the creases on her wrists had creases. 'Shall I get ye something else? Only Captain Pierre insists ye must have everything ye want.'

I glanced at Rowan. 'You know Captain de la Croix?'

'Lord love him! That's why I know to treat ye right. He's not one for bringin' women into our rooms.'

My stomach twisted. 'Please understand . . . we're not like that. I'm waiting for my brother-in-law. He has all my money. I . . . I can't think what's keeping him.'

She stopped, a shrug to her shoulders. 'Yer brother-in-law? Look, I'm not one to pry, an' I don't tattle – not if I want to keep our business, which I do, as it's a good business – but it's very late and how I see it, is this: ye've had a narrow escape. Now, ye've no money *at all*?'

'My brother-in-law *is* coming back . . . he *will* pay. I can't think why he's taking so long. Please don't think . . .' I glanced at Rowan. 'Please don't think . . .'

I must breathe, I must not panic. Rowan reached for the dirty dishes, swiftly piling them on to the tray. 'I can work fer ye. I can do anything . . . scrub floors . . . clean the grates. I can wash pots . . . prepare vegetables . . . make the beds . . . do the laundry. Only please . . . may we stay?'

Her large eyes looked distraught in the candlelight. The landlady took her hands, turning them over, holding them to the lamplight. Red, raw hands, hardly soothed by the balm she had applied to my skin. 'Ye're used to hard work, I can see that . . . an' I believe ye to be a good girl.' She smiled a toothy smile. 'Ye must be that proud of yer daughter. I'd give ye both work if I could, but I've no need fer anyone.'

She kept Rowan's hands between hers. 'But I can tell ye one thing: they're hiring up at the Hall. They asked me fer recommendations an' ye can say I sent ye. Mrs Bolitho – got that? Ye'll have to be up at five, mind. The cart leaves at five thirty.'

It was as if a bolt shot through me. I could hardly breathe. 'Which hall?'

'Pendenning Hall – it's three miles distant. Other side of the river. The family are returning an' they need to shake out the dust sheets. There's been neither sight nor sound of them fer two years an' the house needs waking up. They want maids . . . grooms . . . cooks.'

'We'd like to be considered . . .' I had to keep my voice steady. I must stay composed, yet I could sense I was about to giggle. A surge of laughter was rising in me. Madness. I must fight this madness.

Rowan was smiling. 'Please, Mrs Bolitho . . . put our names down. My mother's Marie Barnard and I'm Hélène. We can be at the cart for five thirty. Where does it leave?'

Mrs Bolitho's chins wobbled as she nodded her approval. 'From the slip opposite the Ferry Inn. There's no list, just tell them I sent you. Be sharp, mind. There's plenty wanting that work.'

'Will they pay by the day?'

'Yes, my love.'

Rowan's smile would have melted ice. 'Then ye shall have my earnings every evening.'

I clasped my hand over my mouth. One minute wanting to laugh, the next wanting to cry.

We settled beneath the covers, the sheets rough, smelling of woodsmoke. 'Who's that?' Another knock on the door and Rowan slipped from the bed, clutching the cover around her. 'Who is it?' Hearing only a muffled answer, she turned the key, opening the door a fraction.

'It's Marcel.' His candle cast shadows on the wall behind him. 'I'm so sorry to leave you like that – but for the kindness of the landlord! May I come in?'

I pulled the blanket from the bed, crossing the room to stand by Rowan. 'Where have you been? Did you find Cécile Lefèvre?'

He looked drawn, suddenly shivering, and in the darkness I saw his boots were wet. So, too, his trousers and jacket. The door closed behind him. 'The address is merely a disused linhay on the cliffs towards the cove. No one was there so I took my chance.'

He took off his jacket, reaching for a towel to wipe his face. 'We've a way of signalling. There's usually someone watching – to await any signals – so I gave the signal. I can see why they use the linhay. It's on high ground before the path dips and is visible for miles. We only signal twice, then we must hide.'

A small puddle was forming on the floorboards beneath him. He pulled off his boots, emptying each into the jug on the washstand. 'I was just turning back to secure your room when

I saw a returning flash. It was the signal I was expecting, but on the other side of the river.'

'In Porthruan? How could you be sure?'

'The night's so clear – almost as bright as day. I needed to see it repeated, so I hid near the linhay willing them to flash a second time. I saw it again and ran to the quayside but the last ferry had just crossed and there was no one to take me – no boat I could use. I had to swim.'

'You *swam* the river?'

He nodded. 'I tried to find my bearings and waited where I thought the lamp had been swung. Yet there was nothing.'

'Maybe they were watching you, not knowing if you were one of them. Have they seen you before?'

He looked drawn, the lines on his face deeper in the candlelight. 'I'm sorry, may I?' He pulled off his wig and ran the towel over his soft grey hair. 'No. We never meet. We just leave messages. I was searching for a hiding place where they'd leave their instructions. But there was nothing. I must have mistaken a chance flash for a signal. When I returned the river was full – the wind had freshened and the waves were considerable, so I followed the river upstream to where it narrows and I swam back.'

Without his wig he looked older, his short hair forming a grey halo over his scalp, and tears pricked my eyes. Joshua would have been his age now, maybe a bit younger. He would have been fifty-five and have grey hair just like that. 'You're soaked. Have you eaten? You must get out of these wet clothes.'

'They've given me a room, though they're not well pleased.

How did you manage to persuade them to let you have this room?' He must have caught the glance between us. He held up the candle. 'What is it, Madeleine? Have they overcharged you? What tariff did they say?'

I felt gripped with fear. The same fear I felt when all men questioned me: the sudden pounding in my chest, the acid burn in my stomach. If he was cross now, he would be furious at the truth. Rowan stepped forward, leading me back to bed. 'We don't know the price,' she said softly. 'The landlady didn't tell us — but I'm sure she hasn't overcharged. She seems a nice lady.'

I took courage from her strength. 'You must get dry, Marcel. Thank you . . . for everything . . . we can talk tomorrow.'

After he had gone Rowan locked the door and jumped into the bed. She tucked the bedsheets back in place, plumping up the pillow. 'He can't stop us,' she whispered. 'He'll be asleep when we get on that cart.'

Chapter Eight

A gentle sea breeze, a chorus of birds in the trees behind the house; a slight chill in the air, no sound of seagulls, just the songbirds, the calls of the cockerels, the sheep bleating on the other side of the river. A handful of women were hurrying ahead of us, the tide not yet turning, and I breathed in the smell of dried seaweed. The air smelled so fresh. A child of the sea, I had run barefoot along our sandy beach, the salt air making me strong. Now I was as fragile as a sparrow, every bone in my body aching, my joints and movements painfully stiff. My mind seemed muddled, my thoughts elusive. I had to concentrate, control my hatred of Charles Cavendish. Yet the sea air would strengthen me, I would get better.

'There... over there. Looks a bit crowded.' Rowan ran ahead, pushing her way towards a horse and cart. A stout man was holding a piece of paper, women telling him their names, pleading for him to allow them a seat on the cart.

He shook his head. 'Ten on the cart. No more.'

He turned away but Rowan clasped her hands, her eyes

desperate. 'Mrs Bolitho sent us specially. We've a *reference*. Mamm and me are good workers – Mrs Bolitho sent us specially. Please, sir . . . please . . .'

'Mrs Bolitho? Ye've a reference?'

She nodded vigorously and he indicated the cart. Scrabbling up as fast as we could we squeezed on, ignoring the glares of the women around us. I gripped my hands under my cloak. They would not recognise me at the Hall even without my bonnet and lace, but even so, I pulled it lower. I did not want anyone gaping at my disfigured lips and the blood blisters on my cheeks. Two young women were to sit on the driver's seat, another four permitted to walk behind. 'That's all fer today. I'll be back Monday. Day after that, they'll be hiring groomsmen – tell that to yer menfolk.'

We pulled away, watching the stooped shoulders of the retreating women as they walked back along the river. A man was watching us from the ferry slipway and my heart jolted. He was waving, bowing an elaborate greeting, his unkempt hair falling across his face – Thomas Pearce, the silk pedlar from the stagecoach, staring at me with a knowing smile.

Horrible man . . . a man with no morals . . . a thief if ever I saw one.

Our fellow passengers stared in astonishment and Rowan gripped my hand. 'Yes, and very lucky we are to be rid of him.' She smiled at their sea of faces. 'I'm Hélène, and this is my mother, Marie.'

There was no further conversation, just drawn expressions and pursed lips, and I watched the familiar riverbank. The road turned, the wheels splashing through the ford. I could barely breathe as we began the achingly familiar journey up the long drive. The trees would soon part and we would see the cattle, the sheep, the oaks my husband had planted. We would see my favourite spot where we had sat on Turkish rugs to drink fine wine from crystal glasses.

The huge folly rose above us and Rowan stared transfixed, a stillness in her face I had not seen before. She said nothing but stared back at it, keeping it in sight until we came to a stop. The back of the house, not the front. I hardly recognised the vast array of outhouses, the storerooms, the red-brick stables and imposing coach house with its huge clock tower dominating the courtyard. Fire burned within me, flames of hatred threatening my composure. I had always been driven to the front entrance with its magnificent fountain and grand portico; taken everywhere in a fine coach, Joshua's four perfectly matched greys the envy of his London friends. Not that I liked horses or had ever chosen to ride one. Horses, like men, were never to be trusted.

Herded like sheep, a maid ushered us through the back door and along a corridor to the servants' hall. Waiting in line, the women tidied their hair and straightened their skirts, and I searched the maze of doors. Rooms led left and right – the kitchens, the pantry, the scullery; the laundry room, the ironing room, the butler's pantry, the cold store – rooms I had never visited. The pounding in my chest was unbearable, resentment making me light-headed. Rowan slipped her hand through my arm. 'We're to be seen by the housekeeper, Mrs Pumfrey – *and* the steward.'

Soon I would stand face to face with Phillip Randall, Sir

Charles's steward – the man who had murdered my husband. They were sitting behind a large table and I forced myself to look. 'But he's not Phillip Randall.'

The woman in front turned round. 'Randall's dead.' There was venom in her voice. 'Lynched, an' a good job, too. The man was evil.'

'Lynched . . . who by?'

'Vagrants . . . four years back, or more. He whipped them too many times so they strung him up. His body was found in the river. Mr Troon's steward now.'

Anger shot through me, the ground seeming to slip beneath me. I felt winded, my chest crushed. Phillip Randall would never stand trial for my husband's murder. We reached the huge table and I tried to breathe. A stern-looking, middle-aged man dressed in a jacket and green tweed waistcoat was staring down at a ledger. His white shirt was linen, his necktie held in place with an enamel pin. His brown hair was short, a pair of glasses perched on the end of his nose. He already looked displeased, but when he saw my veil his mouth tightened.

I held out the reference Rowan had thought to make me write. 'Mrs Bolitho sent us . . . I've good references.'

The housekeeper was in her early forties, her gown navy blue, her hair fastened tightly beneath a lace mobcap. Though dressed severely, there was a rare kindness in her look, as if she was more used to smiling than frowning. 'We need maids with *strength*, Mrs Barnard. I believe you've wasted your time. Your daughter may be of some use to me, but not you.'

I tried to copy the way Rowan spoke. 'My daughter's able

to beat a carpet an' take down hangings. But . . . if ye read the letter, I believe it tells ye I'm good with books. Mrs Bolitho sent me on account of the library.'

Mr Troon read the carefully worded reference I had re-written several times. His eyebrows rose and he passed it to Mrs Pumfrey. Her look sharpened. 'Your husband was a book binder?'

'Yes . . . he restored damaged books. We went all over grand houses cleaning an' seeing to the books. People think dusting's all that's needed, but dust don't show up the jiggers, or the damage done by silvers. We've seen whole books lost, yet they look fine on the outside.'

'The library here is very well cared for.'

'Indeed, Mr Troon, I'm sure that's the case. But my husband taught me to look for what others don't think to look for. It's not just keeping the sun off and dusting with clean cloths . . . or getting the spacing right to allow air to circulate. Ye need goose feathers and hog's hair brushes to find jigger dust. We've seen whole parchments destroyed on the inside with no damage to the outside. Once, we found a last will an' testament so badly destroyed, it couldn't be used.'

Despite my fear, I wanted to giggle. Jiggers were what I called the insects that bit me in the night. Maybe I had lost my reason? The enormity of what I was doing terrified me, so why want to laugh? Fourteen years planning my revenge, and I might ruin my chances by *baying like a wolf*.

Mrs Pumfrey glanced at Mr Troon. 'You're an educated woman?' I heard her ask.

'No, Mrs Pumfrey. I don't read nor write. It's the pages

an' bindings I look at. But that don't make me stupid. I love books an' I wish with all my heart I could read and write.' I wiped my eyes with my sleeve, my borrowed accent rather more convincing than I had expected. 'My husband was a good man – he loved his books – but he weren't good with money. We need the work – Hélène an' me . . . we're hard workers. I'm begging ye, please.'

A nod from Mrs Pumfrey and Mr Troon wrote our names in his ledger, swinging the page round for us to make our mark. I knew to sign it with a shaky cross and Rowan followed my example. Mrs Pumfrey pointed Rowan to a group of girls about her age. 'I take it you're thirteen? We'll hire you for two weeks in the first instance. Prove you're hardworking and respectable and we'll keep you on. Join them . . . over there. You'll have a room upstairs and a half-day off every other Sunday.'

She pointed me to the group of older women. 'The rest of you will be hired by the day. From six to six with two meals a day. I expect you to work hard but not on an empty stomach. You'll get ninepence a day and you're out at the first sign of trouble.'

Mr Troon closed the ledger, staring at me over the rim of his glasses. 'You're to come with me. What will you need?'

'A goose-wing feather, hog's hair brush, saddle soap . . . a pail of warm water . . . soft linen cloth . . . an' a small bowl for drowning the jiggers and silvers. A magnifying glass . . . an' most important: burned roach-allum and flowers of brimstone.' He looked unconvinced. 'That's to get grease spots off the pages.'

Rowan came to my side. 'She means to give me a bed...
take me on proper,' she whispered. 'I don't mind...but I'll
miss ye terribly.'

'Maybe just for one night?' I looked round, frightened I
might be heard. 'You could ask about Phillip Randall? Just one
night?'

'What about ye? Will ye be all right?'

I nodded, though the thought of being without her filled
me with dread. Mrs Pumfrey pointed her back to her group.
'You're to start upstairs and work down *room by room*. All
bed hangings and blankets to be stripped and shook from
the windows... pillows to be beat, carded, and if necessary
remade with pure feathers. Every mattress needs checking –
some might need re-stuffing with fresh hair.' She paused. 'Let
me warn you now – you'll be searched at the end of the day
and if anything's found you'll be had for theft.'

Her voice followed us as Mr Troon led me down the
corridor. 'All walls and ceilings to be swept with feather
brushes... the wainscoting's to be wiped with hot soapy
water and dried with a *clean* cloth. All carpets to be taken out
and beat. If they're too heavy, they're to be hand-brushed with
stiff brushes dipped in soft water. Grease and stains are to be
rubbed with fuller's earth...'

Mr Troon's large strides were leaving me behind and I
hurried behind him, weaving between a group of footmen
carrying ladders. Everywhere was commotion, instructions
echoing down the corridor. 'Silverware's to be taken to the
butler's pantry. Under-maids to carry the buckets of water
upstairs. Fireplaces first. Then the wardrobes.'

I only knew the vast rooms we had lived and entertained in; a bride of twenty, I had taken everything for granted, but these back corridors were unfamiliar, a maze of passages and stairs I never knew existed. Mr Troon opened a door and sudden recognition tore my heart. I felt giddy, needing to steady myself against the wall.

The hall with its familiar sweeping staircase and huge front door lay before me, the marble floor exactly how I remembered it. The same mahogany sideboard with its huge china vase; the table with claw feet and silver tray for letters. Dust sheets were being removed from the longcase clock and I looked round, expecting to see my portrait. Instead, the smirking face of Charles Cavendish confronted me and bile rose in my throat. Flames scorched my chest. *A little rest, my dear, with doctors to cure you of your grief.*

A footman was halfway up a ladder, cleaning the vast gold frame of the man who had incarcerated me without a backward glance. One look at those pinprick eyes and I wanted to climb the ladder and claw them out. Scratch at him. Rip him to pieces. Expensively attired in formal wig and silk clothes, he stood with my beloved Pendenning Hall behind him, and I stared at the greed in his eyes, the self-satisfied gloat that had haunted me for the last fourteen years. Mr Troon was waiting by the library door and I breathed deeply. *I'm not mad — not insane. I'm justifiably enraged — as anyone would be in my situation.*

The dining-room door was open and an icy hand gripped my heart. My portrait had been moved and I stared at the beautiful woman with blonde hair curling under her large straw bonnet. She was smiling back at me with joy in her heart, and tears stung my eyes. I was about to tell Joshua that another heart was beating within me.

'Mrs Barnard? In here, if you please.'

Pain cut me like a knife. I stood in the doorway hardly able to speak. 'This doesn't smell good. The room's musty – the air's stale. Open the windows but keep those end blinds down.'

He opened the French windows and the gentle sea breeze blew across the terrace, filling the room with the scent of honeysuckle. The leather chairs were still under dust sheets, a soot-stained canvas across the marble fireplace. In the corner, Joshua's writing desk lay covered with a heavy blanket, and I forced the hatred from my voice.

'I ought not start until the fire's swept.'

Chapter Nine

He shrugged. 'Start anyway. I'll get the fireplace swept and cleaned. There'll be no soot or dust on the books. Do you suggest I have the shelves fumigated?'

I walked slowly round the room, sweeping my finger across the top of the books. 'I do, Mr Troon. Silverfish are rarely seen but there's no doubt they're here – doing untold damage. Fumigate the shelves an' take up the carpets to beat out the eggs. You'll have to take down the drapes an' beat them, too. The book bindings may look sound, but silvers an' jiggers eat the glue . . . whole books can fall apart.'

I pushed the steps along the rows of books, looking up at the top shelves. 'I'll do these first, then the other side away from the fireplace.'

These were Joshua's library steps, imported especially from Italy – upholstered in the finest Italian leather and delicately inlaid with gold. Mr Troon hurried from the room and I gripped the polished wood. I had underestimated the pain of being here, feeling Joshua in the room, hearing his voice.

I could see him smiling at me, holding open a book by the French window, showing me etchings of French monasteries. Most of the books had been here when his father bought the house, but these shelves contained his books and I clutched one to my heart.

Everything interested him – Roman statues, fine paintings, bone china, not just the wine that had brought him such wealth. His father had established the business and Joshua had sourced the finest wines – Madeira, port, the superior wines from Papa's vineyards. His visits had grown increasingly frequent, lasting long enough for Joshua to court me. *You must know my regard has long deepened to the sincerest love.*

He was enraptured. Twenty years my senior, he was a slave to the joyous girl who wanted nothing more than to spread her wings. He wanted to take me to Paris and the opera, the London season, yet I had never left Pendenning Hall. There was so much he had planned. I could see him standing by the fireplace smiling back at me. *China clay's been discovered on Polcarrow land and I'm going to build a new quay to load the ships.*

It was as if he was there, holding out his hands to me. *All I need do is dredge the river deep enough.* I shut my eyes, feeling him fold his arms around me. He was going to form a partnership with the man who owned a creek – an old retainer of the Polcarrows who was willing to embark on the scheme. *We'll charge harbour fees.* I could feel him kiss my forehead, his passion rising. *A small expense, but we'll reap huge rewards.*

He would sit me on his knee so I could turn the pages of his catalogue. *What would you like next, little songbird? Let me spoil you*. I fought my tears. The sun was glinting on the lake and I breathed deeply. This was not where I needed to be. I needed to search Sir Charles's study. Four shelves were cleaned but the metal taste in my mouth was back. I put my finger to my lips. My gums were bleeding, my handkerchief insufficient to stop the flow. I felt dizzy, my head spinning.

'Are you all right, Mrs Barnard?'

I had not heard him come in. 'Slight dizziness, Mr Troon ... that's all.' The truth was I could hardly move, my joints so stiff I could barely climb the ladder. 'Maybe ... I should stop until you've swept the chimney?'

He nodded. 'There's a cart leaving shortly. I'll give you half pay. Come back on Monday when the chimney's swept.'

I gathered up my feathers, my handkerchief to my lips. 'Thank you, sir. Will you tell my daughter I'm coming back?'

In Fosse, the river mouth stretched before us. 'Take it careful. Let me help ye.'

The cart driver pulled the horse to a stop and helped me alight. I had no strength, walking painfully back to the inn, missing Rowan more than I could imagine. Laboured breathing followed me up the stairs and I turned to see Mrs Bolitho holding out a key. 'Yer brother-in-law's below. He's not happy. I didn't tell him where ye were. Took ye on, did she?'

I took the key she held out. 'I can't thank you enough. Here, I've got sixpence for the room.'

My own key. In my hand. I could lock and unlock the door as often as need be. I sat hunched on the bed, trying not to laugh. My lips were moving as I held the bloodied handkerchief to my mouth. The day's exertion had proved far harder than I had expected. I felt torn to a shred, wanting only to rest. Pouring water from the jug, I washed my face, soothing fresh balm on to my lips and scalp. A bowl of oranges lay on the table and I ate two, the juice stinging my lips as I licked it from my fingers. Marcel Rablais was so good to me.

He was sitting in the corner of the crowded back room, smoke curling from his pipe. He looked angry and I immediately saw why. Thomas Pearce rose and left him, staring back at me as he made his way around the tables. Marcel Rablais pulled out the newly vacated chair. 'I only know where you've been because Thomas Pearce told me. Why didn't you tell me last night, Madeleine?' He looked more hurt than cross.

'Because you would have stopped me. I needed to see my old house.' I sounded calmer than I felt.

He wiped the sweat from his brow. 'I want to keep you safe, Madeleine, that's all.'

'I'm sorry . . . I'm not what you expected – I'm even a disappointment. All these years of searching for me and you see me as ungrateful.'

He looked tired, dark circles beneath his eyes. He was badly shaven, a cut beneath his chin, his wig unbrushed, dust on his sleeves. He shook his head as if addressing a wayward child, even a slight smile. 'I knew when I followed your defiant scratchings on the walls that you were a determined lady. I like that . . .'

His eyes darted across the room, his voice dropping. 'But I'd advise you not to go to Pendenning again. Where's Rowan?'

'They took her on. We can get her any time. Marcel . . . I need to go back.'

A flash of exasperation, a shrug of his shoulders. 'I think that's very unwise, though I can't deny the money will be useful.'

'There's still no message?'

'The linhay's the only address we have. It must be their point of contact. I've searched it thoroughly – I've been observing it all day. I'll sleep there tonight.'

'Have you so little money you can't afford a room?'

He drew a deep breath. 'It's not that. I think I'm being watched.' Despite the heat in the room, I felt a sudden chill. 'There are those desperate to find Cécile Lefèvre. Maybe I'm being too cautious – maybe it's Cécile Lefèvre's men who are watching me. She has to decide if we're here to flush her out or contact her.' He glanced at a man sitting in the corner and his mouth tightened. 'He was on the coach with us. He's been watching me. If he's one of us, I'll know soon enough – we've ways of making ourselves known. I'll recognise anyone Cécile Lefèvre sends, but I have to say this delay is unusual.'

The man turned his back and resumed his meal. 'You think something's wrong?' I asked.

There was fear in his eyes, a new tension. 'Something's very wrong. There's a chance we may have been infiltrated. Oh no, he's coming back!'

Thomas Pearce was weaving his way between the tables, holding a large tray. Sliding it in front of us, he removed three goblets of wine and a plate of congealed food. Wiping his nose with his hand, he drew up a chair. 'Eel pie and mashed potatoes for you, Mrs Barnard. A hard day, was it?' He thrust a knife and fork towards me.

Despite my loathing for the man, my hunger was too great to refuse. 'I hope you've put this on our account?'

Some attempt had been made to clean his nails. He was wearing a new shirt, though not a clean one. He reeked of tobacco; several particles of food were trapped in his unkempt beard. Stains darkened his waistcoat, mud on his boots. He tossed back his greasy black hair. 'I've a much better plan.'

I looked at Marcel, as if I had missed something.

Thomas Pearce finished his drink, wiping his mouth on his sleeve. 'It's all right, I won't squeal. Only it's a bit obvious. I've a much better plan. It's foolproof – and it *works*. You win, I win. And no one gets hanged.'

The eel pie churned my stomach. Marcel's mouth tightened. 'I don't know what you're implying. Leave us, please – what you're thinking is misjudged. Please, leave us.'

A smile, a nod. Disregarding Marcel's wishes, Thomas Pearce reached into his bag and brought out a leather sample book. Flipping through the pages of silk squares, his voice dropped to a whisper. 'I've seen it so often. You get rooms you can't afford, so you seek a position as a maid in a grand house. After a few days of hard labour you gain their trust. You watch and wait and when the time's right you steal a candlestick ... or a silver bowl ... linen or fine lace ... anything you can slip beneath your bodice.'

I stared, aghast. 'How dare you?'

'A gentlewoman fallen on hard times? A concerned *brother-in-law* ... a child left to see which pieces might or might not be missed? It's not exactly original. It's been done too many times. The housekeeper will search you – and you'll hang.'

He turned the last page. Pressed against the back cover was a square purse made of silk and fastened with a row of pearl buttons. He opened each button slowly, in such a way I knew the contents would not be buttons. 'You need *ingenuity*,' he whispered. 'You need to draw them in. Make them come to you.'

We were too incredulous to speak. The silk purse was open just wide enough for us to glimpse a nest of diamonds, some the size of thumbnails.

'That's got your attention.' He opened the bag wider. 'Diamonds from the alluvial deposits of Arraial do Tijuco – that's Brazil to you and me. Well, two of them are, the rest are crystals taken from rather a fine chandelier that just *happened* to break.' His moustache curled as he smiled. 'It's worked before. The tailors tell me who's got money – who the greedy ones are. The unscrupulous ones. Then we send along a grieving widow whose husband's just been murdered by the natives on the land he owns on the confluence of the river where they sift for diamonds.'

His weasel voice was soft and utterly terrifying. 'She tells them she's desperate to sell the land. She's too scared to go back. She has certificates to prove ownership . . . the bill of sale . . . everything. It gets them every time.'

'How dare you!' Marcel's eyes were blazing. 'Leave us. Never speak to us again.'

Thomas Pearce held my gaze. I saw Charles Cavendish's

portrait in my mind and a rush of hatred burned my cheeks. Why not steal from the man who had stolen everything from me? False diamond deposits in place of a false dredging company?

I shook my head. It was not his money I wanted, but his ruin. I wanted his disgrace. I wanted Charles Cavendish behind bars.

Chapter Ten

Sunday 8th June 1800, 9 a.m.

The church bells chimed nine. I felt as if I had been beaten with a stick. 'I've brought yer breakfast.' Mrs Bolitho bustled in with a tray laden with porridge and a large jug of freshly squeezed juice. 'Captain Pierre says I'm to give ye as much freshly squeezed lemon and lime as I can.' She glanced at the bowl of oranges. 'And I'm to keep that filled.'

'The oranges are from Captain de la Croix?' I reeled in horror. 'Mrs Bolitho . . . I can't accept anything more from him. Please . . . take them away.'

She took no notice, placing the tray on the bed, plumping up the pillows, pulling back the curtains to a bright sunny day. 'He said ye'd say that – an' I'm to leave it anyway. Ye've made a conquest of our captain, my dear. And why not? Captain Pierre's a *lovely* man. Not only is he handsome and strong, but he's that kind. Didn't charge me nothing for mending my clock. So there ye are.'

'You know him?'

'Well enough to recognise a good catch when I see one. He

don't just live off his shilling and six a day – he's got friends in high places.' She bent closer, her bosom in danger of escaping her bodice. 'His carvings sell fer a good price – *two guineas* the last ship went fer. He didn't tell me, but 'tis common knowledge.'

'Why does he come to Fosse?'

'Sir Alexander Pendarvis appointed him agent to all the prisoners. He does all sorts – sees to their conditions, an' the like. He's not just a prisoner – he's *favoured*. An' if he's taken a fancy to ye then snap him up, my girl. All that lovely manhood goin' to waste!' She paused by the door. 'I'll have hot water sent up and something fer those scabs on yer head. I know just what ye need.'

The clock struck eleven, twelve. The hot water soothed my hands, the soft yarrow balm smoothed over every inch that I could reach. The itching seemed less violent, the redness not so brutal. The lime juice hurt my gums but I had slept well. My stockings and bandages were washed and hanging by the window, but I missed Rowan. I felt lost without her. Yet the sea sparkled, the salt air drawing me to the window. The sea would heal me. Pulling down the lace on my bonnet, I stared at the key in my hand. My *own* key. It was hard not to giggle as I held the banisters and crossed the taproom.

The tide was high, the clear blue water lapping the stone steps on the quay. Ships were moored against the side, their rigging hardly swaying. The sun sparkled on the water, dazzling my eyes as I lifted my veil, and I breathed in the world that had been kept from me. The linhay must be up the cliff road towards the newly fortified battery. I had made a small parcel of food for Marcel – I felt sure he was not eating enough – and I decided to take it to him now.

Everywhere looked changed. Street lamps lined the road, fine new brick houses, a row of cottages, and almshouses where there had been fields. New wharfs had been built, several large warehouses. Yet the sea was the same, stretching out as far as I could see; the seagulls were the same, the heat of the sun beating down from a cloudless sky. I had forgotten the smell of salt on the breeze, the sheer beauty of the flowers. Bright red poppies danced back at me, tall stalks of pink foxgloves, a swathe of ox-eye daisies; everywhere infused with the scent of honeysuckle and camomile.

Stopping frequently to recover my breath, I reached the brow of the hill, the road plunging steeply to a small cove below. I scanned the cliff beside me. The linhay must be the ramshackle building just visible behind the rock. Picking my way across the rough grassland, I stared at the stone walls. Roof timbers arched to the open sky, the brick floor carpeted with daisies and wild thyme. It must once have been used as a home, for an old brick oven stood at one end, a hearth and fireplace, the outline of the chimney.

No one would think to come here unless they were so directed. Marcel must not have seen me or else he would have left his hiding place to greet me. I looked around. Skylarks were singing above me, the air filled with the scent of thyme crushed beneath my feet. Where would Cécile Lefèvre leave her message? I lifted up a broken pot and looked inside the bread oven. An old wooden bucket lay on its side, an overturned stool with only two legs, but nothing to find. Just scattered sheep droppings and butterflies warming their wings on the crumbling stones.

Below me lay the familiar cove with its jagged rocks and arc of sand, and sudden longing tore my heart. To feel the sand again, to watch the waves... To pick up shells and breathe the smell of seaweed... Anyone seeing me hurrying down the lane would see a sick woman crippled by aching joints, but inside I was a bride with the wind in her hair. Behind those very rocks, Joshua had drawn me to him, kissing me, wanting me, increasingly impatient to get me alone.

Sobs racked my chest, tears flooding my cheeks. To be here again. To be free. To have escaped my pigpen. The air was so fresh it almost hurt to breathe, yet I gulped lungfuls of the salty air, laughing, crying, blinded by the brilliance of the sun's reflection. Reaching for great handfuls, I let the glistening sand slip through my fingers. I never thought to be here again. Never thought to be free again.

A white flash caught my attention and I stared across the water to the rocks beyond. A seagull was struggling in the water, trying to free itself, the waves forcing it against the rock, and panic seized me – a seagull was trapped in a rock-pool, unable to fly. I could feel my heart beginning to pound, the stirrings of suffocation. It was trapped like a bird in a cage. Like a bear on a chain. Like a woman forced into a filthy pigpen. I had to set it free.

Lifting my skirts, I waded out into the shallow cove. The water was cold, the salt stinging the wound on my ankle. Suddenly, I felt my shoe sucked into the soft sand. I had thought the surface much firmer but my shoe felt gripped, as if pulled from beneath me. Shaking my foot seemed to make it worse. I was sinking deeper, my other foot also in danger of getting sucked beneath the sand. I heard someone shouting, a voice carrying across the water. A man's voice with a definite French accent.

'Mrs Barnard . . . wait. Don't move.' It was all I could do to keep my balance. I could hear him splashing behind me. He was right beside me. 'Don't struggle or you'll sink deeper.' He had stripped off his jacket and the sleeves of his white shirt glowed bright in the sun. His black hair was ruffled, falling over his forehead, his hand reaching out to steady me.

'Captain de la Croix! I should have thought to take my shoes off.' I gripped his hand, struggling to pull my foot free but my shoe remained firmly stuck.

'Let me retrieve it.' With one arm round my waist, he leaned forward, gripping my foot, pulling my shoe free. 'There . . . one moment.' Holding it at arm's length he shook out the wet sand and handed it back. He held me steady but my hand was trembling, my chest squeezed of all breath. We would be too late.

'Hurry, please . . . that poor seagull is trapped. Please, you must save it.'

He saw the stricken bird and withdrew his arm, wading out towards the rock. The water was deeper than I thought, up to his thighs, but he kept striding on. He reached the seagull and held it up and I stifled my cry. It lay stiff and white in his hands, not the slightest movement. 'Oh no . . . no . . .'

The need to free it had been so powerful. A trapped bird, unable to fly. I could feel myself shaking, a sense of agitation growing. My heart was jumping, thumping, pounding with sudden irregularity and I fought to breathe. Everywhere seemed too vast, the seagulls too loud, the sky too high. He stood smiling across at me, holding up the dead bird. 'A piece of white driftwood. But I must admit it looked very like a seagull struggling against the rock.'

I burst out laughing. I could not help myself. I was laughing too loudly, too irrationally, and I knew I must stop, yet the more I laughed, the more I wanted to cry. I felt light-headed, dizzy, completely petrified.

'Mrs Barnard . . . let me help you.' His arm slid round my waist, his hand on my elbow. 'Let me get you back to dry land.'

Standing on the shore, the dizziness began to pass but the sense of fear remained. 'I'm sorry . . . it was very foolish of me to make you get so wet.'

'Think nothing of it . . . it's my pleasure, though I wish I had managed to free a seagull for you. May I ask if you're all right?'

'Sudden dizziness – that's all. The sun on the sea hurts my eyes . . . it's very bright. I think I've walked too far. I'll be all right in a minute.'

His hand remained firmly on my elbow. 'May I help you back to the inn?'

'No . . . thank you. I'm perfectly well now.' My pulse was slowing, though my heart was still pounding, my breathing less shallow. It was the space that had frightened me, the vastness of the ocean, the screeching of the birds. The height of the sky.

He removed his arm, stepping away. 'Only, I saw you leave the town and I thought . . .'

I stared at him through my lace. 'You thought to follow me?'

His eyes filled with the same regret I had seen on the coach. 'No, madame. I'm permitted to walk one mile out of town each way. Every day, I walk as far as this cove and back to the Ferry Inn. Twice a day, in fact — if not more often. It's my greatest pleasure. I was not following you, I merely saw you leave as I set off for my walk.'

His trousers clung to his thighs, his sleeves sodden, a flush to his cheeks, his hair glistening, and I looked away. 'Please don't think me ungrateful. I'm grateful for both your concern and your generosity . . . but I can't accept anything more from you. My brother-in-law doesn't take kindly to your interference. We must never meet like this again.'

'As you wish.' His voice held sadness, a stiffness in his manner as he pointed me up the beach. 'At least, allow me to see you on to the road.'

'That includes oranges, Captain de la Croix.'

He reached for the jacket he had left lying on a rock. 'Once a ship's captain, always a ship's captain — forever vigilant for the signs of scurvy. You will get better, Mrs Barnard, and quickly, too. Just eat as many oranges as you can, and drink the juice of lemons and limes.'

His hair was ruffled by the wind, dark lashes framed his eyes. He held up his hand to shield them against the sun — the deepest blue, the colour of the sea. His complexion was browned, his hands strong. A man in his prime, yet held captive just as I had been. Buttoning his jacket, he seemed suddenly shy, as if his state of undress embarrassed him. I, too, wanted him to put on his jacket, not stand there with his white shirt open at the neck and slightly untucked at his slim waist. I did not want to see the kindness in his eyes, nor hear his consideration for my welfare. Because he was lying. All men were liars. He was a Republican spy, his only intention to trap my brother.

Above us, soldiers in scarlet jackets watched from the fort. One seemed to be holding a telescope to his eye and Pierre smiled. 'Do they think I'm about to steal a rowing boat and row home?' His laugh sounded hollow, a sadness in his shrug as two more soldiers ran down the battlement steps. 'I'm officially allowed this far . . . yet they obviously don't like me being so near their fortifications.'

My restlessness was increasing. I wanted to hold my head in my hands, curl up in a ball. Somehow I managed to stare ahead, ignoring his polite bow and stammered good wishes. I was foolish, very foolish. I had no idea how poor my sight had become, how turning my head and trying to focus would make me so dizzy. I was trembling inside, desperate to get to the safety of my room. Without Rowan, I felt adrift. I needed her strength. I needed her with me.

'Are you well enough to walk back . . . ?' A man was loading his cart outside the cottages by the beach. Pierre walked towards him, calling over his shoulder. 'I'll ask if he can give you a lift back to town.' The man nodded and Captain de la Croix returned quickly to my side. 'He says he's happy to drop you off at the inn. May I assist you on to the cart?'

'Thank you.'

He knew I was ill and was using it to further his purpose. If I looked angry, so much the better. It would deter him from believing me his fool.

Chapter Eleven

Pendenning Hall
Monday 9th June 1800, 6 a.m.

The early mist promised a warm day. The cart took the turning to the back of the house and I clasped my hands with equal measures of dread and excitement. I had hardly slept, but lay listening to the chimes of the church clock. My hem was still wet, my sturdy shoes stiff with salt and uncomfortably damp. Rowan was waiting for me by the kitchen door and seeing her made my courage swell. Her smile pierced my heart.

'I've been waiting for ye... I have to go now, but Mrs Pumfrey says we can sit together for our meal.' Two other maids stood behind her and I yearned to embrace her, yet I felt suddenly awkward, not knowing how a mother would act. She stepped forward, flinging her arms around me and I stifled my cry. 'I've a bed in the attic and I don't mind the work.' She smiled at the two girls behind her. 'And I've made friends.'

She waved goodbye and I followed my fellow passengers to the servants' hall. Once again, Mrs Pumfrey stood by the table taking their names, but Mr Troon stepped out of his office and drew me aside. 'We fumigated as you suggested and Mrs Pumfrey's seen to it you have all you need.'

I hung up my cloak, following his long strides down the corridor. This time, I was prepared, filled with purpose. I had to find evidence that Sir Charles had fabricated the dredging company to ruin my husband. I stared up at him gloating down at me from the wall. *I will have redress, Charles Cavendish. I will see you ruined.* The library smelled of lavender, a hint of burnt rosemary. The dust sheets had been removed, two white goddesses glistening at each end of the marble mantel-piece. Joshua's painted globe from the Netherlands stood in one corner, his favourite Italian leather armchair in another.

'We've hung up lavender and mint.' Mr Troon looked tired, distracted, taking off his glasses to rub his eye. 'The drapes are down and the carpets have been beaten.'

'May I suggest bunches of bay leaves? Insects don't like the smell of them.' There was nothing for me in the library. If I was to find anything I would have to search the study. 'I should finish by lunchtime. Shall I start on Sir Charles's study after that?'

'No one goes into Sir Charles's study.'

I tried to quell the thumping of my heart 'With respect, sir, how d'you know the silvers haven't took up there? They go straight for old papers. No jiggers...silver moths? What about mice?'

'There's no mice.' He wiped his other eye. Both were red-rimmed and puffy. He wore the same smart jacket and green tweed waistcoat, but the cuffs of his white shirt were grey, his necktie less pristine. His hair looked dusty, and I shook my head.

'There were mice droppings along the back shelves here. It's no trouble if ye'd like me to look. I'm happy to do it. Like I said, what looks right often isn't.'

He sneezed loudly and turned to leave. At the door he stopped, blowing his nose on his handkerchief. 'Perhaps, you should take a look at Sir Charles's study. After your meal. Quarter past two – I'll have to lock you in, mind . . . and just the bookshelves, nothing else.'

There was barely any dust on the books, a few cobwebs but little sign of damage. Crumbling the scrapings from the floor of my room on to the muslin cloth, I hoped it would look like an influx of jiggers. Being prepared had made it no less painful; the bell clanged and I returned Joshua's beloved portfolios to the shelves, wiping away my tears.

Rowan was waiting for me in the servants' hall. Her cheeks were glowing, not a trace of dirt on her face. Mrs Pumfrey had rubbed goose fat into her hands and insisted she washed her hair with honey and warm wax. She looked bright-eyed and excited, squeezing next to me along the table. We were to eat in silence. Mrs Pumfrey believed in feeding her maids, making sure we ate everything, insisting we flushed the dust from our throats with a quart of small beer. Our plates scraped clean, she sat regally at the end of the table watching the huge oak clock. On the stroke of two we were allowed five minutes' free conversation and the noise level began to rise.

I pulled up my veil and Rowan squeezed my hand. Her dress was a little too big for her, her white apron and mobcap crisply starched. It made her look younger – nearer eleven than twelve.

'Ye look so much better,' she said to me. 'Yer lips aren't so cracked . . . and the itching's stopped?'

'My fingers don't ache . . . look, my joints aren't so stiff.'

'All because of lemons and limes?'

Mrs Pumfrey rose from her chair. 'Clear the plates. Take everything to the scullery.'

We rose in unison, collecting our dishes, filing through a door and down the stone steps into the old kitchen. It was now the scullery, the grilles of the windows too high to see through. Wooden racks lined the walls, a row of large sinks down one side, three doors leading from the other. At one end, the old fireplace retained its kiln and bread ovens, though none were in use. There was a door to the wine cellar, another to the larder.

'That's always locked,' whispered Rowan. 'On account of people cutting off a slice or two when they pass – all cooked meats are locked away, though it's the footmen do it, not the maids!' She had colour in her cheeks, real joy in her smile. 'I'm in a room with Beth – that's her there – and Ella. She's Mrs Pumfrey's favourite and, honest to God, she's lovely. She reads us from the Bible, an' we have hot milk and buttered toast at night. 'Tis hard work, but I've not been . . .' She took a deep breath, smiling as she bit her lip. 'I've not been anywhere I feel so . . .'

'Happy?'

She nodded and a pang of jealousy twisted my stomach. We were taking our turn to wash and rinse our plates. She seemed so settled, as if she had found her new home, and I fought my terrible sense of emptiness.

'Here, put yer plate in this rack. Now we needs go to the privy... then wash our hands to be ready on the dot of quarter past.'

We joined the queue for the privy, standing in the courtyard with the sun glinting on the large clock and bathing the stones in golden light. Men rolling barrels across the cobbles paused to raise their hats and wink at the line of smiling maids, carts stood waiting to be unloaded: sacks of potatoes, a basket of chickens. Rowan seemed suddenly hesitant, as if undecided whether to speak. 'Madeleine... ye know I loved ye to draw me the folly? Well, it's as if I remember it. Not remember it as such, but I've held the shape... the arches... in my mind, an' now I've seen it, I feel certain I remember it.'

'But you're from Bodmin – you've never left the moor.'

'I was *found* on the moor. I don't know how old I was, nor who my real mamm was. The woman I called Mamm found me under a rowan bush – that's why she called me Rowan. She took me in and I loved her as my own.' She swallowed but did not cry. 'When she died, I had no one... not till ye came.'

A sharper twist this time, and I tried to smile. 'You think you might have come from *here*?'

Her large eyes brimmed with hope. 'Maybe my mother was a maid here? Why else would I remember the exact same folly? But there's more, Madeleine. Ye've no idea what I've heard about Phillip Randall. He was cruel an' wrongful.

96

He whipped vagrants an' forced people off the land. He was hated . . . no one has a good word for him. They *lynched him* – they strung him up to die. On his birthday, too!'

'When was that?'

'Back in, oh what did she say? 1796, in July . . . the third. I remember that because I like the number three. There are three of us in our room.' We reached the privy. 'I'll meet you back in the scullery,' she whispered as we parted.

I leaned against the privy wall. *She wants to stay. Dear God, she wants to stay.*

Back in the scullery we joined the line of maids waiting to show Mrs Pumfrey their clean hands, unstained aprons and tidy hair beneath their white mobcaps, but I could not match Rowan's spirits. 'That leads down to Sir Charles's wine cellar,' she whispered as we stood by a stout oak door. 'Phillip Randall was a *unprinced* knave.'

'Unprincipled?'

'That's the word. Ella says he spent hours locked in the wine cellar drinking Sir Charles's wine. Every night he went there to *check the wine.* Hours, he spent – sometimes till the early morning. And another thing: he had *women* to stay in the little cottage. He took them bottles of wine. Ella saw him do it. And she never lies. Madeleine, what is it?'

'Just the thought of my cottage . . . Joshua had it built for me – somewhere we could go to take tea in. Rather like a grand doll's house to play in, really.' I tucked a loose strand beneath her cap. 'See what else Ella can tell you. I'll see you later when I get on the cart . . . but now, I'm allowed into the *study.*'

97

Her eyes widened, her hand flying across her mouth. 'Never?'

I wanted to kiss her cheek but held back. Resting my hands lightly on her shoulders, I stood fighting my growing hollowness. 'Between us, we're sure to find something we can use.'

She skipped off and the hollowness turned to pain. *She wants to stay.* I should have said how much I missed her. How important she was to me. That I loved her as my daughter.

Chapter Twelve

The door to Mr Troon's office opened. A brief nod of his head and I hurried behind him, my determination rising as he unlocked the study door. It smelled musty, airless, the drapes drawn shut. He drew back the curtains and light flooded the room. It was just as I remembered it – Joshua's polished elm desk, his glass-fronted bookcases, his two cabinets with neatly labelled drawers, even the expensively commissioned painting of his racehorses still hanging above the fireplace. I put down my basket. 'I'll need the windows opening... and fresh water. Shall I check the cabinets?'

'Everything stays locked – just the bookshelves. Not the cabinet.'

'The French windows stay locked?'

'Yes. And I'll search you as you leave.' He sneezed again, blowing his nose. 'I'll give you two hours. Go and fetch your clean water – hurry.'

Returning with my bucket, I saw he had rolled up the carpet and several footmen were carrying it out. The lock turned behind me and I flew to the desk, pulling at the drawers. They remained firmly locked and I ran to the cabinet. Firmly shut. But what did I expect? Even the windows were to remain locked. I could see Joshua sitting at his desk, always be-wigged except in the bedroom where I would run my fingers through his short brown hair. Me a bride of twenty, him an experienced man of forty. He was in his prime, he was handsome, he was witty, he loved to dance. He loved the opera, his London townhouse, his horses, and he loved me, Madeleine de Bourg, his little songbird to be adored and spoiled.

I stared at the desk, blushing at the memories. The way he ushered out the footman, the way he locked the door and drew across the curtains. His urgent need as he lifted me on to the hard wooden surface. Afterwards, he would sit me on his lap, kiss my hair and plan our next purchase – a statue for the terrace, a secret bed in my little cottage.

Sudden distaste made me purse my lips. A return of the hollowness.

The glass-fronted bookshelves were crammed with catalogues, rows of ledgers labelled by the year. A key was in the brass keyhole and I opened the glass door to a musty odour, but no sign of mould. Lifting out books dated fifty years earlier, I glanced through details of who lived in which cottage, the rent charged, the tithes, the late payments and debts. Other ledgers detailed the costs of repairs, the wages of journeymen, the itinerant labourers brought in to clear the fields of stones.

The two cupboards looked to have the same brass keyhole and I slipped the key from the top of the cabinet into one of them. The lock turned and I stared at the shelves crammed with papers and letters held between leather bindings. Scrolls squeezed above piles of maps and I picked up the magnifying glass, my hand trembling. The bundles were tied with black ribbon, the dates clearly marked: 1780, 1781, 1782. But that was before my husband inherited the estate. I needed 1783 onwards.

I ran the magnifier over the shelves and a box spilling over with letters caught my eye – 1785, the year we were married. Lifting it out, I spread them in a fan, panicking which to read first. They were letters from the bank, letters to the bank – letters from Sir Charles to Joshua, letters from Joshua to Sir Charles. I picked up another set and they swam before me – letters from several attorneys, their language growing increasingly threatening. Joshua's angry letters back, further letters threatening bankruptcy, and I fought to breathe. Letters telling Joshua the bank was withdrawing its support. There were to be no more loans; all monies to be repaid or he would be imprisoned for debt. Another letter contained an inventory of what must be returned through non-payment, a final notice to declare himself insolvent.

I reached for my bucket, retching into it.

There were more letters detailing long lists of debts, unpaid accounts running into hundreds of pounds. Letters detailing the sale of the London house, the sale of parcels of land from the Pendenning estate. Letters from Sir Charles warning Joshua to be more frugal – to curb his extravagancies. Letters from Joshua begging Sir Charles for another loan.

I picked up the next letter and thought I might faint. It was from Joshua, begging Sir Charles to take the house as surety, pleading with him to put his name on the mortgage deeds. The bank was foreclosing and the bailiffs would soon arrive. I could not breathe. We had been married a month, I was his adored little songbird.

The magnifier trembled in my hands. Another letter . . .

Pendenning Hall
Porthruan
25th April 1785

My Dear Charles,

I have a plan which will reverse the situation I find myself in. Indeed, I believe we shall both be handsomely rewarded. You have proved my most loyal and trusted friend. Thank you for taking on the mortgage of Pendenning Hall and securing me another loan. Within six months, I shall be a Member of Parliament and be in a position to further your political ambitions. It will be my prime concern.

A few false speculations have severely dented my finances and my young wife is as extravagant as she is silly. But who can resist the charms of these little French beauties? I have racked up the rents and had the poorest tenants evicted. There will be economies among my staff and I shall sell several of my paintings. The London house is now sold, though it has hardly touched the debt, which continues to mount.

However, I believe we must speculate to accumulate so here is my proposal. I have discovered the white clay on Polcarrow land is porcelain clay – sought by the potteries in the north. There is none of this clay on my land but by complete chance, a small creek on Polcarrow land is in the ownership of an old steward.

He has no intention of selling but that should not deter us. His age is against him and we can work on him. I propose to build a harbour on his land, or at least several jetties. Ships must pay their harbour dues! Such a plan would supply us with a profitable income for the foreseeable future. I propose you a 50 per cent share of the first three years' takings, dropping to 20 per cent thereafter for a term of twenty years. How say you?

However, as the creek dries with the tide I propose to dredge the river to a sufficient depth in order that ships may access the jetties at all tides.

I beg you to invest with me in this: £500 on the same terms as our usual agreement should suffice to begin with, though I have yet to ask a dredging company for detailed costs and reckonings. I may require more.

My regards to Lady April, though I know where your affections lie. We must take another foray to Paris and see what delicacies we can find. I only write that as I know you burn your letters. I have found wives, especially silly little frilly ones, can be very inquisitive.

I remain, your loyal friend,
Joshua

Silly little frilly ones . . . *as extravagant as she is silly*. I reached for the bucket, heaving with the pain. It was his writing, his signature, the paper on his desk that he had pushed aside so hastily. I could hardly hold the next letter, let alone unfold it.

Richmond
London
4th May 1785

Dear Joshua,

I have grave disquiet about your request for further credit.

I believe your scheme might work — indeed, it appears to have great merit, but I feel you're overreaching yourself. Mortgages on property are one thing, speculation on dredging a river quite another. Certainly, the dependence on a creek you do not even own seems highly dangerous.

I advise you against this scheme and I must caution you. After your mortgage, your debt to me exceeds £4,000. Another £500 would see you unable to pay your interest and I believe that to be too great a risk. Indeed, that does not include your debts to the bank, your unpaid subscriptions to the club, and a certain rent taken out for Mrs O.

Lady April desires a country residence and within the year I will set about the purchase of my own estate. Despite my reticence, indeed, because of it, £500 is all I will offer you, though I beg you not to take it.

I'm only prepared to go against my better judgement because I fear you will seek the money elsewhere — from someone who would not offer the same low rate of interest. That would ruin you, Joshua, and as your friend, I cannot take that risk.

£500 and £500 only — on our usual terms — but there will be no more credit. Your house and estate will be in jeopardy if you take out further loans.

My regards to your wife.

I remain your cautious,
and not a little daunted, friend,
Charles

The room was stifling, the windows locked with no air circulating. How could he lie to me like that? Bankruptcy beckoning, yet still borrowing from Sir Charles? Was he insane? Begging Sir Charles like that, offering him political rewards. Insulting me, calling me names, blaming me for his extravagance. I had to stop myself from screaming. Clamping my mouth, I started walking the room, turning, striding, twisting round. Backwards and forwards, like the last fourteen years, but it was now Joshua I was cursing. My *beloved* Joshua, the house in jeopardy even as he knelt before me and offered me the world.

Father had asked me if Joshua was no longer trading and I had dismissed it, convincing him it was because Joshua had sufficient wealth – the income from the estate, the rents, his properties in London. An inheritance from his parents. I needed to retch again, my stomach stabbed by a thousand knives.

The clock struck the half-hour; Mr Troon would soon arrive. I must stop wringing my hands, stop pacing the floor. I had seen too many inmates bang their heads against the wall, yet that was exactly what I wanted to do. I wanted to scream, throw every object I could find, sweep the contents on the desk to the floor. I felt on fire with anger, with incredulity, betrayal ripping my stomach. Charles Cavendish, the man Joshua told me was greedy and manipulative – a bullying director of the East India Company – was, in reality, a loyal friend who warned him against such foolishness.

I sank to my knees, fumbling through the letters. Who was Mrs O? Why pay her rent in London when he was married to me in Cornwall? There was one letter I had not read and I picked it up, my cheeks burning. It was from a firm of Dutch dredgers and I stared at the date. Exactly two months before Joshua drowned in the river.

> *Belgrave Square*
> *London*
> *21st March 1786*
> *Van der Watling Dredging Company*
> *Established 1770*

Dear Mr Pelligrew,

Thank you for your enquiry as to the availability and feasibility of my services.

I can furnish you with extensive references for my completed works, which include numerous canals in Bruges, Holland and the Stroud Water Navigation project in Gloucestershire.

Most recently, I have redirected my expertise into dredging sea-channels and widening harbours. My work is there for all to see, should you desire a trip to Rye or to Rochester. I cannot undertake any prolonged project for the next six months, after that, however, I shall be at your disposal.

I foresee little impediment to dredging the river in question and building a harbour wall in the creek you outline. Indeed, I have a particular expertise in widening and dredging rivers.

However, I must warn you, though I am extremely competitive in my pricing, the expense of such an undertaking would, I believe, amount to more than your proposed sum of £500.

I employ twenty men to cart away the debris. I use two barges with mud mills driven by horses, and there is constant need to replace the bucket scoops where the ground is firm. Notwithstanding the extra costs involved if we strike rock, I envisage at least six months' duration to complete the works from start to finish.

Obviously, I need to survey the river before I can offer further assurance of my services, or my estimated costings. Any work undertaken can only proceed after a thorough inspection of the riverbed. Therefore, I propose to visit you at my earliest convenience to complete this survey.

I remain your obedient servant,
William Van der Watling

Scooping the letters back into their leather pouch, I tied the ribbon with shaking hands. I remembered it so clearly – Joshua, utterly delighted that the dredger had agreed his terms, had opened a bottle of his best wine. I could hear him as clearly as if he was in the room: *A trivial expense for such lucrative reward. Shall we name the harbour after you, my love?*

He was a liar, a fraudster. A speculator. Nothing was as it seemed.

I must have fumbled everything back into some sort of order. I must have locked the cupboards and started dusting the open shelves. Never had I felt such anger. Everything had been a lie. Even Joshua's love for me. I heard the lock turn and Mr Troon stood at the door. 'Found anything?'

My hands were still shaking, my face flaming. 'A few mouse droppings . . . a few dead moths.'

'Are you all right, Mrs Barnard? Only you don't look very well.'

'No, I feel suddenly . . . not well at all.'

'You've a fever?' He glanced into the bucket. 'You've been sick?'

The room was spinning. Hateful, hateful room. 'I do feel a little hot . . .' I had to leave this house of lies. Leave and never come back. I hated every book, every painting. Hated the desk, the scene of such violation. 'I wonder if I may leave, Mr Troon? I don't mind walkin' back, but I've come over rather unwell.'

'Yes, leave at once . . . We can't have sickness in the house. There are plenty of carts going back to Fosse, best get the next one.' His voice came and went as he hurried me to the door. 'Only return when you're well again, Mrs Barnard. If at all. You'll get three-quarters of a day's pay.' He counted out some coins and ushered me into the courtyard, pointing to a step at the furthest end. 'Wait there. A cart will leave soon enough.'

I sat, gripping my shawl. Gripping it and gripping it. I would never return to this house of lies.

Chapter Thirteen

Fosse, 5 p.m.

My legs dangling over the back of the cart, I watched the lake and folly disappearing from view. I had borne such hatred for the man who tried to warn Joshua, yet it was the exact opposite – Joshua's debt to Charles Cavendish had been the ruin of us, not Charles Cavendish's greed. He had lent Joshua money *against* his better judgement. Fourteen years I had planned my revenge, fourteen years of loathing Charles Cavendish, yet I had been so wrong.

'I'll drop ye at the ferry,' the driver called over his shoulder.

Maybe I had acted like a madwoman? Of course I had screamed. Finding Joshua lying face-down in the river had turned my mind. Of course I had wailed. I was mad with grief; my husband, my baby, my house, everything ripped from me. Of course I had accused them of murder. Yet for what? For a lying husband who thought me no better than a plaything.

The ferry was in sight and I knew I must compose myself. I must stop wringing my hands, stop my tears, cease speculating who Mrs O might be. The cart pulled over and I slipped from the back. 'Thank you.'

The driver did not answer but flicked the reins. The ferry was busy, men with oxen carts preparing to squeeze on to the wooden raft. Across the river, the Ferry Inn was lit by the last rays of the sun, yet Fosse lay in shadow beneath the steep hill. The pain was returning, new hatred burning my heart. Nothing was at it seemed.

'Mrs Barnard?' From out of nowhere, Thomas Pearce stood by my side. Odious man, with his sly smile and his firmly clasped bag. Not a silk pedlar, but a thief! 'So it's happened as I said it would – you were caught. No, if you'd been caught, you'd be arrested. Let me guess... they suspected you, but they gave you a chance. I hate to say it, but I told you so.'

I stumbled forward. He had taken me by surprise and my heart began thumping. He stayed beside me, intimidating me with his weasel voice. 'Tried to steal a candlestick, did you? And failed?'

I ignored him, staring at the ground as I hurried along the river road, but he ran ahead of me, turning round, stopping me, laughing as I tried to sidestep him. He had changed clothes, he looked smarter, a little cleaner, but his hair was still lanky beneath his large hat, his beard still greasy and overgrown. 'Come now, *Mrs* Barnard. Don't pretend otherwise. I know you're interested in my scheme. I saw it in your eyes. Back there in the inn. I caught your look when I mentioned the diamonds. You couldn't hide it – you want what I'm offering and you want it badly.'

'I want nothing of the sort. I want nothing more to do with you.' My shoes were rubbing, my blisters making it hard to walk. All I wanted was to get to my room, yet he ran ahead, once more barring my way.

'You'll get a good cut. And you'll get new clothes. I'll do everything that's needed – I'll get the certificates printed – that's not a problem when you know where to go. You get to agree what gentleman you want us to approach. Your cut will be – let's agree . . . a third? You can't quibble with that.'

'Leave me. Please. I want nothing from you . . .' I was going to cry. Any moment, I was going to howl. Joshua had never loved me. He was lying. All men lied.

Thomas Pearce's face hardened, his voice grew cruel. 'You need money for a ship to France. That's what you want, isn't it? *To get to France.*'

I hurried past him. Beside me was a row of elegant merchants' houses with fine iron railings and beautiful front doors – the smarter end of town, with their windows overlooking the river to the fields opposite. I thought I had left him behind but he was playing with me. Once more he ran ahead, swinging round to confront me.

'Perhaps you've a ship in mind? Perhaps you're waiting for someone? Only, your *brother-in-law* doesn't have the money he needs, does he?' He stood smirking in front of me, but his eyes were not laughing. 'Expensive business, persuading someone to take you to France. Listen, my plan's proven. We don't sell anything, we just give them one small diamond and ask for a *deposit for goodwill* while they check the quality of the diamond – or crystal, as it happens!' He seemed to think that was funny. His laugh was wild, fuelled by drink. 'They give us a *deposit*, and we scarper. It never fails.'

I tried to ignore him but he grabbed my arm and I winced with pain. 'Take your hand off me. Please . . . unhand me.'

His grip tightened. 'So, you'll think about it? I thought you might.'

The pressure of his grip, his horrible, forceful voice. I could feel my senses begin to spin. This was how it started – shouting at me, grabbing my arms, shaking me, making me answer. Forcing me to admit I was mad. That I was insane. That I was not a fine lady. That I was an upstart, pretending to be a fine lady. And yet they were right all along, I was not a fine lady. It was all lies – my husband a fraudster every bit as dishonest as Thomas Pearce. The road was spinning, my legs giving way beneath me. Sinking to my knees, I clutched my bonnet. If I shrank to nothing, the beatings seemed less severe. He stood over me, hovering like one of the attendants. 'Go away . . . please . . . go away.'

I heard running footsteps, a man's angry shout. 'Leave that poor woman alone. Leave her. Get away or I'll call the constable.'

I could do nothing but crouch on the cobbles, clasping my bonnet. Everything was lies. Nothing was true. Joshua had not loved me, he had wanted to parade me on his arm, have me at his disposal – his fancy French conquest. The songbird he had trapped.

Someone was speaking: a soft, woman's voice. 'Come, my dear . . . come, compose yourself. He's gone. Forgive me, but I saw it all from my window. Do you know the man?' Her hands were on my shoulder, such kindness in her voice, and I could not speak, the tears I had been holding back streaming from me. I could only howl into her proffered lace handkerchief. It smelled of lavender, and my sobs grew fiercer.

'Help me, Sam. Perhaps, take her other arm?'

'Right-o, Mrs Pengelly. Though she's as light as a feather. Shall I carry her?'

The kind voice again, a gentle hand brushing a strand of my wig from my cheek. 'Would you mind if my man carries you, my dear? Only it doesn't seem you're able to walk.'

I did not want to walk, or if I did it would only be to wade out into the river and never come back. Joshua did not love me, he had been playing with me. I was a silly, frilly plaything – an excuse for his extravagance. I felt myself lifted in strong arms, felt the careful negotiation down a flight of steps. A door opened, the delicious aroma of baking, and my sobs took hold.

If they had not been so kind, I could have dried my tears sooner. Heaven knows I had been drying my tears for fourteen years, yet I seemed unable to stop – crying from hurt, from loneliness, from the cruelty of an unlived life. Unlived, unloved, every memory now tainted by untruth.

'A little brandy, my dear? Sam, why not pour the lady a small glass?' The woman's voice was as gentle as her eyes were loving; soft wrinkles radiated across her forehead, her greying hair tied loosely beneath a straw bonnet. A beautiful, warm face, which made it even harder to stop crying.

We were sitting at her kitchen table, another woman sitting

113

opposite me; a large, round-faced woman with red cheeks and equally greying hair, though not so neat. It was wispy, abundant, barely held in check under her large mobcap. Her arms resting across her ample bosom, her apron covered with flour, her concerned eyes were staring at me from behind a pair of round spectacles. 'She needs feeding, that's what.'

'Perhaps a plate of your ham, Mrs Munroe?'

'And lardy cake. The poor woman looks half-starved.'

Freshly baked bread lay on a rack, a black kettle whistling on the stove. A huge pine dresser took up most of one end of the room; shelves along the other walls were crammed with gleaming copper pans and neatly arranged fish kettles. Everything in neat rows – jelly moulds, jugs, pewter tankards and china dishes, and huge bunches of herbs hanging from hooks; a basement kitchen with two windows too high to see through, and a back door leading to a small courtyard. A staircase entered one corner, a lamp burning in another. A rocking chair stood by the stove, a large black-and-white tomcat watching me through half-closed eyes.

'I must go . . . but thank you . . .' A fresh burst of tears. It seemed I could not stop.

'Wait a while. Wait until you feel better.' A plate was placed in front of me, a beautifully embroidered napkin, and I laid my head on my hands, my emptiness so unbearable it cut like pain. 'Try a little . . . it will keep your strength up.'

A beautiful china plate. A silver fork. A fine bone-china cup and saucer. A crystal glass. The lady of the house had a local accent, she must be a rich merchant's wife. 'There's no need to tell us who you are – or who *he* was. Just get your strength back, my dear. We won't pry. I'm Eva Pengelly, and this is Mrs Munroe, and Sam.'

Now I saw her properly, I could see she was dressed to go out. Her pelisse was soft grey muslin, open at the front and sides and trimmed with black lace. Her gown was dotted-grey, her straw bonnet trimmed with yellow ribbon. A silver brooch glinted on the lace at her neck and a pearl-drop earring swung freely from each ear. A basket crammed with jars and brown paper parcels lay on the table next to her. 'I've stopped you from going out . . .' I whispered.

'Not at all, my dear. Most of my day is spent planning an excuse to visit my grandchildren. This time, it's to bring them Mrs Munroe's strawberry tartlets and her latest recipe – *cherries en chemise*.'

'*Cherries en chemise?*' A stab shot through me, a memory of a lifetime ago. I must have gasped. I certainly started crying again. '*Cherries en chemise?*'

'I'm sorry, my dear. That was very insensitive of me. I can hear by your accent you must be French. Would you like one?'

'No . . . not at all. I couldn't possibly . . . I must go. Thank you for your kindness.'

Mrs Munroe was clearly offended. 'Nonsense. Of course you must try one. In fact, you can be the judge as to whether they pass muster. Besides, I can make plenty more for Lady Polcarrow.'

Another painful stab, this time at the mention of my once-loved friend. 'Lady Polcarrow? You know Lady Polcarrow?'

Colour rose in Mrs Pengelly's cheeks, a slight shrug to her elegant shoulders. 'She's my daughter,' she said softly.

'Your daughter? How can that be?' I must have sounded shocked, but I was shocked. Shocked and rather thrilled. 'You mean you're her *stepmother*? Forgive me, but—' I stopped. I could not tell them Alice Polcarrow had been my friend, or could I? I was tired of pretence, tired of being hidden away. Alice Polcarrow had been my friend and, just then, I needed a friend. I needed the truth about Joshua Pelligrew.

Mrs Pengelly seemed suddenly shy. 'She *is* my daughter . . . and I agree, not many women from our walk of life catch the eye of a man like Sir James . . . but, there you are. My daughter has great intelligence, enormous beauty, and is a match for anyone. We live in changing times . . .'

Had I offended her? It was the last thing I wanted to do, yet I could not understand. 'Sir *James*? Forgive me, but how can that be? Do you refer to Alice Polcarrow?'

She smiled a smile a true beauty. 'Why, bless me no! You're referring to Sir James's *stepmother*! Alice Polcarrow has re-married. My dear, you're shaking . . . This news has obviously come as a shock. You must have been away quite some time not to have heard? Sir Francis's son – Sir James Polcarrow – and my daughter have been wed for seven years. They live in Polcarrow House now.'

'So Alice Polcarrow no longer lives in Fosse?'

'No . . . she's *Alice Reith* now . . . She's wed to Matthew Reith and they live in *Truro*.'

Mrs Munroe had been watching us, staring rather too intently at me. She resumed her seat, but her piercing eyes made my heartbeat quicken. There was something in her look, her fierce concentration on my twisting hands. 'I used

116

to be an under-cook up at the Hall,' she said in a way that matched her look. 'Up at Pendenning, many, *many*, years ago. When Lady *Alice* Polcarrow used to visit there.' The more she stared, the more I could not speak. I could do nothing but wring my hands. Her voice softened. 'I'm not wrong in my thoughts . . . am I?'

No words would come. Yet for all the world, I wanted them to know.

She leaned forward. 'I am right, aren't I? You're Miss *Madeleine* . . . our lovely young bride who used to sing like a bird. Our Miss Madeleine from up the Hall?' Her intense gaze flamed my cheeks, and I could only shrug, burying my face in Mrs Pengelly's proffered handkerchief.

'Bless my soul . . . I remember your concerts on the terrace – we'd hear you start to sing an' we'd come running. We'd hide behind the wall and watch ye. All those important people . . . the rich food, the wines, yet all they came for was to hear ye sing. And ye'd dance . . . and see us watching and ye'd smile and dip us a curtsy. And that made us love ye so.'

Behind my veil, tears streamed down my cheeks. A lie. Everything had been a lie.

'We'd make all manner of fancy frangipane, and ye'd tell us to make extra for the servants' hall. I'm right, aren't I? Ye're Miss Madeleine.'

I had to do it. I had to lift my veil. Shutting my eyes, I heard her sharp intake of breath.

'Bless my soul. Well . . . like I said. Ye need feeding. Ye've escaped from France?'

Mrs Pengelly was clearly surprised. 'You're *Madeleine Pelligrew*?'

I had longed to hear myself called by my name, yet now there was a horrible emptiness to it. 'I didn't go to France ... I never left England. I can't tell you where I've been because I don't know the names of all the places they kept me. I'm free now, but I was held against my will. Doctors had me locked away – they deemed me a danger to others. My crime was heartbreak, my *madness* stemming from the grief of losing everything I loved. But I'm certified sane again ... two doctors ... signed papers ...'

Both reached for my hands, their grips firm, their unspoken fury filling me with courage. Mrs Pengelly dabbed her eyes. 'You poor, dear love. I knew *about* you, of course, but I only ever saw you from afar – glimpses of you in your carriage, or the back of your bonnet. We thought you'd gone back to France. May I ask where you are staying?'

'At the Ship Inn.'

She caught her breath. 'Surely not? It's very rough there, not at all suitable ...'

I rose to go, slipping the veil back to cover my face. 'No, it's very comfortable. Mrs Bolitho has been wonderfully kind. I must go. Please may I ask you to tell no one who I am? I need to keep my whereabouts unknown. I don't want anyone to know I'm here ... I'm calling myself Mrs Barnard ... my daughter's a maid up at the Hall. She's not my real daughter ... but she's come with me.'

'A maid at the Hall?'

I caught the look that passed between them. Sam had been standing by the door. He was smartly dressed in a tweed jacket despite the warmth of the kitchen. His cream neckcloth was

118

tied neatly, his red waistcoat fastened with brass buttons. Also in his mid-fifties, his hair was grey, thinning on the top. He had a long face, a strong physique, slightly stooping shoulders and perfectly polished boots. 'I'll see ye safely back to the Ship Inn, Mrs Barnard.' He smiled shyly. 'Lest ye get set upon again.'

Mrs Pengelly also rose. 'Mrs Pelligrew . . . it may be comfortable, but it seems wrong for you to be staying at the Ship Inn. Alice Reith is a very good friend of mine – she's family. She's my son-in-law's stepmother, though there's little difference in age. I believe she'd want me to offer you my help, and I'd like to – for myself. Won't you stay with us? At least until you get settled somewhere other than the Ship Inn?'

'I . . . I . . . don't . . . that is . . .' I knew I must decline. I must stay hidden in my room. I must force my way back up the steps and never see them again. Yet their kindness felt like a mantle, the warmth of their concern thawing fourteen years of coldness. 'Maybe for just a couple of nights?' I whispered.

Relief flooded their faces. 'Excellent. Sam will collect your luggage from the inn.'

I lifted the veil back from my face. 'I've no luggage – only a bowl of oranges. Please give Mrs Bolitho these.' I held out the six pennies Mr Troon had given me.

Mrs Pengelly showed no sign of surprise, merely smiled and nodded at Sam, who shut the door carefully behind him. The clock on the wall struck six and the cat stood, turned in a circle, and sank down again. 'We were living in Porthruan when your husband *died*,' she said. 'My husband was a shipbuilder . . . he, too, is no longer with us.'

My stomach twisted. It was the way she paused on the

word *died*. 'What did they say about my husband's death? It must have been talked about?'

Her eyes plummeted, a slight swallow. 'That's all a long time ago.'

'What did they say? Please don't hide anything from me.'

Her hands covered mine. 'There's always talk. I believe they tried to keep things quiet but the town knew well enough. Your husband's ruin was widely known . . . rather than face prison . . . they said he took his own life.'

'Took his own life?' I had to sit down. Never had I thought that. Never that.

'The town understood how hard it was for you – hard enough to cause the grief you suffered. But you're better now, my dear?'

I nodded. I even think I smiled, but I was not better. I was worse. Sir Charles had tried to shield me. No one had even alluded to the truth. But why incarcerate me for so long?

I slipped from the smooth sheets, pinning back the shutter, opening the sash to gaze across the river. It was two in the morning, the moonlight shimmering across the black water, and I breathed in the freshness of the night. Mrs Pengelly had reeled in horror when I told her the truth – that I had been incarcerated, bound in cloths with my arms pinned to my sides. That I had been drenched with cold showers, made to vomit, kept in dark cupboards. Treated no better than an animal until my prayers had been answered and my brother's friend had come to my rescue.

Only Rowan's kindness had kept me sane; the compassion in her smile lighting the darkness, her sweet look of encouragement as she entered my pigpen. Were they treating her well? I was missing her dreadfully, yet maybe I was being selfish. She seemed so happy. She had even made friends.

Mrs Munroe had made me bowls of nutritious soup, plied me with her *cherries en chemises*. Sam had taken my shoes to polish, and the cat, Mr Pitt, had jumped on to my lap as if welcoming me to his house. There was only Tamsin, the housemaid, left to meet: she was visiting her grandmother but would be back tomorrow.

'Your brother's friend has clearly done his best under very difficult circumstances...' Mrs Pengelly had said as she bade me goodnight. 'But, forgive me, my dear, your gown is very ill-fitting and it must be rather hot. Shall I find you a lighter one? I'm proprietor of a school of needlework – it bears my name, though I don't teach there as much as I used to. Their work is of a very high standard. The girls sew practice gowns and alter dresses, and I'm sure I can find you a more suitable gown for this warm weather. Shall I find you one, my dear?'

A week ago I would have thrown back my head and laughed at the absurdity of being offered a new gown, yet now her kindness seemed overwhelming. I held the sleeve of her nightdress against my cheek, breathing in the scent of lavender. Perhaps I should pinch myself that it was not one of my dreams. The faintest breeze caressed my cheek, the town deserted, not a soul in sight. A sudden flash in the shadows caught my eye and I peered down from the window.

There was nothing to see, no one there, just a beached

rowing boat pulled high on to the riverbank. I looked again, my eyes straining through the darkness. Surely I could see a large hat and a pair of crouching knees? The flash came again, moonlight glinting on metal, and I could just make out the shape of a sleeve, a hand holding a fob watch. I pulled away quickly, my heart thumping. A man was crouching against the side of the hull and by the way he was facing, he was watching the house.

Chapter Fourteen

Coombe House, Fosse
Tuesday 10th June 1800, 9 a.m.

The same nightmare haunted my sleep: I woke to the same terrible panic. Always, I would be wading out through the muddy water unable to reach Joshua; the water heavy against my skirts and impossible to push through; Joshua, lying face-down, his arms drifting by his side. Always, I would be shouting, turning round, crying out to the group of men watching from the riverbank; always they would be laughing, their grotesque jeers turning my blood cold.

The dream always unsettled me. Mrs Munroe was bustling about, stirring her porridge, smiling at the cat, and I could hold back no longer. 'Mrs Munroe, I believe I know what your answer will be. Was my husband considered *honourable*? Was he considered a gentleman?'

Her lips pursed as she stopped her busying. 'It's not fer the likes of me—'

'Was my husband liked? Please, Mrs Munroe, I need the truth.'

She heaved herself on to the chair beside me, a frown as she shook her head. 'No, he weren't liked . . . and he weren't a gentleman. The maids were warned to go around in pairs . . . if you know what I mean?'

I swallowed hard, a bitter taste in my mouth. 'Go on.'

'That's all, really – that and no one in the town offering him credit. He ruined too many businesses. He put the rents up so high a lot of people went hungry . . . he turned old folk from their homes. So no, he weren't liked, not one bit.'

'They must have been thrilled when Sir Charles took over the estate?'

'Thrilled?' She threw back her head, laughing loudly. She looked incredulous. 'Dear me, you really don't know, do you?'

'I know Sir Charles was a good friend to my husband.'

She shook her head all the harder. 'Friends with a man who'd stab you in the back as soon as look at you? No, Miss Madeleine, he's a friend to no one. Charles Cavendish is only out for himself. That man is hated more than *anyone*. Least your husband was a lecherous fool! Sir Charles Cavendish is no fool – he uses and he abuses, everyone's that scared of him. There's not one person with a good word to say about him – especially Sir James and Lady Polcarrow.'

My heart was pounding, my loathing for Charles Cavendish returning. 'Why's that?'

'Devious . . . he is. A devious man. He bought land unlawfully from the Polcarrow estate because he wanted their clay and he wanted to build a new harbour. He thought to profit from Sir James's clay but Sir James stopped him.' Her voice dropped to a whisper, a comforting scent of lilac as she drew closer. 'I shouldn't speak of it, only 'tis common knowledge. Sir James took Sir Charles Cavendish to court and hung him out to dry. Least, Mr Reith did. That's Alice Polcarrow's husband – the one Mrs Pengelly told you about.'

The kettle whistled and she rose. My pulse was racing with a strength I had not felt for fourteen years. 'Devious, you say? Mrs Munroe, would you think me mad if I believed Sir Charles *deliberately* encouraged my husband to be in his debt . . . and that he set up a fraudulent dredging company to increase that debt?'

She had her back to me, holding the kettle in two hands as she filled a silver coffee pot. A delicious aroma filled the kitchen. 'No, Miss Madeleine, I'd say that's exactly what he *would* do.'

It was like light flooding the room. Like fog lifting. My husband was a fool. He was vain and he was weak. His lack of propriety, licentious behaviour, frivolity and utter stupidity had made him the perfect target for Charles Cavendish's greed. It was so obvious – I almost laughed. Make a man like that heavily in your debt, murder him, and as his main creditor take everything he owned.

'There now, how about some more toast?' Mrs Munroe put another piece on my plate.

Sir Charles knew my husband would be unable to resist his loan of five hundred pounds and he fabricated a dredging company to dupe him. He had written saying he was going to buy an estate, but his real intention was to move into Pendenning Hall and take Joshua's place as the Member of Parliament. He spread rumours that Joshua had taken his own life, and his plan would have worked only I saw Phillip Randall walk away from the murder site and I needed to be silenced.

The toast caught in my throat. I could hardly swallow. Charles Cavendish would find a way to silence me again. The sound of footsteps made me look up. A maid was coming down the stairs with a bucket and mop.

'Ah, there you are, Tamsin – just in time to take Mrs Pengelly up her coffee.'

In her early twenties, Tamsin was tall, a slight awkwardness in her gait. Her dress was spotted muslin, her starched white apron tied in a large bow behind her back. Her mobcap was edged with lace, her shoes shining. She jumped when she saw me, water spilling from her bucket. 'Oh, good morning, Mrs Barnard. I hope you slept well.' She had the same habit Rowan had of putting her hand in front of her mouth, but whereas Rowan's teeth were straight, the large gap between Tamsin's front teeth made her whistle as she talked. 'I'll just mop that spilt water.'

Putting down the bucket, she reached for the mop but Mrs Munroe held out her tray. 'No . . . here . . . I'll do that. Take this up . . . but mind you don't spill it.' Her eyes followed Tamsin up the stairs, her face relaxing when she reached the top. 'Mrs Pengelly likes to take coffee in her room, then I hear ye're going to Elowyn for a new dress?' She ran the mop over the spilt water. 'She used to sit just where you're sitting – Mrs Pengelly taught her everything.'

We followed the river road back towards the ferry. I knew the Old Forge from before and was surprised it was to be our destination. Mrs Pengelly smiled, her crinkling eyes framed by the white silk handkerchief holding her straw bonnet in place.

'Of course, you'll remember it as a working forge. William Cotterell – that's Elowyn's husband – does fire it up every now and again. He's an engineer.'

'And Elowyn's a dressmaker . . . Does she teach in your school?'

Mrs Pengelly slipped her arm through mine. 'Sometimes – when time allows. Then, of course, there's . . .'

The road was busy with a steady line of carts streaming by and people walking in the sunshine. I loved her soft voice, her smiles of greeting to those we passed, the respect with which everyone nodded and curtsied. There was no false air about her; her son-in-law was the richest landowner in Fosse, yet she greeted everyone with the same courtesy, pointing to her husband's shipyard with the same shy pride as she spoke about her dressmaker's. Their names were lost on me, her happy chatter drifting over me. The fear was still with me, but a far stronger emotion was twisting my stomach. *You have robbed me of this, Charles Cavendish. Robbed me of everything.*

'. . . William needed somewhere for his engineering works and it seemed the perfect solution. Elowyn's dressmaking business has never been so busy, and what with Sir James opening his mine . . .'

I must concentrate. I must not let my mind wander. The sky seemed too vast, too many eyes staring at me. Too many names I had no hope of remembering.

'Are you all right, my dear? We're nearly there.'

I had to breathe. The vastness of the space was making me panic. 'I'm just a little hot . . . Sir James is opening a mine?'

'*Reopening* the old mine because William has redesigned the

127

old engine.' She smiled her enchanting smile, the soft lines on her face crinkling. 'And everyone going to the ball needs a new gown! Elowyn's never had so many orders.'

'Forgive me... why so many orders?'

A sudden questioning glance, a look I had grown used to seeing. I was alone in my mind too much, missing whole chunks of conversations, yet she seemed to understand. 'My daughter's giving an opening ball for the mine and just about everyone's been invited. It's the talk of Fosse.' She stopped, a nod of gentle encouragement. 'Are you all right to go in?'

An archway above the iron gates led to a path that divided into two — one to the back of the Old Forge, the other to the front door of the dressmaking establishment. Yellow roses hung in profusion round the door, a painted sign — *Elowyn Cotterell, Bespoke Dressmaker, Patronised by Lady Polcarrow and Lady Pendarvis* — secured to one side. Mrs Pengelly pushed open the door and I breathed deep for courage.

The room was bright and airy, Elowyn Cotterell as kind as she was beautiful. An efficiency in her manner, she swept forward, welcoming me, showing no signs of the distaste she must have felt for my dress. A large pine table took up the centre of the room, a huge cabinet with boxes of coloured satin and silk ribbons taking up one side. Two large windows let in the sunlight, a painted screen in one corner, several dressmaking dummies in the other. Rolls of pastel silks lay on the table and I fought my sudden envy. Elowyn had the thick blonde hair I had once had.

Her dress was simple yet elegant: a delicate lemon sprig with a scooped neck and cream lace at her elbows. She spoke softly, kindly. 'We've an assortment of gowns to suit every taste. Some are given to us, some are sold to us . . . and we've several *practice gowns* the seamstresses make. Any one of them would be suitable.' She sounded respectable, professional. 'They're mainly light cambric or fine cotton – some are silk . . . some are muslin. All of them would be so much cooler. I'll bring them down. They'll need taking in, mind, but I'm sure I'll find you something you like.'

I fought my tears. 'Thank you.'

At the foot of the spiral stairs, she hesitated. 'May I suggest I make you a turban as well, Mrs Barnard? Your wig looks . . . *heavy*. It must be very hot.'

Mrs Pengelly smiled her encouragement. 'Elowyn transforms everyone who enters here. Some of her ladies come all the way from Truro!'

Elowyn returned with gowns spilling over her arms and Mrs Pengelly helped her lay them on the table, spreading them out, tweaking their creases, and I stood staring at the light material, loving every one of them. Would I dare wear anything so light? 'They're beautiful . . . all of them.'

Elowyn pulled round the screens and I bit my lips as she started to undress me. The itching may have subsided but the scars where I had scratched myself until I bled were as brutal as ever. 'It's not lice . . .' I whispered. 'I'm not infested. I'm just very sore. I'm told it's scurvy.'

If my scars shocked her, Elowyn showed no sign. Her tone remained matter-of-fact, a reassuring smile. 'Then you'll soon get better . . . but maybe a high-necked gown – worn with a lighter jacket? How about this one?' She held a blue sprig muslin gown against me. 'This makes your eyes look very blue and the lace will be gentle – it won't irritate your throat.' She paused. 'May I take off your wig?'

I waited for her gasp but it never came.

'Nowadays women don't need to wear such heavy wigs. Our turbans are perfect for thinning hair – they're much less bulky and far kinder to sore scalps. We just add curls down the sides to make it look like there's hair beneath . . .' She picked up the wig. 'I could cut off some locks from round the base and use them round the turban?' She paused. 'But, to me, your skin looks much lighter . . .' She lifted my chin with a gentle finger. 'Your skin is fair . . . is your hair naturally blonde?'

'I . . . haven't had hair for so long . . . but yes, I once had long blonde curls.'

I wiped the tear from my cheek. Her voice was soft, her eyes full of understanding. 'I have a drawer full of curls and locks to suit *all* complexions – would you like me to choose one that's just a little darker than my own hair?'

I nodded, forcing back my tears. Her kindness was overwhelming, her smiles and chatter filling the room as she began to measure me. It was better than my dreams. Better than all my dreams. I had forgotten the intimacy of female friendship, the quiet laughter, the gentle ticking of the clock, the ringing of children's laughter in the courtyard outside. I had forgotten what it felt like to have someone treat me with such respect. She put away her tape measure, snapping shut her box of pins.

'That's all done. I hardly like helping you back into your old gown, but it won't be for long. We'll have this finished in no time.' She replaced my wig, smiling at me. 'Come through to the back and join me in a glass of Madeira.' She smiled at Mrs Pengelly. 'I was taught by the very best and only the very best will do. We always serve cake and a drink. We're not so much dressmakers as . . .' She linked her arm through Mrs Pengelly's. 'How would you describe us?'

Mrs Pengelly's answer pierced my heart. 'Friends who look after each other.'

A burst of sudden laughter echoed through the open window, excited screams ringing across the yard. Children were calling out, chanting rhymes. At a fresh burst of explosive giggles, Elowyn raised her eyebrows and shook her head. 'Honestly, that poor man – but they do love him so.'

The back room must be their family room. The ceiling was heavily beamed, a stone fireplace at one end, a table with chairs in the centre. A large dresser stood crowded with plates, two windows overlooking the yard outside. The Old Forge lay immediately opposite, a covered well in the centre of its courtyard. The sun was shining, lighting up several red-brick buildings, glinting on their brightly painted doors.

A man was standing by the well, a fair-haired girl on his back, two boys holding him by the hand. A large white scarf was tied across his face, the boys turning him to make him dizzy, and we drew closer to the window watching this bewitching scene. The two boys obviously deemed him dizzy enough because they let go of his hands, shrieking as they ran away. He had taken off his jacket, the neck of his white shirt loose. Beneath the tied scarf his hair was dishevelled, his sleeves rolled to the elbow. Strong, lithe, a man in his prime, and my heart thumped.

The golden-haired girl on his back was directing him, telling him which way to turn, the two boys darting towards him, running back, hoping to be caught, and I tried to quell the rush of pleasure seeing him had brought. Elowyn opened the small leaded window and leaned out. 'That's enough now!'

Her words were lost to screams of delight. The man reached forward, scooping up first one boy, then the other, tucking them both under his arms as he swung them round. Their squeals grew louder, his swirling getting faster, until the golden-haired angel on his back shouted for him to stop. She freed him of his blindfold and they stood laughing and gasping. Elowyn shook her head, once more leaning out of the window.

'That's quite enough! Leave poor Captain Pierre alone!' She hid her smile. 'The children adore him. He'd make such a lovely father.'

She poured our drinks and I took the glass, trying to hide my agitation. I wanted to leave, but there was more laughter, the sound of running footsteps, and I tried to stop my rising panic. He was at the door, dipping low to avoid bumping the child's head on the lintel. His presence filled the room, a physical presence, and I fought the memory of his arm slipping round my waist.

A huge smile lit Mrs Pengelly's face. 'Ah, Captain de la Croix, we're just having some refreshments. This is such a lucky coincidence. May I introduce Mrs Barnard, who's lately arrived in Fosse?'

Chapter Fifteen

Elowyn told the children to wash their hands and sit at the table, handing them each a drink and a buttered bun, and I stood staring at my hands. The last time I had seen him I had acted so foolishly. Captain de la Croix seemed equally agitated, rolling down his sleeves, fumbling with the top buttons of his shirt. He stood, formal and awkward, his obvious discomfort in complete contrast to his earlier playfulness.

Mrs Pengelly reached forward, helping him arrange his cravat into some semblance of order. 'Well, now! Meeting you like this? I didn't know you to be in Fosse, Captain Pierre?'

He ran his hand through his tousled hair, jet black, except for the slight greying at his temples. 'A coincidence indeed.' He attempted a smile, accepting the glass Elowyn held out. 'Thank you, your good health, ladies.'

Dark, heavy brows; a strong face – straight nose, firm chin – yet a face that could change in an instant, one moment smiling and compassionate, the next stern, his eyes wistful and unreadable. He caught my glance and I turned away. I had not replaced my bonnet and my face was bare for him to scrutinise. I could feel my cheeks burning, a flush of shame creeping up my throat.

He handed back his finished glass. 'I brought a chronometer down... one I mended for Sir Alex... I would have gone back... but one of Lady Pendarvis's clocks isn't keeping time. The mechanism's faulty and it's proving very hard to mend. And... while I was here, I thought to visit William... to ask about the dials he wants me to make.' He was talking quickly, an uncertainty in his voice I had not heard before.

'It's lovely to have you back, Captain Pierre... Don't even think of leaving before you visit us in Coombe House. Mrs Munroe's been practising her French fancies. Ever since you mentioned *cherries en chemise* we've had them every night!'

His laugh was genuine, deep and throaty, a quick glance in my direction. 'I'd be honoured. Thank you.'

I knew I must say something, Mrs Pengelly must hear from me that we had already met. 'Captain de la Croix was on our coach... from Bodmin... we've met before... on the coach.'

He seemed to be regaining his composure, his manner growing formal. 'How is your daughter, Hélène? And your brother-in-law? Are they enjoying the sea air?'

I nodded, answering perhaps more curtly than I should. 'They are both well, thank you.'

He reached for his fob watch, flicking it open. It was the same movement I had seen the night before and as he stared at the large silver dial, snapping it shut, the room began to swim. I thought I might faint. His bow was formal. 'I must leave you now, it's been delightful. Mrs Pengelly, Mrs Barnard...

134

Mrs Cotterell, thank you for your kind hospitality . . . goodbye, children.'

He stepped back, bowing once again, the children racing after him, skipping by his side as he retrieved his jacket. Through the window, we watched him place his hat on his head and walk to the gate, and I tried to keep calm. Watching me at my window. Following me here. The hesitancy in his voice, that downward glance – did he think me so stupid? Liars do not look you in the eye. Liars always give themselves away – like glancing down at the mention of the clock. All men were liars. All men.

There was no doubt in my mind: he had stopped Lady Pendarvis's clock and removed a small part of the mechanism. It was the perfect excuse for him to stay in Fosse to watch us.

We walked back slowly, Elowyn's borrowed parasol shading me from the burning sun. Mrs Pengelly was talking happily, yet I could not shake off my emptiness. The golden-haired girl had reminded me of a portrait of my sisters – the three of us in our best silks, our hair shining like halos even though we had been naughty and run from our nursemaid.

A lady waved from the other side of the road. She wore a powder-blue gown and a long-sleeved jacket, her straw hat tied under her chin with blue ribbons. Her parasol was edged in lace, a small boy and a young girl dancing by her side. Equally joyous, they laughed and skipped, keeping up with their mother's hurried steps, and a stab of envy made me catch my breath.

Her curtsy was graceful, her blue eyes smiling back at us. 'Good day, Mrs Pengelly... a lovely morning.' She pointed to the Old Forge. 'Forgive me if I don't stop — only I'm late for my fitting.'

It was like the sun coming out, then disappearing behind dark clouds. We stood watching her hurry her children to the Old Forge, where there would be more laughter, more joyous games, more buttered buns and chatter. More laughter and love — *Friends who look after each other* — and I fought the lump in my throat.

'That was Mrs Pendarvis. Her husband's a naval captain. They have a house in Falmouth but she often comes to visit her mother-in-law in Admiral House.'

The lump made it hard to speak. 'She's very gracious.'

'She is. And very lovely. We're all glad it worked out so well.' We had reached her house, the black iron railings glinting in the sun. She stood on her front step. 'There was a time when we thought she was to marry Viscount Vallenforth — but she married for love. You can imagine the scandal! Her parents disowned her...'

A wave of hatred soured my smile. 'Who was she?'

'Before her marriage she was Celia Cavendish — Sir Charles's eldest daughter — though I believe neither he nor Lady April speak to her now. Are you all right, my dear?'

My wave of hatred might be passing, but my fear was mounting. This town was too small, everyone knowing each other's business. He was devious and I must not underestimate his cunning; Charles Cavendish would find me and have me locked away again.

Sam stood smiling as he opened the door. Bowing, he held out a note on his silver tray. It was addressed to *Mrs Barnard, Coombe House*. There was no seal, only candlewax keeping it closed.

Dear Marie,
    Please meet me to explain.
                Your obedient servant,
                François Barnard

Chapter Sixteen

There was no wind, the town baking beneath the hot sun. Mrs Pengelly was insistent I should stay out of the heat, Sam equally convinced he should accompany me in case I was set upon again. I assured them both I would find François Barnard in the Ship Inn and promised to return straight away. Still, she was right. Despite the shade of my parasol, my gown encased me like a furnace, my scalp burning beneath the heavy wig.

It was no cooler in the inn. 'Why, bless me, my dear. He's not staying here. He's not said where he's gone.' Mrs Bolitho smiled at me. 'So ye knew Mrs Pengelly all this time?'

'She knew my husband . . . she's been very kind, as have you, Mrs Bolitho.'

Without a breeze, the pavements stank of fish guts, offal from the butcher's and tar burning in the shipyards. Voices rang across the still river, the sound of banging and clanking echoing through the streets. Flies buzzed around piles of horse dung, the mules restless, flicking their tails. Sheep huddled under the shade of a solitary tree, and I knew I must climb the hill to the linhay. Yet despite the searing heat, I felt stronger, less breathless, walking up the hill with more vigour than before. Skylarks were singing, butterflies dancing, the scent from the flowers drenching the air, and I stared out at the horizon. The sea was so still it could have been glass, the gulls resting on the surface. So far, so good. I looked up and felt the fear return. I must look for clouds, for the birds. It was just the sky – just the vast blue sky, yet even so, I could feel myself beginning to weaken. From now on, I would not look up.

The linhay was in sight and crossing the rough grass, I walked slowly round it, picking my way over the fallen stones. Marcel was not there. He would be watching me, waiting to see if I had been followed. The path was deserted and I settled in the shade against the stone wall. I had forgotten how strong the scent of flowers could be, how delicate their petals. How the cliffs looked so treacherous, how they formed such jagged points. I heard a cough behind me. 'Marcel, you made me jump!'

He wore no wig, his hat shading his unshaven chin. His jacket was in his hand, his shirt crumpled. 'Madeleine . . . you left the inn. I was so worried . . .' He spoke softly, no sign of anger, just an incredulous shrug and a flash of real hurt.

'Mrs Pengelly wouldn't hear otherwise. Thomas Pearce was pestering me outside her house – insisting I join him in his hoax. She saw him accost me and offered me refuge . . .'

'But why offer you refuge? Madeleine, you do understand how dangerous this is for us?'

'Yes, I do. They recognised me from before but they know you only as François Barnard. I haven't told them your real name and they don't know my release was unlawful . . . they believe me discharged under your care and they're grateful to you. They know you're taking me back to my brother and they've promise to call me Mrs Barnard. They're just being kind. You have so little money and I thought with Rowan at the Hall and me at Mrs Pengelly's . . . you could take a room . . .'

He stood by my side, staring out across the sea. A frown creased his brows. 'My dear . . . of course I want you to be with people who treat you as you should be treated. The inn is very rough . . . I can only apologise for my lack of funds. Of course, I wasn't meant to be like this. It never takes this long.'

He looked gaunt, dark shadows beneath his eyes. Whereas I was feeling new strength, he looked tired and unkempt, new anxiety in his voice. 'There's been nothing. No sign at all. Something's wrong.'

Fear sliced through me, a terrible sense of guilt. He was risking his life for me. 'How long should we wait?'

'I don't know. Cécile Lefèvre will take her chance when she can. We have to be ready — available for every outgoing tide. *Day and night* we must be prepared to drop everything and board her ship. She may be out there now, waiting for the wind.' His eyes skimmed the horizon. 'Just out of sight. That's why staying with Mrs Pengelly is . . . well, awkward, to say the least.' He turned, and I saw fear in his eyes. 'How can I alert you? How can I get you *both* to the ship on time?'

'Mrs Pengelly knows I'm to leave.'

'And have her come to see you off? Have her know which ship you're on and where you're heading? My dear Madeleine, it would be like handing your brother to them on a plate.'

'My window's at the front of the house – it overlooks the river. It's the first window on the first floor. I'd hear you if you threw a pebble. I'll leave the window and shutters open.'

He reached for my arm, pulling me into a recess behind the stone wall. 'See who's there?'

Captain de la Croix was standing at the brow of the hill, staring across at the linhay. He began crossing the field, standing knee deep in the long grass. We watched him bend as if watching butterflies, and Marcel's voice dropped. 'He visits daily. I see him from my hideout above. Always snooping round . . . staring across the sea, as if he's waiting for the same boat. He's a ship's captain, he knows this is the lull before the storm and the wind's coming.'

'He's watching the house, too. He knows I'm staying with Mrs Pengelly . . . Marcel, I'm wrong about the window. Always send a note; *never* come to the house because he'll be watching.'

'You've seen him?' I nodded and his mouth clenched. His swallow made my heart race. 'For a while now, someone has been shadowing me, always turning round when I turned round. I don't know how they've found me but it seems they have. In which case, I've put all our brave men and women in danger.' I had to sit for the sudden weakness in my legs. He ran his hand across his mouth. 'I can only hope Cécile Lefèvre knows we're here – that she's hiding. Perhaps she's waiting for Pierre de la Croix to return to Bodmin.'

Pierre de la Croix had left the field and was walking down to the cove. He was taking off his boots, rolling down his stockings, wading out into the water. To everyone else, a lonely figure staring out at the horizon, but to us the man who had the power to rip my family apart.

'Go now...while he has his back to us. I'll send a note.' Marcel removed his hat, running a crumpled handkerchief over his short, damp hair. 'Madeleine...I'm very glad you've found comfortable lodgings with Mrs Pengelly. Forgive me if I sounded angry.'

'Marcel?' I could hardly bring myself to ask. 'I need more time – just a few more days. There's something I need to look for in the house. And I need to see Rowan – I need to talk to her.'

He must have seen the tears in my eyes, the way I could hardly say her name. His eyes held mine. 'Is France the right place for her? Maybe it's best for her to stay behind if she has employment – and as for returning to the Hall, let me warn you against it. Your brother can advise you. He will seek redress.'

⚭

I walked back, grateful for the shade of the houses. Marcel was wrong: my brother would be powerless against a man like Charles Cavendish. The quay was busier than usual, a number of carts lining up and blocking the riverside, but the inner road looked free, and I crossed the market square, passing the town hall with its overhanging gables and stone seats. Notices were pinned against the walls, men slowly filing past. Some warned against the threat of invasion, others calling for volunteers. A large reward caught my attention and I stepped closer. It was brighter than the other notices and looked to be newly pinned. Just one look and the blood drained from my head.

THEFT OF DIAMONDS. TEN-SHILLING REWARD.

A reward of ten shillings is offered for any information regarding the theft of jewels from Mrs Enrique Gonzalez on Saturday 31st May in Cranborne.

More was written below but I had no time to read it. A hand reached from behind me, ripping off the notice, and I swung round. Thomas Pearce was scrunching it up, hiding it beneath his jacket, and I caught the challenge in his eyes. There was threat in them, the unquestioning insistence that I was to tell no one. His voice was fierce, as icy as his stare.

'Don't even *think* about claiming this reward. I've got money enough to get us out of here. You get me a ship, I'll give you a diamond.' He looked over his shoulder, turning his back as a man passed. 'Perhaps you've got one ready to leave?' I shook my head, too scared to speak. He was doing up his jacket, his long tapering fingers with their filthy fingernails pulling at the buttons. 'Win, win – that's how it works. We both need to leave England. You tell your *brother-in-law* to get me a ship, and I'll tell no one you're Madeleine Pelligrew, *a madhouse runaway*.'

I felt breathless, a terrible pounding in my chest. The street was too hot, the gutter foul and stinking. There were too many people – too many horses, the shrieking of the seagulls piercing my ears. He drew out his fob watch and flicked it open. 'You better get back to Mrs Pengelly . . . I believe she takes her tea at five.'

The same flick of the wrist as he snapped it shut. The same movement as the night before. He knew who I was – *Madeleine Pelligrew. Madhouse runaway.*

Chapter Seventeen

On the cart to Pendenning Hall
Wednesday 11th June 1800, 5.30 a.m.

A whole day to see Rowan – a chance to talk. Mrs Pengelly understood my need to return to the Hall, though she did not want me to go. Mrs Munroe had left me a jug of squeezed lemon juice and a ham roll wrapped in a damp cloth, and I ate it hungrily, clutching my borrowed cloak. The wind was fierce, a gale from the north howling down the river, whipping the river mouth into a frenzy. It was what I had prayed for – borrowed time. No ship could enter the harbour: even Marcel must give up hope of Cécile Lefèvre arriving today.

We followed the same routine, signing my name with an *X*, a pleasant smile from Mrs Pumfrey, a nod of approval when Mr Troon saw I looked recovered. I gathered my cleaning utensils, once more hurrying behind him down the corridor. I felt stronger, clearer headed. All men lied, I should have known Joshua would be no exception.

'Shall I finish the study?'

'No, Mrs Barnard. The study's finished – there's just this last wall of books in the library. I believe you'll notice a difference

– we've had the room aired.' He glanced at the clouds scudding across the sky and seemed relieved. 'Finish those books today and that'll be all.'

'You're expecting Sir Charles and his family?'

He shook his head. 'Not if he's coming by ship.'

A rich smell of beeswax greeted me. The dust sheets had been removed, a set of plump cushions adorned the chairs. Candles had been placed in the crystal chandelier, a huge Chinese vase by the marble fireplace. Mr Troon stood watching me, as if by seeing what I did he could instruct his staff to do the same. I, too, had stood watching the book cleaners when I had been mistress of this house. I knew exactly how it was done. I began tapping the first book, collecting the dust on my clean lint, examining the shakings with my magnifier. I pursed my lips, frowning as I held the book over my basin and caressed the pages with my goose feather.

He finally left and I sank back on my knees, the scent of lavender drifting from the carpet. It was just as well these were not my husband's books. Now I felt stronger, I wanted to rip every book he had bought to pieces.

Most of them were arranged vertically but some of the larger ones on the bottom shelf lay horizontally, and a set of bindings caught my eye. They were behind the large leather chair shielded from general sight – either that or they had been placed there after someone had read them in the chair and they had remained ever since. I looked again. They were not books, but leather folders similar to the ones in the study. I reached for the magnifier. Definitely similar folders, containing accounts and letters.

Hiding from sight behind the chair, I lifted the first off the shelf, my excitement giving way to disappointment. Just page after page of settled accounts – dating from 1786, *after* Sir Charles had taken over the running of Pendenning Hall. Letters sanctioning rent cuts or promising new almshouses; letters allowing a poacher to go free, sanctioning a pension for a butler, money sent to clear the main town sewer. I had to look again. There was such disparity in these accounts. The exact opposite to what Mrs Munroe had implied.

I reached for the next, confused by the generosity of Sir Charles's gifts – letters sending money to the church, to tenants for the repair of their cottages; letters from grateful recipients, thanking Sir Charles for such considerate terms on their loan. Such generosity. I lifted the next letter and my head spun. It was from an attorney in Bristol.

> *Willoughby & Son*
> *Attorneys, established 1760*
> *Broadmead*
> *Bristol*
> *December 1787*
>
> *Dear Sir Charles,*
> *In reply to your recent enquiry, I can inform you that both Dr Melrose and Dr Taylor have been delighted with the progress made by Mrs Pelligrew. Such has been her full recovery that they feel it is no longer necessary to continue her treatment. They have certified her in sound mind, her well-being restored, and she has requested to return to her family in France.*

She would like me to thank you for your generosity and the kind interest you have taken in her welfare, yet you must understand the delicacy of the situation. She does not want to have anything more to do with you as she blames you entirely for her husband's ruin.

I believe in the circumstances it best for you to no longer write to me to seek assurances that Mrs Pelligrew is well. She wishes all correspondence to end.

I remain your obedient servant.
George Willoughby

I tried to steady my hand. *Bristol*, and I had requested to return to France? I had to breathe, stop the room from spinning. Charles Cavendish had sought and been assured of my welfare? All these years I had accused him, hated him, and yet all along he had thought me safely returned to my family? The words blurred before me – *your generosity . . . kind interest you have taken.*

The door opened and I manage to scramble the letters back into their folder. I had just enough time to slip them on to the shelf and pick up my cloth. Dipping it into the warm water, I dabbed it against the saddle soap. It was not Mr Troon, but a footman holding a set of crystal decanters on his tray. He nearly dropped them as he jolted. 'Blimey! Didn't see ye there!'

I gripped my cloth. I had got it all wrong, all these years harbouring false hatred. Someone must have assumed my identity and *pretended* to be me, and I must have become her. Of course, no one believed I was a fine lady – they thought me to be *her*. I fought my dizziness, the terrible rage boiling inside me. Two more footmen entered and began cleaning the windows. One opened the French window and I ran on to the terrace. *Keep from crying . . . keep from shouting.*

The top of the trees were swaying, the clouds racing across the sky, and I breathed deeply. Was it an accident or had someone been bribed to swap the two of us? Two weeks ago, I would have shouted and screamed, maybe even laughed, but now I knew to breathe deeply. All my hatred, all my plans for revenge directed at a man who had done his best for me? The pain was so fierce it cut like a knife. Nothing kept me here. The moment Marcel sent word, I would return to my brother and meet my nieces and nephews. They were my family – they would have my love. Rowan must stay behind. She had found where she belonged and it would be cruel to bring her with us to France.

She waved at me from across the hall, leaving her friends to rush and sit next to me. Reaching for my hands, she put them to her lips and after just one day apart, I saw the change in her. Her eyes were brighter, her cheeks full of health, her black hair plaited into coils beneath her mobcap. Her hands looked less raw, her fingernails clean. She ate hungrily, wiping her bowl with her bread. At last we could talk and she burst forth, hardly knowing where to start.

'Ye look that well, honest. When they said ye took ill, I was that worried; but ye look . . .' She peeped under my veil again. 'Ye look *pretty*, Madeleine. Honest, there's no need for yer veil. Yer skin looks so much better.'

Her happy chatter was accompanied by smiles across the table from her new friends. Even Mrs Pumfrey smiled, and

I fought the ache in my heart. It was the right decision. I would leave her here where she would be happy. But perhaps I should ask her?

'So ye see, it's not bad at all. Sometimes we get caught laughin'... we have to put our fists in our mouths.' We stood in the queue for the privy, the wind whistling round the court-yard. 'Madeleine, ye know ye wanted me to find out everything I could... well, did ye know there's not one painting of Celia Cavendish in the house? That's Sir Charles's eldest daughter. Ella says it's because they had a terrible falling-out. And what's more, Ella says she was here when Miss Celia *was said* to have become *unwell*.'

She clapped her hand across her mouth, her eyes full of excitement. She glanced round. 'Ella says she saw a man *carrying* a woman over his shoulder that night. And that man was *Phillip Randall* and Ella says she swears to God that the woman was *Celia Cavendish*.'

I stared at her. 'She was carried out to a waiting carriage?'

Her huge eyes widened. 'Yes. Carried all floppy over his shoulders... and *forced* into the carriage. Ella didn't know what to do. She told Mrs Pumfrey and Mrs Pumfrey told her *to leave it with her*. She made her swear to say nothing to no one. But Miss Celia *never* came back. Never, ever stepped across the door again. And they *never* speak her name... and her portrait was taken down.'

Carried all floppy. Just like I had been. Bundled out of this very house just two days after I had found Joshua's body. Drugged by Phillip Randall so I could not push him away; bound and gagged so I could not scream. Was that really on the direction of the doctors? I had been expecting to take up residence in a house on the estate – a kind gesture from Sir Charles until I found my feet – but that never happened. I was deemed too mad with grief to see anyone. Too dangerous to others. To be taken for treatment until the wildness passed.

'Madeleine . . . don't ye see? Ye used to tell me all the time that ye were wronged, that ye'd been taken at night. That ye'd been carried out against yer will. And it happened to her. What if she was sent to a madhouse, too? What if Sir Charles had wanted to put her away, just like he did you?'

'Maybe Ella saw wrong . . . maybe Celia Cavendish was eloping.'

Rowan shook her head. 'Not according to Ella. There was all sorts going on round that time – Sir Charles and Lady April said she was unwell . . . they tried to stop any rumours that she'd eloped but no one believed it.'

'Why not?'

She glanced round, her hand covering her words. 'Because a footman read something . . . a private letter . . . and something didn't sound right.'

'A footman read a private letter?'

I must have sounded horrified. She giggled, pointing me forward. We were nearly at the privy door. 'Madeleine, ye do know, don't you, that servants read everything they can find – especially *here* with them away all the time? Mrs Pumfrey reads all manner of books from the library, honest, and they go through their drawers looking for diaries and secret love letters – not everyone, of course, but the ones what read do.

And Ella says the very next day a footman read something in Sir Charles's study that gave him to believe Sir Charles had his daughter *put away*.'

The door of the latrine opened and she gestured me forward. 'Ye go first. I'll see you back in the hall.'

She had waved me goodbye, smiling down at the jam tart Ella had given her. *It's because Mrs Pumfrey's so pleased with me*, she had whispered. *I'm happy here, honest I am – an' I'm happy to stay as I know ye'll come back fer me*. Her smile had seemed genuine but there had been so little time to talk; the cart was leaving and the bell summoning her to the servants' hall.

Mrs Pengelly sat on one side of her stone fireplace and I sat at the other. Her drawing room was charming, the two large windows giving views right across the river. It was bright and airy, decorated with striped cream wallpaper. The chaise longue was furnished in gold and blue, as were the two chairs with their finely curved backs and claw feet. A large gold mirror hung above the mantelpiece, a set of painted china ornaments sitting beside a gold clock. Yet my mind was elsewhere.

I needed to be sharper. Charles Cavendish was far more devious than I had thought. What if he knew servants read what he left out for them to find? I felt jumpy, unable to settle. We had eaten well, drinking hot chocolate from Mrs Pengelly's delicate china cups, but my mind kept straying from our conversation. Finally, I could bear it no longer. 'Was Celia Cavendish ill for a while?' I asked.

She looked perplexed. 'No, my dear – I don't believe so.'

'Do you know there are no portraits of her in Pendenning? Rowan told me the family never speak of her.'

She put down her cup. 'That is the truth. Father and daughter have not spoken to each other for many years – though I didn't know that about the portraits. The rift, I believe, stems from her refusing to marry Viscount Vallenforth.'

'Was Celia Cavendish away for some time?'

A frown creased her forehead, her eyes shrewd, as if knowing there was more to my questions. She was wearing a grey poplin dress, an intricately embroidered silk shawl tucked around her shoulders. Elegant and demure, yet I had heard her laugh with such gaiety. There was no laughter now, just deep concern. 'You've been very quiet since you came back. What's troubling you, my dear?'

I was meant to find those letters, meant to be duped along with everyone else. Sir Charles knew servants read what they found and he used that knowledge, counting on them to spread what he wanted known. Leaving receipts and bills where they would come across them – in bookcases with easily accessible keys, on shelves behind chairs, everything left as if by accident. A raft of fabricated letters carefully selected to show him in a good light, making the servants believe what he *wanted them* to believe. Feeding them lies – his good works, his concern, his generosity and interest in people's welfare. All carefully positioned lies. Joshua had said Charles Cavendish burned his letters, yet Charles Cavendish had kept those he needed to cover his tracks. Letters to prove he was a concerned friend. False letters.

I hardly heard Mrs Pengelly. 'Is there something you want to tell me, Madeleine?'

I had to tell her. 'No doctors saw me before they incarcerated me — Charles Cavendish falsified the certificates and had me dragged straight from the house . . . drugged. Within months, he moved me to *another* madhouse and changed my name. Thereafter, he moved me every two years with the sole intention of preventing anyone from finding me. Each time, I was given a new name and the conditions worsened. He sought to make me mad and he very nearly succeeded.'

Her eyes widened, a slight catch to her breath. 'Why would he do that . . . ?'

'Because he arranged for my husband to be murdered. Joshua did not take his own life. He was heavily in debt to Charles Cavendish — though I had no inkling at the time. My husband was clever in many ways, yet unbelievably foolish in others. Charles Cavendish knew he could manipulate him into debt. He wanted our house, our land, and access to Sir James's clay.'

'Many want what others have. But they don't murder for it.' Her voice was wary, slightly clipped.

Dear Lord, she thinks me mad. I had to keep my voice steady. 'His plan would have worked, only I told him I suspected my husband had been murdered. I told him I saw a man coming from the riverbank only ten minutes before I found my husband inexplicably drowned in the river. The man I saw was Phillip Randall. He knew that I'd take it to the authorities — that I'd call for an investigation — so he had to silence me.'

'This is a very grave accusation. Do you have any proof?'

153

I shook my head. 'None whatsoever. Mrs Pengelly, there *was* a time I sounded mad. Maybe I even acted mad, but I can assure you I'm not. I believe I was on the very edge of insanity but for Rowan's kindness... She brought me back from the brink.'

Her voice was soft, yet filled with such strength. 'I believe you to be in sound mind, Madeleine.'

Tears filled my eyes. 'François Barnard believes so too. He searched for me and finally found me.' I fought the thumping in my chest. 'But I have to tell you... he *falsified* the certificates that claimed I'm sane. He helped me escape... I wasn't set free.' The clock on the mantelpiece chimed nine. The shutters were drawn, the silver tray on the table awaiting our empty cups. Perfect tranquillity, except for the thumping of my heart.

Her mouth tightened. 'I think it's time for me to send for your old friend, Alice Polcarrow, and her husband, Matthew Reith. He's the foremost attorney in Cornwall. He will arrange for two doctors to examine you.' A tear rolled down my cheek and she reached forward, clasping my hands. 'They'll be thorough, though. Totally rigorous. They'll need to be convinced of your sanity. Are you ready for that, my dear?' She waited, but I could not answer. 'Shall I send for Alice and Matthew Reith?'

I nodded, the words *totally rigorous* sounding so brutal. I would have to train my thoughts, not allow my mind to wander. I must ask no more questions about Celia Cavendish, yet I felt certain she had suffered the same fate. Had she been sent to a madhouse and yet managed to escape?

The wind funnelled down the river, whistling against my casement, rattling the panes. Large ships lay tossing in the heavy swell, the smaller boats hauled on to higher ground; even so, there was little protection from the black water raging against the banks. Securing the shutters, I sat at my dressing table.

Usually it was too painful to look in the mirror, yet now I leaned forward. Perhaps the oranges and lemons were working. My eyes seemed to have lost their bulge, my lips were no longer cracked. The sores round my mouth were healed and the web of fine lines on my cheeks seemed to be fading. I still had no eyebrows, very sparse lashes, and the same bitter mouth. Rubbing salve on to my lips, I smoothed lemon-scented lanolin on to my cheeks, staring back at the eyes in the mirror. They were hard, brittle, full of mistrust.

A soft knock on the door, and Tamsin stood with fresh candles, smiling as she replaced them in the top drawer.

'Tamsin, do maids like working up at the Hall? Is Mrs Pumfrey considered fair?'

The light shone behind her, her frizzy hair a halo around her. 'I believe they like her. She's strict, mind, but she's not cruel. There's some been there a long while. Ye're thinking of yer daughter?'

I nodded, trying to hide my emptiness. 'I need to know they'll take care of her.'

Chapter Eighteen

Tamsin glanced out of the window. 'Yes, 'tis her. There now – she said she'd be here at ten. Whoops...' She seemed to lunge instead of walk, spilling the water in the jug, the soap slipping from her hands as she tried to grasp it. 'There... got it.' She had been busy all morning, running up and down the stairs carrying jugs of hot water. With my bath finished, and Elowyn downstairs with my new dress, I felt strangely nervous, like a bride preparing for her wedding.

'I'll get that put away.' Tamsin abandoned her attempts to tuck back her red hair. 'There now... Whoops...' Her foot caught my dressing gown and she stumbled forward, swilling more water from the basin. Her already flushed cheeks turned crimson. 'Are ye all right? Only I'd better get this downstairs.'

Footsteps sounded on the stairs, voices discussing the fortunate break in the weather. Mrs Pengelly sounded excited. 'Go on up. Mrs Barnard is in your old room.'

'Can I come in?' a voice called through the open door. My gown over one arm, a hatbox under the other and a bag over

156

her shoulder, Elowyn came sideways through the door. 'I'll put these on the bed. There now. Good morning, Mrs Barnard.'

She must have seen the tears in my eyes. I could not help it. I was newly bathed, smelling of lilac soap, my borrowed chemise beautiful. My fingernails were no longer bitten, my itching gone, and I was about to be given a new gown. Mrs Pengelly smiled from the door. 'We've brought in the looking glass and Tamsin will come back and give you a hand. I'll see you downstairs.'

Elowyn unwrapped the gown and I slipped off my dressing gown, standing in front of her in my chemise and borrowed stockings. 'They've sewn it beautifully,' she said as she held up the gown.

The pale blue muslin caught the light, and I ran my fingers over the row of pin-tucks. It had a high waist, a trim of cream lace at the collar, the sleeves ending below the elbow with a small cuff decorated with blue satin and matching lace. On the bed lay a cream jacket with long sleeves, a soft round neck and blue buttons.

'They had plenty of fabric after taking it in and the girls like making buttons.' She smiled, holding the gown against me. 'You're going to find this much lighter.' She hesitated, placing it back on the bed. 'Mrs Barnard . . . before you put this on, may I suggest a few simple touches?' She had a gentle way of talking. Leading me to the dressing table, she pulled out the stool and invited me to sit. Daylight was never kind, even more so as my dressing table faced the window, and I sat unable to look up. She lifted my chin.

'A number of my ladies have smallpox scars. Some have

157

disfigurements and unsightly birthmarks... and over the years I've perfected several aids to help.' She took a small box from her bag. 'I've brought some salves with me. They're made from the purest beeswax and will be gentle on your skin. Here's some powder to lighten your complexion – just a gentle mix of potato starch and chalk – and a touch of rouge to highlight these lovely cheekbones of yours. To finish, I've several shades of lip salve. May I show you?' I closed my eyes, feeling her soft fingers rub my cheeks, the dab of a brush, the touch of balm on my lips. 'There... what do you think?'

Her powder reduced the redness, her hint of rouge giving me a look of health. Even my lips had been cajoled back into a delicate shape. Pulling the cork from a small bottle, she picked up a fine brush. 'Now, for your eyebrows. This burnt cork is steeped in resin so it won't smudge – just don't touch it until it dries. I'll leave you these... you only need a touch – here, where your eyebrows should be. Like this... very, very, softly. You don't want them too dark.'

Her tiny brushstrokes were transforming my face, the exact shape of the arch where my eyebrows had once been. 'Don't cry,' she whispered. 'I tell all my ladies not to cry – or else I have to start again!' She stood back, admiring her handiwork. 'Two things – don't try to re-create your eyelashes, just put a tiny dab of white powder on your lids... like this.'

The lightest touch on my eyelids and I fought my tears. She had brought light to my eyes, a brightness to my face, and I gripped my hands, determined not to undo her hard work. I would never be the beauty I had once been, I was much too gaunt; but I was no longer a gargoyle, just a thirty-five-year-old woman who had lost the last fourteen years of her life.

She picked up the gown. 'And the second thing I need to say is that when hair grows back after a period of loss it can grow back thinner and maybe a different shade – sometimes white, or grey. I've seen that several times . . . so best be prepared.'

I smiled. 'I'll be happy with any hair.'

She smiled back. 'Did you lose your hair from shock? I've heard that happens.'

The gown fitted me perfectly and I could see she was thrilled. Turning me round, she plumped out the top of the sleeves. It felt so light, such a sense of freedom. A small pleat opened at the bodice, a cream insert, my stockinged toes peeping from underneath.

'No . . . wait . . . don't look yet. I've several pairs of shoes you might like to try – and we have your turban. In fact, we have two – one in the blue, and one in cream silk. One for the day, and one with pearls for the evening.' She lifted both from the hatbox, helping me on with the blue one. Pulling it lower, her smile grew. 'There . . . now you can look,' she said, handing me the handkerchief she had ready.

I could not speak. No need to wear my heavy wig. Soft blonde curls peeped from either side of the turban, two small feathers held in place with pearl pins. 'Now . . . these shoes . . . this leather is much softer. Good, they seem to fit . . . try these ones, too.'

She was adamant I keep both the satin slippers and the leather shoes, but I shook my head. 'I can't have both . . . I can't afford these . . .'

159

She remained resolute, pursing her lips. 'Mrs Pengelly won't hear no.'

I was overwhelmed. *Friends that look after each other.* So much kindness, so much warmth and care. 'I can't thank you enough.'

Her eyes held mine. 'It's why I'm a dressmaker, Mrs Barnard. Why I'll never stop. I may work all hours, but I could never deny myself this pleasure.'

Footsteps ran up the stairs and Tamsin stumbled through the door. Elowyn stood to one side. 'Well, Tamsin, what d'you think?'

Tamsin's hands flew to her mouth. 'Oh my goodness... ye look so beautiful... like a real lady. Honest, it's like I hardly recognise ye. Wait till Mrs Pengelly sees ye like this!'

The sun streamed through the two large windows, Mrs Pengelly's dining room every bit as elegant as her drawing room. A portrait of her husband hung above the wooden mantelpiece, an embroidered fire screen in the fireplace. Paintings of ships adorned the walls, a series of charcoal sketches, a glass-fronted cabinet full of china. The clock struck two and she adjusted her glasses. 'Had you heard... did you have knowledge of it?'

I nodded. 'Rowan told me what she knew and the attendants used to taunt me. They said I should consider myself lucky, that if I was such a fine lady I could be awaiting the guillotine.'

'How very heartless.' Mrs Pengelly took a deep breath. 'After they beheaded the King, the Revolutionaries unleashed such terror. The Queen was beheaded and no aristocrats were safe – the bloodshed and atrocities were barbaric.'

'You say there are lists? Names of people I might know?' Despite the heat, I felt icy cold. The horror behind her words sent shivers through me.

She nodded. 'There are lists of names. I'm sure there are many in London who you could talk to. Thank goodness your family was spared and your brother survived.'

'He must have persuaded them he shared their ideals. He's been given a position of trust.' My pulse quickened at the thought of his capture. There was too much to take in. *The Courier* lay open on the table, Mrs Pengelly quizzing me for some time. I had answered correctly – George III was on the throne and William Pitt was First Minister, but I had no idea of the assassination attempts on the King's life.

She nodded. 'The doctors will be rigorous in their questioning. They may ask you about it – it's very shocking and only a couple of weeks ago. The first attempt was in Hyde Park, but the bullet missed and hit a man standing beside him. The second attempt was in a theatre in Drury Lane. He fired another two bullets but according to *The Times*, a man knocked his arm and the bullets hit the panel behind the King. Such a narrow escape.'

'Who was he?'

'An ex-soldier...wait...I do know his name. James Hadfield – I believe he's insane but the rumours are that he was put up to it by the French. They have spies in London – placed as agitators to stir up unrest and undermine the government. Many believe *they* were behind it.'

Ice cold gripped me, a terrible hatred of the new regime. 'Why is France marching into these countries? Who *is* Napoleon Bonaparte... how can he wield such power?'

Slipping off her glasses, she rested her elbows on the table, the tips of her fingers beneath her chin. 'He's a general from Corsica – from minor nobility. He's powerful and, it seems, unstoppable. Last year, he abandoned his troops in Egypt and returned to Paris and declared a *coup d'état*. He just disbanded the Directorate in charge. He had the military behind him and just marched in and declared a new regime. He's called his regime a *Consulate* – and he's declared himself *First Consul.*'

She was using words I had never heard before and must have seen my panic because she put her hand on mine. 'It changes by the day. I only know this because I discuss it with my daughter. The Revolutionaries set up the Directorate and it's *them* that General Bonaparte ousted.'

'He has that much power?'

'So it would appear. Rose says General Bonaparte commands both parliamentary and military power. But so far, we still control the Mediterranean. Their armies are strong but we possess greater naval strength. We've constructed an effective blockade and we're holding strong.'

The sun was glinting on the river, a slight lessening in the wind. 'Do you think they'll ask me this?'

'I don't know. We can go over it until you're confident you'll remember.'

The front page of the *Courier* was next to me. '*Naples is on the side of the British and with us controlling the Mediterranean,*

General Bonaparte has taken his army to cross the Alps. Is that the only way he can invade the northern states of Italy?'

She slipped her glasses back on. 'Yes. No doubt we'll hear more about that. Are you all right? Shall we stop our lesson for now?' A dull ache throbbed at my temples. It was hard to concentrate, facts and names jumbling in my head. Outside, boats were drifting up the river, a cormorant spreading out its wings. A group of swans was swimming to the other side. Mrs Pengelly saw me looking out of the window. 'Would you like to take a walk, my dear?'

'Maybe the fresh air might help clear my head. And I need to see François to explain why I'm dressed so beautifully.'

'He'll be delighted by how well you look. Go and tell him – only don't be *too* long.' There was a lightness to her tone, a slight purse of her lips. 'I've invited Captain de la Croix to take tea with us . . . at five.'

'Captain de la Croix?'

I turned to hide my sudden blush as I folded the newspaper. The sudden rush of pleasure at the sound of his name disarmed me. He was a dangerous man: he would question me about Marcel, about my brother; he would ask me about my parents and where I lived. The thumping in my chest grew unbearable; he had followed us to the dressmaker and now he was to take tea with us.

Ships were entering the harbour, taking down their sails, dropping their anchors. Six hours until the outgoing tide. Six hours before Marcel might call for me.

Chapter Nineteen

A soft breeze caught the feathers on my turban, my new shoes in no danger of getting soiled. Rain had washed the cobbles free from manure; the shops were busy, a group of women waiting to buy bread. They were staring at me, nudging each other, and my anxiety spiralled. I should have stayed in my old gown, worn my hideous wig and my hat with a veil.

The rain had brought freshness, the fragrance of the flowers almost intoxicating. Marcel would be watching from his hideout above the linhay, and I would tell him Captain de la Croix had been invited for tea. I looked round – there was no sign of him, just a handful of women carrying baskets of clams, a man with a barrow of stones, and a group of soldiers returning to the fort.

The wind was stronger on the clifftop, rippling the grass around the linhay, making the ox-eye daisies dance. Pink foxgloves stood sentry against the stone walls, a profusion of scarlet poppies in the field beyond, and I breathed in the smell of thyme, revelling in the sheer beauty of the place. The storm had been a godsend, yet I needed more evidence if I hoped to persuade Matthew Reith to investigate Joshua's death. A shadow passed behind the stones and I hurried forward. 'Marcel...'

My greeting died on my lips. Pierre de la Croix had his back to me. He swung round, his eyes widening, a sudden blush reddening his cheeks, and I turned away, disconcerted by his gaze. 'I'm... sorry. You startled me, Mrs Barnard. I wasn't expecting anyone and...' He tried to compose himself. 'How... very... *well* you look. How very... I hardly... that is... How very lovely to see you. ' He bowed stiffly. His shirt was unbuttoned at the neck, his sleeves billowing, caught by a sudden gust of wind. I could see him standing on the deck of a ship, tall, commanding, and I turned to hide the burning in my cheeks.

To be looked at like that again – to see such admiration in his eyes. My blush was from shame, from fury that my response had been a rush of pleasure. He was a Republican officer in the regime I detested. 'Are you searching for something?' I managed to ask.

He shrugged, smiling his shy smile. 'I was watching a very fine beetle.' He seemed somehow vulnerable, but I knew not to be fooled by his boyish innocence, nor by his concern for my well-being, his oranges and limes, his paying for my room. They were all a ruse to fool me. He must have followed Marcel and been searching the linhay, guessing this was where Cécile Lefèvre would leave her message.

'Do you make a study of insects, Captain?'

'Not in any great depth, but I have plenty of time on my hands to observe them: a prisoner on parole must occupy his days somehow. The flowers are so beautiful, especially here where they're sheltered from the wind... Look... in this crevice. If I could paint I would like to capture their image — just like this.'

Like the images I held in my mind for fourteen years, my nightly visits round the flower beds in the gardens of Pendenning Hall. But it was never my garden, never paid for by my lying husband. The pain was sharp, stabbing. All men lied. All men, and this man among them. He reached for his jacket, quickly buttoning it, pulling his hat low over his brow. No longer flustered, but a frigate captain. 'Mrs Pengelly said you were French. Where about in France are you from?'

I knew I must stay calm. I must breathe slowly, stop the thumping of my heart. My brother's life depended on him believing us Republicans. 'We never say we're French. It's too dangerous to admit — you understand that, don't you?' He nodded and I felt a surge of courage. 'It's not like we're *émigrés* to be pampered and run after. My family are tradesman in Saint-Malo. They've worked hard all their lives — and you, Captain de la Croix?'

His jaw clenched, a swallow as he gazed across the sea. 'From Montagne-Charente.'

'A landlocked region, yet you joined the navy?'

A wistfulness entered his voice, a tightness round his mouth. 'A fifth son must find employment where he can. I was fortunate to be appointed *Aspirant* on the frigate *Diadème* — a midshipman in our navy. I was nineteen. I'm now forty-three and I've never returned to my place of birth. The sea became my home.'

His words pierced me like a knife. I, too, left home and never returned. I had to harden my heart, ignore the sadness in his voice. 'You've done well, Captain – *Capitaine de Vaisseau* is a great achievement, and serving our glorious country must have brought you great pride. Do you never think to escape? Our navy needs you more than ever. You're not held in prison – you have ample opportunity to bribe someone to help you escape.'

A hardening of his mouth. 'I've sworn an oath. I've given my parole and I'll never break my word.'

I knew to sound convincing. 'What's an oath to our enemies when we have *right* on our side? Our glorious ideals of *liberté* and *égalité*. We've freed ourselves from tyranny and now we must free others. Those who rise to power should rise not from birth – not from divine right – but through *merit*. Captain de la Croix, do you not thrill at the thought of our great general marching across the Alps?'

'Indeed I do . . .' His voice was hoarse, his frown deepening as he stared out to sea.

'Our country needs you back . . . our navy needs experienced officers to command our ships – we must break this blockade if our troops are to have access to the Mediterranean. You must be desperate to return to duty.'

He remained staring out to sea. 'My ship was taken as a prize, Mrs Barnard, and as such I bear the consequences of great shame. Had she sunk, I might be honoured with another command, but a *capitaine de vaisseau* who hands his ship over to the enemy is never given another command. The disgrace is absolute.' He swallowed. 'My navy days are over and I would be foolish to believe otherwise.'

A knife twisted my stomach. 'I'm sorry, I didn't mean to sound so harsh.'

'No . . . not at all. I've had plenty of time to consider the disgrace I'll face on my return. And as for serving my country? I've been held prisoner for four years, and though I no longer command a ship, I believe I still serve my country. I have the honour of representing my compatriots held prisoner alongside me . . . appointed by Sir Alexander Pendarvis to visit the prisons and compile reports of their conditions, their food, their welfare. I speak for those who fought for our country . . . for the captains of merchant ships and their families imprisoned with them. I convey their requests and their complaints. I mediate for them, and make sure their letters are sent.'

The church clock in the town chimed the half-hour and he reached for his fob watch. 'Did you know I've been invited to take tea with you and Mrs Pengelly?' He sounded tentative, as if the idea would displease me.

'Yes . . . she did mention it.'

'I came to pick her some flowers. She loves ox-eye daisies and these are the best I can find. They're sheltered from the wind . .' He began picking them, laying them carefully over one arm while reaching for the next, and I bit my lip, forcing back my tears. I wanted to cry with the pain, cry for my family, for my country, for everything that had been and could never be again. 'Not long now . . . just a few more.'

168

I had to turn away. His voice, his gestures, his straight back and broad shoulders, so like my father, and now his words taking me back to my childhood. I was ten years old, skipping by my father's side, my father holding the plump grapes between his fingers. *Not long now . . . just a few more days and we'll start the harvest.* He had the same dark hair, the same frown of concentration. The same flicker of sadness when I persuaded him to let me marry the man I loved.

We hardly spoke as we walked back. He held his flowers in the crook of his arm, crossing over to the other side of the pavement to shield me from the passing carts. He doffed his hat to many, returning smiles from women and waves from children, everyone smiling back as if he was their friend, and my regret returned. I had been too impatient to leave my parents' home, too eager to taste the delights of London. Too much in love with the thought of love. Too ready to spread my wings and fly.

Outside Mrs Pengelly's beautiful red-brick house, a sudden hoarseness entered his voice. 'Back in the linhay, you called me *Marcel*. I . . . apologise . . . if you were expecting to meet someone else and you found me instead.'

I shook my head, cursing my foolishness. *Marcel, not François.* Already he knew too much.

Mrs Pengelly was delighted he had accompanied me back. Settling him between us, she started talking about her adored granddaughters and new grandson, and I sat with my hands clasped, desperate for his visit to pass. He sat straight-backed and formal, asking after each grandchild, remembering their favourite toys, delighted her grandson was now sitting up. Tamsin brought in a jug for the flowers, casting him an adoring look, and he smiled in greeting.

Mrs Pengelly was trying to draw me into the conversation but I could not speak. I had put my brother in grave danger: Captain de la Croix would trace Marcel; Cécile Lefèvre would be caught because of my stupidity. My nephews and nieces would lose their father. I had to stop myself from twisting my hands, stop the thumping of my heart. Time was passing so slowly, no sign of a tea tray. No sign of him leaving.

'Have you known each other long? Mrs Barnard told me on the coach she had friends in Fosse but I had no idea it was you. Such a lovely coincidence – both of us knowing you . . .' He glanced at his hands but he did not fool me. This was the beginning of his questioning, an interrogation would follow.

Mrs Pengelly seemed to sense the coldness between us. Pierre de la Croix was not looking at me, and I was certainly not looking at him. A note of hesitancy crept into her voice. 'We didn't know each other but my husband knew Mrs Barnard's husband. It was a long time ago now.' She must have seen my cheeks burn as her voice softened. 'I believe he was interested in shipbuilding.'

I breathed deeply. Commissioning a ship he would never own, not that it mattered because he had no money to pay for it. Footsteps scuttled behind the door, Sam knocked and opened it. He bowed formally, beaming with pride. 'Tea is served, Mrs Pengelly.'

Pierre de la Croix stood as if to attention. 'This is indeed a rare treat. Mrs Pengelly – you've gone to a lot of trouble.'

Eva Pengelly raised her eyebrows. Leaning towards him, her

voice dropped. 'I'd like to take the credit but Mrs Munroe and Tamsin have been unstoppable . . . and Sam's polished the glasses and decanted our best brandy. I've not seen them so happy in years.'

More shuffles and giggles sounded in the hall and my heart froze. We were clearly going to take tea in the dining room. Captain de la Croix held out his arm and Mrs Pengelly beamed. 'Thank you . . . please take Mrs Barnard through.'

I slipped my hand on to his proffered arm and he stared ahead, tall, upright, wearing the uniform of a Republican officer. No hint of a smile, just leading me forward like a guard to the guillotine. At the door, his eyes widened in pleasure. The table was covered in a lace-edged tablecloth, a polished silver candlestick gleaming in the centre. Our places were laid with fine bone china, the crystal glasses sparkling. His voice faltered. 'How beautiful the table looks.'

Sam drew out Mrs Pengelly's chair and Pierre de la Croix drew out mine, his hand burning my back as I took my place. The three of us sitting in splendour, the silver urn ready to be poured, Sam hovering over his gleaming decanter. More footsteps, more excited whispering, followed by silence, before Mrs Munroe and Tamsin swept in with their trays laden with elaborate dishes. They had changed into their best dresses, both with fresh aprons and newly brushed hair. Bursting with pride, they placed their plates carefully on the table, smiling coyly at each gasp of admiration.

At last, they stood back and Mrs Munroe pointed to each delicacy in turn. 'That's *oeufs en neige* . . . and these are *îles flottantes* . . . Here we have *cherries en chemise* – the captain's favourite – and you must remember these, Miss Madeleine? I made them especially from my old cookbook . . . and I can tell ye for sure, they don't have anything like this up at the Hall.' She folded her arms across her ample bosom, a sniff of pride as she lifted her chin. 'Least not now, they don't. Not like the old days.'

They stood proudly watching us taste their hard work. All my favourites, yet for all that they could have been sawdust. My cheeks were burning, my stomach twisting. Mrs Pengelly had not noticed Mrs Munroe's mistake; she was talking happily, laughing, trying everything, and so was Pierre de la Croix. He seemed utterly delighted, sampling cake after cake, dipping his spoon into Mrs Munroe's *crème anglaise*, assuring her that her soft twirls of meringues looked just like clouds. Sighing with pleasure, he told us he could not remember the last time he had tasted such perfect *îles flottantes*. She had used exactly the right amount of nutmeg and they were light enough to float, and if I had not felt so consumed with fear, I would have done the same.

'No . . . no, I can't manage another morsel!' There was real joy in his face, genuine happiness as he repeatedly thanked them. His rich laughter rang across the room. He could manage nothing more to eat, but maybe a drop of Sam's brandy?

Yet every mouthful made me want to vomit. A flicker had crossed his eyes, a sudden stiffness when he heard Mrs Munroe call me Miss Madeleine. It would take him no time at all to connect a *Miss Madeleine* to Pendenning Hall. No time at all to discover that my brother was le Comte de Charlbourg.

Égalité

Chapter Twenty

The clock in the hall struck eleven and I glanced at my writing, delighted it was getting neater. 'I mainly forget names – but writing things down helps me remember.'

A sweet smile of encouragement and Mrs Pengelly folded the newspaper. 'James says we'll soon be united with Ireland. Most people believe it will give us greater stability but I know my husband wouldn't approve. He was a Radical, Madeleine, he believed in the freedom of man.'

I could hardly hide my astonishment. 'He supported the French Revolutionaries?'

She shrugged, a slight rise to her eyebrows. 'In *principle*, yes. But not how it developed – not the bloodshed. His ideal was for men to be free from tyranny and oppression... which is why he'd hate to see the Irish crushed so brutally. The problem lies in that two years ago the French attempted to invade us *through Ireland* and most people in England, especially our government, feel it's vital to crush any rebellion – to curb further association with France.'

'In case the French try to invade through Ireland again?'

'Yes . . . but I have to admit to some sympathy for these Irish Catholics. I believe they *do* have reason to protest. It's very hard. Our Protestant troops are imposing laws on them yet they do pose a danger to England.'

I picked up my pen. 'Who has rebelled?'

'Presbyterians, too, not just the Catholics. Many of the leading families are now denied the power they once held. They're angry at being shut out of important decisions – and we have to remember most of the Irish are not Anglican. They see their country as being seized by us . . . which is why my husband wouldn't approve. He was one for proper representation – a vote for each man.' Her voice softened. 'Have you had enough for a while?'

The truth was I could not concentrate, my thoughts drifting constantly to the dream that had woken me. Not my usual nightmare but a dream leaving me even more unsettled. Even now, I felt myself blush. Pierre de la Croix had been holding me in his arms, our heads resting on a soft pillow. A breeze had been blowing the light curtain at the window, the room filled with the sound of the sea. A bunch of ox-eye daisies were beside the bed, his chest bare. His strong arms had been round me, his fingers playing with the bow on my nightgown.

'Perhaps we should stop for a while? Madeleine, are you all right, only you look a little flushed?'

'Maybe I am a little warm.' Playing with my bow, twisting it through his fingers, his hand slipping beneath the soft cotton.

She flicked open her fan. 'Borrow this. You look very hot,

my dear. Perhaps a walk would do you good? Here, stand by the window. Open it a bit more.'

Even now, my body tingled as if woken from years of sleep. 'Maybe some fresh air would help . . .' His lips burning my neck, my ear, my lips, and I had thrilled at his touch, not wanting him to stop.

'Should I call someone? You might have a fever.'

'No . . . I just need a little air.' The clouds were heavy, with no sign of sun; yet the air was warm as I lifted the sash. A woman was hurrying down the street, her two children held tightly in each hand. She turned, flashing me her radiant smile, and I waved back. Waving to a Cavendish! Three weeks ago, the thought would have had me howling with laughter, yet not today. Today, I felt intrigued by Celia Cavendish.

'Is Captain Pendarvis at sea?'

Mrs Pengelly joined me at the window. 'I believe he's between ships at the moment – awaiting his new command. They're coming to the ball, so you'll meet them both there.'

I needed to talk to Marcel. He had not been at the linhay the last time I visited, yet the thought I might see Pierre de la Croix made me reluctant to leave the house. I could put it off no longer. 'Perhaps a short walk might help me clear my head. I won't be long – just a breath of air.'

Sam wanted to accompany me but I declined his kind offer, walking quickly to the linhay, glancing constantly over my shoulder to make certain I was not being followed. The linhay looked deserted and settling myself on the old stones, I searched the hawthorn bushes further up the cliff, desperately hoping Marcel would see I was alone.

'Madeleine, at last.' He appeared as if from nowhere.

'Marcel, where have you been?'

'I've had to be very careful. I don't want to be seen.' He paused. 'Your gown is . . . very beautiful. You look so *well.*' His compliment was followed by a sudden frown. His eyes held mine, a hint of fear in his voice. 'Does Captain de la Croix know who you are? He had tea with you, I believe?'

'I didn't tell him but I think he might have guessed. The cook knew me from before . . . I think he heard her call me Miss Madeleine.'

He drew me into the linhay. He looked older, his wig abandoned, his new growth of beard flecked with grey. He had changed back into the jacket he had worn when we left the madhouse, his hat pulled low. He clasped his head in his hands, they looked rougher, dirtier, his nails no longer clean.

'Then he'll know. He moves in the highest circles . . . he has the ear of Admiral Sir Alexander Pendarvis and holds a position of great trust. As such he can ask questions others can't. His network will know your name and will connect you to your brother. We're in a very dangerous situation, Madeleine.'

'He might not—'

'No, believe me. He *will* know. We've suspected for some time they have someone in Bodmin. No – don't cry . . . please, don't cry. If I sound angry it's because I wish I could have offered you more. This waiting is unnerving. It's never like this. Never.' He stared across the sea, new determination in his voice. 'I need to find a ship . . . we have to leave. I have to get you to your brother – we have to warn him.'

Kittiwakes were calling above us, gulls circling a fishing boat entering the river mouth. The sea was grey, the waves building, white froth swirling against the rocks below. *Let there be another storm . . . let me stay a little longer.* At least until I could persuade Matthew Reith to take up my cause.

'You need to be ready at all times. I can't chance anyone seeing me now – it's too dangerous. If they ask after me, tell them I've gone to Redruth for a couple of days. Do they know you're returning to France?'

'We haven't spoken at length.' The thought of saying good-bye to Rowan was ripping me in two, my future hollow at the thought of leaving her; yet to bring her with me would be too cruel. My love for her was selfish. She was safe. She was happy. I could only bring her uncertainty. I had a family of my own. I had nephews and nieces. 'How does my brother live? Does he oversee the vineyards? Do they have servants . . . and live in our old house?'

He looked saddened, staring down at his hands. 'They live well enough – they still own your parents' home, but things are *different*. His work sees him in Saint-Malo for long periods at a time and they have a townhouse there. The vineyards have been *acquired* by the Commune and he has no control over them. He still *owns* the land, but in name only. The produce is for the people. He's watched constantly . . . and presided over. He's doing everything he can for his family and the country we once loved.'

'And you? Will you stay or return to England?'

His tired eyes searched mine. He looked on the point of tears. 'I've lost all my family. I only have my work. In Britain,

I can salvage what I can by helping others flee the tyranny. It's my duty, and I'm proud to serve my country.'

He stood up, throwing back his shoulders as if to regain his composure. 'Cécile Lefèvre usually sends her ship via Guernsey. We'll wait another twenty-four hours, then we'll leave. Madeleine – don't come here again. That blue gown is very beautiful, but too visible. I watched you leave the town and others would have seen you, too. The colour's too distinctive – it draws the eye.'

I hardly heard him. *He's watched constantly . . . presided over. He's doing everything he can for his family.* 'Marcel . . . what if I don't want to . . .' I turned, but he was gone, my words dying on my lips. *What if I don't want to return to France?*

I knew he was watching from his place of hiding. I had been a fool not to wear a cloak. I had put him in great danger. He was risking his life for me and I had shone like a beacon, directing all eyes up to the linhay. I should have taken him food, I should have offered him money. Why could I not think straight?

Three tall masts rose majestically above the quay, a host of people pushing past with trolleys. Shouts were echoing across the water, yet another blockage caused by mule packs queuing to get to the wharf. The crush was building so, once again, I took the inner road to avoid the confusion. I hardly dared glance at the town hall with its wooden pillars and notices. It was as if I knew another notice would be pinned there.

This time it was far more terrifying.

MURDER HUNT

A Reward of One Guinea is offered for any information
regarding the Murder and Theft of Jewels of
Mrs Enrique Gonzalez
who died as a result of a Vicious Stabbing which
took place on Saturday 31 May in Cranborne.

Chapter Twenty-one

I shut the door, and leaned against it. Thomas Pearce was a murderer as well as a thief. I had seen it his eyes, that cold look of evil. He would be a blackmailer, too. Through the open door, I could see Mrs Pengelly asleep in her chair and I tiptoed across the hall to seek refuge in the kitchen. Immediately, I felt safe. The kettle was about to boil, the cat watching us from the rocking chair, and I breathed in the smell of fresh bread. Drawing up a chair, I took a raisin from the bowl.

Mrs Munroe smiled, laying down her rolling pin to pick up the butter knife. Tamsin stood eagle-eyed next to her. 'So cover it in more butter – nice and thick, mind . . . a good coating, then ye sprinkle it with cinnamon – like it says in my book.' She pointed a floury finger to her recipe book. 'There, see, Miss Madeleine? Then pick up one end an' fold it into the middle – like this, about one third. Then the other end. Can ye follow?'

The recipe was written in a flowing hand and a joy to read. 'Yes, I'm following. You have very neat writing, Mrs Munroe.'

She sniffed. 'Yes, well. That's our Rose's writing. She copied out all my old recipes, bless her heart. I can write, but not like that. Not like Miss Rose. Now, take over from me, Tamsin. Hold the rolling pin *lightly* . . . ye've got to be firm but with a light touch.'

Tamsin was clearly concentrating. Frizzy red hair escaped her mobcap, flour dusting her flushed cheeks. She seemed hesitant, wiping her hands on her apron before gripping the rolling pin. Mrs Munroe grimaced. 'A little lighter, love. Don't squash all the air out. It's to be light an' airy. Go on . . . that's better.'

I turned the pages of the beautifully written recipes, a space between them for her to write her notes. 'Are some of these from when you worked at the Hall?'

She nodded, clearly reluctant to take her eyes off the dough Tamsin was squashing. Her round glasses glinted, her cheeks pink. Beneath her lace-edged cap, her wiry grey hair was held back in a chignon. 'I kept my recipes in my head, but Miss Rose suggested I wrote them down. My writing wasn't up to it so that's her present to me.'

I smiled back. 'Mrs Pengelly tells me Lady Polcarrow insists all her maids learn to read and write and she teaches the seamstresses in the sewing school how to keep accounts.'

'Aye, that she does.'

'Mrs Munroe, how many servants do you think read up in the Hall?'

Tamsin seemed to have passed muster as Mrs Munroe sat down, folding her arms across her chest. 'More than they think!'

'Do servants read private letters and things left lying about?'

She leaned back, a slight purse to her lips. 'Course they do – specially up at the Hall. If they didn't read things, they'd know nothing. There's a lot goes on that no one knows the half of.'

She seemed reluctant to continue but I knew to press her. 'It's not like I'm ever going to have a grand house again. My husband died a pauper, Mrs Munroe – for all my sumptuous surroundings, I owned as much as I do now.'

She shook her head, her soft laugh making Mr Pitt look up. 'Bless ye, my love. Ye'll soon find yer feet. Ye just have to see the way Captain Pierre looks at ye to know ye'll not be lonely fer long.'

Fire burned my cheeks, a sudden memory of my dream. 'What do they do – up at the Hall? Do they read books from the library . . . private diaries? Tell me.'

'Those that read tell the others what's going on. There's never no stealing because if ye steal, ye're out. But there's fun to be had trying on the mistress's clothes . . . her jewellery, her hats. Some like to try on her silk stockings . . . in the laundry, mind . . . not from the drawers. And there's usually a bit extra cooked that sees its way to the servants' hall. Mind you, it's always better when they're away.'

She stood up, hovering behind Tamsin. 'That's more like it . . . See, ye're getting there. I think we'll use this one – not like yer last three attempts! Now, sprinkle the dough with the raisins.' She reached for the bowl and stopped. 'Miss Madeleine – ye've nearly finished them!'

The bowl replenished, the raisins were placed on the rectangle of dough and Mrs Munroe sat back down. She leaned back, folding her arms once again. 'The footmen used to slice off pieces of the cooked meats, but we loved the sweet sugar – the honey and candied fruit. Cook knew we were up to no good, but we always found a way of slipping a jar of her jam up to our room.'

'I'm sure she didn't mind.'

'No – nor should she! It was innocent enough compared to what she was up to! Like buying our silence, really. The odd jar of honey left out.' She shook her head, her smile broadening.

'What was she up to? Go on . . . you can't stop there.'

She leaned her ample bosom on the table. 'Not a word, ye promise?' She glanced at Tamsin, who shook her head. 'Well, she an' the head gardener – they've both moved to other employment, but I'll say no names – well, they used to send a young lad through the smoke hole to the cellar. Poor boy, he was one of the under-gardeners and thin as a rake, but he got them bottles an' bottles and *no one ever knew*.'

'They sent him into the wine cellar? How come?'

'It's part of the old house – the old kitchen before it was expanded. It used to be the smoke house – they'd fire up the wood fire an' the smoke used to go through the gap an' fill the cellar. They used to smoke eels there – mackerel and hams, too – and duck breast. They've the new smokery now but that was the old one.'

'So when my husband built the new kitchens they used the smoke house for his wines?'

'Well, it were nice an' cool down there. And convenient for the butler. But they left the smoke hole open for *ventilation*.'

'And no one ever checked to see if any wine went missing?'

185

'Not back then, they didn't. They do now. Most certainly they do now.'

The clock struck four, the kettle whistling on the stove. Tamsin stood smiling down at her raisin ring. 'Shall I put it in to bake now, Mrs Munroe?'

'No . . . leave it by the fire to rise, my love. An' don't burn yerself like last time. Here, use this thick cloth.'

The scrubbed pine table, the jars of sugar and raisins, the patchwork quilt resting on the back of the rocking chair, the basket full of knitting. I fought the emptiness surging through me, the terrible sense of loneliness. It was so different from what I knew. I hardly ever ventured into the kitchens of our French house and never during my short stay in Pendenning Hall. I felt safe here, cherished; I would not swap Mrs Pengelly's beautiful house for any chateaux or grand country estate, would not swap the affection and love I had found here for the empty grandeur of a place that never felt like home. Yet I must. Cécile Lefèvre was risking her life for me and my brother had been searching for so long.

I could picture Rowan next to me, eating the raisins, smiling up at Mrs Munroe. She would love Mr Pitt, Tamsin and Sam. My emptiness felt like pain. 'From what Rowan tells me, it's still going on – or at least it was. She said Phillip Randall spent whole evenings in the cellar drinking his way through Sir Charles's best claret! Often until the early morning and not only when Sir Charles was away.'

Mrs Munroe's eyes sharpened. 'Well, he hated the man.'

My heart missed a beat. 'Phillip Randall *hated* Sir Charles? I thought he was devoted to him?'

This time there was no ringing laughter, no warm smile. Her lips clamped. 'Then you thought wrong. Phillip Randall put it about that he liked and respected Sir Charles, but those that know know different. They detested the sight of each other.'

A prickle ran down my spine. 'Then it's no surprise Phillip Randall spent every evening drinking Sir Charles's best claret. He probably wanted to work his way through the lot.'

She shook her head, her lips tighter. 'No, Miss Madeleine. Not Phillip Randall. I don't know what he was doing in there but it weren't drinking. The man didn't drink. Not a drop. Those that know used to watch him. He'd take a drink and *pretend* to drink it, but he never touched a drop. They say,' she glanced at the door, 'that he kept himself sober to keep one step ahead of Sir Charles.' Her voice dropped. 'They say *he knew too much.*'

I stared back at her, my heart beating but not with anxiety. It was beating with excitement. With absolute conviction. 'Why did he spend hours alone in a cold cellar?'

'That man was a law unto himself. Could have been doing anything.'

'Maybe he was just checking the wine? How long would that take?'

Tamsin was struggling with the heavy iron skillet, her raisin ring in danger of sliding to the floor. Mrs Munroe leapt to her feet and I knew I must leave them to their cooking, but as I reached the door, I heard her answer.

'No more than twenty minutes – just to dust and check none's blown. Half an hour at the most. Now steady, my love. Let's not have this one on the floor as well.'

Her candle held high, Mrs Pengelly paused at my bedroom door. 'Are you worried about her? You say she's happy, but if you'd like to... why not bring Rowan back here? I'm sure you'd rather be together.'

Her shawl was embroidered with exquisite flowers, her nightdress edged with lace. A delicate row of pin-tucks lay across her breast, mother-of-pearl buttons at the cuffs of her long sleeves. I reached for the edge of her shawl, lifting it to the candlelight.

'I used to sew like this and I used to sing. I used to play the piano. Mrs Pengelly, I can't trespass on your kind hospitality for much longer...'

'Of course you can, my dear. In fact, I *insist* you stay until you find your feet. It's my pleasure to have you – and Alice and Matthew Reith will soon be here. I've had a note to say they'll stay at Polcarrow.'

The kindness in her voice, her gentle understanding, made it hard to speak. 'My brother's been searching for me. He believed me happily remarried, but when he heard nothing he sent François Barnard to find me. He's never given up on me – never. He's my family... I have nephews and nieces I've never seen—'

'You think I don't understand? You're French, yet you don't recognise the country you left all those years ago. You've emerged from great wickedness to find France a different place. Of course I understand. Does Rowan like sewing? If she does, I can offer her a position in my school of needlework

'– you don't have to go, my love. You could stay here, in Fosse, and teach French and singing. There are plenty of proud parents who want their daughters to learn the piano.'

She was voicing my thoughts, making them sound possible. 'And you'd allow me to pay for my board and lodging? Until I earn enough to take rooms?'

Her long grey hair lay in a plait down one shoulder, her face soft in the candlelight. 'I'd rather you remained as my guest, but I understand – if you decide to stay, then in one month's time you can give me a shilling a week.'

A new life with Mrs Pengelly as my friend, rooms of my own, Rowan with me every night. I would work my hardest to make them proud of me. 'I'm sorry, I don't mean to cry.' I kissed her soft cheek. 'I'll take the cart – I'll wear my old dress. I need to tell her I want to stay in Fosse.'

'Sam will take you—'

'That's very kind, but I must return as the Mrs Barnard they know.'

'I understand.' She frowned at the open casement. 'Night air is dangerous, my dear. It's too damp . . . Do let me advise you to shut your window against the chill. Fasten your shutters. This dreadful habit you young people have of allowing in the night air is very worrying. Windows are for shutting and shutters are for bolting. Don't go letting in that sea air or you'll catch a chill.'

I walked swiftly to shut the window. I felt stronger, resolute, thinking clearly for the first time in fourteen years. I did not sleep, but kept pacing the room. It was as if I had come alive, my senses finely tuned. I felt restless, like a coiled spring, as if some instinct was finally coming to fruition. I could not put my finger on why my mind was racing.

Why did Phillip Randall spend so long in the cellar? Suddenly, I stopped.

Lying on my bed, I began envisioning the old kitchen. Rowan had pointed out the wood fire and I could picture the smoke hole. I remembered a woman used to come to trap cockroaches – that would do it. I would persuade Mrs Pumfrey to let me search. A quick lift of the woodpile in the courtyard below and I would find woodlice and earwigs, maybe even mice droppings I could take with me.

Like the gardener's boy I was as thin as a rake. I could fit into the smoke hole. I could search the cellar. Three weeks ago I would have roared with laughter at the thought of picking up insects, but not now.

Not now, Charles Cavendish. Not now.

Chapter Twenty-two

Rowan looked aghast. 'But surely you can't?'

The scullery was cold, shafts of sunlight filtering through the grilles of the windows. Plates lay gleaming in the wooden racks, the three large sinks now empty of water. 'I can . . . I just need you to take the stool away once I'm through. If there's a grille blocking my way, I'll just back out and drop to the ground – I only need help getting up.'

She bit her lip. 'Mrs Pumfrey set you to work in here?'

'Not *work*. I asked her for work . . . I burst into tears and begged her. She said there was none, and I said I was good at finding roaches and mice. I asked her if she'd like me to have a quick search in the larder and storerooms and I found several earwigs and woodlice and told her I suspected an infestation of cockroach, so she asked me to set traps.'

Her hand flew to her mouth, a nervous giggle. 'And she agreed?'

The maids had left their plates to dry and were taking their place in the privy queue. This was our only opportunity. The door to the dairy was closed, so too the larder. The cooks were busy in the kitchen and most of the footmen had left the servants' hall. Taking off my hat, I studied the circle of red bricks above the bread oven. There was no grille, just an earthenware jar on a slate shelf. The kiln had not been lit for years, the bread ovens used for storage.

Putting the stool on the hearth, I reached for the jar, lifting it carefully. It was heavier than I expected and I needed all my strength to dislodge the slate it had been resting on. At last, it gave way and I saw a thin black tunnel. 'When I'm through, replace the slate as it was.'

Rowan's eyes were fixed on the door, her cheeks drained of all colour. 'Why don't I go instead?'

'No, I'm just as thin as you – and I'm putting you in enough danger as it is. Mrs Pumfrey will wonder where you are but she won't look for me. Come back when you can – if I'm caught, deny all knowledge. Do you promise?'

I stood on the stool, reaching forward, my shoulders just small enough to fit through the hole. 'There must be a ridge – a gap, something I can grip.' Tiny particles crumbled in my hands, the edges rough, the thick dust itching my nose. I could feel a row of bricks and searched for a crack. No light shone from the end, just a black tunnel leading nowhere. My wig brushed the surface but there was just enough room to lift my chin. 'I need you to hold my legs – maybe I should push against you?'

Glad of my long sleeves, I took my weight on my arms. Rowan's grip was strong and I pushed against her, my heavy skirt constricting me from bending my knees. Even so, I could just about wriggle forward. Rowan sounded relieved. 'Your feet are through – you can't be seen.'

I heard her replace the slate and jar and pulled myself forward, seeing nothing but darkness. The tunnel smelled musty, dusty, retaining the faint odour of woodsmoke. I must have gone eight feet, no more, and felt the stones change back to brick. I stretched out, feeling a sharp edge of what must be the end of the tunnel. The air was colder, filled with the aroma of wine like my father's cellars. There was nothing to stop me, no grille, just another open circle of bricks and I curled my fingers round the entrance, pulling myself forward until my shoulders broke free.

Nothing but blackness, no light even beneath the door, and I reached into my bodice, drawing out Mrs Pengelly's tinderbox I had practised lighting long into the night. The flame caught and I held it against my candle, my hand steady though my heart was pounding. In the flickering light racks of wine lay neatly stacked – shelf upon shelf of wooden racks holding rows of bottles. Below me was a large barrel.

Blowing out my candle, the cellar plunged back into darkness but I had seen enough. I must breathe, keep the demons at bay – the blackness, the rats, the pain of being cramped in an airless black void. I was stronger now, my mind clearer – I would not let the fear return. I would take my weight on my hands and slide carefully down the barrel until I touched the flagstones.

Reaching out, I gripped the top of the barrel and slipped into the darkness, my palms outspread. My hands felt the cold floor and I walked myself forward, diffuse light filtering through the smoke hole behind me. The shelves looked grey in the half-light, the corks of the bottles pointing at me, and I bent first one knee, then the other, standing up, confident that any light from my candle would not be seen.

The tinder struck, and I held up the candle. There were no windows, just worn flagstones with steps leading up to a door to the scullery. Slates hung against the racks, the date and names of the wines written in chalk. The barrel was behind me, a chair beside it, and I caught a glint of brass. It was no ordinary barrel but smooth and highly polished, the light catching a brass keyhole with a key inside it.

I turned the key. Not just a barrel, but opening up to form a desk – no doubt one of my husband's extravagant purchases. The polished wood was inlaid with green leather, a quill and inkstand on one side, a blotter on the other. A shallow shelf circled the writing space, a selection of crystal glasses glinting in the light. So, too, a silver cork opener. Three drawers lay below, each with a matching brass keyhole but no key.

Putting the candle on the top, I drew the chair closer, thrilled the same key fitted the top drawer. It turned easily, and I drew out a large leather-bound ledger. It was the wine register, detailing every purchase: when the wine was bought, where from, the cost, and on which shelf the bottle was stored. Pages and pages, going back years – *Madeira, Bordeaux, Château Margaux, Château Lafite* – everything recorded in minute detail, the latest being Sir Charles's three cases of port from Oporto in July 1799.

I replaced it in the top drawer and tried the second. Once more, the key fitted and I drew out another register. This time it was the record of the wine drunk, detailing every bottle taken from the cellar: the date taken, by whom, who consumed it, and whether it was considered good quality or inferior.

Dates I was there, evenings I remembered; lavish dinners we had hosted, scores of bottles drunk by those with a franchise – Joshua smiling, insisting someone had to buy their votes. I turned the page – 27th July 1786, the day *after* I had been taken to the madhouse. Sir Charles Cavendish had wasted no time at all and a new butler was named. I looked carefully, adjusting the candle. It seemed strange – every entry from then on was not signed as taken by the butler as I would expect, but taken and signed for by Phillip Randall.

The sight of his signature made my stomach twist, yet I looked again. Every wine was taken from the shelf by Phillip Randall – until July 1796 when the butler had resumed his duties. Phillip Randall's last entry was on 2nd July 1796: *Two Bottles Château Grimaud 1789; taken by Phillip Randall; consumed by Sir Charles Cavendish and Sulio Denville. Considered very fine.*

I shivered, but not from the cold. The next day he was dead, lynched by the angry vagrants he had evicted with such scorn. Yet the name Sulio Denville looked familiar. Flicking through the register, I could see similar entries – *Two bottles of wine taken for the consumption of Sir Charles and Sulio Denville.* The named jarred. Why name Sulio Denville so often, when no other guests were named?

Replacing the ledger as I found it, I tried the third drawer. The key turned easily but there was little in there – a knife to sharpen the quill, a fresh bottle of ink, several new candles, and I reached further into the drawer, stubbing my fingers. Not a whole drawer, but a third of the size of the ones above.

A shiver ran down my spine. I was in the chateau, showing Joshua Maman's bureau. *Look . . . a third of a drawer because there's a secret drawer round the back.* What if Joshua had copied Maman's bureau? Reaching round the barrel, I pulled it away from the wall. It was a huge hogshead barrel intended to carry salted pilchards across the seas and had not been moved in years. I gripped tighter, shifting it slowly, instinctively knowing Phillip Randall had moved it every night – behind a locked door, with no one to watch or listen. No one to witness where he kept something he did not want anyone to find.

With the back exposed I could just make out a drawer. No brass keyhole, just an inconsequential hole and a slightly deeper crack between the planks of wood. The candle flickered and I caught my breath. The flame glowed again, and I put the key into the hole, turning the stiff lock. The drawer was deep, stuffed full of leather books and I picked up the top one, opening the first page.

In the case of my untimely death, please be assured that this is the true and honest account of all my dealings with Sir Charles Cavendish.

Chapter Twenty-three

It was a diary. The front page dated 1795, and I flicked to the last entry.

> *2nd July 1796: Sir Charles is staying in the cottage. As usual, none of the servants are aware of his presence and assume the food and wine I take there are for my own consumption, and that of my mistress. His discussions with Sulio Denville were private and I heard only snippets. However, I believe Sulio Denville has been summoned, not to deal with the vagrants who have been more demanding of late, but for a far more sinister motive (see 10th May 1795).*

I flicked back the pages.

> *10th May 1795: Once more, Sulio Denville has been summoned. Sir Charles has returned to Pendenning without the knowledge of his servants and sleeps in the cottage. I have warned Mr George Silverton that Sir Charles will not*

tolerate any further investigation into his land deals and any
attempt to take him to court will result in Mr Silverton's ruin.
However, Sir Charles believes a man like Mr Silverton needs
to be taught never to question him again. Therefore, Sulio
Denville will see to it that a member of his family has an
accident (see 7th November 1793).

I could barely breathe. The candle was guttering and I needed to light another. Fumbling with the key, I unlocked the third drawer, bringing out a fresh candle. It caught, and shadows leapt across the dusty bottles. *He knew too much.* It was as if Phillip Randall was peering through in the darkness behind me, wanting his diaries to be found – writing everything in neat readable script, all his entries cross-referenced, accompanying letters dated and numbered, slipped carefully between the appropriate pages.

I reached back into the hidden drawer, taking out the other five diaries. The dates were on the front, the same warning about his untimely death. I found 1793–1794 and turned the pages to 7th November.

His name was there again – Sulio Denville, *summoned* every time Sir Charles needed '*assistance*' *to be rid of someone.* I skimmed the next entries and a name caught my eye: *Celia Cavendish found listening to our conversation.*

I had to breathe, stop my heart from the hammering. Two letters had been inserted and remained folded, Phillip Randall's writing on the front of each. *This is the true letter to Dr Fox in Fishponds, Bristol, written by Sir Charles but signed using the forged signature of Dr Hunter.* The next said the same only with the name of *Dr Bentley* and the addition of *Both letters accompanying Celia Cavendish to Maddison's Madhouse were copies.*

I stared at the entry.

Friday 22nd November 1793. Today I received 100 guineas from Sir Charles for the successful removal of Miss Celia Cavendish, under the name of Mrs Eleanor Morpass, sent for an indefinite period of time in Maddison's Madhouse, Bristol. Also paid were Walter Trellisk 50 guineas, and Augustine Roach 30 guineas.

Every word in the diaries was neat and concise, Phillip Randall laying bare Sir Charles's dealings, even as he admitted his own part in them. Fear filled me, yet I could not stop, turning back the pages to the day before my husband was murdered. Had Sir Charles summoned Sulio Denville to kill Joshua? A voice drifted through the smoke hole and my heart hammered.

'Madeleine . . . ? Madeleine are ye there?' Rowan's whisper was faint but sounded urgent.

I reached up, whispering back: 'Yes, I'm here.'

'Ye must hurry . . . quick. The family's back. They're in Truro – on their way here. A messenger's been sent ahead. Quick.'

Locking the secret compartment, I heaved the barrel back in place and replaced the register and wine record exactly as I had found them. Only one candle was missing and there was perhaps the smell of the beeswax, but nothing else looked disturbed. The books were cumbersome and would be difficult to carry. I needed my hands to pull myself along, so I reached back, looping up my skirt. The fold formed a pocket and I placed the books in the loop, pulling the material tight, tying it in a firm knot at my waist.

'Wait . . . someone's coming.'

I stood poised on the barrel, ready to reach forward, knowing I must not kick it over as I pushed myself off it. There was no sound from the scullery but Rowan could have been called away or someone might be in there. I had to wait, I had to keep calm, plan what I must do. The evidence was overwhelming. Phillip Randall feared he faced death by the hands of Sulio Denville – and just one day before his death Sir Charles had summoned Sulio Denville. He may have been lynched, but not by the mob.

'Come . . . Madeleine . . . come now.' I caught the fear in her voice and wriggled forward. She was clearly petrified but trying to be brave. 'If I cough it means someone's come in. Hurry. There's footmen in the butler's pantry but there's no one here.'

Inch by inch, elbows then toes, the diaries were cumbersome but it seemed easier the second time. The light from the scullery lit the tunnel and I forced myself along, reaching out through the brick smoke hole. Her hand caught mine, gripping me tightly, and I emerged into the empty room.

'I'll slip forward . . . hold me as I come down. Is the door shut?'

'Yes . . . but there's people in the hall.' Rowan let go of my hands, reaching up to hold my chest, strong, secure, taking my weight as my toes slipped from the hole. She staggered back but remained upright.

'Quick . . . I must undo this.' Untying the knot in my skirt, I grabbed the diaries. 'Where's my basket? These are too big to put down my bodice. Where's my hat?'

Picking up my basket, she hurried it back to me and I wrapped the diaries in a rough cloth. Footmen were gathering in the servants' hall, orders being shouted, the sound of running footsteps. Brick dust covered my skirts and my sleeves and I tried to brush it off.

'This won't come off... it's stained... I can't be seen like this. We'll have to leave.'

Rowan replaced the slate and bowl. She looked ashen, her eyes fixed on the door. 'Not through there... here... out this door. It goes to the stables but there's no horses yet. Sir Charles has come early. Everyone's in a terrible state.'

The door opened to a small yard. A group of stable boys were standing by the well listening to the coachman's frantic instructions. Opposite, the stables looked empty. 'We must walk, Rowan, not run... as if we've been sent there for a reason. I'll go first – when it's clear.'

A laden wagon rumbled into the yard, two gardeners sitting on the back alongside crates of vegetables and sacks of potatoes, and I drew back, letting it pass. It pulled up by the back door to a flurry of activity and I took my chance, walking slowly into the stables. The cobbles were neatly swept, the wooden stalls strewn with fresh straw. No doubt the stable boys were being given instructions to collect the horses from the nearby farms, but for the moment we could hide there. Light footsteps followed me. 'I'm here, Rowan. In this one... further along.'

Rowan sank into the straw beside me. 'What are they?'

'Phillip Randall's diaries . . . but they're more than that. They're written *against* Sir Charles – all his dealings recorded. *Everything.* As if he was planning to use them against Sir Charles. They're dangerous, Rowan, unbelievably dangerous.'

Her hand flew to her mouth as footsteps passed the entrance. 'Will ye hide them here?'

'No . . . because I'll never get them back. Once the horses are here – once Sir Charles is back.' Fear caught my whisper. 'Rowan . . . I'm going to have to walk calmly away from the house. If I look like I'm hiding something, they'll search me.'

She nodded, wide-eyed. 'They're in a terrible spin. The family's nearly here. And there are dogs at night. They'd run after you.'

'That's why I have to chance it. Go back to your duties and act perfectly calmly. Say my illness has returned and I thought it best to leave . . .'

She reached for my hand, tears pooling in her eyes. 'But I want to come with ye. Please. I don't want to be here if ye can't come an' visit. Please . . . let me come with ye.'

In the midst of my fear, my heart nearly burst. 'I'd like that that too . . . but Rowan, you have to stay now, just for tonight. I'll send for you tomorrow. I won't come myself because I can't be seen here – but I *promise* I'll send for you. I can't risk them finding you with me.' I put her hand to my lips, kissing it softly. 'One more night. Just one, I promise. And then . . . we won't go to France . . . we'll stay in Fosse. I'll teach piano or French . . . we'll take rooms . . . we'll have our own home.'

She flung her arms round me, a tear trickling down each cheek. She could not speak but nodded, smiling as I held her against my thumping heart. I had to think which was the safest way out of the grounds. I would cut back from the house and head towards the folly. It was further to walk but the trees would shield me from view. Once at the folly, the small path would take me through the woods and down to the river.

'Rowan, go now... stand at the entrance and cough if you think everyone's too busy to notice me leave. If anyone's looking, stop to do up your lace. Either way, return to the kitchen and if anyone asks what you've been doing, say you love horses and wanted to pet one. Can you do that?'

'Yes.' Her courage was all I needed.

At the entrance she coughed loudly and I gripped my basket, slipping from the empty stall. She reached the kitchen and I walked swiftly across the cobbles, leaving the shouts and activity, the barking dogs, the oxen harnessed to an empty cart. The coach-house clock struck four and I walked through the hens pecking the dirt. I did not hurry, nor did I look back, though my legs felt as if they might crumple beneath me. The diaries in my basket could bring Sir Charles to justice, but just as easily they could lead me straight to the gallows.

Chapter Twenty-four

If anyone was watching they must believe me unwell. I bent double, pretending to retch, wiping my mouth before walking slowly on. I hardly needed to pretend; I felt sick, my heart pounding, my breathing too fast for comfort. Yet I knew to walk slowly, not look up at the sky. Once I reached the small gate, I would take the path and follow it alongside the wood – *the bluebell wood*, as I used to call it.

Only the gardeners could see me now. Dappled light filtered through the branches, the path steeper, twigs crunching under my shoes. Sulio Denville had been summoned only days before Phillip Randall was found murdered. The servants knew nothing about Sir Charles's clandestine visits, he kept himself hidden, no doubt arriving by night. Rowan told me Phillip Randall had used the cottage to entertain his women, yet it was Sir Charles who had slept there. But why stay there and not in the main house?

At the top of the hill, the house was lost to view and I bent to catch my breath. The enormity of my find was suddenly overwhelming. I must not falter, but take one step at a time. All I had to do was to cut down the hill and climb the rough pasture to the folly. It rose before me, my memories now soured with hatred – Joshua enticing me up there, his whispers not of love, but of intent. Drawing me behind the columns, his grip growing painful, forcing me against the cold marble and me, staring back at Venus as she witnessed my humiliation. My marriage was a mockery. Not love, but possession.

Unhindered views stretched before me, the heavy clouds racing, the sea darkening. The horizon was growing indistinguishable, a band of grey mist approaching from the west. The wind was freshening, white crests building at the mouth of the river. Waves foamed against the base of the cliffs, the cottages of Porthruan huddled on one side of the river, the church spire dominating the slate roofs of Fosse on the other. Next to the church, the turrets and arched windows of the ancient house of Polcarrow stood grey and squat.

A commotion made me pull sharply back, and I stood peeping from behind the marble columns. Three carriages were hurtling down the drive leaving a trail of dust. Sir Charles's entourage had arrived.

Racing down the hill, I searched for the small path – it would be here, I just had to find it. It was further down than I remembered and I ran to it, taking cover beneath the thick canopy of leaves. Branches snagged my dress, knocking my bonnet, but I would not stop. I kept running, twisting along the path to the river. I caught glimpses of the wading birds scuttling across the banks and knew I was nearly there.

The tide was almost out, the centre of the river dark. I

stood at the edge of the ford, knowing I would have to wade across. No one was there, no prying eyes or tongues that would talk. Poles marked the depth – it was less than a foot at the edges and would be deeper in the middle. It would be over my knees but the surface beneath it would be firm, the tide slow, and I hitched up my skirt, holding my basket high.

Phillip Randall knew exactly what he was doing. Even if no one found his diaries, he had left clues in the wine record – recording when Sir Charles was in the cottage by the wine he had ordered. Recording who was with him by repeating only one name, the person Sir Charles had drunk with: Sulio Denville, his hired murderer.

They fussed around me as I knew they would, their concern at my wet shoes and stockings both loving and attentive. Tamsin kept filling the copper for hot water to bathe my feet, Mrs Munroe heating soup and toasting bread, Sam pouring me a glass of mead. Yet all I could think of were the diaries hidden beneath my pillow, the terrible fear Sir Charles might come banging on Mrs Pengelly's door.

Warm and snug in the kitchen, I sat with Mrs Munroe's favourite blanket across my knee, Mr Pitt purring heavily on my lap. Mrs Munroe handed me another plate of buttered toast. 'Course she'll be welcome. As soon as Mrs Pengelly comes back from Polcarrow, she'll tell ye so herself. How old is she?'

'I'm really not sure. Eleven, maybe just twelve? She doesn't know for certain. Her mother died up on the moor. She was found under a rowan tree by her dead mother's side. A woman

206

found her and took her in, but she had very little – she was almost destitute. Rowan told me she didn't speak for a whole year after she was found. It must have been so awful for her.'

'And the woman who took her in? Where's she, then?'

'She was a maid where I was held – both of them were. But she was never in good health and she died, leaving Rowan to fend for herself. Rowan was too young to go anywhere else so she stayed, but they treated her harshly. Yet she was *so* kind to me . . . her kindness saved me. I asked her to come with me – I couldn't leave her.'

'Course you couldn't leave her! Bless her dear little heart. Makes me weep to think on it. Poor little thing, lying by her dead mother's side.' She wiped her eyes. 'Course she'll be welcome here. Course Mrs Pengelly will take her in.'

I must wait, show my appreciation, not jump at every sound. Their kindness was overwhelming, yet the diaries drew me like a magnet. I could barely sit still, only Mr Pitt had no intention of moving and Mrs Munroe was once again filling the toasting iron. Above us came the sound of the front door opening and Sam jumped to his feet, rushing up the stairs to greet Mrs Pengelly. She entered the kitchen, Sam holding a large parcel behind her.

Her immediate concern I had caught a chill reassured, she settled next to me at the scrubbed pine table and smiled at Tamsin. 'Go on . . . open it – it's for you. The girls have made lovely work of it – we just need to finish the hem and add any bows or lace you might like.'

Tamsin's cheeks deepened to the colour of her hair. 'I . . . I can't. Honest, I can't.'

'You can, my dear. And you must. Mustn't she, Mrs Munroe?'

Mrs Munroe's ham arms folded across her starched apron. 'Indeed she must. And ye're to put yer name forward for Queen of the Fete just like everyone else – Sir James made that clear. *Every* unwed man and woman is to enter for King and Queen of the Fete.'

Tamsin stared down at the unopened parcel. 'Are ye going to put yer name forward, Mrs Munroe? And Sam?'

Both nodded, Sam looking up from the silver he was now polishing. 'Course we will. And we'll both be wearing our very best. Miss Rose is that insistent, she'll not hear otherwise.'

Mrs Pengelly reached for my arm, tapping it gently. 'And you must put your name forward, too, my dear. *Every* unwed man and woman in Fosse is to put their name into the hats. It's for the fete Sir James is holding – for the opening of his mine. There's to be hog roasts . . . and dancing . . . and wrestling. And all number of competitions. And the King and Queen of the Fete will rule over us. We must do exactly what they say.'

Mrs Munroe slid the parcel nearer Tamsin. 'They'll lead the dancing and have crowns and special thrones . . . just like when Sir James opened his lock.'

'And in the evening there'll be the ball at Polcarrow.' Mrs Pengelly leaned closer. 'Rose wants you to come, my dear . . . She's already invited Captain Pierre.'

It was not just Tamsin whose cheeks were burning, both of us blushing, both shaking our heads. Tamsin fumbled with the string, tying it into a tight knot, and Mrs Munroe reached forward with a pair of scissors. 'There, now.'

Tamsin stared at the soft cream gown, her hands flying to

her mouth. 'I . . . can't. I just can't.'

Mrs Munroe's arms remained firmly folded. 'Can't let Oliver Jenkins see ye look so pretty? Get away with ye! 'Tis the perfect chance. Like it or not, young lady, ye need to talk to him – ye need to show him ye like him. Honest, my love, he comes here, stopping at the door, desperate for a glance of ye . . . and ye spend all morning fidgeting, and all over the place . . . glancing at the clock, unable to concentrate, yet the moment he gets here, ye run into the pantry and won't be seen!'

Tamsin's blush deepened, her eyes fixed on the soft folds, the scooped neck and delicately puffed sleeves. 'He's delivering his father's meat . . . he don't come to see me.'

A deep intake of breath, a shake of Mrs Munroe's head. 'And pigs fly, do they? Course he comes to see ye. His father usually delivers here, so why suddenly send his son? He's *asked* to come, that's why . . . And ye too shy to even say *good day*! What are we going to do with ye?'

Mrs Pengelly beckoned Tamsin nearer, her voice soft as she held the dress against her. 'Lady Polcarrow is adamant we all come . . . but you've no need to dance . . . and you *don't* have to talk to Oliver Jenkins if you don't want to. Miss Rose just wants you to enjoy the day like everyone else.'

Tamsin ran her fingers across the fine cotton. 'It's too good for me . . . honest. I'll just trip up an' ruin it . . . I'll catch it on something. Ye know how clumsy I am.'

Mrs Pengelly shook her head. 'Gowns are for wearing . . . and tears can be mended. We'll hem it a bit shorter so you don't catch your shoes.'

She turned to me. 'Madeleine, before I forget. Matthew and

209

Alice Reith have asked if it would be convenient to visit tomorrow. I told them eleven o'clock.' Her eyes held encouragement and I tried to hide my fear. I was listening for a knock on the door, for the barking of dogs. 'Are you all right, my dear?'

'Sir Charles and his family have returned to Pendenning. I saw them arrive. I hurried away. I had to leave Rowan . . . but she doesn't want to stay. I . . . I told her—'

'That she could come here? And so she must.' Mrs Pengelly glanced at Sam. 'Sam will fetch her first thing tomorrow. See if you can borrow the cart, Sam.' She reached for my hand, firm, encouraging, lending me courage. 'Perhaps you should write a note to Mrs Pumfrey to let her know it's safe for Rowan to go with Sam. What is it, my dear? You look most unwell.'

Under the table, my knees were shaking. If Charles Cavendish found out I had been cleaning the books in his study, he would come after me and search my room. The buttered toast lay like a rock in my stomach. 'I can't write to Mrs Pumfrey because she mustn't know I can write — I said I couldn't read so that I could search the library, and she'll know I was lying . . . she'll tell Mr Troon and Charles Cavendish will find out I've been back to the Hall . . .'

Her arm slipped round my shoulders. 'Shh, hush . . . breathe deeply . . . There now. We won't let any harm come to you. Sam can take something Rowan will recognise. Why not your old hat with the lace? They'll know it's yours and so will Rowan. Come . . .' She felt my forehead with her palm. 'He won't find you . . . He doesn't know you're here and we'll soon have those certificates to prove you're sane. Matthew Reith will arrange everything tomorrow.'

Chapter Twenty-five

The shutters firmly bolted, I slipped between the sheets, placing the candle on the table beside me. We had retired early to bed, our simple supper of cold meats and pickles taken quietly in the dining room. I had been poor company, yet Mrs Pengelly seemed to understand, reading me her favourite poems before we headed up the stairs. The house seemed quiet, no light showing beneath her door, and I could wait no longer.

Drawing out the diaries, I spread them in a half-circle on the bed around me. Two of them spanned just one year, the others covered two years, and I reached for the earliest – 1786 – opening it at the first page.

> *24th July 1786: Sir Charles Cavendish has informed me that he has every expectation of acquiring the estate of Pendenning Hall, in County of Cornwall and, as such, has led me to the expectation of being offered the post of his steward.*
>
> *This post, I have accepted, as from today. Hereafter I shall*

record all my dealings with Sir Charles faithfully and truthfully. The purpose being that I am concerned Sir Charles has
instructed me to dispose of all letters, accounts, and records
of negotiations I make on his behalf that could be considered
injurious to his interests. All records must be given direct to
him, or burned.

This does not sit well with my conscience. Therefore, I
intend to record everything here for my own protection. Where
I cannot keep the original, I will make copies of all correspondence and I will record my dealings in their entirety. It is
my belief that powerful men like Sir Charles must, in time,
turn on those who know too much. This diary is, therefore, to
serve my own interests, even while I serve Sir Charles's.

The diary bulged with letters and I turned to the day I had
been forcibly removed from Pendenning Hall.

26th July 1786: I have this day escorted Mrs Madeleine
Pelligrew for treatment at Maddison's Madhouse in Bristol.
Although I would like to say she went willingly, I was obliged
to use a measure of force which I found distasteful. There is
little doubt her sanity has been gravely affected by the death
of her husband and the loss of her estate. However, I have not
been aware of any visits from either one of the two physicians
who have certified her as insane. (See accompanying letters.)

A wave of anger scorched my cheeks. He had shown no
remorse at the time, no sense of wrong. He was writing his
diary for his own purpose, making out he was an unwilling

accomplice. I had to control my fury. Two letters were slipped between the pages and I caught my breath. They were signed with the same forged signatures he had used for Celia Cavendish. The words blurred before me, each letter detailing my descent into madness, my unreasonable behaviour, my howling, my screaming, my scratching and kicking. With them was a receipt.

Mrs Madeleine Pelligrew, admitted from Cornwall.

One Year's Advance to be paid in full.

Daily treatment from an eminent physician trained in the ways of the insane *£15*
Board and lodging to include food, clothing, bedding, fuel, lighting, laundry and airing of personal linen *£22*
Personal attendant's wages *£2*
Extra for double aspect room with closet *£4*
Daily visits from A Lady of Good Virtue *£1*
Mortuary fees and funeral expenses in the unlikely event of death *10s*

Total due *£44:10s*

Signed by Phillip Randall, 26th July 1786

A date was added to the bottom – *1st December 1786* – and I turned the pages.

1st December 1786. Today I visited Maddison's Madhouse to enquire after the well-being of Madeleine Pelligrew, only to be told she had been discharged to the safe custody of her brother. I was unable to take any record of this, but can confirm the names of the two physicians who certified her as sane — Dr Emmet Smith and Dr Oberon Dennings.

My request for a refund for the next six months' fees was forcibly denied. I have written to Sir Charles for his response, wondering why her brother did not come first to Pendenning Hall to enquire about her whereabouts.

There was a forward date — *See 10th August 1787* — and I reached for the next diary.

10th August 1787. I have today forwarded this letter to Sir Charles. He will believe it unread, because I have perfected the art of reclosing seals so as to make them look unopened. It is as I suspected — the brother has no knowledge of his sister's whereabouts.

The words swam before me. It was written in English.

Malouinière du Clos-Poulet
Saint-Malo
2nd August 1787

Dear Sir Charles,

I write with increasing concern that we have heard nothing from Madeleine since her husband's tragic drowning. We have written a number of letters to the address you

214

have given and we remain grateful for your generosity in housing her at your own expense. However, our concerns mount and we would like to be reassured of her well-being. Her father is gravely ill and we urge her to visit him. I propose to visit her within the next three weeks with the hope of persuading Madeleine to return with me. May I enquire as to whether you will be in Pendenning Hall over the next three weeks?

Your obedient servant,
Joseph Emery de Bourg

My dearest brother, desperate for me to come home. The forward date at the bottom read — *See 1st September 1787* — and I flipped quickly forward.

1st September 1787. Today I intercepted another letter from Mrs Pelligrew's brother. Sir Charles must have written from London and I have no record of his correspondence, but this is a true copy of the response it brought.

Malouinière du Clos-Poulet
Saint-Malo
21st August 1787

Dear Sir Charles,
    Your letter brings us great sadness, yet great relief. That my sister was brought to the brink of insanity is distressing in itself, but that her despair was so great she refused all succour and victuals seems a violent and woeful lack of supervision. The loss of her child, her husband, and her estate

*would render any woman helpless and not in sound mind, and
we should have been informed.*

*However, we are relieved and grateful she has found new
happiness and financial stability. Her new husband, being a
physician, will, we hope, both understand and cherish her. We
await their visit. In the meantime, please send us a forwarding
address where we might contact her.*

*I remain Your Obedient Servant
Joseph Emery de Bourg*

The irregular beats of my heart were stronger, a return of my
agitation at the thought that my family thought me ungrateful, uncaring. I wanted to scream with the pain. Father was
gravely ill, yet they believed me happily remarried with no
interest in my dying father. He died believing me callous. The
injustice of it. The cruelty of it. I would have rushed to his
side. I started pacing the room, my head between my hands.

Sir Charles must have directed everything from London –
employing someone to move me, paying less each time until
I was just another insane pauper – a blight to society. I could
not stop my tears. It was so painful, so cruel. Falling to the
floor, I gripped my knees. I must have cried out. Someone
was knocking at the door, coming quickly to my side. 'Madeleine . . . my dear . . . what is it?'

I could not speak. Mrs Pengelly held me as I sobbed against
her, her arm firmly around my shoulder. 'There now . . . hush,
you're safe.' She must have seen the diaries as I felt her stiffen.
Reaching for one, she held it up. 'What are these, my love?
Is this why you crossed the ford in such a hurry?' Her arm

slipped from me and she opened the first. '*My true and honest dealings with Sir Charles Cavendish.*' Her gasp sent shivers down my spine. 'Where did you find these?'

'In the wine cellar . . . I crawled through the smoke hole like Mrs Munroe said the young gardener had. The barrel had been made into a desk. These were in the secret drawer behind.'

'What on earth made you look there?'

'Phillip Randall didn't drink . . . and he didn't entertain women. Rowan told me he spent hours every evening in the cellar – yet Mrs Munroe said he didn't drink. So I wondered what kept him there so long into the night. *He* held the keys to the cellar, not the butler. Only he had them – so he could keep things from prying eyes. He knew Sir Charles could search his office . . . and his rooms . . . but he'd never think to search the wine cellar.'

She picked one up as if it burned her fingers. 'What are they? Accounts?'

'No, they're diaries – of his dealings – or rather Sir Charles's dealings. They contain everything. I've barely read them but they're full of Sir Charles's lies. He told my family I was remarried – to a doctor, who was treating me.'

Her colour drained, a bite to her lip. 'Are you sure no one saw you take them?'

'No one saw me.' I reached for my handkerchief. 'I've not read them in detail . . . they're full of letters and receipts.' I turned to the first page. 'Look . . . there are letters from physicians who don't exist. And attorneys who don't exist. Why does he have them?'

Her voice was a whisper. 'Because Sir Charles wrote them.'

My heart thumped. She understood, she believed me. 'There are entries about land deals and a threat to someone's life. Do you know a man called Sulio Denville?'

Her lips tightened, a nod of her nightcap, and I saw the sudden fury in her eyes. 'He brought about my husband's ruin. My husband built a cutter for the Revenue. It was an unpopular decision among many in the town — a fast cutter in the hands of excise men was frowned upon, as you may imagine. But his men needed work and the ship was complete. Only it wasn't insured and Sulio Denville, our *nightwatchman*, slipped it from the quay without a backward glance. My husband was ruined and imprisoned for bankruptcy.'

'In the diaries, Phillip Randall seems to suggest Sulio Denville is Sir Charles's hired killer.'

Her voice was sharp, bitter. 'I can believe that — and so will others.'

'He records dates when Sir Charles summoned Sulio Denville — only Sir Charles stayed in the *cottage* not the Hall so no one knew he was in Cornwall. He was in the cottage the day before Phillip Randall was found dead, and I know that because Phillip Randall records Sir Charles drank wine with Sulio Denville.'

She shivered, dropping the diary as if she could not bear to hold it. 'We have to give these to Matthew. Are you certain no one saw you take them?' Her chest was heaving. 'What if someone finds the drawer empty? Sir Charles will know there's been a theft . . . he'll make enquiries.' She ran her hand across her mouth. 'We have to get these to Matthew.'

'They were in a secret drawer — unopened since Randall's

death. No one knew they were there or they'd have taken them already.'

'Phillip Randall was a cruel man. Do you think these were to appease his conscience – or was he planning to blackmail Sir Charles?'

'I don't know. He says in the diary he knew nothing about my whereabouts – that it was Sir Charles who kept moving me.'

She gripped my hand. 'We need to get Rowan out of there. Matthew will advise us . . .' The chill in her voice made my stomach turn.

'Do they know Sam up at the Hall? If so, they'll know straight away that he'll bring her here. We can't risk that.'

Candlelight flickered across her nightgown, lighting the lace trim round her nightcap. She looked more worried than she wanted me to believe. 'Everyone knows everyone in a small town. We'll have to ask someone else to collect her – someone she knows and trusts.'

'Mrs Bolitho from the Ship Inn knows her.'

She shook her head. 'She's a good woman but best not ask her.' Her hands rested as if in prayer. 'What about Captain Pierre? He was on the coach with you – Rowan knows him, doesn't she?'

'No . . . he mustn't know . . . we can't trust him.'

Her eyes widened. 'My dear, why ever not? He's an honest, honourable gentleman . . .'

'But he knows who I am. He heard Mrs Munroe call me Miss Madeleine . . . there was talk of the Hall . . . how things *used to be*. He knows, or he soon will.'

'But he made no reference to it. I'm sure it went right over his head. I had a visit from Lady Pendarvis this morning and she would have said something. She gave no indication Captain Pierre asked about you or the Hall.'

Tears stung my eyes. 'We *can't* ask him.'

She took my hand. 'My dearest, neither Lady Pendarvis nor Captain Pierre will judge you for what's been done to you.' She sounded genuinely surprised, almost hurt. 'Lady Pendarvis will have your best interests at heart – she of all people will understand. She can give you names of people you might know – addresses and introductions to her friends . . . *émigrés* who've settled in London.'

The beating of my heart was too strong, the pounding too painful. I fought to breathe. 'Lady Pendarvis is of *French aristocracy*?'

'Very much so. Her brother's the Marquis de Barthélemy – the family are up in London . . . her brothers, her nephews and nieces. They were fortunate to flee the terror, though I believe not all her family survived.'

'And she allows Captain de la Croix into her confidence? She tells him everything?'

'I believe they have differing opinions on several matters, but they both think very highly of each other.'

I tried to calm my panic. The walls were crushing in on me, a terrible sense of suffocation. I needed to fling open the window, feel the breeze on my cheeks. Pierre de la Croix had positioned himself well – worming his way into the one household that could lead him to so many. It was worse than I thought – far worse. My brother was in grave danger. So, too, my nephews and nieces.

She reached round, gathering up the diaries. 'I'll put these where my husband used to hide his money. They'll be safe — just in case anyone saw you leave. Sir Charles has no restraint. Nothing will stop him barging into my house and searching every room.'

I thrust the last diary into her hands. 'I mustn't put you in danger...'

'We'll give them to Matthew — he'll read every last word of them. Leave it to him. Now, the best thing for us is to try to sleep.'

She shut the door, my fear almost overwhelming. Pierre de la Croix knew the truth; he did not need to ask Lady Pendarvis. There were enough people in Fosse he could charm with his false smile and his lonely eyes. Enough people to tell him Madeleine Pelligrew's brother was le Comte de Charlbourg.

Chapter Twenty-six

Saturday 21st June 1800, 9 a.m.

I tried not to twist my hands or pace about the room, yet every minute seemed an hour, every new sound of wheels giving rise to a rush of nervous expectation. Carts were heading towards the market, men pushing a steady stream of barrows from the surrounding farms. The early sun glinted on the river, the water reflecting the azure blue of the sky. Already the warmth of the sun showed on the men's faces; flushed and squinting, they formed a long procession into town.

Sam was watching from the front steps and called through the open door. 'That's them now – caught behind that oxen cart.'

Mrs Pengelly put down her embroidery and we joined him, standing on tiptoe, just able to glimpse the top of Pierre's tall naval hat. The cart moved forward and I fought the quickening of my pulse. Pierre was smiling, pointing across the river, clearly enjoying Rowan's delight in the two swans with their cygnets. She was obviously at ease, smiling back at him, standing up on the cart, and I knew at once he would have wheedled out our secrets.

Sam swung round, his glance at Mrs Pengelly almost incredulous. Returning his look, she seemed perplexed, staring at the cart with fixed concentration. Tamsin was just behind her. 'Get Mrs Munroe,' Mrs Pengelly whispered, her voice strangely hoarse.

Again she fixed her eyes on Rowan, who had sat back down, wearing no bonnet, her black curls framing her flushed cheeks. Still her eyes seemed too large for her face, yet they were lit with pleasure, her excitement making her wriggle on the seat.

'Bless my soul,' Mrs Munroe said from behind us. 'It's like we've turned back the clock.'

Tamsin's hand flew to her mouth. 'Ye don't think it is, do ye?'

I looked round, stunned by the tears in their eyes. Mrs Pengelly retrieved her handkerchief, dabbing her cheeks. 'She's the spit of him – how many times have we watched Billy on that cart – with just the same big eyes and long nose? The same black hair and high cheeks. She's the image of him.'

Sam had reached the cart and was pointing back to the house and Rowan seemed suddenly shy, lifting her hand to wave in a demure manner. Behind me, Mrs Munroe wiped her eyes. 'Bless her dear little heart. Ye said she was found up the moor? Her mother dead? She has to be Billy's sister. It's as if Billy's on that cart. The likeness is extraordinary.'

Sudden jealousy pierced my heart. She was Rowan, *my* daughter. 'Who's Billy?' I whispered.

Mrs Pengelly slipped her arm through mine. 'Billy came to

us some seven years ago. He was a vagrant child – separated from his sisters and badly beaten. He was twelve when he was brought to us – on that very cart – though he looked ten. She's the image of him. Billy's sisters would be twelve and nine now – he's nineteen. He's apprenticed to William Cotterell – he lives with them at the Old Forge, though he's away studying to be an engineer.'

My jealously almost overwhelmed me. Rowan had a family. Her own family. 'What would be her name – *if* she is Billy's sister?'

'Betsy,' they said in unison.

Mrs Pengelly smiled. 'Elizabeth is the oldest, and Bella was the youngest – Betsy and Bella.' The cart was almost at the front door and she put her hands out, stopping the others from rushing forward. 'Let her get settled. Don't frighten her with our thoughts. Madeleine, my love – why don't you greet her for us?'

Pierre handed the reins to Sam. 'Here we are. Thank you, Sam.' Helping Rowan from the bench, he towered behind her. 'Safely delivered . . . and I believe very glad to be here.' He smiled down at her, bowing politely. 'I'm honoured to have been of service.'

His glance at me was shy by comparison, tentative, a formal nod before he smiled at Mrs Pengelly. 'No one tried to stop me, though I had my permission slip ready.' He held up a letter. 'Sir Alexander kindly gave me a pass but it wasn't needed.'

I could not return his civilities and turned from his smile. All morning I had been imagining how I would run to Rowan, embrace her as a mother would, take her hand and introduce her to the household, but that was stolen from me now. She was stolen from me. She would be theirs, not mine. I tried to smile, holding out my hands. Of course I wanted her to find her brother. Of course I was happy; it was just the shock, that was all. The shock and the certain knowledge that I would now lose her. She did not need me – they would take her in. She would be embraced as one of them – lost to the gaiety of the Old Forge. She would love Elowyn, just as everyone else loved her. She would work as a dressmaker.

Mrs Pengelly held out her hands. 'Come in, dear. We have a room all ready for you . . . Mrs Munroe's been baking . . .' She glanced at the empty cart, realising Rowan had no luggage. 'We've a cat who looks very grumpy but he's as soft as butter . . . Do you like cats, my dear?'

Rowan smiled and nodded but seemed reluctant to go through the door, turning to me with a look of panic. 'It's all right,' I whispered. 'You can use the front door.'

Mrs Pengelly smiled at Pierre de la Croix. 'Won't you join us, Captain Pierre?'

He must have caught my sudden glare. His smile faded. 'No . . . perhaps another time . . . thank you. You must get Rowan settled.' He bowed stiffly, walking swiftly away.

Rowan stayed close to my side, following us down the steps and into the kitchen. 'There now!' said Mrs Munroe proudly. 'I've made you some lemonade . . . and I've added just a touch of mint. And sugar, mind! I had a terrible sweet tooth when I were a girl.'

Tamsin stood beside her, her smile radiant as she pointed to her raisin cake. 'An' I made ye this . . . I hope ye're hungry.'

Everywhere smiles, tears in their eyes, the three of them welcoming Rowan as if for the last seven years they had been expecting her to walk through their door. Laying plates on the table, they fussed around her and I watched her respond with smiles and grateful thanks. I added my own, my emptiness growing. I could not offer her the warmth and love they offered – nor the stability. I must be happy for her, glad I had been the means of bringing her here. It was not my loss, it was her gain.

Lemonade and cakes were piled on to the table, but midmouthful Rowan stopped, rising from her chair as if thunderstruck. Hurrying across the kitchen she stood next to a charcoal etching of a young boy with black curly hair, huge eyes and a straight nose. 'Who's this?' She put her finger to the glass, tracing the contours of his face.

'A friend of ours – he lives at the Old Forge. He's going to be an engineer. That etching was done five years ago.'

She had lost all colour, bewilderment in her eyes as she turned to face us. 'It's like I've seen him before. Like I know him. I remember the folly and it's like this boy was there. It's just a quick picture in my mind . . . then it goes . . . just a boy running towards the folly . . . It's like I've seen him before.'

I helped her back to the table. Mrs Munroe followed, slipping the picture from the wall and placing it in front of her. 'Does the name Jonny sound familiar?' Rowan shook her head. 'Do you think you may know a boy called David? Or Tommy? Could his name be Eddy?'

Rowan shook her head to all three names. 'No . . . I'm sorry. Perhaps I'm wrong.'

Mrs Pengelly put her hand on Rowan's. 'How about the name Billy?'

Rowan jerked round, a sudden gasp. 'Billy? Billy... That sounds right. Yes. *Billy Boy*. I remember that name.' Her face clouded. 'No – it's not Billy Boy.'

'Could it be Billy *Bosco* you remember?'

Her eyes widened. A lift to her voice. 'Billy Bosco... maybe. I don't remember anything before I was found. But saying that sounds somehow right.'

'My dear... seven years ago Billy Bosco was brought to live here after suffering great brutality. We took him in. He's nineteen now and for the last seven years he's been searching for his lost sister.'

She gripped my hand. 'Searching for his sister?'

Mrs Pengelly lifted the mirror from the wall, placing it in front of Rowan. She held the portrait next to it and we stared at the two almost identical faces. 'Billy's sister Betsy was lost on the moors... and we're struck by how much you look like him. He must have been about your age when this was drawn. Look, see, my love...? You've got very similar eyes... and noses. And, well, seeing you on that cart made us all think you were Billy.'

Tears pooled in her eyes, her mouth beginning to quiver. She gripped my hand tighter. 'You think he might be my brother?'

Mrs Pengelly nodded. 'He *may* be. But my sweet love, *if* you are the sister we've all been searching for then I have some very sad news. When Billy was separated from... Well... back then he had *two* sisters. And two years ago we found that Bella

Bosco — aged three — had died up on the moor. We found her name but your name's never appeared in any registry. You were lost without trace — but Mrs Pendarvis has never given up her search.'

'Mrs Pendarvis?' I did not mean to sound so sharp.

Mrs Pengelly's pearl-drops swung as she faced me. 'Celia Pendarvis witnessed Billy's beating. She's Billy's patron. She paid for everything. She got him into Truro Grammar School — and though Billy lives with Elowyn and William, Celia Pendarvis has always paid for his upkeep — including their search for his sister. She's never stopped searching — she even sent someone all the way to Ireland. She's never given up.'

Mrs Munroe was showing Rowan a book of etchings, Tamsin clearing the table, and though I tried to join in, I could not concentrate. I felt winded. Rowan's voice broke my thoughts. 'Betsy?'

I reached for her hand. 'We'll try to trace the lady you knew as your mother . . . back to where she found you under the rowan tree. The lady who died will be buried some-where . . . they'll find her name . . . and maybe they can trace her back to Bella. I'm sure there'll be a way of finding where you've come from.'

Her face crumpled, her cry breaking my heart. 'But I like Rowan . . . Please don't make me be called Betsy.'

I held her to me, a fierce pain shooting through me. 'You *are* Rowan . . . we love you for being Rowan. No one wants you to be anyone else. If Billy is your brother, then he'll be happy to call you whatever name you choose.'

Mrs Munroe picked up the huge black-and-white cat. 'I

think Rowan's the prettiest name there is. You're Rowan to us, my love. And it's only for Billy's sake we'd like ye to be his sister. How about you meet Mr Pitt?'

Rowan clutched the cat to her. 'He's lost half his ear,' she said, kissing his soft fur.

'Doesn't matter if ye have half an ear, one leg, one arm . . . All that matters is that whoever steps into my kitchen knows they're welcome. How about I show ye the pantry? There's a barrel of biscuits in there . . . and Tamsin will show ye the yard. No, keep hold of the cat. I can see he loves ye.'

Mrs Pengelly glanced at the clock. 'Goodness, it's nearly eleven. How this morning's flown. Matthew and Alice will be here soon. I'm afraid we'll have to leave you for a while, Rowan. Will you be all right for an hour or so?'

She turned at the foot of the stairs, watching Rowan stroke Mr Pitt. 'I hope she'll be happy here . . . You don't think we've given her too much of a shock, do you? Only with her seeing Billy's portrait . . .'

'I think it's been a shock to us all,' I replied, following her up the stairs.

She opened the front door to a blast of warm air. Looking to the right, she raised her arm and waved. 'There they are . . . always right on time.' Her hand slipped through my elbow. 'You've nothing to fear. You're looking so pretty, my dear – Alice will recognise you at once. And Matthew only *sounds* fierce . . . once you get know him, you'll find him quite charming.'

Chapter Twenty-seven

Alice Reith held out her hands and the years slipped away. She had welcomed me with the same vibrant red hair and shy smile as a grieving widow of twenty-two when I had visited her in Polcarrow as a young bride of twenty.

'Madeleine... I'm so sorry... I'm completely horrified. Eva's told us everything and it breaks my heart.' Tears pooled in her eyes, a frown creasing her brow. 'It's... so cruel...'

Mrs Pengelly ushered us all into her drawing room, shutting the door behind her, and Alice gestured to her husband, a tall, slender man with short greying black hair. 'This is Matthew, my husband.' She sounded strained, reaching for her handkerchief. 'I failed you, Madeleine... I kept asking after you ... I kept visiting the Hall, but each time I went to see you, they turned me away.'

'You had your son to look after... you couldn't have done more.' The years had been kind to her. I knew her as the anxious young widow of Sir Francis Polcarrow, jumping at her own shadow, petrified of her brother, Robert Roskelly, yet now she looked radiant, her abundant red hair pinned in a coiffure. The green ribbon on her straw bonnet accentuated the colour of her eyes. A happy face, no sign of hard lines around her mouth or hatred in her eyes. 'Mrs Pengelly tells me Francis is studying Law,' I said, a stab of envy twisting my stomach.

She nodded, smiling quickly at her husband before her frown returned. 'The last time I went to the Hall, I spoke to Sir Charles himself. He said you were struck with terrible grief . . . that your husband had taken his own life . . . and you were going back to your family.' She reached for my hand, drawing me to the chaise longue. 'He assured me your welfare was his prime concern . . . that he'd arranged your passage on a ship and would send a maid and one of his men to accompany you.'

A flood of hatred made my cheeks burn. 'He's been so successful in hiding the truth. He lies and leaves a trail of lies – ledgers where they can be found with letters for his servants to read. Lies fabricating how good he was to me . . . how I found a new life and returned to France. He'll tell you he received a letter from my attorney confirming I was happily remarried and wanted nothing more to do with him, but the reality is he had me taken to Maddison's Madhouse and moved every two years thereafter.'

I know I sounded bitter. I sounded angry, contemptuous. Matthew Reith was looking out across the river, no doubt allowing Alice to talk, yet he turned at the venom in my voice. Impeccably dressed in a well-fitting cut-away jacket and simple silk necktie, his eyes pierced mine. 'Is that conjecture or fact, Mrs Pelligrew?'

Alice reached for my hand, a stern glance at her husband. 'Matthew's so much happier when he can deal in truths — evidence and facts that can't be disputed. He has a fearsome reputation in the courts...' She shrugged her elegant shoulders. 'We're going to help you, Madeleine ... we're going to do everything we can to get you redress.'

I knew to expect this. I had applied Elowyn's creams and potions with such care, outlining my eyebrows, adding colour to my lips. I looked better, but I still had the gaunt face of an ill woman. Of course, he would be searching for signs of insanity. I tried to sound level-headed, calmer than I felt. 'It's not conjecture, Mr Reith. But for the brave people who searched for me and executed my escape, I'd still be languishing in a filthy madhouse – no doubt until I died.'

A flicker crossed his eyes. He was making no attempt to be civil, polite enough, but his eyes looked sceptical, as if he did not believe a word I was saying. 'Brave *people?*' A hint of disbelief. 'I take it your family rescued you? Did they also receive a letter telling them you were happily remarried?'

His tone made me grip my hands. 'Yes, they did. My brother's friend rescued me and—' I clamped my mouth tight, unable to say more. I had to protect Marcel and Cécile Lefèvre. Matthew Reith was making my head spin. He was like the rest of them: powerful, well connected, treating me as if I was lying. I felt unbearably hot, my cheeks flushing. My mind was not the muddle it once was, yet he was intimidating me, making my thoughts jumble, tying my tongue in knots. 'They've ... been searching for me ... my brother's expecting me back in France ... only with this war, it's not that easy.'

'They?'

He had to believe I was sane to arrange for the physicians to certify me. I must not speak of French spies or Cécile Lefèvre's British spies. How Captain de la Croix was not as innocent as he seemed.

'He's here, in Fosse?' I must have looked puzzled. 'Your brother's friend, who rescued you?' he repeated. 'I'd like to talk to him. What's his name? Where is he staying?'

'François Barnard, but he's not staying... That is... he's left Fosse for a few days. But he will return.'

Mrs Pengelly had been glancing between us. Her smile faded; even she must have thought him rather too stern. Alice reached for my hand. 'There are ways of getting to France – via Jersey, I believe. I presume he'll be arranging that.'

Matthew Reith crossed the room, flicking up his jacket as he sat opposite me. He leaned forward and I got the full force of his stare. 'Mrs Pelligrew, I was not in Truro when your husband died but I am acquainted with most of the attorneys in the county and when we received Eva's letter I asked around.' He smiled at Mrs Pengelly.

'It seems there was some agreement – and by this I mean a codicil, a *legally binding* agreement – signed by Sir Charles – that he would house you at his own expense until you married again. I've had no time to investigate this but I believe it may be in your interest to stay in Fosse and *not* leave for France. France for aristocrats is a dangerous place, though your brother has done well to prove the exception. It's your decision, but if I was to unearth this agreement, it may be that you could anticipate lodgings here in Fosse, *paid for* by Sir Charles. Had you heard of such an agreement?'

I stared back at him. There was just the hint of a smile, a warmth in the eyes I had thought so frosty. He must be a good man for Alice to look so radiant; either way, he was my only hope. His eyes hardened. 'In which case, you must assure me that you haven't remarried and that you haven't just arrived from elsewhere – not a madhouse – because you knew of this agreement. You arrived in Fosse with a gentleman of the same surname, your *brother-in-law*, I believe you told the proprietor of the Ship Inn. Word is, however, that he's your *husband*.'

I held his gaze, my heart thumping. I was not in the courtroom and I was not lying. He thought I had fabricated everything. I had to stay strong. 'I have a witness to my release – Rowan, a maid from the madhouse – and I've kept my true name hidden because the moment Sir Charles knows I'm back in Fosse is the moment he'll come looking for me again. Only, this time, I'll be found floating in the river, not incarcerated in a madhouse.'

A sharp rise of his brows, his eyes stern. 'Forgive me, but re-marriage is exactly what Sir Charles will circulate against you. Your late husband was ruined – that's not in question – but why shut you away? Why will you be found *floating in the river*?'

I gripped my hands together. I did not have to like him; I needed only to make him believe me. 'Sir Charles Cavendish shut me away *not* to avoid paying my upkeep but because he orchestrated my husband's ruin and arranged his murder.' The grey eyes turned to steel, a sudden gasp from Alice. 'At the time, I was distressed. I was shouting . . . wailing. I thought no one was listening, but he was. He heard me.'

'Heard what?'

'I told him Phillip Randall left the wood minutes before I found my husband drowned. My husband went to meet the proprietor of a dredging company. He was excited . . . saying he would make us our fortune. Half an hour later he was dead. All these years I've been convinced Phillip Randall lured him there, posed as the dredger, and murdered him on the instructions of Sir Charles. Once he knew I'd seen Phillip Randall, Sir Charles had to silence me. I was the only witness. Two days later, I was drugged, gagged, and taken to the madhouse.'

'There's no chance of prosecuting Sir Charles through Phillip Randall. He was lynched four years ago. Dead men can't speak.'

Mrs Pengelly rose and Matthew Reith followed her across the room, opening the door for her. She thought I would not hear her whisper. 'Maybe a little less hard, Matthew? Madeleine's still very frail.'

Alice gripped my hand. 'I believe you.' The light caught the emerald brooch at her neck. 'But Matthew needs evidence . . . that's why he sounds so severe.'

Once again, I fought my stab of envy. We had both married men twenty years our senior, both young brides with grand houses and estates. We had both been widowed yet she had found love again. She had been enchanting as a young woman, now she looked radiant, her soft face loving, smile lines creasing her eyes. She had her son and two stepdaughters; she had lived her life, yet I had paced away my own.

Matthew Reith resumed his seat. 'You make a grave accusation, Mrs Pelligrew. I need more to go on than your suspicions.

I need times... places... names. Without proper evidence—'

It was as if I had found my voice. 'It wasn't Phillip Randall who killed my husband. It was Sulio Denville, but I believe Phillip Randall either was part of the plan or witnessed my husband's murder.'

His eyes sharpened. 'What plan?'

'Charles Cavendish fabricated a dredging company to fool my husband and he got Sulio Denville to pose as a Dutch dredger – so he could drown my husband when they were surveying the river. I didn't see the murder, and I don't have proof, but I found Phillip Randall's diaries.'

'Found what?' He looked incredulous.

Mrs Pengelly entered, holding up her sewing basket. 'These.' She lifted off her embroidery. 'They don't know these diaries exist up at the Hall. Madeleine found them in the wine cellar.'

Matthew Reith stared, thunderstruck. 'You searched Pendenning Hall?'

'Reading his diaries... I'm convinced it was Sulio Denville who killed my husband. And Phillip Randall knew. I think he saw.'

He picked up the top diary. 'You found these in the wine cellar?' There was new respect in his tone, a warmth in his eyes. 'Mrs Pelligrew... I'm stunned...' He seemed lost for words, a huge smile lighting his face. 'Why keep these... ?' He read the opening inscription. 'Untimely death! I wonder if he was going to blackmail Sir Charles... my goodness... this is extraordinary...'

My voice was firm, my heart leaping. 'Mr Reith, even if I was to legally gain from Sir Charles, I wouldn't accept a penny.

I don't want recompense. I want his downfall. I want people to know the truth.'

Alice took a diary and flicked through the pages. 'Madeleine, you've no idea how useful these will be. Matthew's been prosecuting Sir Charles for years . . . yet here are names . . . letters . . . dates to prove his allegations.'

Matthew was reading with fixed concentration. 'I'll have to cross-reference everything. Every entry will need to be investigated. It'll take time . . . but I believe what he says will prove correct. Phillip Randall felt his life was in danger – look, read this, Alice.' He pointed to an entry. 'But as for Sulio Denville, he's long gone. He's been wanted for seven years. Wanted for the theft of a cutter, kidnap, grievous bodily harm, and for giving false evidence against James Polcarrow.'

The clock on the mantelpiece chimed the half-hour. Alice placed her diary back in the basket. 'You've suffered great wrong, Madeleine, and Matthew will see that you get redress, but it'll take time. What are your plans? Do you mean to stay or go to your brother?'

The hollow emptiness that had been gnawing me all morning returned. I had envisaged our own cottage: Rowan and I living as mother and daughter, coming home to each other, laughing about our day. Discussing my singing lessons, or the French lessons I had given, sitting at a scrubbed pine table, a small but cosy hearth burning, a kitten playing on her lap. Our own rooms with the bedspreads we quilted together, flowers in a vase. Teaching her to read and write, singing carols at Christmas, lullabies my mother used to sing. Collecting beautiful china together, piece by piece.

But she was not my daughter. She had a brother, and I could not compete with the laughter and gaiety of Elowyn's house, nor their rising prospects. William's engineering works were doing well and Billy would soon earn enough to keep her. Far better she lived with them. 'My brother is very anxious to have me home,' I stammered.

Matthew Reith was still reading, his mouth tight. He clamped the diary shut. 'You're right, Mrs Pelligrew. You *are* in great danger. Did you know Sir Charles has returned to Pendenning? There's a rumpus in the Salt Office. He's stormed down to protect his interests.'

The urgency in his voice chilled me. 'Yes . . . I did know.'

He walked to the window, staring down at the street. 'I believe we must meet lies with lies. You say Sir Charles left evidence in Pendenning saying you'd returned to France? That you were not kept in the madhouse?'

'Yes . . . that I was certified sane and no longer wanted him to enquire after my health. If I found it so easily, others would have done, too.'

'Then we must go along with his lies. You must call yourself Madeleine Pelligrew. You returned to your brother and made a new life. However, you recently left France because of the *troubles* and, like everyone else, you're seeking refuge back in England until you can return to your homeland.'

I stared at him. What if Pierre de la Croix had not guessed who I was . . . in which case, I would be exposing everyone to danger. I could not agree to this, not until I talked to Marcel. 'I'm not . . . ready . . .'

Mrs Pengelly saw I was struggling. 'Madeleine needs time

to decide – though I believe it would be a good idea.'

Matthew Reith bowed stiffly. 'It would take courage but it could be done. If Mrs Pelligrew is to stay in Fosse, I believe it's the only way to keep her safe. Sir Charles must believe she was released fourteen years ago. It says in the diary her name was changed many times and she was never called Madeleine Pelligrew. Sir Charles must be led to believe he's been moving another woman from madhouse to madhouse. Mistaken identity is more common than you think.'

Alice pulled Mrs Pengelly's sewing over the diaries and lifted the basket. 'We understand how difficult this is for you, Madeleine. If you like, we could help you fabricate the last fourteen years. I know it's daunting, but it would be possible. Just let us know what you decide. I'll return this basket straight away.'

Watching them walk back along the river, my resolve tightened. I would do anything to see Sir Charles brought to justice, but I would not put a brave and intelligent woman in danger. Cécile Lefèvre had to be kept safe. Mrs Pengelly slipped her arm through mine. 'You did very well, my dear. Are you all right? Only you've gone very pale.'

'I can't assume my real name without discussing it with François. I need to speak to him . . . he's very insistent I keep my identity hidden.'

There was concern in her eyes, no sign of her smile. 'Go now. Take a parasol, the walk will do you good. I'll tell Rowan you'll only be a moment . . . and I'll see what I can find her by way of a new dress.'

Chapter Twenty-eight

The air was warm, no breeze to blow away the flowers' perfume. It hung heavily in the air, the petals burning under the scorching sun. Even at the brow of the hill there was no hint of wind, just the vast blue sea and the flower-strewn clifftops. Despite my parasol, the sun seemed too bright, and I squinted across to the linhay, hurrying through the long grass to seek the shade of the stone walls.

I felt listless, hardly knowing if I wanted to go or stay. Matthew Reith might take years to build up his case against Sir Charles, I should be with my family. I should not remain to harbour my envy, my thoughts of other people's happiness poisoning me. Other people's families. I should return to my childhood home and devote myself to my nephews and nieces. Worse still, what if Marcel had already left town?

Below me, a schooner was anchored perilously close to the rocks, her white sails hanging limp and shouts echoing across her decks. The sailors were taking down the sails, throwing ropes to men in small boats waiting to row them into the harbour.

'They should have done that an hour back. They've anchored now but those rocks are treacherous – they could still founder. They had neither wind nor tide, yet they thought to enter!'

I swung round. Not Marcel, but Pierre de la Croix, and I turned to hide my sudden blush. 'Looking for more insects, Captain de la Croix?'

A smile flashed across his face. He reached for a bag hanging from his shoulders, his voice tentative. 'No. I've been waiting . . . hoping . . . that you might come for your daily walk. I thought perhaps you might bring Rowan.' He opened his bag, the sun on his face, the flecks of grey glinting in his sideburns. His hands were strong, elegant, his fingers fine-boned, his nails clean and well cut. He drew something out. 'I've carved this for you – it's your seagull . . . the driftwood you saw. The shape was already there, I just followed the contours.'

He held out a beautiful white seagull with outstretched wings. He had smoothed it, polished it, mounted it on another piece of wood – the seagull I had seen, taking flight, about to soar free. He had given it life and I forced back my tears. 'Thank you . . . it's beautiful.'

'By way of a peace offering.' His voice was thick, hesitant, his elegant hands doing up the buckle of his bag.

Our eyes caught. 'How very clever you are . . . how very talented. To be able to craft something so beautiful is a rare gift.'

'Mrs Pelligrew, I believe I may have offended you in some

way. I think, perhaps, it's because you believe me a coward? Yet . . . I . . . wish it were otherwise. I would so much prefer your good opinion.'

I could hardly breathe. He called me by my name, he knew everything about me. I grasped the seagull and turned away.

'It wasn't Rowan who told me who you are, it was when Mrs Munroe called you Miss Madeleine. All their talk of the Hall. You have such grace . . . dignity . . . elegance. You have sorrow in your eyes . . . hurt and longing. Please don't shy away from me. If I can be of any assistance, please ask. It would be an honour to help you . . .'

'Thank you, you have already been very kind.'

Something was different about the linhay – a milk churn crammed into a small space. It was half-hidden, pushed into a gap by the disused hearth. The hairs on my arms prickled, a shiver, a sudden absolute certainty. The appearance of a milk churn where no one needed milk? Surely that could only mean one thing? It had been put there to conceal something – a place to leave a message? But what if Captain de la Croix had also seen it and thought the same? What if he had already searched its contents? 'It's very hot . . . I shouldn't have come so far.'

He stiffened, as if stung. 'Let me help you to some shade.'

'No! I must go. I'm sorry. I have to leave.'

I hurried back across the clifftop, stumbling through the flowers, gorse bushes snagging my dress, desperate to draw him away from the milk churn. He stayed close behind, his long strides keeping pace. At the turn in the road, I stopped to catch my breath.

'Madeleine... I've been a clumsy fool. Forgive me... I have little, if any, idea how to address a lady.'

'I cannot stay... I must not. Forgive me...'

A flash of hurt, a tightening of his mouth. 'At least allow me to see you home. You look most unwell.'

I wanted rid of his subterfuge, his lies, the way he followed me, the way I wanted to believe him. The way I had yielded to him in my dream, the way he made my heart quicken, yet I needed to remain civil; he must never suspect me of thinking he was on Marcel's trail. 'I'm sorry, I spoke harshly. Your seagull is beautiful, thank you.'

He smiled, his shoulders straighter, his chin lifting, and I accepted his proffered arm, walking sedately into town. Outside a huge red-brick house with windows overlooking the river mouth, he stopped. Steps led up to a painted door beneath a large portico, on the door a brass dolphin knocker gleamed in the sun. An inscription was carved by the side, *Admiral House*.

'Admiral, as in Admiral Sir Alexander Pendarvis. Apparently it was meant to be Dolphin House but everyone called it Admiral House so they had to change it.' He swallowed, as if suddenly shy. 'Lady Pendarvis has many connections in London. She may know someone who you know.'

He sounded so plausible, as if he meant it, and my mouth turned dry. He knew everything I wanted to keep hidden. Everything. He pointed up to a window with a fine view across the sea. 'I'm very fortunate – that's my room. I watch the ships come and go.' He led me slightly forward, pointing to a boat with a sleek black hull. 'That one riding at anchor is

Sir James Polcarrow's ship. She's called *L'Aigrette*. A ship with a French name, would you believe?'

I tried to keep calm, to smile and nod, shrug my shoulders. There was no doubt in my mind Cécile Lefèvre was in Fosse and had left a message in that milk churn. Had Marcel found it? The wind was too light to sail tonight, but it might return tomorrow. At the door of Coombe House Pierre de la Croix bade me good day. Mrs Pengelly was at the window, her smile lighting her face.

'How well you look together,' she said as I entered the room.

'He *knows* who I am.'

'I'm not surprised . . . he's a highly intelligent man.' She sounded confident, even joyful. 'Maybe you should do what Matthew suggests? Do you believe in fate, my dear? That you were meant to be here, in Fosse, at exactly the same time as Captain Pierre?'

<hr />

I must have smiled, I think I even laughed, sitting with Rowan at the scrubbed kitchen table, sifting through the charity clothes they had been saving for Lady Pendarvis's French prisoners.

Mrs Pengelly smiled. 'Of course you must have a new dress, Rowan. Billy's coming to the ball, so we'll have to have you looking bonny.'

Lace spilled across the table, a collection of colourful ribbons and spools of thread. Rowan picked through Mrs Pengelly's sewing basket, making everyone smile – the first silver thimble she had ever seen, the first embroidered needle case, the first tape measure. Holding up a pair of delicately engraved scissors, she whispered, 'Are they *real* silver?'

Mrs Pengelly held up a length of yellow ribbon. 'Use them to cut this...'

The ribbons cut, Mrs Munroe tied them in Rowan's hair and I must have smiled. I must have told her how pretty she looked. They loved her. Tomorrow, Elowyn would offer her a home and she would be lost to me. Rowan's eyes shone with pleasure. 'But it don't seem right it's only *me* with ribbons. What about you, Mrs Munroe? And Tamsin? It don't seem right it's just me.'

More laughter, more emptiness. We were all to have ribbons in our hair, all laughing and smiling, even Mr Pitt purring in his new green bow. Sam studied his reflection, enjoying the red silk Tamsin tied as a cravat. 'Well, now, who'd have thought it! Quite the gentleman.'

Yet my thoughts were with the half-hidden milk churn. I must leave my shutters open, keep a watch for a note from Marcel. With Pierre de la Croix knowing who I was, it was too dangerous to delay.

Moonlight flooded the room, the waves lapping the riverbank. Lying alert, my ears tuned for the faintest sound, I heard a soft knock and rose quickly from the bed. It came from the door, not the window – a timid knock, and I knew it must be Rowan. She looked pale, her huge eyes searching mine. 'I've never slept alone before. It's like the shadows are watching me...'

I held her to me, kissing the black curls on the top of her

head. 'Don't be frightened . . . come . . . stay with me. I wondered about you sleeping in your own room but Tamsin has her door open, doesn't she?'

She wiped her eyes. 'I'm being silly, aren't I? It's just . . .'

'Not silly at all. It's a strange house and all houses make funny noises at night. Come, my love . . . my bed can sleep two. We'll be very comfortable.'

Tiptoeing so as not to wake anyone, I settled her next to me. 'Are these *silk* sheets?' she whispered.

'Just very fine cotton. Sleep now . . . we've a busy day ahead. You're going to love Elowyn – she has a beautiful little girl and there are always children playing in the yard.'

'Will you sing that song ye used to sing in Pendrissick? I loved to hear ye sing. Ye made me cry sometimes.'

She felt frail in my arms, a child of twelve desperately needing a mother's love. Tears filled my eyes. I sounded strained, singing in more pain than she could ever imagine.

Au clair de la lune
Mon ami Pierrot
Prête-moi ta plume
Pour écrire un mot.

'That's lovely,' she whispered. 'What does it mean?'

'It's about moonlight flooding into a room . . . about two people finding love and having to part. Hush now. I'll sing it again but you must go to sleep.'

She snuggled down, closing her eyes. 'Do you sleep with the window wide open because ye couldn't for so long?'

A sudden pang as I remembered the thin crack in my barred window and Chanticleer heralding in the new day. What if Rowan woke to find me gone? 'Promise me you'll sleep.' I lay fighting my tears. France was no place for her. Her home was with Elowyn and her brother Billy. Marcel would soon contact me, and I would tell him I was ready to leave.

Chapter Twenty-nine

Rowan's breathing steadied to a soft rhythm and I slipped from the bed. Owls hooted across the river, the moonlight glistening on the black water, flooding the town in silver light. Not a breath of wind, no sound of rigging, no sign of Marcel. The church clock chimed, another hour had passed, it was two in the morning and still he had not come. Not knowing was unnerving. I sat bolt upright, straining for the slightest movement. What if the milk churn contained Cécile's instructions and Marcel had left Fosse before he could read it?

Next to me, the seagull on my dressing table seemed so lifelike. Pierre de la Croix had given it life, just as Marcel had given me back my life. It looked poised to fly.

Poised to fly, as if telling me I was not held here, that I was no longer a captive. That I did not have to sit and watch the world through a window but I could spread my wings. Go anywhere – when and where I wanted.

I dressed quickly, shutting the door carefully, slipping down the stairs without a sound. The house was in darkness, all the doors shut, only the ticking of the longcase clock accompanying me as I tiptoed across the hall and down to the kitchen. Embers burned behind the grate, another clock ticking, moonlight pouring through the top window. Making my way across the flagstones to the scullery, I reached for Mrs Munroe's cloak. Mr Pitt watched me through half-closed eyes, flicking his tail as I stood by the back door. I had seen where Sam hung the key and turned the lock, pulling up my hood. I would be gone an hour, probably less.

I crossed the empty road, keeping to the shadows, my soft shoes making no sound. The night was warm, the town silent, only the hooting of the owls as I hurried along the empty street to the market square. Voices drifted from the quayside and I drew back, hiding in a doorway. Two men were smoking pipes, their tobacco smoke drifting towards me, another two leaning against the wall, yet they looked to be nightwatchmen and I hurried on, remaining in the shadows to pass Admiral House.

If Pierre de la Croix was watching he could not see me now, and I breathed in the heady scent of the night. It was like another world; silent, ghostlike, the moon so bright I could see every cobble, every flower, even the leaves in the hedgerows. Silhouetted in silver, the linhay rose eerily in front of me, and I hid against the twisting trunk of a tree blown sideways by the wind. It was as if I had come alive again, the thrill of the night air making my heart race. I held my breath, straining to hear if anyone was following.

I could hear nothing, just the soft waves of an untroubled sea, the barking of a dog. Moonlight glistened on the water, catching the huer's hut on the cliff above Porthruan, lighting the battlements and the cannons poised to protect the river mouth. No sound of footsteps, and I hurried further up the hill, slipping across the field to the linhay.

The night air, the excitement; knowing I could be brave again filled me with such strength. The child in me was still there: the daughter of the sea who would slip from the house at midnight was still there; the wilful young woman who disobeyed her parents to swim with dolphins, who raced barefoot along the sandy beach, her lips tasting of salt, her hair dripping against her shoulders. The foolish young woman who defied her parents to marry a man they did not approve of was older and damaged, but she was still there.

I clutched the dark cloak round me, peering through the gap of the linhay where the window had been. The milk churn was there, yet it looked as if it had been moved slightly. It glinted as I approached. It felt empty. Yet as I held it, something moved inside and I twisted off the lid, turning it to the light of the moon. A small leather bag lay at the bottom and I reached for it, forcing it through the opening, fumbling with the buckle. There was nothing in it and I turned it over, the moonlight catching the intricate pattern stamped into the leather. Marcel must have taken the contents.

Part pleased, part disappointed, I knew to return the bag exactly as I had found it. I began squeezing it back through the top but the base of the bag felt bulky and I opened it again, running my hand over it. There was something beneath the leather. I had to think like Cécile Lefèvre. Act like her. I was walking in her shadow. A prickle ran down my spine, an inner certainty that I would find her message. Pulling away the false bottom, I drew out a wad of papers and held them to the light.

They were clearly written, yet they made no sense. Nothing was legible – they were not in English, nor French, but seemed in a language of their own. I could make nothing of them, just page after page of numbers and letters jumbled in rows, not sentences – *CL28F, AL37B*. It was clearly in code – details of where we were to meet, the ship, the place, the time, protected from prying eyes. I looked round, staring at the shadows. Rushing up here had been dangerous. A faint breath caressed my cheek, a rustle in the grass beside me, and I turned to face the sea. Wispy clouds were streaking across the night sky, the moon less brilliant. The wind was returning and with it would come the ships.

The town would soon be waking and I knew to hurry. Replacing the papers as I found them, I slipped across the grass, once again seeking the shadows, avoiding the oil lamps with their pools of light, keeping to the edges of the buildings. In the marketplace, I held my breath. Something alerted me – a soft tread, the echo of footsteps. I pulled quickly into a doorway and the footsteps stopped.

If I took the river road, I would be seen from both Admiral House and Mrs Pengelly's house, yet if I took the narrow alleys, I would be in danger of getting lost. I drew my cloak tighter, deciding to take the river road. I would walk quickly and be prepared to run. Leaving my recess, I knew my fear was founded. The footsteps started again, getting louder, no longer stopping when I stopped, but growing stronger, noisier, getting closer.

I began hurling myself along the road, the chimneys of Coombe House still some way ahead. I had never run so fast, my breath sharp, painful, yet the footsteps stayed behind me, catching me up. I could hear heavy breathing, a curse. An iron hand gripped me, forcing my arm behind me. The man was panting, as breathless as I was. 'Out for some night air, Mrs Pelligrew? Perhaps you couldn't sleep?'

We were at the side gate of Coombe House, almost the exact place where he had accosted me before. Thomas Pearce glared at me from beneath his huge hat. Clearly dressed for concealment, he wore a thick black cloak, black gloves, a black scarf. His eyes fixed mine, pin-point cruel. 'Where's François? And don't lie. You've been waiting for him... watching for him at the window. When he didn't come, you went to find him. Well, where is he?'

He reeked of brandy, his voice rising as his grip tightened. 'Tell him I need that ship. Tell him I've enough money to pay him what he wants. Tell him I need to leave *now*.'

A shadow moved, a whispered voice behind me: 'You can tell me yourself.'

The grip grew stronger, my arm twisting painfully as I tried to turn. Marcel stepped from the shadows, his face gaunt in the moonlight. He was unshaven, his eyes wary, his mouth tight with disgust. 'Let her go. *Never* lay your filthy hands on her again.'

Thomas Pearce released his hold and Marcel stepped forward, ushering me behind him. 'We want nothing to do with you.' He spoke angrily, spitting out his words, his fists clenching by his sides, yet Thomas Pearce merely shrugged, his reply a disdainful snort.

Reaching under his cloak, he held out a purse. 'Here's thirty guineas . . . you're to get me a ship . . . get me out of here, or I tell everyone Madeleine Pelligrew has escaped her madhouse. It's quite simple . . .' He thrust the bag forward, pushing it into Marcel's chest. 'That's how it works. You need a ship, I need to get out of here.'

'Take your money and go hang . . .' Marcel's voice was rising, and I glanced up at my window. We were making too much noise; Rowan would wake at the commotion.

'I've no intention of swinging from any gallows. The woman's death was an accident – my knife slipped, that's all. My hands are steadier now.' He laughed, taking a swig from the gourd hanging from his waist. 'Least they are for a while yet.'

Above us, shutters were being opened, the sound of a sash window rising, and I knew to hurry. Slipping from behind Marcel, I ran down the back steps, opening the kitchen door. The key trembled in my fingers yet I managed to lock it, rushing to the scullery to return Mrs Munroe's cloak. The sound of hurried footsteps echoed down the stairs and I hid behind the larder door. Someone rushed into the kitchen and by his breathing I knew it to be Sam. Through the crack in the door, I watched him reach for the key with one hand, grabbing a poker with the other. Thundering out of the door, he raced up the steps.

His shouts filled the kitchen. 'Get away with you. Go . . . now . . . or I'll blow my whistle. Drunken louts . . . think to steal something, did ye?'

I had to hurry. Tiptoeing up the stairs, I shut my door without a sound and slipped beneath the covers. I was fully dressed but my instincts were right. Within minutes the door opened and Mrs Munroe's soft whisper answered Sam. 'No, she's not been woke. Bless their dear hearts, fast asleep – both of them.'

Next to me, Rowan's eyes remained closed. Her warm hand reached out, clasping mine. 'Will Elowyn like me, Madeleine? Will Billy like me?'

She turned and slept again, leaving my heart in a thousand pieces. Yes, they would love her, and she would love them.

Chapter Thirty

Sunday 22nd June 1800, 9 a.m.

They gathered in the hall, Mrs Munroe fussing over Rowan, tying the ribbons on her bonnet. She took hold of Rowan's hands. 'Who'd have thought Mrs Pumfrey makes her maids rub goose fat into their hands every night?'

Rowan looked swamped beneath her borrowed straw bonnet and slightly too large jacket. 'We'd gather to say prayers an' she'd get out this big pot and watch us rub it into our hands. She was kind, really – only ye had to work very hard or she'd soon scold.'

Mrs Pengelly was tying the ribbon on her own bonnet. 'Madeleine, how very lovely you look.'

I had taken extra care with my make-up, trying to conceal my sleepless night, yet I was still in turmoil, not knowing if Marcel had found the codes. The day was cloudy, the wind blowing against the tide, rippling the surface of the river. After our visit, Mrs Pengelly would go to church and I would watch for Marcel. Rowan's hand slipped into mine, she even started skipping, and I held my chin high, smiling, wanting her to think it was the happiest of days.

'What if Elowyn doesn't think I look like Billy?'

Mrs Pengelly smiled. 'She will. So will Mr Cotterell. They'll be as convinced as we are . . . or I'll eat my hat!'

A flicker crossed Rowan's eyes. She seemed scared, casting me an anxious look. Yet I knew blood was thicker than water. She had been drawn to my drawings, intrigued by my scratchings in the dirt. Always asking me to draw the folly. She was not sent to me, I was sent to her so she could find her brother. I was being selfish. If I loved her, I must let her go.

They were waiting by the gate, the golden-haired child on William Cotterell's shoulders, Elowyn dressed impeccably in a yellow cotton gown. She had her fists clasped against her mouth, her eyes tentative. Rowan's large bonnet shadowed her face and though we curtsied and exchanged greetings, she remained looking at Rowan as if she needed further convincing.

Mrs Pengelly reached to undo the ribbons on Rowan's bonnet. 'May I take this off, my love?'

The bonnet removed, Elowyn's gasp made the hairs on my arms rise. She stood speechless, tears welling in her eyes. 'Oh . . . I'm sorry to cry like this. It *is* you, isn't it? You've Billy's eyes . . . Billy's nose. Your hair . . . your black curls. Honest to God, it's like when Billy first came to us.' She wiped her eyes with her handkerchief. 'Not that you look like a boy . . .' She laughed, holding out her hands. 'You're as pretty as a picture. Welcome to our home . . . welcome to our family. You're going to love your big brother. He *is* your brother, I'm certain of it.'

William Cotterell was a huge man, tall, broad-shouldered, with dark hair and hazel eyes that crinkled when he smiled. A handsome man, dressed well, with a confident air about him, yet he, too, had tears in his eyes. He put down his daughter and bowed. 'Welcome, indeed. I shall write straight to Billy. He's apprenticed as an engineer. He'll be famous one day, so he's going to need a sister to spend all his money on!' He winked and bowed again, leaving his daughter to take Rowan's hand.

We followed them through the iron arch with its abundance of yellow roses into the kitchen with its smell of cinnamon and vanilla, and I thought my heart would break. The little girl was called Eva, and Mrs Pengelly smiled at her namesake. 'You can help Rowan choose material for her new dress. Are you going to be a dressmaker like your mamm?'

Little Eva shook her blonde curls and Elowyn's eyes rose heavenward. 'She wants to be an engineer.'

'Well!' Mrs Pengelly shrugged. 'I remember telling Rose she would never own her own shipyard!'

Their cheerful chatter filled the kitchen, Little Eva not letting go of Rowan's hand even as Elowyn wielded her tape measure. The happy process was about to start all over again: dresses that could be adapted brought down from above, rolls of material taken from the shelves and spread across the large pine table. Ribbons to be matched exactly, trims chosen, and I forced myself to smile. The wind had been from the north, the outgoing tide would be in six hours' time.

'Shall we decide on this?' Mrs Pengelly held the dotted yellow muslin against Rowan. 'Yellow, like Elowyn's gown? And yellow ribbons?'

Rowan's eyes shone. 'I've never seen anything so beautiful. My very own dress... Will Billy like it, d'you think?'

Elowyn finished writing the final measurements. 'He's coming for Lady Polcarrow's ball. But, if I know Billy, he'll want to come straight away. We'll trace everything back.' She held Rowan's hands against her heart. 'He's been searching for you. But he calls you Betsy. There's been no Betsy found... and that's because your name was changed.'

Rowan glanced at me. 'Does Billy remember my mamm and pa... and how I came to be lost?'

Elowyn sat down, keeping hold of Rowan's hands. 'Your father was a good man. He was a knife sharpener, and a very good one. He took his equipment with him everywhere on a large cart. He had a mule and he travelled across the moors. Sometimes, he'd take you all with him, but usually he left you in your cottage near Truro. Sometimes, he was gone for weeks. But one day, my love... one day, he got set upon on the moor and was badly beaten.'

'Beaten?' Large tears rolled down Rowan's cheeks, and I thought my heart would burst.

'His money was taken, his cart... his sharpening equipment... his mule – all stolen. He became very ill... when they found him, he was suffering from fever. He was a good, hard-working man and he loved you all so much, but he couldn't fight the fever and he died.'

Rowan nodded. 'And my mother? Billy and Bella?'

Elowyn's eyes were glistening. 'With no money for rent, your family was evicted. Your mamm joined people seeking work at Pendenning Hall – they were to clear the fields of stones. The work was hard and the weather was bad and she took ill. Billy nursed her . . . but . . . when she died he looked after you. He did everything to keep you fed and the other vagrants did their best to keep you safe – but they were forced from the land.'

Rowan seemed to be getting stronger, no longer crying but wiping her eyes. 'I knew that – Ella told me.'

'Billy was caught poaching rabbits and badly beaten. When he recovered, he went back to search for you, but everyone had separated – and Mrs Pendarvis – she was Miss Cavendish then – straight away sent a man to search. He found Bella's grave but you had vanished from all record. The lady who called you Rowan could not have known where you'd come from or who you were. She must have been a very kind woman.'

Rowan smiled and lifted her chin. 'Yes, she was.'

Little Eva was climbing on to a chair to reach the window. She waved into the courtyard and I caught a flash of blue uniform. Elowyn looked up and smiled. 'Ah, there's Captain Pierre.'

William Cotterell went to greet him, the two men so alike in their physique. Both were dark-haired, tall, broad-shouldered, though William was shaking his head as if sorry to hear what the other was saying. Within minutes they dipped their heads beneath the lintel. 'I'm afraid Captain Pierre is here to bid us goodbye.'

The room erupted with gasps echoing their sorrow, everyone persuading him to stay. Rowan ran to his side. 'Please stay, Captain Pierre.' She stared up at him. 'I saw the swans again this morning . . . an' I have to show you. They have *seven* cygnets. Not six.'

I had not pleaded with him to stay and his eyes caught mine. If I felt ill at ease, he looked worse – as if he wished he had not seen me. 'I have to leave . . . I've stayed too long . . . I'm in danger of outstaying my welcome in Admiral House.'

William Cotterell put his hand on his shoulder. 'Nonsense, Pierre, they enjoy your company – and even if it were the case, you must stay *here* with Elowyn and me. I'll soon put you to work on another dial.' He smiled coaxingly. 'In fact, I could give you full-time employment. Can't you persuade Sir Alex you're needed here?'

'And forget I'm on parole? William, it's what I'd like more than anything.'

Rowan smiled her sweetest smile. 'Please stay, Captain Pierre.'

He remained adamant, his manner formal. I caught his glance and felt my cheeks flame. There was such admiration in his look, his eyes burning mine before he tore them away. His presence felt too physical, like his hands slipping beneath my buttons in my dream. The room was too hot, too crowded, the blood rushing from my head, and I gripped the back of the chair.

'Mrs Barnard, you don't look well. Are you all right?'

He was by my side, reaching for my elbow, helping me sit. I had to breathe, to stop the room from whirling round. 'Sudden dizziness. I'm better now. Thank you for your concern.'

He remained by my side as the others rushed to me, Mrs Pengelly flicking open her fan, Elowyn reaching for some lemonade, and I breathed deeply, ashamed of my weakness. The clock on the wall struck half past ten and Mrs Pengelly searched my face. 'It's later than I thought . . . it's time for church. Will the walk back be too much, my dear?'

Captain Pierre stood behind me. 'I'd be honoured to see Mrs Barnard safely home. If you're in a hurry, we could walk back more slowly . . . or perhaps I could ask to borrow the cart?'

Elowyn glanced at Mrs Pengelly, a slight rise of her eyebrow. 'That's a very good idea, Captain Pierre . . . especially as *we*, *too*, are on our way to church. *Aren't we*, William?'

Her husband seemed perplexed. 'Are we? Oh, yes . . . we are. What a shame . . . on our way to church and . . . really ought to hurry.'

Mrs Pengelly reached for Rowan's hand. 'Rowan's been looking forward to church, haven't you, my dear? Perhaps we should leave now. Captain Pierre can see Mrs Barnard safely home . . . in their own time.'

My cheeks must have been crimson. They must have thought I felt unwell on purpose, yet my pleas that I was recovered landed on deaf ears. Nothing must stop them rushing to church, and Pierre de la Croix must see me safely home in my own time. One glance at his face and I saw confusion, elation, a look of remorse.

261

Chapter Thirty-one

We stood by the gate watching the others hurry along the road. Rowan turned to wave and we waved back. The bells were ringing, the clouds passing, the sun peeping through a patch of blue sky. Pierre de la Croix stood stiffly, glancing at his feet. 'Mrs Barnard... I've behaved very foolishly. I will return to Truro and no longer intrude on you and your husband. I thought you widowed... I had no idea... I understand, of course, why you do not want my attentions. Please forgive me.'

There was honesty in his voice, pain in his tone. He stood twisting his hands, unable to look at me. 'You've been listening to gossip, Captain de la Croix?'

He ran his finger beneath his cravat. 'When I discovered you were Madeleine Pelligrew I learned you suffered great loss. I hoped to be of assistance to you... yet now I understand you've found happiness again. That you've remarried. And that Mr Barnard is your *husband*, not your brother-in-law. Which makes my... attentions to you... very unwelcome.'

He was staring at the river, watching the ships entering the harbour. Seagulls were calling above us, the sun growing warmer. He cleared his throat. 'Mrs Barnard, do you feel well enough to walk or shall I fetch the cart? I would offer you my arm but . . . in the circumstances . . .' Scent from the yellow roses filled the air, a ginger tomcat jumped from the wall and started purring round Captain de la Croix's polished boots. He bent to stroke it.

'You have a way with children and animals, Captain de la Croix,' I said softly. I wanted to tell him he was wrong, that I was not married and had not found happiness. That I was filled with great emptiness. That my heart was breaking. That loneliness accompanied my nights and envy poisoned my days. That I wished he was not who he was, but someone I could admire.

'That's because I don't have to hold myself in check with children or animals. I can be myself – not conceal my thoughts . . . my family . . . or my connections. With them, I don't have to watch my tongue, nor fear for my life. Children and animals are my refuge. I may wear the uniform of our country, but I do not wear it with pride.'

He looked up and a wave of hope surged through me. He picked up the cat, stroking him gently. 'I can speak freely with you because I know who your family is. I walk a lonely path, keeping my thoughts to myself – never knowing which of my fellow compatriots are Republican spies. When I first saw your husband, I thought he might be one of them . . . but now I understand his hostility towards me was because of my attentions to you.' He put down the cat, straightening, at once formal again. His mouth tightened. 'For which I apologise.'

My mouth was dry, I could not swallow. 'Your family, Captain de la Croix? It seems you know everything about me, yet I know nothing of you. That is how dangerous it is. I have no idea who you are, or whether what you say is true. It could be part of your subterfuge.'

He reached inside his jacket and drew out his fob watch. 'My father gave me this when he sent me to join the navy. I was nineteen, desperate to be a clockmaker, yet he refused to listen to such nonsense. I was the son of a noble family and I was not to disgrace him with thoughts of a trade.' He flicked it open. 'I only wear this when no other prisoner can see it. These are diamonds, and this is an engraving of my family home – Château de la Croix. And here is my name, Pierre Benoît Joseph de la Croix. And behind is our family crest. So you can see why I must keep it hidden.'

The diamonds glistened in the sun, his name engraved beneath an etching of a chateau with turrets and a tall sloping roof; the very proof I needed of his true leanings. 'It's very beautiful,' I whispered.

'When my father gave it to me, I thought only to gain enough money to return to Angoulême and set up my business. I quarrelled with my parents before I left . . . and that is something I shall always regret.' The watch glinted in his hands, his words wrung from him. 'Yet by punishing me, Father saved my life – I survived because I left France. My family . . . my home . . . everything . . . has been taken from me.' He snapped the watch shut, lifting his chin.

I tried to keep my voice steady. 'Have you hidden outside my window and watched me during the night?'

He swung round. 'How can you ask? My attentions may not be welcome, but I would never stoop so low!'

A burst of joy made my eyes water. 'Yet you listen to rumours that aren't true?' He turned, puzzled by my sudden smile. 'I neither remarried nor found happiness. I've been very mistaken in you, Captain de la Croix – and your attentions *are* welcome.'

'You are . . . a widow . . . still?'

I had never felt such joy, such a relief of feelings. It was as if my heart had been freed from its tight clasp. 'Pierre . . . forgive me . . . I had to doubt you because we've had to be so careful. We thought you a Republican spy. Monsieur Barnard is not my husband, nor is he my brother-in-law. He's a friend of my brother and he's charged with taking me to back to my family in France.'

He smiled, his eyes bright between their black lashes. 'Your family has survived? I'm so pleased for you. Your brother is fortunate – or perhaps he's found a way of living with the situation? Living a lie, always watching his back? Because I know how that feels. Hiding your true feelings, never knowing who you can trust. Always being looked on with suspicion.'

'Yes, living a lie, but they seem to have found a way. My brother's married – I have nephews and nieces I've never met. His lands and vineyards now belong to the Commune but he's kept the house and has safe employment.' I put out my hand and he offered me his arm, tall, strong, making my heart pound.

The wind was on our backs, the sun on our faces. His vulnerability, his manners, his kindness, all filled my heart. I had seen the loneliness in his eyes, the hope that one day his emptiness may be filled, and fire burned my chest, my heart bursting, leaping. He cleared his throat. 'I've only just learned that my sister survived. My four brothers . . . my parents . . . my uncles . . . were all brutally murdered.' We had walked slowly yet already the red bricks of Coombe House stood before us. He searched the riverbank. 'Shall we sit on that rock and watch the ships? In the shade of that tree?'

Taking off his jacket he laid it on the rock, his white shirt catching the sun, his brass buttons glinting, and I thought I might die of happiness. Ships were anchoring, the ferryman rowing passengers across the river. Two swans swam past with seven cygnets, and I returned his smile, suddenly shy, as if I was a giddy young woman and this was my first day of courting. 'Why did you stay in the navy? Mrs Pengelly told me many officers refused to fight for the new regime – that they left . . . or joined forces with the British.'

His mouth tightened. 'I believe as many as three out of four of our serving officers left their posts in defence of the old regime.'

'But you didn't?'

'I was too far away.' The wind ruffled his sleeves, his hands clasped around his bent knees. 'I joined as *aspirant* under a friend of a friend. Our ship, *Diadème*, was posted to the Windward Isles – the American Revolutionary War was under way and our colonies were threatened. We sailed immediately. We were to keep the trade routes open and for three years I learned the ways of the sea.' He smiled. 'I'd felt very clois-tered as a child and my punishment wasn't as severe as I'd anticipated. I had a strict captain but a seaworthy ship, and I was seeing the world.'

I nodded, smiling for him to continue.

'At twenty-three, I decided to return but it was not to be. France entered the war against Britain and we were summoned to join Admiral de Grasse. At twenty-five, I saw action at the Battle of Chesapeake.'

'You were there?' It was a battle I had heard so much about.

'A glorious victory. And I was promoted. At twenty-six, I became *lieutenant de vaisseau* – a fully qualified naval officer with enough money to buy as many clocks as I wanted. We received orders to sail home – my sister wrote saying she had lined me up to marry one of her friends – and I was more than ready to return. I'd been away eight years by then, the Peace of Paris was signed, and there was nothing to keep us there.'

He shrugged, the sadness returning to his smile. 'Or so I was foolish enough to believe. The hostilities may have ended, but France's commercial concerns hadn't! Our Caribbean colonies were too valuable to lose – others were casting their eyes on our source of wealth – coffee, cotton, indigo . . . but mainly sugar. Our prosperity was under threat.'

'By the British?'

His smile pierced my heart. 'Who else? Well, maybe the Dutch . . . the Portuguese . . . the Spanish. Everyone fighting over the spoils of war. They needed frigates to patrol the seas and I was offered my own ship – *Capitaine de Frégate* on *Espère* – and I jumped at the chance. Even the name filled me with hope. It wasn't greed, it was pride. I was the fifth son, unsure my father had any real regard for me, yet there I was, captain of a sixty-four-gun ship of the line with five hundred men under my command.'

'He would have been very proud of you.'

'That was the summer of 'eighty-eight. Within a year, the Bastille was stormed and our *Glorious Revolution* was under way. But I knew nothing of that. Not until the first rumours began trickling through and then . . . well, then I welcomed it, Madeleine. I'm sorry . . . Mrs Pelligrew.'

'No, please call me Madeleine.' He said my name so tenderly, yet his words puzzled me. 'You *welcomed* the new regime?'

'Yes, I did. Our ports were Saint-Pierre in Martinique and Pointe-à-Pitre in Guadeloupe, and when I first saw the tricolour cockades worn by the ships' passengers and crews – when I heard their talk of *liberté* and *égalité* – I felt some sympathy.'

'For the slaves?'

'The islands were a tinderbox. They were soon to erupt, but we didn't know that at the time. We heard rumours – reports of atrocities – and we knew tensions were rising. But we didn't know a new war was starting – that *civil* unrest was growing by the day. A surge of uprisings against the governors and plantation owners.'

'The slaves turned on their owners?'

'It wasn't just the slaves. It was all those excluded from making decisions – the *petits blancs* and the free people of colour. People with no voice joining forces to demand *liberté* and *égalité*. And who could blame them?'

His mouth hardened, pain in his eyes. He ran his hand across his mouth. 'It soon became apparent a force was gathering under Captain Lacrosse – ships being sent to *help* these uprisings. The new regime was adamant it was to spread equality and liberty, *not* condone enslavement. I've always abhorred slavery. I saw the barbaric conditions for myself . . . I witnessed the immense cruelty . . . and I was sickened by it. So when I heard the new regime sought to *free* the slaves and offer equality to free men of colour, I felt proud to escort Captain Lacrosse to the Windward Islands. Proud that *we* . . . France . . . were to liberate the slaves.'

'I would have felt the same.'

His hand slipped over mine and I thought my heart would burst. 'We were a long way from home. But soon we heard rumours of the atrocities our new masters were committing. France declared war on Britain and *had* I been in Brittany and known the full truth, I would have resigned my commission. But I was in the Caribbean, surrounded by enemy fire. I had five hundred men to keep safe, I was *Capitaine de Vaisseau* by then – a position of great authority. I thought only to see them safe, then I would relinquish my command. Yet at every port, more rumours abounded – officers I knew hanged or guillotined without trial. Despised as traitors – *four* of my fellow captains guillotined for refusing to support the new regime.'

He swallowed, taking a deep breath. 'I heard my family had been spared, though our lands had been confiscated, and I was desperate to return to them. I had no hatred in my heart *then*.' His hand grasped mine, his mouth tightening.

'What happened, Pierre?'

'My father was Baron de la Croix. Within the same outer walls of our estate was Abbey de la Croix – our family's abbey. The monks were a Benedictine order and my uncle was Abbot – as had been my great-uncle before him. My two brothers were in orders... several of my cousins. I'd been educated by them... spent my boyhood running between their grounds and ours. They used our barns, our stables... their hens pecked around the same well. Our house echoed to the sound of their bells... to the rhythm of their prayers. Father Francis taught me to mend the clocks, Father Paul how to set the sundial.

'When I heard the Assembly had waged war against religion... against Catholicism... against Christianity. That they'd seized all land held by the Catholic Church... destroyed the statues... pulled down the crosses and the bells. Made all nonjuring priests and anyone who harboured them liable to death *on sight*.'

His chest was rising and falling. 'When they started their massacres, their murders... forcing families to reveal the hiding places of the priests and monks... When I heard they'd forced themselves into our house and my father refused to give up his sons and brother... that they'd forced everyone out of our home and hanged each one of them from the church rafters... I could endure it no longer.'

He held his head in his hands, his pain tearing my heart. 'I've carried this alone, Madeleine. I still try to wrestle the image from my mind, but I see it too clearly. I don't hear their screams as often as I did, but the vision remains.'

'And so you let your ship be taken?'

'It crossed my mind. I'd have been strung from my own yardarm if that was the case, and maybe I wanted that. But no. My ship was taken because of illness among the crew. A British ship holed one of our sister ships, she was listing badly and in danger of sinking. We took as many of the crew as we could, but it soon became apparent they were sickening. I'd been vigilant, Madeleine. I never anchored by the swamps, and *never* let my men into any port. I may have no longer wanted to serve my country, but the men were my responsibility and I was determined to do my best for them.

'Yet we'd taken yellow fever on board and the sickness spread. A British frigate engaged us in battle but my men were weak and exhausted. The damage was enough to disable us. When the British boarded, I negotiated my men's release to a hospital nearby and I gave Admiral Penrose my parole. They kept my ship as prize.' All colour had drained from him. 'Madeleine, I've not spoken of this to anyone. You see, it isn't cowardice holding me back, it's disgust.'

Two soldiers walked past in their scarlet uniforms and Pierre got to his feet, reaching for my hand. The church bells were ringing again, people strolling along the river. The others came in sight and Rowan gripped her rather over-large bonnet to run gasping to our sides.

'I'd rather have stayed here with ye.' She stood between us, looking up at us in turn. 'Eva's that naughty! Honest, Elowyn had to take her out as she was climbing all over the pews!' She beamed broadly. 'Elowyn and William have been that kind to me . . . and so have Mrs Pengelly and Mrs Munroe . . . and Sam and Tamsin. I know I'll love Billy.'

'I'm so happy. You have a whole new family...'

Her face clouded with a sudden frown. 'But I can still live with ye, can't I, Madeleine? You and Captain Pierre – like a real family?' Her frown changed to concern. 'Do you have something in your eye, Captain Pierre?'

Pierre tried to clear his throat. 'No... well... no, I think it's just the glare of the sun. Look, you're quite right: seven cygnets when I counted only six.'

She smiled up at him. 'Mrs Pengelly says I'm to ask ye to supper *before* ye go. She says tomorrow. At five o'clock.'

'Thank you, Rowan... tell Mrs Pengelly I'd be delighted ... though I think I won't be leaving after all.'

Our eyes met, my love for him suddenly so fierce it felt like pain.

Fraternité

Chapter Thirty-two

Tuesday 24th June 1800, 3 p.m.

The sound of Mrs Munroe's singing drifted up the stairs, so, too, the rich aroma of onions, carrots, parsley, and the special wine she had found for her *poulet au vin*. Pierre was to join us at five, and I stared at my reflection like a giddy young woman preparing for her first beau. The beginnings of flesh filled my cheeks, my brows neatly arched, my complexion losing its redness, but best of all were my eyes. There was a sparkle in them, a softening, a look of hope. A look of love. I could not stop smiling.

The singing stopped and I heard Mrs Munroe climb the stairs. Slipping from my dressing table, I looked down from the landing.

'Oh, there you are, Miss Madeleine. Only I need more potatoes . . . Captain Pierre's very partial to his potatoes. Likes them cooked in cream and *garlic*.' She must have grimaced. 'Only that leaves ye on yer own.'

'I'll be fine, thank you.'

'Tamsin and Rowan are playin' with Little Eva . . . and Sam's at the brewhouse. And Mrs Pengelly won't be back till four. Will ye be all right?'

'Yes . . . of course. Is there anything I can do to help?'

Her laughter echoed up the stairs. 'No, Miss Madeleine. Just get yerself as pretty as a picture. That man adores ye. Never seen a man so smitten, bless his dear heart.'

I returned to my dressing table, carefully easing on the cream turban with its thread of pearls. My fingers were all thumbs, my body tingling, jittery, my pulse racing. I looked up. Loud hooves were clattering down the road, a horse at speed, a man shouting for directions and I rushed to the window.

The man wore the uniform of an express courier, his horse foaming at the mouth. Digging in his heels, he urged his horse forward and stopped beneath my window. Swinging his leg over the saddle, he slipped to the ground and made towards the front door. An express. Sent here? He was about to bang on the door and I leaned out. 'Can I help you?'

His flushed face looked up, sweat covering his brow. He took off his hat, wiping his sleeve across his forehead. 'I've an express for Mrs Barnard. Does she live here?'

The urgency in his voice made me instantly fearful. 'I am Mrs Barnard. One moment, please.' I felt winded – this was my summons from Marcel. I stared down at him, not wanting to open the door. I did not want to leave Fosse. Not now, not ever. Yet I must go down.

He stood staring back at me. 'I need proof it's you. I'm only to give it to a lady in a blue turban with curls on each side . . .'

'I am Mrs Barnard. I have two turbans.'

He wiped his elbow across his brow. He was a young man,

276

polite yet firm. He shook his head. 'I've very strict instructions.'

'One moment.' I was even more fearful now, unease making my hands fumble. I thrust the blue turban on and raced downstairs, almost missing the last step. I was trying to be rational – the horse was sweating, it had been ridden hard. This express had not come from the harbour, but from quite some distance.

He nodded when he saw my blue turban. 'An' I'm to ask ye Mrs Reith's name. Who she was before . . . and before that.'

I could feel the blood drain from my head. Such precise questions. 'She was Lady Polcarrow . . . and before that she was Miss Alice Roskelly.'

'Thank you. That's all. Here's the express.' He turned and grabbed the reins, nodding in farewell as he led the horse away. My name was on one side, a large red seal on the other. The courier was halfway down the road and I shut the door. Slipping the seal, I glanced at the signature. It was from Matthew Reith and looked to be written in haste.

> *2 Pydar Street*
> *Truro*
> *24th June 1800*

Dear Mrs Pelligrew,

Something in the diaries alerted me to a grave concern. Straight away we returned to Truro and further enquiries proved my suspicion not only true but of the gravest nature. I wish it was otherwise. Madeleine, you must prepare yourself for grievous news.

Your brother was taken prisoner in July 1790 and held

without charge in Saint-Malo dungeons for seven months. A trial was conducted in the prison on 16th January 1791 and your brother was condemned to death by the town's Commune. He was taken from the prison to the town square where he refused to beg for pardon and was hanged alongside twelve other 'traitors'. Your cousin, Etienne St Just, was among those men. Both of them now lie buried in a communal grave outside the town.

Your father died of natural causes the previous year, and the de Bourg estates were seized. Together with your house, they are now in the hands of the Commune.

Madeleine, your grief must not cloud your thinking. Who is your brother's friend? When did he last see your brother? I have further matters to investigate but we shall return as soon as possible. Hopefully tomorrow. In the meantime, do nothing and say nothing, until I have returned.

Yours in haste,
Matthew Reith

The hall floor was spinning: somehow I managed to reach the chair in Mrs Pengelly's drawing room, my heart pounding so fast I thought I might be sick. He must be wrong. My brother was alive. I put my head on my knees, I had to calm myself, to reread the letter.

Yet Matthew Reith seemed so sure. Tears splashed the page. I had no nephews or nieces, no sister-in-law, yet Marcel Rablais had talked of them. He had told me their names, told me my niece was called after me. Why search for me and tell me my brother was alive if he was dead? I needed air. I needed a drink of water.

Making my way down to the kitchen, I leaned against the table, the smell of the cooking pot turning my stomach. The silence was unnerving, my panic growing, a return of the irregular beats to my heart. I needed air, I needed to think. Someone was banging on the front door and my heart lifted. Tamsin and Rowan must be back, or perhaps it was Sam? Running up the kitchen stairs, I opened the door.

A young boy in tattered clothing thrust a note at me. 'Fer Mrs Barnard. Only Mrs Barnard. Is that ye?' I nodded, backing away. I did not want another letter. The boy could only have been seven, dirty-faced, wide-eyed, with gaps between his teeth. He thrust the note nearer. 'Said to give it to ye as quick as I could. Gave me sixpence, so take it ... please.'

My name was written across the front, and I took it from him, glancing down the road to see if anyone was coming. Mrs Munroe waved at me from the corner and I leaned against the wall hardly daring to read. It was not sealed, and tears sprang to my eyes. It was from Pierre.

My Dearest Madeleine,

I entreat you to come. I have news of great importance. Meet me by the steps of the Old Wharf – not the new wharf, but the one reached by Dog Lane. Please, hurry. What I have to say can only be told to you – you alone. Bring Rowan but tell no one you're coming, only please hurry.

Your Obedient Servant, and most loyal friend,
Pierre de la Croix

I held the letter to my heart, a rush of tenderness easing my anxiety. He had discovered the same news — maybe in a discussion with Lady Pendarvis. He understood. Of all men, he understood. Yet Rowan would not be back for several hours and his note sounded urgent. I reached for my jacket.

'Well, bless my soul . . . Miss Madeleine, are ye all right?' Mrs Munroe stared up at me from the bottom step. 'Ye don't look well at all.'

'I am well, Mrs Munroe.' I held up the note. 'Only this is from Captain Pierre . . . he's asking me to meet him.'

Her frown disappeared, her smile broadened. 'Bless ye heart. Go on then — I'll tell Mrs Pengelly ye couldn't wait another moment.' She shook her head, clucking like a mother hen as she squeezed past me. 'Tell him I'm doing him those fancy potatoes . . . no, on second thoughts, let it be a surprise.'

My brother had been hanged and Pierre had found out. Tears blurred my eyes, my breath fast and furious. Dodging the crowds, I did not care that they stared, I saw only my brother hanging from the gibbet in the town square. Murderers, all of them. Seagulls were screeching, a queue of people waiting for the ferryman. A crowd had gathered on the quay, a new catch being packed into crates. Fishermen were mending their nets, men with barrels of water washing the cobbles and I stopped to reread Pierre's note. He definitely said Dog Lane.

I passed the Ship Inn, leaving the crowd behind me. It was quieter on the back streets, and I looked around. There was no one there, I was by myself. I knew Dog Lane from old, knew it as a place no lady should venture down alone. The houses looked even poorer now, with broken windows and paint peeling from the doors, and I glanced at his note again. *Tell no one you're coming, only please hurry*. He would not send for me unless it was important. Ahead of me, the filthy cobbles looked uneven and loose in places, the imprints of heavy boots left in the mud.

I lifted my skirt and stepped forward, trying to avoid the putrid water pooling in the puddles. It was hardly a lane, more an alley, narrowing considerably as I hurried down it. Barely any light penetrated the rooftops, the gables crushing above me, the doorways dark down either side. Pierre should have known better than to ask me to meet him down such an alley; he obviously did not know the town as well as I thought.

I stopped, reluctant to continue. I was less than halfway to the wharf, the place stank of urine, piles of soiled sacks and smashed bottles lying in my path. A cat was watching me from a broken window, a rat scuttling through a heap of rubbish, and I knew to turn back. I would retrace my steps and see if I could approach the Old Wharf from some other way. Footsteps sounded behind me and I swung round. A man was standing at the end of the alley, waving to attract my attention. He wore a large black hat and heavy black coat, his collar turned up at his neck, and my heart lifted. But the alley was dark, he was quite some way away, and as I watched him, my joy turned to fear. His stance was unfamiliar.

'Mrs Pelligrew?' His voice was sharp, urgent. Not waiting for my reply, his arm gestured for me to follow. 'You got Captain Pierre's note? Come . . . quickly . . . follow me. Please, you have to hurry.'

Chapter Thirty-three

The man ran ahead of me, twisting down the steep alley, waiting just long enough for me to see him before he turned the next bend. I was following a shadow, his footsteps, no instructions, only glimpses of his black coat as it disappeared in front of me. The thick walls were damp on both sides, no broader than two men standing side by side, and I stopped to catch my breath. The man was nowhere in sight. All I could see was a flight of worn steps leading down to the river. Water lapped against the stones, the seagulls screeching above me. Across the river lay the town of Porthruan. There was nowhere else to go — only the possibility of retracing my steps.

The river mouth was busy, anchored ships rising and falling in the swell. Two large warehouses rose behind me, a stretch of rocks down one side, the partly collapsed wharf on the other. The timbers were groaning, the wooden poles creaking, and I caught the outline of the black hat and coat. The man was on the wharf, standing by a ship's gangplank. 'You've done well, Mrs Pelligrew. Quick, allow me.' He held out his hand. 'Captain de la Croix needs your absolute secrecy. You told no one you were coming?'

He was a stocky man with broad shoulders and a full black beard. He looked powerful, yet his movements were nimble, jumping on to the gangplank with obvious ease. The ship was a lugger, I knew that from old – a two-masted lugger, about forty-five feet, her bowsprit lifted on to the deck. An everyday sort of ship that had seen better days, but it was not the ship making my stomach tighten. It was his accent.

'You're French? You're a *friend* of Captain de la Croix?' Uneasiness filled me. 'I'd like to speak to him – alone.'

'Of course. That's the whole point – he needs to see you *alone*. Please, Mrs Pelligrew. No one can see you here. Please, allow me.' Again he held out his hand. 'It's my pleasure to serve both you and Captain Pierre.'

It must have been the ship that reeked of mackerel, a pungent stink drifting across the wharf. It was a fishing vessel, just an everyday fishing ship, and I stood rooted to the spot. Every part of me wanted to turn and run. A flash of movement on the rocks made me look round – an urchin boy was fishing with a line. The man must have seen me turn my head; he saw the boy and stormed along the rickety wharf, his fists raised. 'Get away with you. If I see you here again, I'll beat you to a pulp.'

The boy looked terrified. Gathering in his line, he scrambled over the barnacle-covered rocks. 'I'm just crabbin', sir. Ain't doin' nothin' wrong.'

The man's fists remained clenched, yet his voice softened.

'It's dangerous — that's all. You could be swept out to sea. Never crab here again.'

The boy rushed past me and our eyes caught. 'No, sir. Sorry, sir.'

I should have run after him. Dear God, I wanted to turn and run, yet Pierre needed me. 'Will you tell Captain de la Croix I'm here?'

He watched the boy run up the steps. 'And risk him being seen by brats like that? It's too dangerous. Come, I'll help you.'

He began walking towards me, slowly at first, then his pace quickened, his lithe body negotiating the gaps in the planks with quick strides. He came to my side, one hand gripping my waist, the other clamping my mouth. I was caught, lifted off my feet, unable to break away. I tried twisting, wrestling his hands away, but he was too strong. I was kicking, writhing, biting, but with every attempt to free myself his grip grew tighter. I was a feather to him. He held me off the ground, his hand clamping my mouth so tightly I could not scream. I could not breathe, but felt myself carried through the air, those long strides taking me along the uneven wharf and up the gangplank.

The stench grew worse. I could see the open hold, the fishing nets rolled to one side. I tried twisting again, kicking, attempting to break free, but there was no one to see me, no one to help. The warehouses had no windows, we were away from sight. I tried biting his hand but he held me so tightly by the chin it was difficult to breathe. Negotiating the deck, he dipped below some swinging ropes and stopped, holding me above an open hatchway as he shouted, 'Slip the mooring. Start rowing us out!'

His command rang across the deck and I tried to scream. Two men were waiting in rowing boats with ropes attached to the ship. Wearing oiled leather jackets and large hats, they gripped their oars and began to pull. A wooden ladder led down from the hatchway, the interior dark and forbidding, and he thrust me forward, keeping his hand clamped round my mouth. Turning to grip the ladder, he squashed me against the steps and we began descending into the cabin. Letting me go, he forced me on to a wooden seat. 'Forgive me, Mrs Pelligrew. I can explain everything. But you're safe – that's the important thing. Quite safe.'

Without waiting for my reply, he climbed back up the ladder, blocking the light first with his body, then with the hatch cover, scraping it across the entrance to leave me in the dark. There was no porthole, no light, just the stench of fish and of rancid bilges, and I reached out with my hands. I could feel the handrails of the ladder and started to climb, holding one hand above me to feel for the hatch. The grips were smooth yet the hatch felt rough, and I pulled the iron handle, trying to force it open. It stayed firmly shut and I gripped it again, this time with both hands, pulling with all my strength. There was no movement, not even a rattle. The hatch was firmly locked.

Chinks of light showed through a tiny grille, a second one further along; faint light filtered into the cabin and as my eyes grew accustomed to the darkness, I saw two rows of wooden bunk beds with a blanket and pillow on each. A stove stood in one corner, its large black pipe reaching through to the deck above. It was unlit; so, too, the brass lantern hanging from the deckhead. A table took up the central space, a bench down one side, and I slipped onto it, desperate to see through the tiny grilles. They were about two feet wide and four inches deep, protected from the weather by wooden cowls. One faced the stern, the other the bow, and I twisted from one to the other, straining to see out.

I could not see the rowing boats but saw my captor pushing against a long pole, heaving the ship away from the wharf. The warehouses were slipping behind us, the ship beginning to move. I watched him stow the pole and grip the rudder. There was definite movement now, the rise and fall of the waves, and I started shouting, screaming, holding myself against the wooden grille in an effort to be heard. Above me, the seagulls screeched; around me the timbers creaked. The wind was picking up, carrying my screams out to the open sea. Yet my captor heard me. Within minutes heavy sacks were lodged against the grilles and the cabin plunged into absolute darkness.

Like the black cupboard. Like the cellars. I could feel my panic rising, the irregular beating of my heart. I had to stay calm. I was healthy now, my mind clearer – I had to cast away such demons and think. They had not raised any sails, the tide was not at its height; and judging by the boy catching crabs on the rocks, there was at least an hour to go before the tide turned.

A different noise now, the splash of a heavy anchor, and I held my face in my hands, tears of relief making my shoulders heave. We were not leaving, we were staying. I could feel the boat swinging round, the motion easier now we were bobbing to the swell of the current. I slipped from the table on to the wooden bench and stared at the hatch. It was being unlocked, the man returning, gripping the handrails with his back to me.

'You are keeping me against my will.' I tried to sound strong. I must show no sign of fear.

'No, Mrs Pelligrew. You're free to go . . . after you talk to Pierre – he's been delayed. He should've been there to meet you. I promised to act in his best interests, so please, forgive my unpardonable force. I thought you were about to run. My name is Gustave. Here, allow me . . .'

He scraped a tinderbox, lighting a candle. Once it glowed, he reached up to the central oil lamp, turning the brass handle until the flame caught. Light filtered across the cabin and on to his clothes. His hat was pulled low, his beard covering most of his face, and I saw only the briefest glimpse of pale grey eyes. 'We have to wait for Pierre. We have roughly fifty minutes before we have to leave – no more than that. Once you've spoken to him, you're free to go.'

Something in his voice, something in the brief glimpse of his eyes. There was no sincerity in his apology; he was not looking at me but had turned and was examining the chart on the desk. Nothing about this was right. Nothing at all. 'I would like to be put ashore, *now*, if you please. Captain de la Croix will *never* board this ship. It goes against his parole—'

He swung round. 'Madame, are you so very naive? Forgive me, but you must know what's going on? Captain de la Croix has planned this escape for many months. *We* have planned everything to the last detail . . . except, he will not leave without giving you the choice to stay. You are complicating our departure, madame, to put it mildly.'

I searched for words. I felt winded, like being punched in the stomach. 'Pierre . . . is to escape . . . ?' I could hardly take it in. 'He's to return to France?'

A shadow blocked the hatch, a man with his back to me, gripping the handrail and descending into the cabin. He was one of the men from the rowing boat, his oiled leather jacket still wet from the spray. His hat was drawn low, his heavy beard unkempt and greasy. Without looking at me, he reached for a bottle in the rack near the stove and pulled the cork. Taking a long drink, he wiped his mouth with his sleeve. 'Welcome aboard, Mrs Pelligrew. A lovely day for a sail.'

I stared back into Thomas Pearce's bleary eyes and my blood turned to ice. He looked half-drunk, his stare derisory, his laughter turning to a high-pitched giggle. 'Welcome aboard, though I don't suppose the accommodation's to your taste.' He thrust the bottle towards me, his long fingers gripping the neck with filthy fingernails.

Another man was descending the steps. His back was familiar – the slight slope to his shoulders, the sideways tilt to his head. Marcel's leather coat was wet, his hat damp. Removing his hat, he wiped his handkerchief over his short grey hair. 'Madeleine . . . dear lady . . . I hope Gustave has asked your forgiveness? He thought you were going to run. We must leave with the tide.'

He took another bottle, reaching for three pewter mugs, and I watched him fill them with wine. 'We've about an hour before we can sail. Pierre will be here at any moment.'

My throat felt strangled, my voice far away. 'Pierre is coming . . . ? Marcel, I don't understand.'

He handed me the pewter mug. 'I could say nothing, Madeleine, though believe me, I wanted to . . . but so much lay in the balance. We've planned this for a very long time – two escapes at once. I couldn't tell you – not with you making such influential new friends. I had to conceal everything, even from you. But you must know that Pierre is one of us? He's to escape with us.'

Thomas Pierce lay sprawled on the bench opposite. 'And him? Why him?' I asked.

'Our funds are low, Madeleine. We're beggars, not choosers . . . His diamonds will fund further escapes. I'm not as squeamish as you are in accepting his money.'

His eyes seemed sharper than usual, more fox-like, filled with cunning. The edge to his voice was different, a new tight-ness round his mouth, and I gripped my cup, pretending to drink. 'You warned me away from Captain de la Croix. You told me he was a Republican spy.'

'Of course – I had to. That's how we operate. We must never be seen together, never stay in the same inn. Never be seen talking to each other. I had just enough time to alert him . . . to get him on our coach to Fosse . . . but after that, we had to keep our distance. If we'd shown any sign we knew each other, Admiral Pendarvis would have been alerted.' He drew out a chart from the desk drawer, smoothing out the creases. 'Pierre is one of us – some might even say he's the *best of us*. He'll be here soon. We've come to take him home.'

I gripped my hands beneath the table. Everything felt wrong.

So many years of being lied to – a husband who lied, gaolers who lied. They did not look you in the eye, just repeated what they wanted you to know. Louder, firmer, making you believe them. Marcel kept his eyes on the chart, his voice authoritative. 'Pierre is one of us. We've come to take you both home.'

I forced a smile, raising my pewter cup. 'To our escape.' Once more, I pretended to take a drink. 'Is my brother waiting for us in Jersey . . . or in Saint-Malo?'

Marcel Rablais raised his cup in return. 'In Saint-Malo . . .'

I tried to quell the thumping of my heart. 'And my nephews and nieces?'

'Longing to meet their aunt.'

Chapter Thirty-four

Gustave was watching me from the end of the bench, his stare burning me, his huge hands and stubby fingers gripping his mug as if he would strangle it. He kept his hat pulled low, his black beard obscuring his mouth and chin, the collar of his coat pulled up. 'Stay below for your safety. We'll prepare the sails and watch for Pierre.' The three men drained their drinks, reaching for their hats.

Marcel Rablais's voice was curt. 'He shouldn't be much longer. We were expecting him to meet you on the wharf. He said if that wasn't possible, he'd row out as we leave. We'll watch for him now. But Gustave's right. Best stay below – Admiral Pendarvis's windows overlook every aspect of the harbour and your gown and headdress are very distinctive. You'll be seen from the shore. Stay below.'

Seen from the very house Pierre had been staying in as a guest. But why would he risk leaving in daylight – in view of everyone? Nothing seemed right.

They were on their feet, waiting their turn to ascend

the ladder. Something in their looks, the harshness of their voices, made me understand staying below was an order, not an option. The motion of the ship was increasing, the smell of burning pilchard oil enough to make anyone retch, and I held my hand to my mouth. 'Can you turn out the lamp? Please . . . I'm beginning to feel very ill. Please . . . let the fresh air in. The stench of the oil is turning my stomach.'

Thomas Pearce was nearest the lamp. Reaching up, his tapering fingers fumbled with the brass knob. 'You think this is bad!' He laughed his high-pitched giggle. 'Wait till we're out at sea.'

They must not shut me in. They must not lock the hatch. I smiled my sincerest smile. 'Marcel . . . be careful. Please take care. I can't thank you enough . . . I owe you everything – *everything*. You and Gustave . . . putting your lives in danger because of us. Please . . . you must take care . . . don't be seen. Don't let Admiral Pendarvis see you.'

The hatch remained open and I breathed deep for courage. No smell affected me, not after the stink of the sewer, the latrines we had to use, the buckets slopped outside my window. Believe me, Mr Pearce, I had stayed in far inferior accommodation. I rose quickly, making my way to the chart table. By the light of the hatch, I saw the familiar coastline of my childhood, the entrance of Saint-Malo, and I traced my finger along the Rance river. My home. At least in that respect Marcel had not lied.

Yet one of them of them was lying.

Matthew Reith could have been mistaken. The record of my brother's murder was ten years old – names could get muddled, smudged, records wrongly copied. Someone could have had a similar name. My mind was racing. Marcel Rablais was clearly exhausted; this last escape had been difficult from the start: the ship had been delayed, Cécile Lefèvre had taken so long to contact him. He had been kept waiting, his nerves were in shreds. Already his judgement of Thomas Pearce seemed clouded – his need for money outweighing his caution. Yet why take the money?

Surely if Cécile Lefèvre had sent the ship the expenses would have stopped? My heart thumped. Marcel had not once mentioned Cécile Lefèvre since I had boarded the ship. Not once.

A grille lay in the floor at the foot of the ladder – an outlet for seawater should a wave crash against the hatch, and I reached for my cup, tipping my red wine through the holes. Why did Pierre want to escape to France when his family had been so brutally murdered? It made no sense. He had told me he had no home, no family left in France.

The brass clock above the desk showed half past four. Mrs Munroe would be baking her potatoes and stirring her *poulet au vin*, Mrs Pengelly watching out of her window, surprised I was taking so long. William Cotterell's words echoed in my mind: *I'm afraid Captain Pierre is here to bid us goodbye.* Did Pierre mean he was leaving the country?

It made no sense at all.

A shadow crossed the hatch and I slipped quickly to the table, leaning my head on my arms. Someone was descending the ladder, and I groaned piteously. 'Do you have a bucket, Marcel? It's the smell of the fish . . . the oil. I'm going to be sick.'

He opened a cupboard and handed me a large bowl. 'Here . . . use this. Perhaps some more wine will help?'

I nodded, sitting up, keeping my hands across my face. 'Thank you . . . yes, more wine. Perhaps, if I stay still enough, I can keep the sickness at bay.' He refilled my glass, sitting momentarily next to me, and I placed my hand on his. 'Marcel . . . I meant to ask about my cousin, Etienne St Just – he was like a brother to us. We loved him like a brother. Is he well . . . did he marry his lovely Blanche Bellamy?'

His hand gripped mine. 'Yes, Blanche Bellamy, and they have four fine children.'

I breathed deeply. 'And is he one of you?'

His answer was immediate, his hand tapping mine. 'Yes . . . one of us, but you must say nothing. Names are never mentioned. Don't speak his name.'

I nodded, taking my hand from his grip, crossing my arms to lean my head against the table again. One name could get mistaken, but not two. Both names could not be copied wrongly, and Blanche Bellamy was the name I gave a cat who visited my window in one of the madhouses – a white cat, my *Belle Amie*. 'Is there any sign of Pierre?' I mumbled.

'Not yet, and it's worrying Gustave. The tide's slack now. It's about to turn. Are you all right to be left?'

'Yes . . . I think so . . . thank you.'

He hurried up the ladder and a wave of terror made my head spin. He was lying. Lying. Lying. Lying. My heart was pounding, a sudden shaking in my arms. They were not waiting for Pierre; they were waiting to leave without him. Pierre was *not* coming. He was *not* one of them. His note was in my jacket pocket and my fingers trembled as I unfolded it. I had never seen his writing – I had no idea if it was from him or not. They had lured me to the wharf, forced me on to the ship under false pretences. Yet why not let me stay with Pierre? Why force me to leave?

Slipping from the bench, I opened the top drawer of the desk. It was almost empty, just a telescope, a pair of compasses, a notebook and some writing equipment. The second drawer held charts, and I lifted them out, flipping through them, hardly surprised to see most were for France. Replacing them, I reached into the wooden alcove above the desk. There were two books in there – a printed book of tide tables, and a handwritten notebook detailing hidden dangers at the approach to each port. I stared at the writing. It had the same kick to the lower cases, the same loop to the upper cases as the letter in my pocket.

The clock showed ten to five and I tried to stop my hands from shaking. We were not waiting for Pierre, we were simply waiting for the tide. The blankets on one of the bunk beds lay hastily thrown back, only one looked neat, and I recognised the bag Marcel had first loaded on to the cart. Above me, Gustave was shouting instructions to raise the mizzen, the movement of the waves slacker. The tide was turning.

His bag was heavy, his clothes crammed into it in a jumbled mess. I pulled them out, searching the bag, desperate to find something that could tell me who he was. There were just clothes, a pair of boots, nothing else, just the empty bag, but I knew to run my fingers round the base. It would lift, it *must* lift, I just had to dig my nails in hard enough and pull it free.

I began wrenching it, clawing at the leather. At last, it gave way and I saw a wedge of papers. The writing was different from the notebook on the shelf but the contents looked familiar. I had seen the exact same combination of letters and numbers before – *CL28F*, *AL37B* – and here they were again, all carefully copied. Row upon row, page after page; a replica of the notes Cécile Lefèvre had left hidden in the milk churn.

More shouts echoed across the deck, and I crammed the pages back where I found them, quickly replacing the false base. Grabbing the clothes, I piled them back on top, pushing the bag on to the bunk bed. He had copied them, not taken them.

Copied them. It did not make sense. Nothing made sense. Why *copy* her messages, and not take them? My head was spinning, my heart thumping. Marcel had told me it was a *drop* – that he would collect her messages – yet he had left them where they were, and by leaving them, others could find them. That did not make sense – he would be leaving Cécile Lefèvre in danger.

Steadying myself against the table, I tried to think; I had to make sense of it. Sudden pain made me hold my breath, a stab of understanding. Marcel was not working *with* Cécile Lefèvre but working *against* her. He was using me to get access to Cécile Lefèvre. Using me to infiltrate her network of British spies.

Conversations jumbled in my mind. Marcel must have found out she was going to free me. I tried to remember but panic blurred my mind. He had not known where to take me until he read the discharge papers – the disused linhay was a surprise to him. He had expected a house – was that why he had left us that first night? Maybe he was going to abandon us but because he found nothing he had to come back. I clasped my head as if to hold in my thoughts. I had told him who my brother was... who my father was.

Like a fog lifting, I could see clearly now. Marcel was not one of us, *he* was the Republican spy he had taken so much trouble to warn me against. He had left the codes seemingly untouched to make the British *think* they were safe. Cécile Lefèvre must never suspect her channel of communication had been infiltrated.

I felt icy cold, a wave of terror making it difficult to breathe. They needed me away from Fosse – they needed us both away so we could give no descriptions, no details, no trail to follow. Rowan was in danger. Cécile Lefèvre and her circle were in danger. I had to leave the ship. I had to jump. I was a good swimmer and the tide was not yet strong. *Think, think.* If I jumped after the tide turned, I would be swept out to sea. I must show no sign of knowing, no sign of fear.

Reaching for a blanket, I wrapped it round me, pulling it over my head so all my clothes were hidden. They must glean no sense of my purpose – I must look weak from seasickness, not give myself away. I grabbed the bowl, holding it against my chest, pretending to retch as I climbed the ladder.

Chapter Thirty-five

The ship was bobbing with the tide, turning sideways to the river mouth. The river was busier than before, another lugger at the entrance, two large brigs nearer Porthruan. Their flags were fluttering in the breeze, the wind from the north-east, the sun glistening on the water, and I staggered on to the deck pretending to retch. Looking up, I saw the sleek outline of Sir James's cutter anchored below Admiral House. The windows of the house were glinting in the sun. If I stood up and waved, he would not know me.

'We've got tide and wind... another five minutes... maybe ten. I want to be first out.' Gustave had not seen me. He was standing on the prow, staring down at the anchor. The bowsprit was already in place, its rigging swinging loosely across the deck. Nor had Marcel seen me, he was standing by the mast, preparing to hoist the sail. Around me, the river was alive, voices echoing across the water. Every ship was preparing to leave, even those moored against the harbour walls, and I knew I had to hurry. The activity I used to love to watch now filled me with dread. If I jumped too late, a ship could pass right over me.

I had to fight the urge to scream; waving and shouting would have them down on me, and I would be forced below, the hatch locked. The glistening sun hurt my eyes. I would have to jump towards the Old Wharf, where there was less activity. If I swam there I could cling to the poles.

'What the hell?' Thomas Pearce's sudden shout startled me. Furious, he clambered across the deck, staring across the water to the town quay. 'You bloody liars . . . you said he wasn't coming.' His clenched fists flew to his hips, his mouth clamped.

I did not look up but stayed crouched on the deck next to the open hold, the stench of dead fish even stronger here. Thomas Pearce pointed upriver, his finger jabbing the air. 'There. See.' He swung round, his face furious. 'I don't take being lied to.' Marcel and Gustave stopped what they were doing, staring across the river in disbelief.

Both men bounded to his side. '*Merde*. It's him. *Le bâtard*. Shit. Shit.'

There was hatred in their faces, deep scowls and tight mouths, and I reached up, gripping the bulkhead. The blanket was over my head and I peered as if from under a hood. Oars were splashing the water, a small rowing boat low in the river, a man with his back to us, and I thought my heart would burst. A man in a white shirt, his sleeves billowing in the breeze; a man with strong shoulders and a head of thick black hair.

'Shit. Get that sail up.' Gustave's eyes had narrowed.

I tried to keep the excitement from showing, tried to look

seasick. I pretended to retch into the bowl, avoiding his eyes. Pierre was still half a mile away, maybe more, the boat was small, struggling in the waves. I could see him straining on the oars, pulling with all his might.

He was coming for me, Pierre de la Croix, rowing his hardest. He would soon be here. I must keep calm, not shout or scream; if I made any sign of distress they would lock me below. I must moan into my bowl, lie still until he was nearer. If I kept my head down they would think I had no strength to jump. 'Please let me stay, Marcel. I like it here . . . I'm happy here. I'm very grateful to you, but I'd like to stay.' My voice was weak but it carried across the deck.

His face hardened. 'Your brother wants you home.'

Tears began rolling down my cheeks, tears of hope, of love for Pierre. 'Please let him row me back to shore.'

Pleading with Marcel, I did not see Gustave jump to my side. He reached out, and pain seared through me. Gripping me firmly, he began winding his scarf around my mouth. I could not move. I could not breathe, I was suffocating. I had to stop my panic, breathe through my nose. His grip was fiercer than before, more cruel, his breathing laboured. Pushing me to the deck, he stood glaring down at me, his hand raised as if to strike. I thought he would kill me, pick me up and slam me against the wooden deck. I was so slight he could have tossed me overboard, or flung me into the hold. Hatred burned his face, hatred and murder, and I knew by the venom in his eyes that they were going to kill me. Once out at sea, I would be thrown overboard.

I lay whimpering like a dog. Marcel stood at the prow,

scowling at the tiny rowing boat. 'He's a fast rower. Damn him. He's heading straight for us – he knows exactly which ship we're on. We must leave. NOW.'

They leapt across the deck, working in unison, uncurling ropes, getting ready to hoist the sail. 'Help us, damn you.' Gustave shouted to Thomas Pearce. 'Get hold of the tiller. Keep us to wind.'

Thomas Pearce stayed where he was, his eyes wild, glancing from me to Pierre, to me again. He looked terrified, his fists clenching by his sides. Pulling me to my feet, he held me against him and I saw a flash of steel, felt the pressure of a dagger against my throat. His shout rang across the deck. 'You lied to me. You bastards lied – her fancy man's coming.' He was stronger than he looked, his grip pinning me in front of him. 'You said he didn't know about the ship . . . about us leaving.' The steel glinted in the sun. 'Stay still, woman. One move and I'll slit your throat.'

He was like a man possessed, his eyes blazing. I could smell brandy on his breath, feel his body shaking. 'Get those bloody sails up. Get us out of here. We've got a bloody French prisoner rowing right across the harbour for all to see. Straight to us. Right under the bloody nose of a bloody admiral.' He wrenched me round. 'There . . . look . . . there's his ship. The fastest cutter there is . . . and we're in a *fishing tub*. A mile out and we'll have the whole bloody navy clambering over our decks.'

He was shaking with fear, or rage, it was hard to tell; spitting out his words, snarling at Marcel, who shouted from the mast: 'Put her below. We need three to sail this ship.'

Thomas Pearce was deaf to him, swinging me round in his

301

panic. Pierre was halfway to us, his wet sleeves clinging to his arms, the waves breaking over the tiny boat. He looked drenched yet he was coming. Pierre de la Croix was coming to save me.

The dagger at my throat began shaking. 'Everyone can see him – they'll be after him. Damn you. Damn you . . . They'll alert the fort. We'll have cannons firing at us. I'm a dead man. I'll not be caught. D'you hear? I've paid good money. *I'll not swing.*'

'For God's sake, lock her below. Take the tiller. We'll hoist the main and sail on to the anchor.' Marcel was uncoiling a rope, looking up at the rigging. The ship had almost swung round, pieces of wood bobbing next to us on the turning tide. His face strained, his thick muscles tightening as he hauled up the sail. 'Once the sail's set we'll heave the anchor. For God's sake . . . TAKE THE TILLER.'

The grip holding me strengthened, a shout in my ear. 'Can't you see she's got to stop him? She must wave like she's saying goodbye. Like she's leaving him behind . . .'

A hundred yards away the heavy oars splashed the water, the rowing boat plunging towards us. I had to stay calm, think what to do. Thomas Pearce was like a madman, muttering oaths in my ear. 'Don't let him get here,' he shouted. Then a whisper I could not hear. 'I'll not hang!' he shouted louder, followed by a whisper again, hardly audible above the wind. 'Can you swim?'

Definitely a whisper and I nodded. 'Don't nod.' Around us, sails were being hoisted, commands ringing across the decks of the surrounding ships. Everyone was leaving, the sails unfurling, men hauling up the anchors, and I stood straining to hear. Another whisper, increasingly urgent. 'Jump, then, damn you. Be with your bloody captain. But not yet. Wait till I say. Kick me hard and jump towards Fosse.' His grip tightened. 'Don't bloody nod.'

Above us, the white sail was rising, Marcel and Gustave hauling with all their might. Soon it would fill. Another whisper: 'Don't scream or shout... or struggle. If they think you've drowned they won't come back for you. If they think you're alive, they will. I'll let you go – if you let me go. Struggle and they'll come back for you and I'll swing from the gallows.'

He was speaking fast, his voice almost drowned out by the hoisting of the sail. The wind was whistling against the mast, the timbers groaning, and I stood ready. The thought of jumping with a gag was petrifying but I could do it. I could do anything to get off this ship. The sail was starting to fill, the ship lurching to one side. Marcel's shout rang with hatred. 'GET THAT WOMAN BELOW AND KEEP THE TILLER TO PORT.'

Thomas Pearce's dagger flashed, the blade slicing my gag. I felt the pressure released and I gasped for air.

His eyes scanned the waves. 'Kick me *hard*. Look like you've drowned. Don't scream.' He started pushing me along the deck towards the hatch. The ship had swung round and was facing upriver. Pierre was gaining on us, yet he was in the path of several ships; men were leaning over the decks, yelling for him to get out of their way. Thomas Pearce jerked me forward. 'They'll come back for you. Act dead.' A slight pause then a whisper: 'Now!'

I twisted round and kicked with all my force. He lay groaning on the deck and I rushed to the bulwark, keeping my back to the others so they would not see he had released my gag. I knew to jump away from the anchor and out of their path.

Thomas Pearce's yells echoed behind me. Now was the time. Gripping the rail, I knew to swim underwater as far as I could. I took a deep breath, slipping from the side, falling feet first into the foaming water. Ice cold gripped me, my head searing with pain. Bubbles frothed around me, the shape of a dark hull.

Chapter Thirty-six

I began kicking, my gown clinging to my legs; swimming like I used to swim, flipping my feet up and down, my arms pulling me through the water as if diving for shells in the cove by our house. But it was never this cold. I had not swum for fourteen years and never to save my life. The water was murky, seaweed and debris brushing against me, the current stronger than I had anticipated, sweeping me out to sea. I had to struggle against it, swim far enough away from the ship. Cold clamped my head, pain shooting through me. I was at my limit of my breath; I had to break the surface. Blue light filtered above me, below me, nothing but darkness, and I pulled with all my might. Once at the surface, I would have to lie with my arms outstretched.

I was a child again, disobeying my parents, my sisters watching from the shore, shouting for me to come back; floating on the surface, watching the crabs scuttle below me. My sisters knew I was not drowning, merely fearful of my mother's wrath, but they missed so much – the sea life they would never know. The way the rocks glistened, the colours of the seaweed.

I had to stretch out my arms, not kick my legs. Not move my head, keep my face turned away from the hull. Breathe slowly, deeply. I was not drowning, I was in the bay, watching the crabs. I must not swim, but let my face dip beneath the water, and rise again. The water was unsettled, the waves lifting me, the current pulling me. Men were shouting, and I heard a splash.

'Throw another. Upstream of her.'

A barrel wrapped with thick cork bobbed beside me and I let it pass within a foot of my hand. I had to stop myself from grabbing it, breathe slowly, not move. Like in the bay in the hot summers of home. I must spread my arms, keep my legs moving just below the surface. Salt stung my eyes, intense cold creeping up my legs, my whole body numb. My head was splitting, my face half-submerged. Another flotation barrel passed me by, the shouts from the ships getting lost on the wind. I was drifting out to sea. Drifting. Too cold to swim.

Through blurred eyes I saw the vague outline of the lugger, a man on the tiller, two on the deck. The wind caught the sails, filling them, arching, the ship picking up speed. I heard a splash, another and another, my gown clinging to me, dragging me down. Another splash. A wail, a cry that pierced my heart – a heart-wrenching cry jolting me to my senses.

'Madeleine... Madeleine.' Pierre de la Croix secured the oars and was reaching over, his two strong hands gripping me beneath my shoulders. 'Darling... darling... don't leave me.' Tears coursed down his cheeks, he was wet to the skin, his arms lifting me, pulling me from the water. 'Madeleine . . . Madeleine.' I could not move but lay limp in his arms. He was feeling for my pulse, his strong fingers trembling against my neck. 'Breathe, my darling . . . breathe. Come back to me . . . don't leave me.'

He cupped my head in his hands, holding it back, lifting my chin and I felt his mouth on mine, his lips closing over my lips. His breath was warm and I wanted to tell him I was alive, yet I was too cold to speak. Too numb. He put his ear against my chest, his voice pleading. 'Breathe . . . breathe.' His voice caught. A sudden sob. 'That's it. Again. Breathe again.'

'Pierre . . .' I whispered. He cradled me in his arms and I wanted to clutch him, hold him like I would never let him go, but I let my arms hang limp by my sides, my head loll forward. 'They must think I'm dead,' I whispered. We were being carried by the current, drifting on the waves, the lugger pulling fast away. 'They think I'm still gagged . . .'

He seemed to understand, immediately bending as if undoing the scarf, kneeling in the boat with me in his arms. 'They're watching through a telescope,' he said, and I let my head roll back, my arms hang limp. He started shouting, yelling, crying out in pain. 'You've killed her. You've killed her.' His voice dropped, his eyes filled with fury. 'They're still watching . . . wait . . . they're turning to starboard. They're going.'

His shirt was clinging to him, his wet hair streaking across his forehead. The wind was fiercer here, the waves stronger, my body shivering with intense cold. He reached for his jacket, wrapping it round me, folding me in his arms. 'You're like ice . . . you're in grave danger — I have to get you warm.' He reached for his hat, placing it on my head, and I realised I had lost my turban when I jumped. I was shivering too hard to speak, my lips chattering, yet I was used to freezing baths and ice-cold drenches, used to being left to lie all night wet and shivering. No blanket. Just the prospect of another day's drenching as they thought to freeze the madness from me.

He gripped the oars, pulling us swiftly through the water. 'I'll go with the tide . . . we'll pull into the bay.' He was as drenched as I was, stern faced, muscles taut, pulling with all his might. The man I loved, Pierre de la Croix, taking me to the bay where he had rescued the driftwood. If only my teeth would stop chattering. I needed to tell him. 'Pierre . . . we have to hurry . . . I have to warn Cécile Lefèvre.'

He did not hear me. He was glancing over his shoulder, making sure of his course. 'We'll go straight to Admiral House.'

The shaking was getting worse, the force of the wind cutting me like ice. There was not enough flesh on me to withstand the water for so long. 'We have to warn her. Marcel is a spy for the Republic. Cécile Lefèvre is in great danger.'

Soldiers were watching us from the fortifications, whistles blowing, ships unfurling their sails and heading out to sea. The tiny cove was in shadow, the cliffs ringing with the sound of gulls. He did not hear me but pulled with all his strength, guiding the rowing boat round the rocks towards the safety of the sand. I could hear him grunting with the effort, forcing the boat through the surf. Jumping from the side, he pulled it on to the tiny stretch of shingle and reached for me. Lifting me in his arms, he ran across the shore and up the cliff road.

He was breathless as we passed the linhay, but kept running, holding me tightly, my own arms too cold to cling to him.

The red bricks of Admiral House rose before us. 'I'll go round the back . . . down the back stairs. Straight to the kitchen. There's a hearth there. You'll soon be warm.'

A dog was barking, the sound of footsteps, doors opening, surprised gasps, and I tried to make them hear me. 'We have to warn her. She's in great danger.' More voices, anxious this time, getting louder and softer, someone addressing me but I could not answer. The shivering was getting worse, taking hold.

'Upstairs . . . into the green room. There's a bed and warm blankets ready . . . a warming pan . . . and there's a fire newly lit.' The voice was kind yet authoritative, tinged with a hardly discernible French accent. 'We saw everything from our window.'

I felt myself carried up the stairs into a warm room. A maid curtsied. 'Yes, Lady Pendarvis . . . everythin's on the bed – warm clothes, a housecoat. Several towels and there's hot water comin' up.'

Pierre said something. No, it was not Pierre but another man's voice. A stern voice. 'Captain de la Croix, if you'll come with me. I believe you understand you can no longer consider yourself a guest here. You've violated the terms of your parole and are now my prisoner. No further attempt to escape will be tolerated. My soldiers are armed and have instructions to shoot on sight.'

Chapter Thirty-seven

Admiral House

The chattering of my teeth made it hard to speak. I was encased in warm blankets, a towel wrapped around my head, my feet in hot water. A maid was rubbing my back, another handing me a delicate china cup filled with hot chocolate, but my hands were shaking too violently to hold it. The lady they addressed as Lady Pendarvis was pacing by the window. 'Good. You are getting some colour back in your cheeks. Not so deathly white.'

She stood silhouetted against the light, tall, elegant, dressed in dark green silk. Her hair was drawn into a chignon, two feathers in her headdress dancing as she turned to stare out to sea. I caught the glint of an emerald brooch and matching earrings. She held her jewelled lorgnettes to her eyes, her mouth tightening. 'No sign of them, my dear. I'm afraid your friends have left you for dead.'

I shook my head. 'They're . . . not my . . . friends . . . Lady Pendarvis . . . please, I need to—'

'You need to get warm. What were you thinking jumping

310

from that ship when you obviously cannot swim?' She glanced at the maid. 'Hannah, I wonder if we can find a suitable gown for Mrs Barnard?'

'Perhaps in the charity trunk – there's a pile been delivered.'

'And one of my headdresses – perhaps the pale blue silk?' She returned to the window, flicking open her fan. She had helped the maids undress me and provided everything I needed, yet she was clearly upset. 'How could he row out like that?'

'I'll see what I can find.' Hannah bobbed a curtsy.

The door shut and I fought my tears. 'Lady Pendarvis, Pierre wasn't trying to escape. He was rescuing me . . . they were leaving without him . . .' I stopped. Her frown had deepened. At any other time, I might have enjoyed the company of the well-connected Marie St Bouchard-Bouley. I knew who she was – everyone in Paris knew who she was. Her brother was the Marquis de Barthélemy, my father had known her father; yet as her eyes pierced mine I felt a surge of fear. Pierre was clearly in danger. 'Lady Pendarvis . . . I can explain—'

'Captain de la Croix knew the consequences of his actions. Prisoners on parole are forbidden on *any* ship.' She shrugged, turning from me. 'I *saw* him . . . we cannot condone any prisoner trying to escape, especially one we have extended such hospitality to. Captain de la Croix was our *guest.*'

'They weren't going to take him . . . they were leaving *without* him . . . that's why I jumped.' She had eyes like a hawk, a nose like a bird of prey. She would have talons to match. I watched the slight rise of her perfectly arched eyebrows, a tightening of her mouth. She was not a woman to offend.

'Who are *they* exactly?'

I needed to tell her to alert the navy, that a spy ring was operating under her very nose. To send a ship after them. That they had copied secret codes, that lives were now in danger. I needed to alert Cécile Lefèvre, but I had seen that look too many times. I had shouted and screamed, pleaded and spoken rationally, I had spent fourteen years telling the truth only to be met with that same look. If I was to save Pierre, I must be careful no one thought me mad. 'My brother wants me back in Saint-Malo. He sent his friends to bring me home.'

A knock on the door, and Lady Pendarvis resumed looking out of the window. Hannah was holding a hat box, the young maid beside her hardly visible beneath a pile of gowns. 'There's a choice to be had.' She seemed to have been crying. Helping lay the gowns on the bed, she wiped her eyes. 'One of these looks to be nearly your size. It's got a tie . . . so we can pull it in.' She looked round, her eyes full of compassion.

So, too, Lady Pendarvis. She looked stricken. Sweeping from the room, she turned at the door. 'Thank you, Hannah. When Mrs Barnard is ready, perhaps you could show her into the drawing room?'

I stood holding the highly polished banister. 'Are ye all right, Mrs Barnard?' Hannah smiled in encouragement and I took a deep breath. The apricot satin gown shimmered in the light, the bow tied firmly behind a cream trail. Lady Pendarvis's blue silk turban fitted me perfectly and Hannah had found a matching embroidered shawl. I was beautifully dressed and was glad of it. I wanted their respect; I needed to look confident, even though my legs felt weak.

The house was grander inside than the exterior had led me to believe. It was richly decorated, a grand staircase swirling down one side, a row of family portraits on another. The sun shone through an oval window, lighting the last two paintings, and I stared at the first – a young naval captain, handsome, assured, the gold braid glistening on his uniform: Captain Edward Pendarvis, tall, commanding, with short brown hair, a chiselled chin, and fine long fingers holding a scroll.

But it was the lady in the next portrait that caught my attention. It was as if some invisible thread drew me to her. Celia Pendarvis looked refined, extremely elegant, her chestnut curls framing her face. She was staring down at me, the look in her stare not so much haughty as intelligent. Her eyes held challenge, as if she was not used to being crossed. She had paid for Billy's education and searched for his sister. She had not spoken to her father since he had sent her to the same madhouse as he had sent me.

'This way, if you please.' Hannah tweaked a crease from my gown. Her bottom lip began to quiver, another wipe of her eyes. She glanced at the footman. 'What's he goin' to do with him?'

The footman shook his head, his expression equally dismal. He opened the door and cleared his throat. 'Mrs Barnard, my lady.'

A sea of faces turned to me and I tried to steady myself. They were not sitting but standing, formal, stiff-backed, and I felt the frostiness in the air. Pierre was by the fireplace, tall, upright, his hair freshly brushed, wearing a clean white shirt, a new jacket and breeches. He looked immaculate, his silk cravat tied in a small bow. Our eyes caught and I thought my heart would break. His smile was warm, stoical, his chin held high, as if he knew the consequences of his actions and would do the same all over again.

The short, slender man by the fireplace must be Admiral Sir Alexander Pendarvis. Standing close to Pierre, his grey wig was tied in a black bow at his neck, his silk jacket cut away to reveal an exquisitely embroidered waistcoat. Only the ebony peg below his left knee took me by surprise. Everything else was exactly what I expected: a frown, a fierce penetrating look.

Walking to a chair, he indicated for me to sit down. 'Mrs Barnard, are you quite well? You've been through a terrible ordeal.' His words were kind, though his voice held caution, as if he was about to interrogate me. He cleared his throat. 'Captain de la Croix will spend tonight in the gaol here in Fosse and will be taken to Bodmin tomorrow, where he will be imprisoned until we arrange transport to Norman Cross. The penalties for attempting to escape are severe. As Captain de la Croix is well aware.' He held out his hand. 'This is Major Hyssop from the fort. He alerted us. He saw everything.'

I was not prepared for my rush of anger. 'But Pierre wasn't escaping . . . he was rescuing me. Pierre is totally innocent of this charge. The men on that ship were—' I stopped. I had to be certain not to make matters worse. Major Hyssop was glowering at me, his mouth held tight.

His eyes sharpened. 'Captain de la Croix said you were

forced on to the ship by a man you believed to be your friend. That you were taken against your will.' He had a high-pitched voice, a thin mouth and heavy sideburns. He must be sixty or more, stout and red-faced.

'Yes . . . that's true . . .' I could hear my heart thumping. Any talk of spies and I would implicate Pierre. Most especially, Matthew had warned me not to tell anyone of my brother's death. I must remain as Mrs Barnard and say nothing about Cécile Lefèvre.

Major Hyssop was clearly more powerful than I thought. He seemed to be the one leading the charge. 'Captain de la Croix states your brother sent for you, and that he thought you'd changed your mind about going. That you wanted to stay here. Captain de la Croix has led us to believe that his action in taking the rowing boat was simply to *rescue* you when you jumped.' His voice was sharp. 'Were the men on that ship sent to help Captain de la Croix escape?'

'No . . . no . . . far from it. Pierre had *no* knowledge of the ship – or of my brother's . . . intentions.' I was in danger of getting muddled; his voice was like every other powerful man – mistrustful, cynical, making out I was lying. But I was not lying and I was not mad. I just needed time to clear my head.

A voice behind me, kinder now, but ringing with authority: 'Mrs Barnard, do sit down. This must be very hard for you. I fear you do not understand the consequences . . . *Anyone* found helping a French prisoner to escape is liable for severe charges.' Lady Pendarvis glanced at her husband. 'Do we need this written down, only Mrs Barnard must not be subjected to interrogation without cause?'

'I'm afraid we do. We're talking here of a conspiracy to free Captain de la Croix. I can't let this go. Admiralty rules are very clear and must be followed to the letter – and the fact that Captain de la Croix was a guest in my house makes it even more vital I investigate this thoroughly.' He glanced at the Major. 'Major Hyssop was preparing to use the cannons. He was watching from the fort. He witnessed Captain de la Croix trying to reach the ship.'

Pierre's voice was respectful, yet firm. 'I had no prior knowledge of the ship, Sir Alex. I was expecting to dine with Mrs Barnard at five o'clock at Coombe House. I rowed out to the ship because I was told Mrs Barnard had been forced on to the ship under duress and I wanted to confirm she was going willingly.'

Sir Alex shook his grey wig. 'You risked your parole, Pierre . . . for . . . ?'

Pierre's eyes held mine. 'For the very great regard I have for Mrs Barnard.'

Pain ripped through me. I had never loved like this before. Never felt such strength of feeling, such overwhelming need to defend this lonely, honourable, kind, compassionate, heart-broken man who had become so dear to me.

The room was the sort of room I used to imagine in my prisons. The windows afforded fine views across the sea, a collection of delicate porcelain arranged on the mantelpiece. A pianoforte stood in the alcove, a richly woven carpet, elegant silk drapes. Sir Alex held his hands behind his back. 'We need to get this clear. You *hadn't* arranged to meet her, Pierre – you were on the quayside and an urchin came racing up, telling you the lady he'd seen you with over recent days was being forced on to a ship?'

Pierre nodded. 'Yes. That's correct. The boy was crabbing on the rocks behind the Old Wharf and saw Mrs Barnard demanding to speak to me. He said she looked scared and he'd watched her being forced on to the ship. He knew she was a particular acquaintance of mine. He told me which ship it was and my only thought was to reach her on time.'

A smile lingered over Major Hyssop's lips. 'My men have seen you give coins to these urchins. Do they keep you informed about what's going on in the harbour – which ships are leaving, perhaps?'

Pierre shook his head. 'No, Major Hyssop. And I don't give them coins; I give them small trinkets I carve from driftwood or bone. They sell them for food. I consider them very fine boys – they have nothing, and I have very little to give them, but their conversation is precious to me. Their acceptance of me as a person, not an enemy, is priceless.'

A deep intake of breath, almost a sigh from Sir Alex. 'And there just happened to be a rowing boat right in front of you with the oars left in place?'

'I can swear on oath that was the case. No doubt you'll find out who left it there.'

Major Hyssop's high-pitched voice rose. 'I'm sorry, but this farce must end.' He reached into his jacket pocket. 'I have here a letter alerting me to the fact that you were planning to escape. We've been watching you, Captain de la Croix. We know you seek to use your friendship with Sir Alex – or should I say *abuse* the trust he places in you. You have been

317

seeking to escape . . . and you have been detected.' He held up a letter. 'We've been expecting it. My men have been trailing you.'

I gasped in horror. Sir Alex was also clearly shocked. 'May I?' He took the letter, an immediate frown creasing his brow. Pierre looked stricken, yet somehow remained poised. Sir Alex glanced at his wife. '*Dear Major Hyssop, For several years we have been watching Captain de la Croix and believe him to be other than he seems. We believe he is planning an escape and will take with him to France vital information gleaned from his close association with Admiral Alexander Pendarvis. He must be stopped. Your obedient servant, Marcel Rablais.*'

'No. Absolutely not! I deny this emphatically. I can swear on my innocence . . .'

I could hardly breathe. *Marcel Rablais.* They must not see me recognise his name. He must have written the letter when we arrived. Sir Alex handed it to his wife, a look of hurt in his eyes. 'Do you know this man, Captain de la Croix?'

'No, Sir Alex. The letter is a lie. I give you my word, my only thought was to ascertain whether Mrs Barnard was going willingly.'

A snort from Major Hyssop. 'This letter is proof. It was a very clear warning – and I acted accordingly.'

Hurried footsteps ran across the hall and the door opened. Without waiting to be announced Mrs Pengelly came rushing in, tears streaming down her cheeks. Her hands flew to her chest. 'Oh, my dearest, you're safe! I heard you'd drowned.' She reached for her handkerchief. 'It's all over town . . .' She sank into a chair. 'They said Pierre couldn't save you.'

318

Lady Pendarvis rushed to her aid, but Major Hyssop watched her from across the room. 'Fortunately, he did. May I ask why Mrs Barnard left the house, Mrs Pengelly?' His voice was soft, coaxing, the exact hammer blow I was expecting.

'I wasn't there. I was with Lady Polcarrow and I only just missed her leaving . . . Mrs Munroe said she'd received a note from Pierre and had rushed off.'

Chapter Thirty-eight

The colour drained from Pierre's face. He looked suddenly gaunt. 'I sent no note.'

Mrs Pengelly looked puzzled, turning to me. 'Mrs Munroe said you'd got a note from Pierre?'

The room was spinning. 'They're accusing Pierre of trying to escape...' I could hardly speak. 'But he wasn't. He was only seeing if I wanted to go or not. The note was *signed* from Pierre but it wasn't from him. It was written by a man called Gustave – as a ploy to get me on to the ship. They wouldn't leave without me... they held me captive... we saw Pierre rowing out and it was only because Thomas Pearce cut my gag that I was able to jump at all. He had a dagger at my throat but he must have had some good in him because he let me go. I couldn't have jumped with the gag.' I was talking too fast, the words jumbling together.

Mrs Pengelly gasped. Even Pierre looked distraught. 'A dagger at your throat?' Major Hyssop pinned me with his grey eyes. He was a horrible weaselly man. No, not a weasel, a ferret — ferreting out the truth. Only this was the truth, and he did not believe a word. 'Who is this dagger-wielding *Thomas Pearce*?'

'A diamond thief... and a murderer. He needed to leave England because he'd be hanged if he was caught. He'd paid a lot of money for his passage and when he saw Pierre rowing out he became distraught. Quite rightly, he thought everyone would be alerted — that naval ships would come — that you'd fire your cannons from the fort.' I stared back into his disbelieving eyes. 'He told me to jump — he said Pierre would pick me out of the water. He cut my gag and told me when to jump. Lady Pendarvis... you were watching... you must have seen that?'

She nodded. 'I saw you jump. And I saw three men on the ship.'

Yet their glances looked incredulous, all of them thinking the same thought: *a murderer... a diamond thief?* I felt sick with fear. No one would believe me; they would trace me back to the madhouse, find my forged discharge papers. Nothing I could say would help Pierre; everything I said would hinder him. 'You saw Thomas Pearce, Mrs Pengelly — he was the one who attacked me outside your house. Tell them you saw him.'

'Oh, yes, I saw him. A horrible man, I can vouch for that. Oh, dear love... don't cry.' Tears splashed my cheeks. I had been all right until she showed such kindness.

'Did you know these men, Pierre? This murderer... these friends of Mrs Barnard?'

Pierre swallowed. 'Yes, Sir Alex. I had met them but I didn't pass much time with them. I would not say I knew them.

Certainly not the man called Gustave. But the others I had knowledge of...'

Major Hyssop eyes were pinpoints. 'When did you meet them?'

I held my breath, sensing Pierre's tension. 'We met on the stagecoach to Fosse... from Bodmin. We were fellow travellers.'

'How very convenient. You all just happened to get on the same coach?'

Mrs Pengelly gripped my hand. 'I'm sorry, but you can't possibly think Pierre was attempting to escape. That's complete nonsense.' She was clearly angry, yet the major seemed to shrug it off, staring intently at Pierre.

'When did you first meet Mrs Barnard? Was she, too, on this stagecoach you just happened to be on?'

'She was, Major. Once in Fosse, we went our separate ways. Only I came across Mrs Barnard again when Mrs Pengelly kindly invited me to take tea.'

Mrs Pengelly swung round to face Sir Alex. 'Surely... this is going too far?'

Her eyes were pleading, yet Sir Alex remained formal, shaking his head. 'Eva, this is not something we can shrug off. Admiralty laws are crystal clear – the terms of parole are *indisputable*. There can be no avoiding arrest. Major Hyssop was warned and his soldiers saw everything from the fort. Captain de la Croix must be taken prisoner.'

All colour drained from her face, yet her voice was strong. 'No, Sir Alex... not everything. The view from the fort only covers the river mouth... you can't see the quayside from there. They didn't see what the whole town saw. The whole town saw a man intent on saving the life of the woman he loves . . . that he acted swiftly, with no thought to his own life, nor to the terrible consequences that could follow. Isn't that the truth, Captain Pierre?'

Pierre nodded, his chin lifting. 'It is the truth, Mrs Pengelly.'

The footman entered, a discreet cough as he announced the constable was waiting in the hall. Pierre stood proud, addressing Sir Alexander Pendarvis. 'May I speak with Mrs Barnard alone for a moment?'

My heart hammered as I fought my tears. Sir Alex shook his head. 'I'm afraid that's not possible, Pierre. Admiralty law states you can't be left alone to talk . . . to confer . . . or to collaborate. Both of you will be questioned separately – you must understand that.'

Lady Pendarvis stood by my side. 'But we're not so heartless, are we? I believe they will speak only words of love.'

'Rules are rules and I must follow them to the letter.'

The quiet authority returned to her voice. 'What if you allow me to stay with them, and Eva, too? Your Admiralty laws would be complied with . . . let Major Hyssop keep his handcuffs unlocked a little longer.'

Sir Alex must have felt the same reluctance. Pointing the way for Major Hyssop to precede him to the door, he nodded. 'Ten minutes. With both of you present.'

Across the river, the town of Porthruan glinted in the evening sun. Lady Pendarvis sat elegantly on the piano stool, arranging her silk gown around her. She had her back to us, her right hand idly picking out a Mozart tune I remembered playing. Mrs Pengelly went to her side, discussing what music she should play, and a wave of gratitude brought tears to my eyes. They decided on a piece and music filled the air. Pierre stepped forward, shy at first, then reached for my hands.

'Pierre, I'm so sorry . . . you shouldn't have . . .'

His hands tightened around mine. 'I would do it again without a moment's hesitation. The only thing that matters is you're alive.' He looked down. 'I believe you know how much . . . how very *dear* to me you have become.' He glanced up, his eyes burning. 'When we met on the coach, I felt such compassion for you. Your bravery . . . your vulnerability. You had such courage. When you smiled at me . . . when your hands shook . . . my heart felt bruised.' He lifted my hands to his lips.

'It was as if an arrow shot straight through it. You were starving, your sores weeping and painful, yet you had such dignity. Your brave smile, your proud eyes, your whispered *thank you*. I was drawn to you . . . drawn from that very first moment. I thought my heart was breaking until I realised it wasn't breaking, it was *filling*. Filling with love for the first time in my life.'

He brushed away my tears. 'I could think only of what you must have suffered. I thought I'd lost all chance of love – I thought only to love as an uncle or a godfather, but that day in the linhay when I turned and saw you – you were like a butterfly emerging from its chrysalis – and the pain of what you must have gone through pierced my heart. I know you'll tell me everything one day – in your own time – but that day, when I turned and saw you, I knew I had been waiting for you all my life. I've never loved before, I've admired women and respected them, but it was like waking from a half-sleep. Like my body had lain dormant and my heart had never been tested. I could not stop looking at you – loving your bravery, your incredible dignity under such hardship. I could not stop thinking of you.'

His finger rested beneath my chin and I smiled up through my tears. 'I loved you, too, Pierre . . . your kindness to me . . . your genuine concern. I felt drawn to you from first sight. I had to hide it . . . deny it from myself. I had to persuade myself that you meant me harm, but Rowan knew better. My heart knew better.'

He reached down, his lips softly brushing mine, and in that moment I did not care about propriety or decorum. I did not care if anyone saw us. I loved this gentle man. I loved his compassion, his manners, his charm. The way he held himself so formally, the way he unbuttoned his shirt to chase children round the yard. The way everyone loved him. His lips sought mine again and I felt such need to hold him, to cling to him like in my dreams, only in my dreams I was not crying. 'Hush, darling Madeleine. Hush.' He held me tightly and I knew I must tell him the truth.

'Marcel Rablais is François Barnard. He helped me escape from a madhouse.'

His grip strengthened. 'I knew it would be enforced imprisonment of some sort. You have been cruelly dealt with. Scurvy from neglect. I knew you'd been forcibly held. Yet Marcel was no saviour. Right from the start he wanted me out of the way. He must have written that letter the day we arrived.'

'I was held for fourteen years. Pierre, what I'm about to tell you will make you question my sanity. But it's the absolute truth. Marcel Rablais and Gustave are Republican spies... they were *not* friends of my brother. They must have discovered I was being sought by a lady called Cécile Lefèvre. I don't know her as I've never met her but I believe she helps British spies carry information to France. And back *from* France. It's *her* they wanted to find.' I was whispering too fast, trying to make sense of it myself. 'She left us a message in the linhay. They intercepted her codes but they only copied them and left the originals so she thinks they don't have them – they want her to think no one has intercepted them.'

Lady Pendarvis's fingers were racing across the keys, but still his voice dropped. 'I believe you.' He kissed my forehead, glancing at Lady Pendarvis. 'Do you play the piano, my darling? I have so much to learn about you – do you sing... do you paint?'

Sudden pain made me clutch him tighter. 'Will you have a fair hearing? Will they imprison you?'

His lips brushed my forehead again. 'Under the terms of my parole, I can expect all privileges to be removed. I will be imprisoned. Sir Alex may understand my intentions were only to save you, but others like Major Hyssop won't be as lenient. Don't cry, darling Madeleine. Be strong for me. All I ask is that when this war's over, you'll allow me the honour of searching for you. I don't expect you to wait for me, but if you would allow me the opportunity to—'

'Of course I'll wait, Pierre.' I blinked through my tears. 'Of course I will. To think you're imprisoned because of me – in some foul stinking goal . . . rife with fever. Pierre, you *shouldn't* have risked this. I can swim. I could have swum to shore only he told me to pretend to drown or they'd come back for me. To save *his* life. I'll never, ever, forgive myself.'

'No, darling . . . it was nothing to do with you jumping. I was in that rowing boat well before you jumped. I broke my parole *well* before you jumped.'

He was trying to shield me; he was not being entirely truthful. Escaping prisoners could be shot – breaking his parole was one thing, rowing out to a ship quite another. Pierre reached inside his jacket and I felt the smooth outline of his silver watch pressed into my palm. 'Keep this for me . . . keep it safe,' he whispered.

The door opened and Lady Pendarvis kept them waiting until she reached an appropriate finale. A constable stood next to Admiral Sir Alexander Pendarvis, behind him Major Hyssop, red-faced and grim. He stepped forward, a pair of handcuffs held in both hands. 'Captain de la Croix, I'm arresting you for attempting to escape. You've broken the terms of your parole and you're to come with me.'

Pierre nodded. Putting my clasped hands to his lips, he kissed them softly. I was the custodian of his secret and I nodded, needing no words. He stood upright, proud, taking a deep breath as Major Hyssop strode across the room. I heard the handcuffs clank, the twist of the lock, and I thought my heart would break. Sir Alex stood, grim-faced and silent, following Pierre out through the door.

Mrs Pengelly came rushing to my side. For such a gentle woman, her face was livid. Lady Pendarvis's feathers fluttered, her hawk eyes glistening. Gliding across the room as if on air, tall, elegant, her movements one of a woman half her age, she glared at Major Hyssop's retreating back. 'Pierre's shown great courage, great love and great *recklessness*. We have all become very fond of him, but the fact remains he has broken his parole.'

There was something in the way she held her long neck, the slight rise of her perfectly arched brow. Her hawk eyes softened and I felt a flutter of hope. 'We need to find that boy. And we must find the owner of the rowing boat. Sir Alex will not be able to defend Pierre without their evidence.'

Mrs Pengelly slipped her arm through mine. 'Come, Madeleine.' She turned to her friend. 'Pierre would never abuse your hospitality like that, Marie. He'd never put you in such a difficult situation. '

Her lips remained tight, a nod of her feathers. 'We both know that. Go now . . . hurry. Find the boy and keep me informed.'

At the door, a young boy with flushed cheeks darted in front of us, bowing swiftly. 'I'm so sorry, I didn't mean to bump into you.' He held up a clenched bunch of ox-eye daisies. 'Only these are for Grandma.'

Behind him a nursemaid was holding the hand of a small girl, a second bunch of flowers grasped in her hand. 'And these are for Grandpa.'

Mrs Pengelly smiled. I think she said something but I could not respond. All I could do was clutch my handkerchief against my face.

No moon, just the blackness of the night, the heavy clouds obscuring the stars. Rowan's steady breathing filled the room and I held Pierre's watch to my heart, to my lips, to my heart again. No one had seen me, nor had anyone followed me. I had slipped back into the house without making a sound.

The milk churn had been where I had left it, the bag with its secret codes still hidden from prying eyes. No one had disturbed it and I had left my note, leaving Cécile Lefèvre in no doubt as to what had happened. If I was right, she would act swiftly, cancel the codes and be in time to warn everyone of the great danger they were in. I had marked my letter *URGENT*, giving them a description of the ship, and the names of Gustave and Marcel Rablais. Thomas Pearce, too. I had detailed everything, including the chart that had been open on the desk.

I had signed it *A well-wisher*, and I would have to leave it at that.

Chapter Thirty-nine

Coombe House
Wednesday 25th June 1800, 9.30 a.m.

Sam shook his head. 'They say he could be one of the Penrow boys – they've a shack on the cliffs. We've got two names of people who saw him talkin' to Captain Pierre, but the description they give fits them all. Any one of those urchins could be the boy.'

Running his hand through his greying hair, he looked tired, the same sadness reflected in Mrs Munroe's eyes. They remained red-rimmed and downcast, Tamsin's likewise, both women peering over the rims of their yarrow tea. None of us had slept, all of us harbouring the same vision of Pierre, handcuffed, marched from the gaol to the awaiting carriage.

'You think the boy's keeping away because he's frightened he's in trouble?'

Sam nodded. 'A lad like that would be scared of his own shadow. If he's one of the Penrow boys, he'll think we're comin' after him fer stealing. I'll go straight to the shack and see what I can find.' He handed me a piece of paper and I glanced at the names. None were familiar. 'Seeing as we have these names, could ye give it to Mr Reith? Maybe he can help?'

I nodded. 'Does anyone know who owns the rowing boat?'

'Those I talked to said it was left just minutes before. That it weren't there long – not like it was left ahead of an escape. Just chance, like Captain Pierre said it was. Their names are on the list... here, these last three names.'

'Thank you, Sam.' My voice caught. Always on the edge of breaking, the lump in my throat was making it hard to speak.

Rowan stood defiant, her words exactly what we needed: 'People know Captain Pierre's a good man...that he was only savin' ye. Sam's got another list, haven't you, Sam? There's people who heard Captain Pierre shout that the ship should be stopped; he called out yer name. Why would he shout like that if he didn't want to be seen or heard?'

A pot was hanging from the fire and Tamsin got up to stir it. We needed Rowan's belief, her absolute conviction Pierre would be released. It was nearly ten o'clock and Sam straightened. Doing up his jacket, he tidied his necktie. 'Better get ready, Mr Reith's always on time.'

The gathering clouds suited my mood, the rain threatening, hovering over the town; grey, bleak, the wind whistling up the river, making the trees sway and the foam spray. Matthew Reith handed his umbrella to Sam, Alice shaking her head, assuring us that it was only the faintest drizzle and nothing too heavy.

The door shut behind them and Matthew drew two of

331

Phillip Randall's diaries from out of his bag. 'I should have been here sooner. I hoped to warn you. Who were they, Mrs Pelligrew? Why take you forcibly? Why pretend they knew your brother? Can you make any sense of it?'

I sat opened-eyed, hopefully looking bewildered. 'You are absolutely certain my brother was hanged?' That morning I had watched my reflection, perfecting my responses. No one must believe I knew they were French spies, or they would think me mad.

'I'm so sorry . . . I'm afraid it's irrefutable. I've checked too many lists for it to be a mistake. Both your brother and your cousin were hanged . . . and here's the evidence that Sir Charles *knew*. It's this letter that alerted me. Of course I needed to verify it, which is what took me back to Truro.'

He unfolded a letter, handing it to me with a look of concern, and I stared back into his formidable eyes. If I was lying, I would look away and be unable to hold his gaze. I kept my eyes on his. He held out the letter. 'It's from your family's attorney.' He saw me hesitate. 'It makes very grim reading, Mrs Pelligrew. I wonder if I may spare you the details . . . though, of course, if you want—'

I shook my head. 'I'd rather not know the details. It's sufficient to know its content.'

Glancing at Alice, he flicked his coat-tails and sat down on the high-backed chair. She looked as distraught as Mrs Pengelly, her beautiful red hair twisted in a coil behind her neck. The green of her gown seemed to drain her cheeks of colour, but her words were firm. 'Matthew's about to ask you something and I'd rather couch it in gentler terms: are you certain Captain de la Croix had nothing to do with your abduction?'

This time there was no need to hide the truth. I stared back into her beautiful hazel eyes. 'He had nothing to do with my release and nothing to do with the attempt to take me to France. He's entirely innocent – his only crime is... of putting my life before his.' The lump in my throat caught, my eyes welling again. 'Please help him... Please, Matthew. You're held in such high esteem – they'll listen to you. We've got names of people who saw the boy run to Pierre... and names of men who can swear the boat had been left only *minutes* before. People heard Pierre shout that he wanted the ship *stopped*.'

Mrs Pengelly reached for her handkerchief. 'You know Pierre's too intelligent to plan an escape like that. Why shout out? Why let the whole town see him when he could have just slipped from the Old Wharf with no one watching?'

Matthew Reith's frown deepened. He shook his head. 'Eva... we're all very fond of Captain de la Croix. If I could, I would defend him. But I have no jurisdiction over naval matters. None at all. The Admiralty have their own courts – their own laws. It is entirely in the hands of the Transport Board. They set the rules and ensure everyone abides by them. Sir Alex can only follow these rules. His reputation's at stake. They already say he's too familiar with Captain de la Croix. I believe others will be summoned to take this hearing.'

'But these names?'

Matthew Reith glanced at the list. 'Meaningless without a full statement, under oath, signed by the person and witnessed by *two* people of impeccable standing in the town. You need *irrefutable* evidence. Witnesses must give exact times, exact descriptions. Each statement must be taken alone — and by that I mean *not* in the presence of another witness. Everything must be *exactly* recorded: who was present at the interview, when it took place, who witnessed the signatures or marks.'

Mrs Pengelly nodded. 'Perhaps Lady Pendarvis will help us — no one can doubt her standing? And Rose will help.' She adjusted her glasses and took the list. 'Clarity and precision — we understand. No *conjecture*, just facts. And when we have the statements, you'll reconsider and represent Pierre?'

Again Matthew Reith shook his head. 'I'm an attorney . . . No, don't look like that, Eva . . . Believe me, I'd hold no sway. The best person to represent Pierre is Sir James Polcarrow. It's his harbour — his constituency. He'll have far more influence in this matter.'

The clock on the mantelpiece chimed the half-hour. Reaching into his leather bag, he drew out a pile of papers. 'Mrs Pelligrew, returning to matters in hand. I've searched my father's papers. He was involved with your husband's case . . . not solely, but his advice was sought and, therefore, I have access to several letters and was able to peruse the files.' He smiled, glancing again at his wife. 'Or rather *persuade* them to let me have them.'

She smiled back, and my stomach twisted. Not with envy, not with my previous pangs of jealousy, but with the deepest fear. I could see Pierre on a straw-strewn floor in a crowded cell, his arms around his knees, his dark head bent. I knew, too well, the stench of stale air, the overcrowding, the stink of the straw. I could see him lifting his dear face, see his dignity, his quiet acceptance of his fate.

'Do you remember me saying there was a codicil to your husband's will?'

I had to force my mind back. 'Sir Charles Cavendish would house me at his own expense if my husband died?'

'That's exactly what I found — among other things.' He held up a closely written page. 'You were to have a house of your choosing — in Fosse, or on the estate . . . or Porthruan, to the sum of three hundred pounds a year. Until you remarried.'

I reached for my fan. 'Joshua was very reckless — he knew he was on the edge of bankruptcy.'

Matthew Reith frowned. For such a handsome man, he needed to smile more. This was good news, not bad news, but even so, I found myself frowning back. 'I won't take a penny . . . not one farthing. Don't pursue this, Mr Reith. I want you to bring him to justice — for everyone he's manipulated and had murdered.'

Relief crossed his face, a glance at his wife. She reached for my hand. 'Madeleine, are you certain?' There was something in her manner, an easing of her shoulders. They had been so tense and yet now she smiled, both of them looking as if a burden had been lifted, as if they were concealing something.

He cleared his throat. 'You must get certified as sane. Once I have those certificates I'll be able to call you as a credible witness. Only when I have you in the witness box will I reveal the truth.'

'And how long may that be?'

'The evidence needs careful sifting. I have to have absolute clarity – there's no room for error. No place for ambiguity.'

Mrs Pengelly removed her glasses. 'Madeleine wants to remain known as Mrs Barnard. She's petrified Sir Charles will find out she's escaped. She's welcome to stay here for as long as she likes.'

I caught a glance between Matthew, with his dark clothes and professional bearing, and Alice, with her silk and fine lace. An intuitive look, speaking without words.

'What is it you aren't telling me, Mr Reith? Or must I ask to read these papers?'

His look of shock turned to a half-smile, a slight rise to his eyebrow. He shrugged, a sigh escaping as he looked at his wife. 'We were hoping to shield you from this.'

'I don't need shielding. He didn't break me, Mr Reith, though he tried his hardest. I'm stronger than I look.'

'You were married in Saint-Malo?'

'I was.'

'Your husband never told you marriages outside of England are not considered legal? That they have to be repeated back in England or else the marriage is considered void?' He stopped. 'You're smiling, Madeleine . . . you aren't shocked?'

I could not help myself. Months ago, I would have laughed. 'We weren't married in the eyes of British law?'

'That is the case. And Charles Cavendish knew this, which is why he was happy to sign the codicil. He was never going to give you a house.'

I felt no pain. No anger. 'And Mrs O . . . Who was she?'

This time both eyebrows rose. 'Mrs *Owen* lives in London

with her son. She, too, thought she was married to Joshua Pelligrew, only he married her in Spain. I believe there might have been others.'

Just the ticking of the clock, the sound of a cart passing. The drizzle was clearing, even a patch of blue sky. I shrugged, lifting my chin. 'I thought I loved Joshua but I had no notion of *real* love. I do now. I know what it is to love with all my heart and all my soul. Which is why I want to be known as Mrs Barnard. Anything linking me to Pendenning Hall and the madhouse will jeopardise my evidence for Pierre.'

His brows knitted, a shake of his head. 'I wish that was possible – but it can't be. The physicians will need to know the truth.' He was sifting through his papers, finding the one he wanted. 'But here's the good news. I found this among the papers Joshua deposited with his attorney and I doubt very much if Sir Charles knows it exists.' He looked up, rare excitement in his eyes. 'A formal marriage settlement between your father and Joshua Pelligrew.'

Chapter Forty

Matthew Reith held up the stiff parchment. 'You knew about this?'

'No, I didn't . . . My father was reluctant about my marriage. He came to the wedding but he never hid his displeasure.'

'Yet he paid handsomely – a generous dowry of three thousand pounds. That, of course, was swallowed by your husband's debts . . . but read this last paragraph: *Any jewellery Madeleine de Bourg brings to this marriage remains solely in her possession. In the event of her death, the entire collection is to be inherited by her daughters, and in the unlikely event that she has no daughters, the jewellery must return to the de Bourg family, who remain the custodians of these family jewels.*'

The page swam before me – my father's signature, together with his seal, Joshua's signature below, followed by two other names and two further seals. 'I thought my jewellery had been used to pay off Joshua's debts.'

'They haven't listed the individual pieces of jewellery – or if they did, it's become separated and is missing – but it states clearly the value is upwards of seven hundred pounds. Unfortunately, we can't ask Nathaniel Kemp, your husband's steward, because he's been dead for years. He died soon after in sorry circumstances. I believe he drank himself into a ditch.'

'Papa was protecting me...' Tears flooded my eyes. 'I persuaded him to let me marry Joshua. He thought I might elope if he refused.'

Alice drew a deep breath. 'We need to find your jewellery. Can you remember it after all this time?'

I nodded. I could give her a list of anything she wanted. It was how I kept my mind from wandering – the flowers in the garden, the trees in the estate, the paths round Pendenning, the maze in my parents' home. The rivers I knew, the cities I wanted to visit. That eggs made omelettes, meringues and soufflés. The songs my mother used to sing. My jewellery in their silk-lined boxes, the gems sparkling as I imagined them against my skin.

'It was a beautiful *parure* – an emerald, ruby and diamond necklace, blue sapphire earrings... a diamond flower brooch ... a ruby shoulder clasp... diamond hairclips.'

'Could you draw them and perhaps paint in the stones?' Matthew's eyes bore mine. 'As near to their actual size as you can remember? If we give them a list they could claim it's fabricated – but to have them looking lifelike would greatly assist our search.'

I nodded. 'When may I expect your physicians? You've chosen kindly, I hope?' I did not quiver under his scrutiny. For once, I was ready to face any amount of questioning.

He glanced down. 'I've chosen *wisely*, not kindly. They are both unknown to me but they are experts in the field of insanity. If they certify you as sane, there can be no dispute. When we take Sir Charles to court, there must be no—'

'*Ambiguity*. Just undisputable facts.' I smiled.

He collected his papers, bowing formally, taking his wife's arm, and I caught a glimpse of the man behind the mask. His eyes held mine, compassionate, respectful, his voice flooding me with hope. 'Set up your office. You'll need a score or more of reliable statements if you're to defend Pierre. Find the boy, and the man who left the rowing boat. If anyone can get Pierre a fair hearing, it will be you, Mrs Pelligrew.'

To have lived the last fourteen years wanting only to hear that name, it was almost laughable. 'I'm known in the town as Mrs Barnard, and I'd like to keep that name – for now, at least.'

His eyes sharpened. 'I think that's a lost cause. The physicians will need to know the exact nature of your situation.'

'Please, Matthew. Send them to certify me as Mrs Marie Barnard.'

'Servants talk.' He turned to Mrs Pengelly. 'They listen at doors and hear things they shouldn't. Word will get out. I'm surprised the whole town doesn't already know. I need your assurance that not one word we've discussed will leave this room.'

Mrs Pengelly rose to ring the bell. 'I understand.' The door opened and Sam stood ready to escort them to the door. 'Thank you, Sam. Mr and Mrs Reith are just leaving.' Waving to them through the window, Mrs Pengelly pulled the bell pull again. 'Sam, bring everyone up. Everyone – including Tamsin and Rowan.'

We heard their footsteps and waited as they filed into the room. Rowan rushed to my side, slipping her hand into mine. Sam shut the door and Mrs Pengelly cleared her throat. 'Thank you . . . now, tell me truthfully, have any of you let slip the fact that Mrs Barnard is Mrs Pelligrew? Other than when Captain Pierre was here?'

Vigorous headshakes followed her question. They stood grim-faced, surprised, Tamsin with sudden tears in her eyes. 'No . . . not said a word . . . No,' they repeated.

'And Elowyn? Does she know?'

Again, firm shakes of their heads. 'No . . . not from me . . . not at all.'

Mrs Pengelly breathed deeply. 'The situation is this: Madeleine's husband was a profligate gambler and she can expect nothing from Sir Charles. Even so, there's a glimmer of hope . . . some slight chance . . . but it's vital we keep her true identity hidden.' She smiled at Rowan. 'Miss Madeleine will soon be examined by two physicians who have to prove she's in *sound mind*. We all know she is, but we have to make sure no one links her to the madhouse. She's Mrs Barnard and her husband was a book binder.'

Rowan nodded, smiling back at me, and Mrs Pengelly continued: 'They won't ask you if they don't see you. So, my love, stay in the kitchen when they come. Madeleine, tell them about your jewels.'

I cleared my throat. 'Mrs Munroe, you said there was no stealing up at the hall – that theft warranted immediate dismissal? How does the housekeeper know when a theft occurs?'

341

Rowan smiled up at me. 'Mrs Pumfrey has everything in her book. She knows just where to put things. We'd clean an' polish, then she'd open the trunk and place everything exactly where her book said it should go.'

Mrs Munroe nodded. 'That's right. Everything's recorded in the housekeeping book . . . everything down to the last teaspoon.'

I fought my surge of hope. 'What about personal jewellery? Would Sir Charles's wife, or any of her daughters, disclose what jewellery they had in their dressing table?'

Again Mrs Munroe nodded. 'What isn't locked away in the steward's office is recorded. Ye have to understand it's to protect the servants. The mistress could just as easily pretend something was stolen when it wasn't even there. Good housekeepers know to record *everything.*'

Mrs Pengelly glanced at me. 'That's what I thought. Any jewellery not put in the safe, but kept in their dressing tables, is recorded in the housekeeper's book?'

'Everything gets written down. There's a lot to being a housekeeper. Watching yer back is the first thing ye learn.' Mrs Munroe sniffed, a sudden beaming smile. 'Course, if we're goin' back to when Miss Madeleine was there, it would be in the old housekeeper's book in Mrs Pumfrey's office. No one would have thought to move it.'

'And if the mistress was to leave the house unexpectedly?'

Mrs Munroe smiled back at me. 'I wasn't there then. But if they found ye gone, the first thing they'd do was check the dressing table an' take yer jewellery to Mr Kemp. The housekeeper, Sarah Nicholls, would have seen to that. Mr Kemp would lock it in the safe and make a careful list. It'll be in his records — as well as in the housekeeping book. Everything will be on their lists.'

'I believe Sir Charles dismissed them both?'

She pursed her lips. 'They were both discredited. Once disgraced, they couldn't find work. They left the county.'

'Mr Reith said Nathaniel Kemp had died.'

'He took to drink and Sarah Nicholls left Cornwall for the north.'

'So we have no one to ask.'

There was a gleam in her eye, a sudden sniff. 'Well . . . that's not entirely the case. Maybe I could take a day or two's leave, Mrs Pengelly? I've an old friend in Redruth I've not seen fer a while.'

Chapter Forty-one

Mrs Pengelly straightened the crisp pile of papers, looking round the room. 'They can sit with their backs to the window. I'll sit here, and Miss Madeleine can sit here. Perhaps, Tamsin, you should fetch more blotting paper – and more ink?'

Tamsin curtsied. 'And lemons. Mrs Munroe says she'll make lemonade for them. She's making oatcakes with raisins – she said I should serve them something when they've finished.'

Dressed in his Sunday best, his red silk cravat perfectly tied, Sam had polished his boots and washed his hair. Positioning two further chairs in one corner, he straightened. 'I have the list, Mrs Pengelly. Fifteen names. Are these chairs right here?'

On Sam's insistence we had taken the silver from the sideboard, Tamsin had polished the furniture and the room gleamed. The smell of beeswax was to be inviting, not intimidating, and Mrs Pengelly had everything ready. She stood back, nodding her approval. 'I don't know who to ask to witness the statements. Rose wants to, but she can't if Sir James is going

344

to represent Pierre. It must look impartial. We need someone from the town.'

Sam was talking to a man in the hall, their voices drifting through the open door. 'Well . . . that's very kind . . . perhaps . . . just one moment.' He stood in the doorway. 'It's Oliver Jenkins, Mrs Pengelly. He's come with a list of his own. He says people don't like what's happened to Captain Pierre.' His mouth trembled. 'He says they don't think it's right he was arrested.'

'Oliver Jenkins?' Mrs Pengelly glanced at Tamsin's suddenly scorched cheeks. 'Let him come in.'

Tall, lanky, with a crop of frizzy hair, Oliver Jenkins looked to be in his mid-twenties. Eyes down, twisting his cap, his cheeks were the colour of Tamsin's. 'Forgive my intrudin', Mrs Pengelly, only there's a lot of talk in the town. People don't like what's happened to Captain Pierre. They put their names down – here, I've a list of those who saw everything. Only they think someone should . . . *know* . . . an' I thought, well, I knew Captain Pierre often visited here . . . an' I was hoping that I might help him in some way. He weren't escaping. All of us knows that.'

I fought my tears; so, too, did Mrs Pengelly. She took the list, her eyes widening. 'But there's . . . nearly thirty names on this list! We have our own list . . . another fifteen. That's very helpful. Thank you, Oliver.'

'Only Captain Pierre isn't an enemy to us. He's a kind man – he's . . . well, he's liked fer *himself* because he's a good man.'

I had to hold back my tears, his words burning my heart. Oliver Jenkins risked a glance at Tamsin and smiled shyly, all of us smiling, trying not to cry. Sam coughed, straightening his cravat. 'I'll copy these names on to one long list. We're to start taking evidence, Oliver. I might need yer help.'

'Father says I can spend whatever time I need. Honest, the town's not happy. I can get more names – they saw what they saw. Captain de la Croix was shoutin' to *stop* the ship. He called to alert Sir James – he wanted his cutter to follow them out.'

Mrs Pengelly reached for her handkerchief. 'He wanted Sir James's ship alerted?'

'Yes, Mrs Pengelly, *L'Aigrette* was anchored close by. I've thirty men who'll swear to that. It was busy on the harbour an' he shouted at the top of his voice for the ship to follow. People heard him and they watched him row out. That's what they want recorded – that he shouted *before* he took the oars.'

'Thank you, Oliver . . . and please thank your father. Sam will need your help to bring everyone here in turn. It's going to take some organisation.'

Another knock on the front door and Sam went to open it. A man's voice, footsteps, someone standing in the doorway, and I caught a glimpse of a well-built man with greying brown hair, good quality clothes and strong working hands. A prosperous man of the town.

'Thomas . . . how lovely to see you.' Mrs Pengelly rose, smiling at me. 'This is my dear friend Thomas Scantlebury – he's a shipwright. He runs my husband's boatyard. Well, it's his boatyard really, but he won't change the name.'

His eyes crinkled behind his glasses. 'Or rather your daughter won't let me!'

'Thomas, may I introduce Mrs Barnard?'

His bow was respectful, his physique strong for a man of his age. 'Delighted to meet ye, Mrs Barnard.' He turned round, surveying the room. 'I don't know if I can be of any help, Eva, but I saw what happened. The whole town saw it and not one of us think it right. I know Captain de la Croix was a friend of yours . . . and I was talkin' to Reverend Bloomsdale. We think we should instigate some sort of appeal.'

The lump in my throat was set to choke me, my tears hard to keep back. The whole town was uniting behind the man I loved; he was their enemy, a proud captain in the French navy, but they saw only his goodness, knowing him for the man he was. I clutched my handkerchief to my face, hardly hearing what they said. Mrs Pengelly pointed to the chairs where Mr Scantlebury and Reverend Bloomsdale would sit, Sam comparing the names on the list, Tamsin showing Oliver Jenkins where she was going to lay out the jug of lemonade and plates of oat biscuits. I put my hand on his silver watch hanging from a chain beneath my gown and shut my eyes.

I could feel Pierre holding me. It felt so real, and I knew in some dismal prison he, too, would be shutting his eyes, reliving our last embrace. My love, his love, reaching across the miles, our souls united. Never again to part.

The mahogany clock on the mantelpiece chimed eleven and Mrs Pengelly turned in surprise. 'Goodness, we'll be late.' She smiled up at her dear friend, Thomas Scantlebury. 'We can't keep Elowyn waiting. That niece of yours is a terrible stickler for timing.'

Rowan skipped along the road, her hand in mine. Mrs Pengelly was smiling, holding her bonnet as she hurried by my side. This time, I welcomed the women's smiles, their passing nods and bows, their curtsies and kind expressions. Their looks of concern. The town was united, several shaking their heads; Admiral Pendarvis had been heavy-handed, arresting a man they knew was doing no wrong.

Mrs Pengelly stopped to catch her breath. 'Captain Pierre's been visiting Fosse for four years and everyone would like to see him happy.' Another acquaintance looked as if she was about to stop us, so she hurried me on. 'I'll be right behind you,' she whispered.

The door of the Old Forge was ajar, Elowyn surrounded by dressmaker's dummies covered with white sheets. 'No one must catch even the smallest glimpse of another gown. I've promised all my ladies their gowns won't be seen until the ball.' Her dress was immaculate but her hair was coming loose beneath her lace cap. Her cheeks were flushed, the table spilling over with silks and ribbons. She took a deep breath. 'Forgive me, Mrs Barnard, I have your gown under...' She peeped under several of the sheets. 'Yes. Here. Rowan, lock the front door ... just in case anyone comes in.'

Elowyn was clearly taken aback by the dress I was wearing, but tried not to show her surprise. 'Your gown is very beautiful...'

'Lady Pendarvis had it in her charity trunk. I don't think anyone's worn it. There's hardly any allowance in the seams so Mrs Pengelly thinks the previous owner must have become with child.'

'Very likely – which is why I always allow plenty of allowance in mine.' She stopped, her voice breaking. 'Oh Mrs Barnard, I've heard, of course – everyone's heard.'

Crossing the room, she held out a piece of paper. 'This morning, three of my ladies brought in this signed paper – they saw everything from their windows. Most of the houses overlook the river and I asked them to give me names of any other ladies who might have been watching.' She straightened. 'William's going to write to Sir James. They say Pierre wanted the ship *stopped*. Lady Pendarvis is my very generous patron and I owe her everything, but we believe Sir Alex acted wrongly when he arrested Pierre.'

She led me behind the screen, helping me undo my gown. Holding it to the light, she examined the stitches. 'This is very well made ... very fine. There ... I'll get your new gown. I'm thrilled with it. We'll make you another turban. I understand you lost your other one in the river.'

Mrs Pengelly arrived but a sadness prevailed, none of us feeling like laughing or gossiping. She insisted on a new dress for Rowan, promising her that Lady Polcarrow would let her watch the dancing from the top of the stairs. There was going to be dancing on a podium and she needed a pretty dress. We hardly heard the first knock, but the second knock was louder. Elowyn hurried to open the door.

'Billy ... Billy ... by all that's wonderful ...'

A deep, throaty voice answered. 'I came the moment I heard. I've tried Coombe House but they say she's here? Elowyn ... is it really her?' His voice grew muffled: I guessed he was taking off his coat and hat.

'We've no doubt... but see for yourself. She's a lovely girl an' the spit of you at that age.'

Rowan's cheeks paled. Gripping her hands against her chest, she looked like a rabbit caught in a trap. I could see hope, fear, the desperate wanting in her eyes. Elowyn pulled back the screen and any doubt I had that she was Billy's sister vanished with his smile. He was taller than the etchings led me to believe, broader in the chest, a man not a youth, but he had her exact same nose, the same wavy black hair. The same big eyes, the same hope. Dressed smartly in a brown corduroy jacket and breeches, he walked towards her, holding out his hands. 'So... you're my little sister, Betsy?'

Her tentative smile grew broader, tears welling in her eyes. 'That's what they say... I've so little memory... just a boy with dark hair turnin' round... going rabbitin'. But I remember the folly... an' when I saw the drawing of ye, it was as if I knew ye. Like my heart was opening... like I felt happy.' She put her hands in his and he held them to his heart.

'Betsy... we've been searching for you.' He let go of her hand, reaching for his handkerchief. 'Never too old to cry ... just don't let William see this.' He laughed, smiling back at us, then noticed me and bowed. 'Your servant, madam. Billy Bosco, at your service.'

Elowyn stepped forward. 'This is Mrs Barnard. We have her to thank for bringing Rowan to us. Billy, Rowan doesn't know herself as Betsy. She's been brought up as Rowan and wants us to call her that.'

'I understand. You remember nothing of our parents?'

I could not be jealous of this charming man. He was tall,

350

strong, bursting with purpose. They almost mirrored each other. Rowan would grow tall like he was – she would be as refined and educated, her manners as charming. There was no envy in my heart, just a flood of pride.

We watched them in the courtyard, Billy showing Rowan round, winding up the bucket from the well, taking water to the pig in the pigsty. He showed her the forge, William greeting him with a warm embrace, laughing with him, teasing him, getting Billy to fetch him a tool from the wall. Every step they took warmed my heart. She was not *sent* to me from Heaven, but *lent* to me. She saved me and I would never stop loving her. But she belonged with her brother.

Elowyn joined them and we knew to leave Rowan with them. Mrs Pengelly reached for her basket and we stepped into the courtyard, but Billy came bounding over. 'I've just been told about Pierre. Mrs Pengelly, we have to do something.' He frowned down at me. 'I'd like to help. What can I do? There must be something . . .'

Mrs Pengelly's eyes held such love for him. 'Billy, do you remember your hiding places round here – the best shelters . . . somewhere a vagrant boy might still hide? An urchin boy warned Pierre that Mrs Barnard was on the ship.'

'Rowan's just told me. And yes . . . I do have ideas where to look.'

'The boy was crabbing on the rocks – Madeleine, describe him to Billy.'

'I hardly saw him. He was less than my shoulder in height . . . thin, painfully thin. Dark eyes, brown hair. Gaunt cheeks. I only saw him briefly. I . . . I didn't see him very clearly.'

'Was he wearing a jacket?'

'No, a shirt. Bare legs and bare feet.'

'Was he wearing a cap? What colour was his shirt?'

'Brown... his cap, too – probably muddy. His face was dirty. But that could be any one of them.'

He smiled and I fought my tears. He was being so kind. He glanced at Mrs Pengelly. 'There'll be something different about him. People assume vagrants all look alike but they don't. Mrs Barnard, if you don't mind... maybe if you shut your eyes and go back in your mind. Picture the jetty.'

I shut my eyes. I could see the boy glancing across at me, but he was just as I had described him. 'It's how I said.'

Again his voice, deep, unhurried, somehow calming me. 'Take your time... take away all sense of fear and just think back. The boy was crabbing... what do you see?'

The sun was on my face, my tight shoulders slowly relaxing. The boy was clearer to me now, but it was just as I had said. 'No, wait... there's something. He had a leather thong around his neck – under his shirt. Yes... a thin leather thong around his neck.'

I opened my eyes to see his flash of pleasure. 'I can find him from that. You just need something.' Rowan had joined us and he bowed to us all. 'It's a while since I've gone *crabbin'*. Now, *limpets* are much easier to collect.' At the gate he turned and smiled. 'I'll find him for you, Mrs Barnard. I promise.'

Chapter Forty-two

Mrs Munroe handed Tamsin a fresh jug of lemonade and she hurried back to the mayhem above. She looked flushed and happy, hardly spilling a drop, and Rowan leaned closer, her hand over her mouth.

'Ye know she's sweet on Oliver, don't ye?' She giggled. 'And he's sweet on her!'

Mrs Munroe winked and returned to her baking and I dipped my paintbrush into the jug of water. 'I had guessed... There, that's the last. I think I've finished.'

We stared down at the painting of my jewellery, every piece of my *parure* reproduced: my earrings with their blue sapphires, the necklace with its green emeralds and red rubies, the intricate gold bows and diamond flower on my brooch. I had drawn the inlaid box with its velvet lining – seven pieces of matching jewellery, lovingly given to me by my grandmother.

'Did ye really wear these? I can't imagine anything so grand.'

'Never all at once. They're to be worn on different occasions.

Some, you'd wear for a ball, but others . . . like this clasp, would be for the day. These earrings were my favourite. See . . . these huge blue stones are sapphires and these are all diamonds.'

'Wait till the ball. There'll be diamonds and all sorts.' Mrs Munroe wiped the flour from her cheek, keeping her hands away from the paintings. 'Ye've done a lovely job. Ye're quite a painter, aren't ye, Miss Madeleine?'

Tamsin came running down the stairs carrying a bunch of ox-eye daisies, and my heart jolted. 'Honest to God, there's more people upstairs than we've room fer. Oliver's got them in line – it's going that well.' She handed me the flowers and a piece of paper. 'So many people wanting the best fer Captain Pierre. These were left at the door.'

'Thank you . . . Rowan, my love, find me a—' I stopped, staring at the note. *To Mrs Barnard, from a well-wisher, C.L.* They were her initials, the flowers picked from the linhay. Cécile Lefèvre had received my note.

Rowan placed the flowers in the jug. 'Mrs Munroe . . . have you a flask we can take water in and a spare basket? Pierre used to pick these flowers up at the linhay. I'd like to take the paints up there and paint him the view he loved so much.'

She nodded, no doubt desperate to have the kitchen table back to herself. Packing a basket, she could not get us away quickly enough. 'Off ye go, both of ye.'

It seemed too painful to go back. Rowan skipped by my side, holding my hand, the air freshening as we climbed the hill. I could see Pierre at every turn, watching beetles and butterflies, his hands on his hips. Wading into the sea with his trousers rolled to the knee. He was in every flower, every call of the birds. Every beat of my heart. As we entered the linhay, the milk churn had gone. I knew I would not find it. Cécile Lefèvre wanted me to know she had received my warning but I would never meet her.

'Are you all right, Madeleine?'

'Let's paint our pictures . . . I'm going to draw those daisies framed by the window. What will you paint?'

She unpacked the basket, drawing out our paper and paints. 'The sea . . . and that ship there. He won't mind if it's not any good, will he?'

Love shone in her eyes. This darling, darling girl. 'He'll love anything you do.'

Never have I painted with more feeling, every stroke bringing him nearer. It was as if the linhay understood my heartache, as if the wind slowly lessened so that the flowers could stay still. As if the sun burst forth to highlight the vibrancy of the poppies, the pink blush of the foxgloves. As if the butterflies knew to linger, the beetles to stop halfway across the bricks. Everything conspiring to bring back the lonely man who had watched them with such reverence.

Our paintings drying, Rowan lay on the blanket looking up at the skylarks. 'I've never just lain an' looked up at the sky. I can hear them but I don't see them.'

I forced myself to glance upwards. No sudden rush of fear, no sense of being lifted, not pulled from the earth and whirled around. No giddiness. No terror. Just a beautiful blue sky and harmless white clouds. As if the linhay had understood that, too, and healed me. 'We'll paint the clouds next time,' I whispered.

On the way home, the windows of Admiral House glinted in the sun and I looked to the room where Pierre had stayed. Major Hyssop and Lady Pendarvis had only seen this end of the river; they had not seen what the town had seen. The door opened and a footman came swiftly down the stairs. His call was slightly breathless. 'Lady Pendarvis would like to see you. This way, please.'

It was not an invitation, it was a summons, and we followed him up the steps and into the spacious hallway. Rowan looked round, petrified, but I smiled in reassurance, putting down our baskets to pick grass from her shawl. 'Head up. And a nice deep curtsy.'

Above us, the portraits of Captain Edward and Celia Pendarvis filled the hall with vibrant energy. The footman stood waiting by the door and I picked up our baskets. It was the same room, the vast windows overlooking the river mouth, the pianoforte in the corner. I could picture Pierre by the fireplace, his arms around me.

'Mrs Barnard, there is something you must know.' Lady Pendarvis was not alone, by her side was a lady of about her height, younger than me, and I curtsied, unable to look away from her piercing blue eyes. 'May I introduce Lady Polcarrow?'

I was thrown by her beauty, searching to find words. This was *Miss Rose*, Mrs Pengelly's daughter. No wonder she had caught the eye of Sir James Polcarrow. She was tall, elegant, with chestnut-red hair, a perfect oval face and dark mesmerising lashes. Her hat was at an angle, her collar high, her maroon jacket short, her cream gown almost clinging to her legs. Rowan's eyes widened.

'Mrs Barnard, I'm delighted to meet you. My mother's told me you're her guest... and you must be Rowan?' Rowan curtsied deeply and Lady Polcarrow flashed an enchanting smile. 'What lovely ribbons you have on your bonnet.'

Lady Pendarvis, by comparison, looked stern, indicating we might like to sit down, her gravity cutting like a knife. 'We have found the owner of the rowing boat. Lady Polcarrow has just this minute told me the boat belongs to her husband's ship. Captain Jago was collecting provisions before he sailed. He's given a very comprehensive account...'

I sat down, suddenly breathless. 'He heard Pierre shout to follow the ship?'

Lady Pendarvis shook her head. 'No, Mrs Barnard. He was collecting barrels of water off the quay and returned to find his boat gone. He went back to the yard to arrange for another rowing boat as he needed to catch the tide. He was in a hurry and left without searching for his missing boat.'

'It's rather awkward.' Lady Polcarrow sounded like her mother. 'Captain Jago plies his trade independently of Sir James. It's a commercial venture – ships must pay their way. Sir James encourages him to trade alongside our need of the ship. As soon as he returned and heard the rumpus, Captain Jago came straight to us.' She smiled, her mesmerising eyes turning serious. 'My husband's convinced of Captain de la Croix's innocence. He believes Pierre's misguided chivalry was well intended – and he says that, in Pierre's shoes, he would have done the same.'

Her smile brought tears to my eyes. 'And Captain Jago's testimony will hold sway?'

'Together with the outpouring of condemnation from the town!' She raised her eyebrows at Lady Pendarvis. 'My husband will be advocate for his release. Sir Alex acted in the only way he could, but Captain de la Croix will have the best representation he can.' Rowan slipped her hand through mine and Lady Polcarrow smiled. 'Be strong for your mother, my dear. Sir James will leave for Bodmin on Monday. He'll need all the evidence by then.'

Lady Polcarrow and Lady Pendarvis were clearly good friends. Lady Pendarvis nodded. 'Pierre is held in a small cell in Bodmin. By small, I mean tiny. It has two other inmates, but he has a window – not that it opens. Sir Alex has arranged for him to wash and change his clothes. Also for food to be brought in. If Pierre can withstand these conditions for the next few weeks, I believe we have a chance to clear his name.'

I had to stay brave. 'Lady Polcarrow . . . would you mind asking your husband to give these paintings to Pierre?'

'Of course.' She took the rolled-up paintings and I turned to Lady Pendarvis.

'And if they find him guilty of attempting to escape?'

I saw the compassion in her eyes. 'It will mean imprisonment. Sir Alex will do his utmost to have him sent to Norman Cross near Peterborough. The conditions may be harsh, but better there than anywhere else.'

Rowan gripped my hand. 'Then we shall follow him, won't we?'

I drew her to me, holding her like I would never let her go. 'Yes, my love. We'll follow him . . . we'll stay near him. We'll visit him every day until this horrible war is over.'

Holding hands, we walked out into the hall. A footman opened the front door, and I would have stepped out but Rowan pulled my hand back. 'Look . . .' she whispered, staring up at the portrait of Celia Pendarvis.

Her intelligent eyes were staring back at us, her expression knowing, lofty, but not arrogant. She even seemed amused. 'That's Celia Pendarvis . . . Lady Pendarvis's daughter-in-law.'

'I know. But look at her earrings. They're like the ones in yer painting.'

I stared, transfixed. I had not noticed them before, but there were my earrings – there in plain sight. Hurrying back to Coombe House, we tore down the steps to the kitchen. My paintings were dry and I scooped them up, rushing them to Mrs Pengelly. She put on her glasses, examining the painting of the large sapphires with their ring of diamonds. She drew a sudden breath. 'Yes, my dear, the exact likeness. She's wearing them in her portrait but now I think about it, I've not seen her wear them for years.' Her eyes held mine. 'She used to wear them a lot. I believe she told me they were a gift from her father.'

Chapter Forty-three

Coombe House
Tuesday 1st July 1800, 2 p.m.

Mrs Munroe stood in her Sunday best, her bag on the floor next to her stout leather shoes. 'Just four days, no more. Tamsin's got her instructions. Ye'll not go hungry.'

Mrs Pengelly ushered her to the door. 'I'm certain we won't. You're to think no more about us. You're to go and enjoy yourself. We'll be perfectly well looked after by Tamsin and Sam.'

'Only the pie needs eatin' first, then the glazed ham. There's newly picked raspberries and I've left a Madeira cake an' there's a rhubarb tart...'

'Sam will carry your bag and see you on to the coach. You're not to think of us. Have an enjoyable visit and let's hope you're successful.'

If Mrs Munroe looked exhausted, so did Sam and Tamsin. Mrs Pengelly had even cut short her visit to her grandchildren. The silver was back in the dining room, the chairs rearranged, the paper and ink returned to the desk drawers. Fifty men and six of Elowyn's ladies had given sworn statements, each saying they had heard Pierre shout out before he picked up the oars. Reverend Bloomsdale had written a character reference, and with Captain Jago and Mr Scantlebury the total came to fifty-nine people, not one of them believing Pierre was attempting to escape. The statements had been packed into a large bag in time for Sir James to take to Bodmin. Yet for all Mrs Munroe's carefully prepared food, I could eat neither breakfast nor lunch. We had less than an hour before Drs Perrow and Underwood would arrive.

Mrs Pengelly smiled at Rowan. 'Best stay in the kitchen with Tamsin. Sam will be back to let them in.'

She seemed as nervous as I was, both of us taking great care with our appearance. I had decided on the soft apricot gown that Lady Pendarvis had given me, my cream turban with the thread of pearls, and my cream jacket. I had pencilled in my eyebrows with the greatest care, applied Elowyn's balm and lip colour. My cheeks looked plumper, and if I could only keep my nerve, I might convince them of my sanity. Mrs Pengelly looked uneasy, a frown creasing her forehead. 'What is it?' I whispered as she shut the door.

'How many Dr Underhills do you think there may be? The name's familiar . . . and not entirely pleasing.'

Fear shot through me. 'Why so?'

'Years ago . . . maybe ten, maybe eleven, a Dr Underhill was in a consortium that commissioned a ship from my husband. The rest were Corporation men – all important men of the town, *all* of them corrupt and self-seeking, lining their pockets at the expense of others.' She paused, a bitterness in her voice I had not heard before.

'Go on.'

'They ordered a cutter, but they were ruthless — driving down the price to barely cover the costs. My husband agreed because his men needed work . . . competition was fierce and yards were falling by the wayside. He completed the ship, paid their wages, but took nothing for himself. Within a month the consortium sold the ship for twice the price.' She swung round. 'That's as may be, I suppose . . . but it's not what's worrying me. At the time, my husband was furious and he investigated the sale of the ship — to find Charles Cavendish had a half-share in the sale.'

'So . . . if this is the same Dr Underhill, you think he'll know Sir Charles?'

'Not necessarily socially acquainted . . . but he certainly had business dealings with him ten years ago. Who knows what other deals they may have struck?'

'Would Matthew know this?'

She took a deep breath. 'He was still in London . . . there was no inquiry into the sale. Nothing was deemed improper. It just fuelled my husband's hatred of Sir Charles.'

'But you'd recognise him?' My heart was racing. None of them could be trusted, they were liars, all of them.

'I never saw him — just his name. I wouldn't remember it except for my husband's fury. He called him Dr *Underhand* . . . said that should be his name.'

The clock on the mantelpiece had barely finished chiming as a carriage pulled up outside the door. Two men sat next to the driver, three more inside, and as Sam opened the door I caught the profile of Matthew Reith. 'Matthew's come with them.'

We watched them shake out their coat-tails, stretching their legs, staring at the door, and I knew I must smile and hide my fear. To keep my hands still, my voice light and respectful. We met them in the hall and Mrs Pengelly pointed to the dining room. 'Please . . . come this way.'

Two men looked to be junior clerks. Both wore black, buttoned-up jackets and starched white cravats. Both had leather bags, respectful downward glances and pale faces. The other two could not be more different. 'Mrs Barnard, may I introduce Dr Perrow?' Matthew was sombrely dressed in black, his white silk cravat neatly pinned with an enamel clip. He smiled politely, indicating the younger of the two men. 'Dr Perrow is from Redruth.'

He was tall, slim, with short black hair and a slight stoop to his shoulders. About my age, his eyes looked kind yet wary, looking over me with professional interest. Perhaps he expected me to be in some attic with spittle on my chin. I curtsied, straight backed, but not too deeply. 'Thank you for coming all this way, Dr Perrow. It's a great imposition on your time. Would you like some refreshments before we start . . . or maybe you'd like to wash your hands?'

He smiled back at me. 'Thank you, but we stopped at the inn just moments ago.'

Dr Underhill had remained outside. He had his back to us, standing at the water's edge as if recalling the ship he had commissioned. Smoke rose from his pipe, his legs slightly apart, his back broad, his stance the stance of a man who

363

would happily cheat a decent shipbuilder, and fear flooded through me. He would trip me up, make me muddle my words. He was like them all. All of them. I took a deep breath. 'Is Dr Underhill going to grace us with his presence?'

Matthew looked stunned but I took no notice. Settling myself at the head of the table, I indicated where I would like everyone to sit. The clerks spread out their papers, arranging their quills, uncorking their ink bottles, and I smiled at Dr Perrow. 'The view is always changing. I love the sea. I was brought up by the sea. Mr Reith, is Dr Underhill going to keep us much longer? I presume I'm paying you all by the hour?'

The astonished glances of the clerks gave me courage. 'I'll . . . I'll . . . see if he's ready, Mrs Barnard.'

Dr Underhill stood red-faced at the door, scowling across the room. Middle-aged, fat-bellied, well-dressed, a gold chain stretching across his elaborate waistcoat, he wore a brown wig, the folds of his chins lost to his cravat, and I fought my fear. I could have been looking at the portrait of Sir Charles. He had the same greedy eyes, the same buckles on his shoes, the same arrogant air. 'So, you are Mrs Barnard, are you?'

I did not rise, but pointed to his empty chair. 'Thank you for coming all this way, Dr Underhill. I appreciate you are very busy men with little time to spare. Mr Reith has, no doubt, told you about my circumstances?'

His piggy eyes glared back at me. 'Mr Reith has asked us to ascertain your *sanity*. He has not told us of your circumstances, however.' He sat down, shifting his belly to face me. 'That, you must tell us for yourself, and . . . *if* we deem you to be of sound mind, then we will leave a signed copy of our statement declaring you as such . . . or we may leave a statement declaring you to be *otherwise*.'

'Perfect.' I smiled, as if he was trying to be witty. They must have no notion of how my knees had buckled as I sat, how hard it was to keep my hands from twisting. I cleared my throat. 'The first thing to record . . . is that I am not Mrs Marie Barnard – that's only what I call myself. A woman of my age does better in society if she's a widow. I was never married to Mr Barnard, and Marie was my mother's name.'

The clerks were writing everything down, both doctors fixing me with a curious look. I knew I must speak with authority. 'I was born Madeleine Eugenia de Bourg and, like so many, I'm an émigrée. I've lost my family, my home in Saint-Malo, and the lands that once belonged to my father – le Comte de Charlbourg. I have nothing but my name and these . . .'

I took my paintings from the side table, spreading them out. 'These belonged to my grandmother. I can only show you a painting of them, but these are why you are here. My grandmother's jewels are worth more to me than money . . . they are all I have of my previous life . . . of my family.' I pressed my handkerchief against my eyes. 'I'm so sorry, forgive me.'

Dr Underhill reached for the paintings, his puffy fingers stained by tobacco. Mrs Pengelly was sitting in the corner, eyes down, her hands clasped. No one had thought to introduce her and I knew she wanted it that way. Matthew Reith remained impassive, staring across the table.

'I've sought representation from Mr Reith because since my husband died, I've lived in pecuniary circumstances. My friends have kindly stepped forward, people are very generous, but what I want is certainty. You see ... I have learned that I was never married to my husband in the eyes of British law. We were married in Saint-Malo, and though he no doubt *intended* to remarry me here in England, our time was cut short. He was drowned ... and I lost the child I was carrying. I cannot believe my husband *intended* me harm but he was reckless and profligate, and I have lived through very difficult circumstances since his death.'

I dabbed my eyes. 'Recently, it's come to my notice that the only thing I can claim as my own – my jewels – may have been tricked from me or, more ruthlessly, kept from me. And that's why I'd like you to examine my mind ... my intellect ... my reasoning.'

Dr Underhill leaned forward, pinning me with gleeful eyes. 'Ah, so you believe someone is after your jewels ... that they will steal them from you? You hear voices telling you they aren't safe? That you, yourself, are in great danger?'

'No. My jewels are perfectly safe. I hear no voices telling me otherwise. It was Mr Reith who suggested I paint them – for clarity ... and precision. Merchants insure their ships and their precious cargos, so I look upon this as a kind of insurance.'

Dr Perrow was watching me carefully. He glanced at his list. 'You hear no voices in your head ... no sense of persecution, that you're being hounded, sought by killers or madmen?'

I shook my head. 'I doubt any of us can stop those thoughts, Dr Perrow. They are what our nightmares consist of. Knowing our families have undergone such terror and we have survived. The pain is unimaginable.'

He coughed, colouring slightly. 'Yes, of course. But forgive me, our questioning must be rigorous. Tell me, why are you going to all this trouble to be certified in sound mind?'

'Because, Dr Perrow, I have been separated from everyone I know for fourteen years. Now I find myself back in society, I realise my jewels are my only hope of financial stability. I must not have others take them from me.'

'You fear people are *watching* you... lurking... hiding behind the doors, in dark crevices... waiting to jump out at you and steal them from you?'

Dr Underhill's breath reeked. I felt like shouting, *Yes, Dr Underhand, stolen from me like everything else. Stolen by men like you. Men who incarcerate women in madhouses. Men who lie and cheat. Men who do not register marriages and trick others out of their due reward.* I had to breathe, I had to rid myself of my fury. I had to think of how this would sound when it was read out in court.

I dabbed my eyes. 'A woman is very vulnerable, Dr Underhill – especially if she is on her own in a different country to her birth and has no husband to protect her. I'd like to believe in the good in everyone – that people don't lie or cheat, that vulnerable women will be protected and not taken advantage of – but I know that's not the case. I also know the claim of insanity is the most powerful tool of all.'

'Well! You believe you'll be *deemed insane* just because someone wants your jewels?' He clearly thought it was funny, but his laughter died on his lips.

'Thank you for your insight, Dr Underhill. That's precisely my point. I call myself Mrs Barnard because under that name,

I can hide my true identity – but as Madeleine de Bourg, rightful owner of jewellery worth upwards of seven hundred pounds, I'm in danger of being deemed of unsound mind by any unscrupulous claimant to my fortune.'

The clock chimed, the scratching of pens stopped. Dr Perrow had been writing but paused. 'You believe that to be true?'

'I know it to be true. That's why I've gone to so much trouble – and expense – to have you examine me. Our fortunes may have disappeared, but fortune seekers haven't. I remain very vulnerable. Fortunately, I have those who know me – in London many knew my family – but what if a man calling himself my cousin should appear and claim my inheritance . . . or a man claiming family debts?'

'You believe he may try to certify you as insane?'

I looked deep into his eyes. 'I'd like to pre-empt such a claim by convincing you I'm of sound mind.'

'Well, we must go through the proper procedure . . . there must be no cause to doubt our findings.' He picked up his list. 'I can see no evidence of mania, dementia or melancholia.' He looked at Dr Underhill, who nodded. 'We can rule out signs of fitting, spasms, uncontrollable tremors of the limbs . . . and general paralysis of the insane. Are we agreed?'

Another nod of the head, a swing of his double chin. 'Agreed.'

'There's no reported evidence of voices heard, no one goading her into harming herself, or anyone else . . . nor is she non-communicative . . . unresponsive . . . nor is she cowering in a corner.'

'Agreed.'

'I can perceive no impairment of intellect . . . no dementing psychosis . . . no loss of cognitive ability.'

Dr Underhill shrugged. 'I agree . . . I can ascertain no loss of reasoning . . . no sense of *undue persecution*. I think this is a waste of all our time. How many women are incarcerated in madhouses for owning jewels?' His hollow laughter sent shivers through me, but I knew to smile.

Matthew Reith remained impassive, likewise making his own notes. He looked up. 'Alas, that's not our business today, gentlemen, though I agree, it would make for a very interesting debate.'

Dr Perrow returned to his list. 'I see no evidence of depressive behaviour, nor wilfulness . . . no undue wandering of the mind, nor an inability to listen and concentrate. No talking to herself . . . no shaking of the limbs, no piercing cries, no shouting, no denying who she is . . . and, to my mind, no indication of moral insanity.'

Dr Underhill searched his list and turned to Matthew Reith. 'Can we rule out evidence of wilfulness and disobedience, do you think?'

Matthew's mouth tightened. 'To whom is she being disobedient?'

'To whom indeed? That's what we're here to find out. *To get to the truth.*'

I knew to smile, remain elegant, refined. Dutiful. To know my place as a woman. Never to step outside my domestic sphere. One day, I would free others from men like this. On my dressing table upstairs Pierre's seagull stood poised to fly. A seagull, not a songbird in a cage; not a woman behind bars. One day, I would free others to fly over the town and look down at the ships and tiled roofs, the winding river, the wooded riverbanks, the fields with cattle.

'Mrs Barnard . . . ?'

'You have more questions?'

'Just to ascertain whether you're aware of the day, the time . . .' Dr Perrow cleared his throat. 'Tell us what's happening in the world, if you would?'

I pointed to the newspaper lying next to Sam's polished silver. 'We've been at war for seven years and there's to be an inquiry into the system of National Defence – the regulations for pay and allowances are being reviewed. At the moment, serjeants receive 1s 6d, corporals 1s 2d, and drummers and privates 1s, but there's mounting pressure to increase that.' I smiled, shrugging my shoulders. 'Napoleon Bonaparte, the Corsican general who's declared himself all but ruler of France, is crossing the Alps to secure Northern Italy because the British blockade remains strong in the Mediterranean. The high duty of salt is causing the pilchard industry to buckle, and now the patent has finally been lifted on the engines, there's a chance that Cornish tin and copper may once again prove profitable . . .'

'That all seems very . . . comprehensive.'

Dr Underhill sniffed. 'King?'

'George the Third.'

'First Minister?'

'Mr William Pitt.'

He reached for his pipe, bringing out his pouch of tobacco.

'One final question.' He looked at Matthew. 'Is the person bringing about the claim whether Mrs Barnard *is or is not* in sound mind satisfied with the examination?'

A slight bristle, a tightening of his mouth, and Matthew looked at me. 'Mrs Barnard . . . you asked for this examination – are you satisfied?'

Dr Underhill roared with laughter. 'It's you I'm asking, Mr Reith. I need your professional assurance there's no *wilfulness* nor *disobedience* on her part. Mrs Barnard submitted to her husband in all matters?'

Matthew nodded. 'I'm entirely satisfied with your examination. You have my robust assurance Madeleine de Bourg showed only devotion and obedience to her late husband. I wouldn't have ventured on this undertaking had I not been totally convinced of the morality and nobility of her behaviour.'

I had just enough strength to thank them and wish them a safe return journey. Any sign of wilfulness and they would tear up the papers and start again. Yet I had done it. No mention of wrongful incarceration, no burning hatred for Sir Charles, no talk of spies or codes and ciphers. No mention of the name Pelligrew or Pendenning Hall. Now they were gone, I found I was shaking.

'Come, my dear . . . sit down.' Mrs Pengelly's eyes were burning.

'My knees were knocking under the table. Look, my hands are still trembling.'

She helped me to a chair. I felt light-headed, as if I might faint. 'You were wonderful, my dear . . . They'll rue the day. Every word you said was true.'

I put my head between my knees. 'I'm more angry than anything . . . you heard Dr Underhill. Only men can speak for us.'

Across the room, Mrs Pengelly looked like any other prosperous widow, a sewing basket on the table next to her, her glasses folded in her hand. Even the miniature portrait of her grandchildren in a silver frame added to her domesticity, but her eyes were resolute. 'That's as may be. My husband held very radical views, and most of my marriage I was frightened by his constant quarrelling. I wanted him to temper his outrage – to be a little less *dissident* in his views – but more recently, I've come to understand his desire to speak out for those with no voice. Fourteen years ago I wouldn't think to question a man's authority, but times are changing. These last years my daughter has influenced my thinking. We must see all women educated.'

My dizziness seemed to be passing. 'Like your school of needlework? There's hardly any sewing done there, is there? Not compared to reading and writing . . . and learning accounts.'

She picked up her sewing, a secretive smile on her lips. 'It's early days, but I believe you'll find a way for your voice to be heard. Maybe not your *spoken* words but your written words? Many will want to read what you have to say.'

She crossed the room, opening the glass cabinet, reaching for a small volume among her books. 'Read this, my dear . . . *A Vindication on the Rights of Women*. Eight years ago, Mary Wollstonecraft wrote a thesis about the need to educate

372

women. Three years ago, she died in childbirth. It is our duty to continue her work.' Handing me the volume, she returned to her seat. 'When the time's right, I'm sure my daughter will find you a sympathetic publisher. Circulating pamphlets are a growing market.' She threaded her needle. 'But only when the time's right.'

The light was fading, a heavy band of clouds threatening rain. We would soon light the candles and ring the bell for tea – a perfect domestic scene, one lady sewing, the other with her hands gently holding a slim book. I took a deep breath. 'Something like . . . *The Power of the Physician's Pen* by a *Person of Standing*?'

'Then they wouldn't know it was written by a woman.'

Courage filled me. '*The Power of the Physician's Pen* by *An Obedient Wife*.'

But for her smile, anyone looking through the window might think we were discussing the price of tea. She pointed her needle at the newspaper. 'Have you read this? I understand the high levy on salt has brought Sir Charles Cavendish rushing down to his warehouses. There's growing unrest – he's raised the price of his salt. The pilchards are soon to run and he's charging three times what the fishermen expect to pay.'

'Is he justified? The tax is quite exorbitant.'

Her earrings swung as she shook her head. 'Sir Charles pay tax?' She laughed. 'Oh Madeleine . . . I just wish Rose had seen you with Dr Underhill. You were quite wonderful. Rose would have so enjoyed it.'

Chapter Forty-four

Thomas Scantlebury stood on the slipway of his shipyard, the masts of his nearly completed lugger looming above us. He wore heavy boots, a leather apron, a tricorn hat, his waistcoat tightly buttoned over his white shirt. A man in his sixties, he had a strong physique, a weather-beaten complexion and eyes that crinkled when he smiled. 'Aye . . . just the last of the caulking . . . there's the final varnish, then there's the wheel to secure. They'll take her upriver to fit the sails and rigging. Ye like her, Miss Rowan?'

Rowan smiled up at him. 'She's beautiful . . . I've never been on a ship.'

Our visit was nearly at an end, the shipyard busy, the noise levels rising. Black smoke billowed from a cauldron of boiling tar, men filling their buckets, balancing along the criss-cross of planks and poles surrounding the hull. The acrid smoke caught my eyes, but Rowan seemed oblivious, smiling and waving to the men as they worked.

374

'We've to build another after this – a brig fer the navy. That'll take a while, mind.'

Mrs Pengelly had clearly enjoyed our visit. 'It's good to see you so busy, Thomas.' Sawyers were planking logs in the saw pit, two blacksmiths hammering in the forge. The day was early, yet already they were stripped to the waist, the sun growing stronger, lighting the coils of ropes by the ladders, glinting on the large windows of the warehouse above us; behind us, a huge anchor lay balanced on a cart. A young man was coordinating the crane to lift it on to the deck, four men turning the heavy wheel. The chain grew taut.

'Clear the yard,' came his urgent shout.

Mrs Pengelly reached for Rowan's hand. 'We mustn't keep you, Thomas . . . we just wanted to thank you. It was so kind of you to give up your time to help Captain Pierre.'

Thomas Scantlebury walked us to the archway at the entrance. 'I've had many a good talk with Pierre. He knows his ships – over the years he's given plenty of sound advice. It's the men that sail the ships that know what's really needed. There's nothing I wouldn't do to help Pierre. Have ye heard anything?' I had to look away. To speak so kindly of Pierre brought tears to my eyes.

'Rose says Sir James has every confidence Pierre will be given a fair hearing. The evidence of fifty-nine people must be fairly compelling.'

'Aye, well. Best get back to work.' He smiled at Rowan. 'Visit us again – an' I'll show you round before she leaves dock. It's a shame we can't call her Rowan. She's another *Dolphin*, would ye believe?'

The town was bustling and I held Rowan's hand, following Mrs Pengelly as she nodded and smiled to just about every passing person. Yet their smiles were not just for her. Each time they greeted her, Mrs Pengelly turned round to introduce me, and each time I was met with the same concern, the same compassion in their eyes, the same kind words.

'Mrs Barnard . . . we're that sorry to hear about Captain Pierre. I can't think of anything more unjust.'

'He don't deserve it – not one little bit. Poor love, he's such a kind man.'

Each way we turned, almost every step. All the women I had previously crossed the road to avoid, the ones I had turned from, expecting their hostility, their censure, their hatred, seemed determined to stop us, even waiting their turn to tell me how highly they esteemed Pierre. How he had mended their clocks for free, how he read to a blind man on the quayside; how he doffed his hat and remembered their names; how he always passed the time of day with them. I felt overwhelmed, fighting my tears. So much love after years of such intense hatred.

'He's meant to be our enemy – if ye read the notices, ye'd think he'd be a savage – but I've had nothing but politeness from Captain Pierre. He's a gentleman, through and through.'

A lady thrust two oranges at me and I held them to my heart. 'Thank you.' Pierre had no idea how much they esteemed him. How much they all cared.

Mrs Pengelly slipped her arm through mine. 'Come, let's get you home.'

The tide was in, the sun glinting on the water. We were

almost at Coombe House when Rowan's happy shout made me look up. 'Look, 'tis Billy . . . He's found the boy.'

She started running, holding on to her bonnet, her ribbons flying. Reaching Billy, he swung her round like Pierre would have done. He was laughing, smiling down at the small boy from the wharf. The boy was thinner than I remembered, younger, his spindly legs too long for his trousers. He was wearing the same scruffy shirt, a filthy waistcoat, his hair curling to his shoulder beneath his worn cap. Eyes wide with fear, he stood cowering behind Billy, and I watched Rowan take his hand, smiling at him as she led him back to us.

He was clearly reluctant, as if at any moment he might run away. 'Ye've nothing to fear,' she said. 'I'll help ye. We're that glad to find ye. What's yer name?'

He seemed too scared to speak. 'Opie. My name's Opie.'

Sam opened the front door, but Mrs Pengelly shook her head. 'We'll go down the back stairs to the kitchen. You look hungry, Opie. Let's see what Tamsin can find you to eat.'

Billy followed us down the stairs, his tall frame blocking the light. Rowan sat Opie at the scrubbed pine table, smiling with encouragement. 'Ye look half-starved, Opie. Don't be frightened. This's Mrs Pengelly . . . this's Tamsin . . . and that's Sam . . . Ye know my brother, Billy . . . and this is Mrs Barnard, my mother.'

I had to turn away, pretend to untie my bonnet. It was the love in her eyes, the way she called me her mother. Billy seemed much at home, reaching into the cupboards for a plate, lifting the top off the biscuit barrel. Tamsin rushed to the larder for the untouched ham, Sam placed a loaf on the table.

Mrs Pengelly dipped a cup into the milk churn and handed it to Opie. He looked overwhelmed, draining the contents, his large eyes watching from over the brim. He wiped his mouth with his filthy sleeve. 'I didn't do nothin' wrong. I only said what I saw.'

Mrs Pengelly pulled her chair nearer. 'And thank goodness you did. You did a wonderful thing, Opie. You're not in any trouble . . . far from it.'

Billy drew up a chair. 'I told you they'd be pleased to see you. No one thinks anything but good of you. Was Mrs Barnard the lady you saw on the wharf? The one you rushed to tell Captain Pierre about?' He nodded, and Billy smiled. 'Here's some ham and bread. Chew it carefully, lad, small bits at a time.'

The boy nodded, his hands reaching out, and I thought my heart would break. This half-starved boy, falling on a plate of food just like I had. I could feel his hunger and the pain that would follow if he ate too quickly. 'How did you know to tell Captain Pierre?' I asked as Tamsin passed him a plate of rhubarb pie.

'I saw ye together by the river . . . on Sunday when everyone's at church. I came looking for Captain Pierre but he was busy with you.' His large eyes welled with tears. 'I came looking – not because of what he gives me but because he talks so nice to me. Wants to know if I'm all right. Not fer what he gives me.' His hand flew to his chest.

Billy's eyes sharpened. 'What have you got round your neck, Opie?'

'I didn't steal it. He gave it me. He said he had no money but if I sold his trinket I'd get money to eat.' He drew up the thong, cradling an intricately carved heart in his hand. 'He makes them from bone. He told me to sell it.'

Billy shook his head. 'When did he give you this?'

'Last time he was here . . . March it was.'

'Opie, you could have sold this for at least two shillings.'

'Didn't want to sell it, did I?' Tears filled his eyes. 'I've never been given nothin' before. It's . . . it's like he cares. Like having someone love me. I've never had anyone so kind to me as Captain Pierre.'

Billy glanced at Mrs Pengelly. 'Seven years ago, I sat at this very table as hungry as you were. I know what it's like, Opie. I know how every day you live on your wits, but not to sell something like this makes you very strong. Who looks after you?'

Rowan slipped her hand on to his. 'Ye can tell them, Opie. They've nothin' but goodness in their hearts.' He must be about eight. His boots had gaping holes in them, his trousers held up with a piece of rope. Mud streaked his cheek, his fingernails black. She nodded in encouragement. 'Ye've no family?'

'I have. I have.' The poor boy looked petrified.

'Where are they, Opie?'

'Back in Mevagissey I've no parents, but an uncle. He got pressed. He got taken. A man came with a shilling an' that was that. Next day, my aunt put me on a ship to Fosse. Said I was to live with my grandfather. She said she'd too many mouths to feed without me eatin' everything.'

'So you live with your grandfather, Opie?'

He shook his head. 'They'd got him in the almshouse. He

379

was being cared for when I saw him. He said how proud he was of me . . . that he loved me, but he couldn't offer me nothing because he was too ill. He said if I stayed, they'd take me . . . they'd have me in some workhouse. He said go back to my aunt.'

'But you didn't?'

Tears welled in his eyes. 'I did . . . I did just what he said. My uncle wasn't always good to us but he was no worse than most. But she was never nice to me. Still, I went back. But they'd gone. The whole family – my aunt an' five cousins had upped and gone. The woman next door said she'd gone back to her mamm an' told me not to follow.'

'So you came back to your grandfather?'

'No. I came back because I like it here. I never troubled my grandfather again, but I saw them take him out. He's in a pauper's grave an' I visit him. I tell him what I do – but I won't let anyone take me.'

'Where d'you sleep, Opie? How d'you eat?' Rowan's eyes were full of tears.

'I run errands, an' I muck out pigs. People give me food fer doin' things for them. I sleep in the hayloft behind the stables of the Pack Horse Inn. The innkeeper must know but he don't send me away. His missis leaves leftover food outside the back door. Many go there. You'd be surprised how many. She puts out what's left of the day. She's very kind like that.'

Mrs Pengelly slid the biscuit jar along the table. 'Opie, Captain Pierre needs you very badly. He's been arrested for breaking his parole – that means they think he was trying to escape – he faces imprisonment until the war's over. We need

380

you to tell everyone what you saw and what you told Captain Pierre on the quayside. They're important men and they'll make you scared... but what you tell them will help Captain Pierre more than anything else. Will you do that for him?'

Opie nodded and Billy smiled, his hand reaching into the biscuit barrel. 'I'll be with you the whole time. How d'you fancy a ride in a stagecoach? We need to go to Bodmin. We may be gone several weeks.'

Tamsin had been busy at the hearth, lifting the lid on the enormous copper cauldron. The steam rose and she jumped back. 'There now! Opie, if you're to save Captain Pierre we better get ye bathed.'

Rowan slipped from his side as if she had lived there all her life. 'Mrs Pengelly... shall I look in here for somethin' Opie can wear?' She lifted the lid of the charity box.

Mrs Pengelly shook her head. 'No, my love. Sam can run to Jenna. Her two boys are forever outgrowing their clothes and she's plenty given her. She'll have something. First, though ... Opie, will you let Sam cut your hair? Let's get you looking like a real gentleman.'

We waved them off, Opie, scrubbed clean beneath a new set of clothes, looking so small next to Billy, and my heart wrenched. Mrs Pengelly saw me reach for my handkerchief and slipped her arm through mine. 'Let's ask Reverend Bloomsdale what he knows about Opie,' she whispered.

Chapter Forty-five

The Vicarage was on the bend behind the church. Built of grey stone, it boasted a sturdy slate roof and a grand front door. I had often thought it sombre, yet today the sun glinted on the brightly painted sash windows, lighting the profusion of roses round the front door. The imposing wall of the Polcarrow estate dominated one side of the garden, a flowering orchard and a flock of honking geese on the other. Mrs Pengelly opened the iron gate and I followed her up the steps. A maid ushered us across the hall and into Reverend Bloomsdale's study. Peering over his glasses, his face broke into a smile.

'Ah, Mrs Pengelly . . . Mrs Barnard . . . what a pleasure this is.' He indicated a large book lying open on the table. 'Here . . . let me show you.' He turned it round. 'Mr Opie Burrows was admitted to the almshouse six months ago. Born in this parish . . . he worked as an itinerant labourer – mainly on the Pendenning estate. His family were evicted from the estate and they found work elsewhere. In Penzance, as it happens. He and his brother became tinners but Mr Burrows returned to Fosse when the mine closed, again picking up work as an itinerant labourer . . . stone picker . . . gleaner, that sort of thing. He was fifty-five when he died of . . .' He adjusted his glasses. 'A *purulent cough . . . muscle wasting . . . and fatigue.*'

Behind him the sun lit his white hair. 'I believe he had a difficult life. His wife and daughter died of dysentery in Penzance. His eldest son drowned while fishing – that's Opie's father – his other son was the fisherman in Mevagissey. The uncle who was pressed.'

With his creased brow and long white hair, Reverend Bloomsdale might be taken as stern, yet his voice was full of compassion. 'Young Opie's mother died a while back – giving birth to her next child – and Opie was taken in by his uncle until the press gang got hold of him. I believe they lived hand to mouth.'

'What was he like – the grandfather?'

'A very sick man. Pleasant and quietly spoken . . . grateful, and extremely concerned about his grandson. We talked at length in March. He told me about the boy – said he'd told him to return to his aunt. He said the boy was eight and would soon be able to help her. We both thought Young Opie had returned to Mevagissey.'

'When did he die?'

'End of March. He was never strong . . . it was never going to be very long.'

The ache in my heart cut deeper. 'Opie's been living off his wits for over three months? You never saw him visit his grandfather's grave?'

A sad shake of his head. 'No, Mrs Barnard — I wish I had. I may have seen the boy around, but I had no idea who he was. I believe Young Opie was terrified we might take him away so he never came forward. He wasn't born in this parish and I think his grandfather instilled great fear of the workhouse in him — he wanted Opie back with his aunt before he died. And who can blame him?'

'Who indeed? But we mustn't keep you any longer.' Mrs Pengelly lifted her basket. 'Reverend Bloomsdale . . . my housekeeper's returning from a few days away and if she finds food left in the house, we'll be in trouble.' She smiled as I lifted my basket. 'There's cold ham and pies . . . and potted crab . . . and a tub of calf's foot jelly. There's two loaves that need eating and a whole apple tart. We'd be very grateful if you'd find a home for it.'

Reverend Bloomsdale reached for the bell pull. 'You're very generous — your gifts of food are always appreciated. Our residents will enjoy this immensely.' His smile turned conspiratorial. 'I know you need to take back your empty baskets because Mrs Munroe will get suspicious!' Walking us to the door, he stood blinking in the sunshine. 'What a glorious day. Will I see you in church tomorrow, Mrs Barnard?' He reached into his pocket, bringing out a small pair of scissors. 'All are welcome, my dear. Captain Pierre often sits at the back. There . . . a red rose for you, Mrs Pengelly, and this yellow one for you, Mrs Barnard. God bless you, my dears.'

A carriage was hurtling towards us, the crest clearly visible, and fear shot through me. Mrs Pengelly gripped my arm and Reverend Bloomsdale frowned. 'Sir Charles is back.

They say there may even be looting. Best get home and keep indoors.'

Putting down my book, I went to the window to see Sam and Mrs Munroe hurrying down the back steps. 'Yes . . . it's them.'

A slight rise of her eyebrows and Mrs Pengelly put down her sewing. 'Rowan, ask everyone to come up – we'll go into the dining room.'

Mrs Munroe looked flushed, fear in her eyes. 'Shut the door, Sam.'

'Come . . . sit down.' Mrs Pengelly sat in the carving chair, her hands grasped in front of her. 'Take your time. You look very distressed.'

Pulling up her chair, Mrs Munroe whispered, 'My friend remembers *everything*. My goodness . . . where to start? There's so much to tell. When the maids found Miss Madeleine gone in the morning, they called her straight away.'

'Your friend was *my housekeeper*?'

Mrs Munroe nodded. 'Yes, Miss Madeleine, *Sarah Nicholls* – if ye recall. Like I said, she did what I said she'd do. She found ye gone so she summoned the steward, Nathaniel Kemp, and they made a list of all yer possessions. All yer clothes . . . yer clock . . . yer jewels . . . yer brush and mirror set. *Everything*.' She glanced at the door even though it was shut.

'He put my jewels in his safe?'

'Yes, but within the hour they were dismissed by Sir Charles. Both of them OUT – with just one month's pay. They were to pack their things and leave. Dismissed for incompetence.'

385

She gripped the table edge. 'But she was far from incompetent. Her list will be in her housekeeping book – they don't change books when there's a new appointment and Sir Charles won't know that. But that's not all.' Again she glanced at the door. 'Two weeks ago Sarah got a message to meet a man in the back after church. There was no name but she goes... and it's Nathaniel Kemp – out of nowhere... like a ghost.'

Tamsin's hand flew across mouth. 'Was he a ghost?'

'No, my love. Alive like you and me... it's just Nathaniel Kemp didn't die. He's *not dead*. I can't tell ye where he is or what he calls himself, because Sarah wouldn't tell me. He just needed everyone to think he was dead.'

My heart was thumping, pounding in my chest. 'Because he was scared Sir Charles would come after him. Just like Phillip Randall felt the need to record everything in his diaries.'

Behind her steel-rimmed glasses, Mrs Munroe's eyes sharpened. 'After they left Pendenning Hall, Sarah never saw Nathaniel Kemp again... not until two weeks ago. But she did have several visits from Phillip Randall and a man she described to me. Honest to God, it made my flesh creep to hear how she described him. Huge, she said he was... a thickset man... neck like an ox – short, stocky with *tattoos on his hands*. Shaved head... a scar. Evil eyes.'

Mrs Pengelly gripped her hands. 'Sulio Denville.'

'That's just what I thought... but that's not all.' Mrs Munroe leaned forward, inviting us closer. 'Nathaniel Kemp was very particular... he wanted to know if anyone had come asking her questions, whether this man – an' I'm sure he's Sulio Denville – had already found her. More importantly, he asked her if she'd told anyone anything *untoward* about him after she'd been dismissed.'

'About Mr Kemp?'

'Yes, Tamsin . . . and the point is they *had* come askin' and she'd said nothing they found of interest. But she'd been that frightened she left for a position in the north. She's been there all this time and only came back once she knew Phillip Randall was dead. I met her a year ago when she returned. She thought she'd put it all behind her. But then two weeks ago Nathaniel Kemp comes out of the blue and wants to know if anyone's come asking more questions about that day. Honest, she's that scared.'

A sudden chill gripped me. The steward at the time of my husband's death had just warned the housekeeper at the time of my husband's death that someone answering the description of Sulio Denville might come asking questions. I clasped my hands over my mouth. 'Sir Charles knows I've escaped. He knows and he's sent his hired killer to ask questions.'

Mrs Pengelly gripped my arm. 'But what do they want the answer to? I don't understand. What is it Sulio Denville wants to know?'

Mrs Munroe glanced at the door. 'Nathaniel Kemp told Sarah that Sir Charles never believed he was dead – despite everything he did to cover his tracks. He said they'd been after him on and off. He kept changing his name and starting up elsewhere, living on his guard, constantly watching his back. But a year ago he saw this man – Sulio Denville – sniffing around. Straight away he hid, and fled straight after.'

She waited, Tamsin pale with fear, Rowan wide-eyed yet

somehow staying strong. Sam nodded and Mrs Munroe bent closer. 'Then three weeks ago, Nathaniel Kemp caught a sudden glimpse of him again. He thought they were off his trail. He thought he'd managed his disappearance well enough to shake off the past . . . but they're devious . . . they're clever. Like playing cat and mouse.'

'Cat and mouse. That's horrid.'

'Yes, Tamsin. But, here's the thing: Sulio Denville's changed his name. Course he has – he's a wanted man! Mr Kemp followed him and saw him working in a brewery in Plymouth Dock. He now calls himself Johnathan Woolacre.'

All colour had drained from Mrs Pengelly's cheeks. She was clearly struggling to keep calm. 'But I don't understand – why would they think to question Sarah again?'

'That's just what I said. I told her she'd have no reason to worry . . . but she started cryin'. She's that scared. She said she thinks it's about what *nearly* happened. All those years ago an' she's kept it to herself. She was that glad of her new job and thought no more about it but now she thinks she should have said something.'

'About what?'

'That morning she was about to dismiss an upper maid. The maid had become,' she glanced at Rowan, '*close* to Mr Kemp. She'd seen him follow her into the wood a couple of times.'

A shiver ran down my spine. 'The *wood*. They used to meet in the wood?'

Sam's whistle filled the room. 'What if they saw – not the murder or they'd have raised the alarm – but what if they saw someone in the wood at the time of the murder? Or . . .

what if they were seen by the murderer . . . at the time of the murder?'

Mrs Munroe shook her head. 'Someone might have seen Mr Kemp but no one saw the maid.'

She sounded so certain. 'How do you know?'

'Because the maid stayed on. And did well. After fourteen years, she's risen to the top. She's become the housekeeper – she's Mrs Pumfrey.'

My chest felt too tight to breathe. 'They know there was a maid in the wood but they don't know it was Mrs Pumfrey. And they think to question Sarah again because now I'm free they know I'm going to accuse them of my husband's murder.'

Mrs Pengelly's urgency cut through my dizziness. 'Sam – you must go to Matthew Reith and tell him everything . . . We can't risk this in a letter.' She reached for Mrs Munroe's hand. 'You've been remarkable . . . quite remarkable. We've got very little time. Any moment Sulio Denville's going to find Sarah Nicholls and question her.' She breathed deeply. 'Go to Pol-carrow . . . ask for a horse . . . and a groom to go with you. Ask for two. Tell Matthew we believe Charles Cavendish knows of Madeleine's escape and he's rattled enough to call upon the services of Sulio Denville – now called Johnathan Woolacre.'

Sam's clenched fists rested on the table. 'But that'll leave you in the house alone. I can't do that. Shall I ask Oliver Jenkins to come until I'm back?'

Mrs Pengelly nodded. 'Yes. Ask Oliver. Hurry.'

Chapter Forty-six

The doors firmly locked, we felt safer in the dining room, Tamsin watching from the window. A steady stream of mules were returning to the fields, oxen carts trundling back to the farms. A yawl drifted on the tide, the trees glowing in the evening sun. Any other evening Sam would be bringing up his silver tray with a sparkling decanter of Madeira. She pressed her face against the window, her cheeks flushing. 'It's Oliver . . . he's coming. I'll go and let him in.'

Standing with fierce concentration, Oliver listened, asking Mrs Pengelly about the locks and back entrances. At once, he straightened. 'We'll bar the kitchen door and I'll jam the back gate. No one will get through to the yard. I'll set up watch here by the window where I can see both ways.' He glanced at Tamsin. 'I'll keep you all safe.'

Mrs Pengelly tapped the tips of her fingers against her mouth. 'We need to warn Mrs Pumfrey she's in danger. Sulio Denville is a man who gets answers . . . he'll terrify Sarah. He's brutal . . . he'll use force . . . he'll make her tell him everything. Oliver, Mrs Pumfrey needs to be told she's in great danger.'

Oliver ran his hand through his frizzy hair. Tall, willowy, he filled the room with energy. 'We deliver meat to the Hall. No one would give me a second glance if I took the cart. I can tell her myself – I can tell her everything or take a letter. But that leaves you on your own.'

He risked a glance at Tamsin yet she was not looking. She was staring out of the window, her eyes widening. Her hand flew across her mouth. 'It's a carriage . . . it's stopping.'

He pulled her back. 'Don't let them see you.' The carriage stopped in the shadow of the house, the gold crest clearly visible. 'It's the Cavendish coach. It's Sir Charles . . . he's been at his warehouse.'

Puffy fingers with a gold signet ring gripped the curtain and I thought I might faint. After fourteen years, I was facing my husband's killer. Older, fatter, he wore the same grey periwig, the same gold embroidery on his waistcoat, the same silk cravat. He had the same cruel eyes, the same thin mouth, and I fought my dizziness. He was staring at the house, looking up at each of the windows. Making sure we saw him. The curtain dropped and the coachman whipped the reins. I held out my arms and Rowan slipped on to my lap. Kissing her hair, I held her tightly. No one must harm her. No one. 'Did he see me?'

'I don't think he could see in – not with the sun behind us. But he's telling us he knows you're here.'

Mrs Pengelly looked petrified. 'Pierre's bravery is all over town. It's in the newspaper . . . Sir Charles need only ask if there's been talk of a French woman.'

Oliver Jenkins watched the departing coach. 'Sam's put his trust in me. My duty is to keep ye safe. Maybe I should take ye all to Lady Polcarrow? No one can stop Sir Charles when he's a mind fer something.'

Charles Cavendish had as good as told me he was coming after me. I hardly heard Mrs Pengelly. She must have been agreeing: '...far safer... with both Sir James and Sir Alex away... no one to counteract his orders. No one to stop him. I think we should all pack a bag.'

There was the sound of running footsteps and Oliver looked along the street towards the town. A knock rapped the front door and his shoulders relaxed. 'It's a boy – just a boy. Looks like he's got a letter. I'll go and see to him.' He opened the door just wide enough to reach for the note. 'Thank ye ...Are ye to wait a reply?'

'No, sir... no reply.'

We heard the bolts draw shut and he returned with a note. Mrs Pengelly held out her hand but Oliver shook his head, handing it to me. 'It's fer Mrs Barnard.'

The letter had no seal, just a thumbprint on red wax. I eased it open.

Dear Madeleine,

My intention has always been to keep you safe. Therefore, expect within the hour Mr Jack Ferries with four watchmen. He is the best there is.

CL

Despite trying to be brave, tears filled my eyes. 'It's from Cécile Lefèvre – she knows we're in danger. She's sending us some guards.' I read them the letter. 'Cécile Lefèvre is the lady who organised my escape.'

I expected their smiles, not their frowns. Mrs Pengelly glanced at Oliver. 'It's the sort of devious ploy Sir Charles would use. You've heard of the Wooden Horse?'

'But how would he know her initials?' Yet even as I spoke, fear shot through me. Someone did know her plans. Someone had intercepted my escape. Someone had told Sir Charles I was free. Rowan was staring at me with her huge eyes, Tamsin standing petrified by the window, Mrs Munroe looked ashen.

Mrs Pengelly shook her head. 'I don't think we should trust this note, Madeleine.'

I stared down at it. 'It's the same writing as the note with the flowers – *From a well-wisher*. Her exact initials.' In an hour Sulio Denville could walk up to our door and we would let him in. Like the Wooden Horse. Yet what if it was from Cécile Lefèvre? I had to think like her. What would she do? 'Maybe there is a way of knowing if it's from her.'

'You know where she lives?'

'She leaves messages... somewhere quite safe. May I borrow Tamsin's cloak... and her bonnet... I'll be back within the hour?' I looked at the note. 'She knows I'll check. That's why she's given us the hour. Cécile Lefèvre means to protect us and I can ask her to protect Mrs Pumfrey.'

Mrs Pengelly's eyes held mine. Finally, she nodded. 'Would you like Oliver to go with you?'

'No. Let him stay with you.'

The last of the sun lingered on the rooftops of Porthruan, the riverbanks muddy in the low tide. Gulls were circling above the harbour, their cries drowned by the shouts echoing round the town. Women standing in doorways grasped their children's hands, shutters were being closed. A crowd was gathering on the quayside, men striding purposefully towards the wharf, and I gripped my basket, taking the cliff road.

I knew to walk slowly to attract no attention. The wind was blowing against my cheeks, the air smelling of the ocean, and I glanced round to see if I was being followed. The town was in shadow, the linhay silhouetted against the red sky. The evening sun was burning the water, turning it scarlet. I was not being followed, and picked up my skirts, making my way across the long grass. As I ran, I knew what I would see. The milk churn was back, the leather bag inside it. Twisting the lid, I lifted out the bag and pulled back the false base. Her note was brief and to the point.

Dear Madeleine,

You would not be the woman I know you to be if you did not confirm the validity of my guards. Sir Charles Cavendish has been asking questions. Stay in Coombe House, Mr Ferries will keep you safe.

Cécile Lefèvre

Reaching into my bag, I took out my own letter.

Dear Cécile,

Mrs Pumfrey is in great danger. Please afford her the same protection.

Madeleine

The shouts in the town seemed angrier. Braziers were being lit, a series of torches held in the air, and I knew to hurry. Dogs were barking, the women no longer in their doorways, but safe behind closed shutters. I walked swiftly, crossing the market square, knowing to avoid the wharf. A group of men were heading towards the warehouses. The church clock struck nine; I had been three-quarters of an hour, no more. Oliver opened the door and I stepped into the dining room, their frightened eyes staring back at me. I held up my note. 'We can trust them.'

It was darker now, the tide turning. Mrs Munroe had Mr Pitt on her lap, Mrs Pengelly sitting stiff-backed, her glasses in her hand. 'If they aren't here by half past, we'll shut the shutters and go to Polcarrow.'

Oliver swung round. 'They're comin'. There's five of them. Shall I open the door to them?'

Mrs Pengelly held my glance. 'Let *one* in and we'll hear what he has to say.'

Gripping a large poker, Oliver went to the door. A man followed him back. In his late forties, dark hair, smart appearance, medium height, slim build, he seemed hardly a match for Sulio Denville.

'Mr Ferries, at your service.' He was quietly spoken, educated, his clothes of good quality. His hands were clean, his nails neatly cut. Reaching into his jacket, he drew out a letter. 'My terms of appointment are quite clear. My men will set their watch.' He smiled at Rowan. 'One in the house, one at the front, and two at the back. You won't see them outside – you'll see the dummy we place against the back door. His hat covers most of his face and we place him as if he's asleep. He's the decoy . . . in case anyone thinks to use a firearm.'

'Firearm?'

He nodded without smiling. 'My men are never seen, but they watch. Four by day, and four by night. I'd like them to come in – they need to see who they're protecting. It's a precaution I like to take.'

Mrs Pengelly nodded. 'Yes, of course. I haven't seen you in Fosse before.'

This time there was a smile. 'We're from Truro . . . St Austell . . . Redruth . . . Lostwithiel. Mainly Truro. My guards are highly sought after. My nightwatchmen are placed all over Cornwall. I run a tight ship and deliver on my promise. I'll keep you and your house safe.'

'And you just happen to be in Fosse?'

'I run a business, madam. My men have families . . . they have homes and loved ones. If someone engages my services but refuses to pay what I ask, I'm open to other offers.' He spoke calmly, no hint of anger or protest, just stating the facts. 'I'll not have my men defend a warehouse full of salt for a man who's not paid the tax but has doubled the price, and who expects my services for less than I ask. My men have families . . . those fishermen have families . . . their pilchards need salting.'

Oliver put down his poker. 'I'll let your men in.'

I knew the answer before I asked. 'Who hired you for us?'

Mr Ferries shook his head. 'A boy came with a note telling me to collect instructions from the bank. We've been paid for two weeks – and there'll be further instructions as necessary. We're to escort you everywhere – shopping, church . . . walks. From now on, we'll accompany you every minute of every hour.'

Oliver held open the door and four huge men filled the room to bursting. Men with broad shoulders and necks like tree trunks. Hats in hands, they bowed their shaved heads, their thick bushy brows rising as each was introduced. The one called Peter reached forward, stroking Mr Pitt with his heavily tattooed hand. 'My little girl has a cat just like this.'

Mrs Munroe handed him the cat, rising swiftly, straightening her apron. Walking down the line of the men, she demanded each show her their boots. Inspection over, she sniffed. 'See ye keep them that way.' She frowned, shaking her head. 'I can see ye all have an appetite on ye. Well . . . best get started.' She nodded to Rowan. 'Rabbit pie to start . . . roast potatoes . . . and gooseberry tart and baked custard . . . Ye can make them a lardy cake. Come – nothin's going to bake itself.'

At the door, she glanced at Oliver. 'I'll give ye a list of the meat I'll need.'

The bedroom was stuffy with the window closed – another of Mr Ferries' precautions. There were pails of water in every room, the shutters barred against the threat of burning bricks. Rowan snuggled against me. 'Why doesn't Madame Lefèvre ever come an' meet us? Ye think she'd just come an' say hello.'

I kissed the top of her head. 'Madame Lefèvre doesn't want us to know who she is.'

She giggled. 'Mrs Munroe's that happy. She makes out it's hard work but Tamsin says she's never happier than having mouths to feed.' She closed her eyes. 'Do you think Captain Pierre is thinking of us . . . wondering what we're doing?'

Warmth flooded my heart. 'I'm sure he is. And now he has the testament of fifty-nine good people and Sir Alex and Sir James Polcarrow to help him.'

'And he has Opie.'

'Yes, he has Opie. We'll write to them in the morning. Lady Pendarvis will see our letters are delivered.'

'And if they do decide to put him in gaol . . . we *will* go to him, won't we?'

She must not see my tears. 'Yes, we'll go to him.' I kissed her hair, this dear, sweet angel sent straight to me from heaven.

Chapter Forty-seven

Coombe House, Fosse
Sunday 6th July 1800, 6 p.m.

The wind was picking up, a battalion of black clouds stacking up over the sea. The sky was darkening, the threat of heavy rain. We chose not to go to church but remained taut and watchful, a rich aroma of steak and kidney pudding drifting from the kitchen. Peter stood by the dining-room window, his presence bringing much needed calm. I could not settle. Nor could Mrs Pengelly. She had been pacing the room most of the day. 'Sam will be back soon. Unless Matthew's not in Truro, in which case he'll have gone to Bodmin.'

Rowan's skill with her pen was growing. 'There, everyone's name. How do you write Mr Pitt?' She was keeping us occupied. She had not seen Sir Charles but I had. I had never forgotten those eyes; they had kept me awake on too many nights.

Peter's voice boomed from the dining room. 'There's a man running towards the house – grey hair, middle-aged, brown jacket, red waistcoat. Might that be your man?'

Sam was on the steps, catching his breath. 'Yes – that's Sam. You can let him in.'

He looked flushed, unusually ruffled, his clothes dusty. He took off his hat, running his hand through his damp hair. 'Who's he?'

'He's Peter. He's here to protect us...' Mrs Pengelly asked Rowan to get the others and she ushered us into the dining room. Smiling at our huge guard, she closed the door. 'Sir Charles stopped outside the house yesterday so Miss Madeleine's friend sent us some guards. We'll talk only in here – nothing must be said outside this room. Take a seat, everyone.'

Mrs Munroe and Tamsin sat in their floury aprons, Sam taking the seat at the end of the table. 'I told Mr Reith everythin' and straight away he gathered up what he needed and headed off to warn Sarah Nicholls. He's certain it's Sulio Denville. He said he can't believe we found him and the name he now goes under.' He allowed himself a smile. 'Fact is, he was that surprised by everythin'. Said he'd underestimated us. Said we'd done better than him.'

Mrs Munroe sniffed, a slight bristle. 'Well, he didn't ask us, did he?'

Sam wiped his head with his handkerchief. 'His plan is to wait for Sulio Denville. He's got the law with him and they'll set a trap. When Denville comes expecting to ask Sarah Nicholls questions, it'll be him that gets the questions.'

Tamsin clasped her hands. 'They'll arrest him?'

'Yes. But Mr Reith says we're to warn Mrs Pumfrey. He says we have to find a way. He says she's in great danger.'

'We've done our best to arrange a nightwatchmen for her. I've asked my friend and Oliver's going there tomorrow. He's going to deliver the meat as usual. Sir Charles is so devious we have to assume everyone's in his clutches. We thought if Oliver goes to Pendenning Hall outside his usual routine someone will report it to Sir Charles – probably his steward, Mr Troon.' Though I spoke with certainty, my fear was rising. 'Oliver's going to talk to Mrs Pumfrey and tell her everything.'

Sam leaned forward, his voice a whisper. 'Matthew Reith says Sulio Denville's been a wanted man for seven years. He's been running from the law but it's caught up with him at last.'

'Thank you, Sam. You've done well. Was there anything else?'

Sam shrugged, a rueful smile. 'Lady Polcarrow saw me askin' fer a horse. She was watchin' when I returned it. She knows I borrowed two of her grooms. She didn't say anything but she knows somethin's up.'

We returned to the drawing room, Mrs Pengelly with her sewing, me with my book. Rowan was downstairs, Sam washed and brushed and holding out his silver tray. The crystal glasses glinted in the candlelight and Mrs Pengelly smiled. 'Better make that three glasses.' She glanced at the clock. 'Tell Peter I'm expecting a gentleman. Sam, you can let her in.'

Within minutes a shadow passed across the window. Sam opened the door and shut it quietly behind the tall, elegant figure of Rose Polcarrow. Dressed in men's clothes, she removed her heavy hat and chestnut curls cascaded around her shoulders. 'Is there something I should know?' she said, bending to kiss her mother's cheek.

'Rose, dear . . . you've already met Mrs Barnard, I believe?'

Rose turned, fixing me with her penetrating blue eyes. Almost mesmerised by their beauty, I rose and curtsied. Her voice was soft, not angry at all. 'First Matthew and Alice come rushing down for a visit, then yesterday Sam goes rushing up to visit them. Mrs Munroe has ordered three times as much meat as she normally does, and you were not in church this morning.' She poured the Madeira, handing us both a glass. 'I don't like not knowing what's going on. Your very good health, Mrs Barnard . . . though it's not Mrs Barnard, is it?'

I took the glass, warming to her bright smile and raised eyebrows. Even in men's clothes, her beauty lit the room. 'No . . . I'm Madeleine Pelligrew, formerly of Pendenning Hall. I'm here to seek justice for my late husband – I intend to see Sir Charles arrested for his murder. Only he knows I'm here in Fosse . . . in your mother's house. We have guards in place and nightwatchmen. Matthew Reith is hoping to set a trap to arrest Sulio Denville and is searching for enough evidence to have Sir Charles arrested. Alice was my friend.'

Rose Polcarrow raised her glass. 'Excellent. Well done. Anything else I should know?'

Mrs Pengelly reached for her sewing. 'Only that Madeleine has formed a strong attachment to Pierre de la Croix and he to her . . . which you already know because you sent James to Bodmin to fight his cause.'

Rose sat, legs apart, smiling back at her mother. 'I sent James to Bodmin because he was getting under my feet. Men do not organise fetes and balls – we do. I needed him out of the house. Anything else I should know?'

I smiled back at this extraordinary woman. Rose Pengelly, shipbuilder's daughter, the scourge of corruption and deceit. 'I don't want anyone to know I'm Madeleine Pelligrew. For Pierre's sake. People need to think I'm *not* an émigrée. If his case goes against him and I need to visit him in prison – or should he be allowed back on parole – his position with the other prisoners would be compromised. A French Republican officer should not fall in love with an émigrée. It's dangerous... and could harm his reputation.'

She had a perfect oval face, high cheekbones, and perfectly arched brows. Yet her beauty lay in the mischief of her smile. 'I gather there were no guards to protect Sir Charles's warehouse. They were *diverted*. A number of angry fish merchants have taken over the warehouse and threaten to ruin the salt unless he brings down his price. There's terrible unrest... and no one there to stop them. Must be very hard for him to have his guards go elsewhere.'

Mrs Pengelly threaded her needle. 'How are my grandchildren?'

Rose drained the last of her Madeira. 'Missing their father and not yet asleep... I better get back to them.' She rose and I curtsied deeply. 'You have my word, Madeleine. No one will hear from us who you really are.' Twisting her hair, she crammed it beneath her huge hat. 'James is doing everything he can for Pierre. We've both grown very fond of your Captain de la Croix.' She bent to kiss her mother again. 'I suppose it's no good asking you all to come to Polcarrow, is it, Mother?'

Mrs Pengelly picked up her sewing. 'So you can keep an eye on me?'

Her smile flashed across the room. 'No. It's just I could do with Mrs Munroe's help in the kitchen...and Sam's very handy at putting up pavilions. You could help sew the bunting...and Madeleine could enjoy the gardens.'

'You need Mrs Munroe's help for the ball?'

I caught the love in Rose Polcarrow's eyes. 'If she's not too busy cooking for your guards.'

Rowan blew out her candle. 'Tamsin's that sweet on Oliver she asked Mrs Munroe if she should let him kiss her! They thought I couldn't hear but Tamsin said, *What if he tries to kiss me?* An' Mrs Munroe said, *Well, why not let him? His father has a good business – he's a catch all right.* Then Tamsin left, an' I saw Mrs Munroe reach fer her handkerchief. She was crying and Sam comes up to her and says, *We always knew we'd have to let her go sometime...an' I think that time's come.* He looked sad an' all.'

'Poor Mrs Munroe. Tamsin came here at fourteen – that's not much older than you. But Oliver's quite remarkable and Mrs Pengelly and Mrs Munroe wouldn't let Tamsin go to anyone less worthy.'

She curled up beside me. 'I wish we could see the moon. Will ye let Captain Pierre kiss you if he asks?'

I kissed her forehead. 'Hush now. If I sing you a lullaby you must be asleep before I finish.' I clasped his watch to my heart and shut my eyes. I could feel his arms folding round me, the touch of his lips.

'Please let him,' she whispered.

Chapter Forty-eight

Coombe House
Monday 7th July 1800, 6 p.m.

The rain lashed against the window panes, the wind howling round the shutters. With the sky so dark, Mrs Pengelly called for the candles to be lit. 'Will he deliver to the Hall in this weather?'

Sam placed the candles round the room. 'He'll deliver in a snow storm. I'm sure he'll be here soon.'

'Are the guards drenched? Won't they come in for a moment?'

Sam shook his head. 'They'll only come in at change-over.'

Within minutes we heard the iron wheels of a cart draw up outside the front door. Mrs Pengelly reached for a candle and I followed her into the dining room. 'Close the shutters,' she whispered.

Oliver had taken off his heavy coat and hat but even so his hair was dripping. Wearing no boots, he rushed up the stairs and we took our places round the dining-room table. Each of us in the same place. Mrs Munroe pulled up her chair and Sam closed the door, placing a candelabra in the centre of the table.

'I spoke to Mrs Pumfrey. It wasn't easy but I whispered she was in danger. She took me into her office and pretended to go through the list price – she left the door open so everyone could see – an' I told her we knew that the old housekeeper, Sarah Nicholls, had nearly dismissed her fer being in the woods with Mr Nathaniel Kemp. I told her that someone had now come asking Sarah Nicholls questions about what she saw the day Joshua Pelligrew drowned.'

'What did she say?'

'I said straight away a prominent attorney was seeking to charge Sir Charles with the murder of Mr Joshua Pelligrew and Sir Charles was desperate to silence anyone who saw *anythin'* or *anyone* in the wood at the time.' His voice was a whisper, his eyes sharp. Beneath his jacket, his cuffs were damp. 'I could see I'd touched on something. She just stared at me, hands a tremor. She looked terrified an' I told her she had to trust me. I think she thought I was sent from Sir Charles – I thought she weren't going to say anythin'. Then I remembered Rowan saying how much she liked Ella so I said I knew Ella's grandmother and to ask Ella. Ella would know I meant no harm.'

'That was good thinking.' Mrs Munroe reached for Tamsin's hand.

'It seemed to work as she started talking. She said Sarah Nicholls had got it wrong – that she weren't close to Nathaniel Kemp at all. He wanted it . . . he was pressing her into a dalliance but she refused. Only he thought to persuade her. He followed her into the wood in order to blackmail her. He'd found out she was taking food to her brother. She came from a large family and was the only one with employment – out of six brothers and sisters. She was takin' food from the kitchens and Nathaniel Kemp found out . . . so he followed her. He was going to use it against her – to make her do what he wanted or she'd lose her job. She had no regard for him. She hated him abusin' his power like that.'

Mrs Pengelly gripped her hands. 'How despicable.'

'That's what maids up at the Hall had to face back then.' Mrs Munroe raised her eyebrow. 'Wasn't just him, as we know.'

Distaste churned my stomach. The maids going round in pairs to escape my husband's clutches.

Oliver cleared his throat. 'She says her brother used to take a boat to the creek and wait fer her. She said she had a way of hiding the food beneath her cloak. I asked her if she'd seen a man in the woods that day and she said she had. At just the time of the drowning. She described him in detail. Mainly because of the tattoos on his hands . . . but she's quite convinced he *didn't* see her.'

'Tattoos on his hands?'

'Yes. A thick-set, heavy man . . . sounded just like Sulio Denville. She hid in a thicket and he passed her by, but she saw him watch Nathaniel Kemp. But what's more important is that her brother was there – and *he* saw him as well.'

'Her brother saw him, too? Would he remember well enough to describe him?'

Oliver leaned forward. 'She says they could. But what's more to the point . . .' He glanced at the door. 'She told me they had seen the same man talking to *Sir Charles* at the river's edge. Right in the creek where the drowning took place.'

I fought for breath. 'When was that?'

'Two days before. Her brother was waiting as arranged – she said she took slices of meat, eggs, bread, potatoes . . . and they saw them both at the river's edge – pointing to places, deep in conversation, as if agreeing on something.'

In the silence the clock ticked, the sound of the rain lashing against the window. Mrs Pengelly drew a deep breath. 'Did she not think to say anything? Didn't she wonder at all?'

Oliver nodded. 'She said she was petrified. She returned to the Hall in a terrible state. She thought she was going to be dismissed, but then both Nathaniel Kemp and Sarah Nicholls were dismissed instead, and she thought she'd got away with it – stealing the food, that is. It was only afterwards when she talked to her brother about seeing Sir Charles at the exact same place where Mr Pelligrew drowned that she became scared. She said it petrified her. She said her brother asked if he should come forward, but they'd only got Sir Charles to go to. By then, Sir Charles had taken over the house and Mrs Pumfrey was given a lot more responsibility. She was acting in place of the housekeeper and doing very well.'

'And she didn't give it a second thought?'

'She said she thought about it all the time, but she knew Joshua Pelligrew was planning to dredge the river an' she thought the man they saw must be the dredger. She was taking reading and writing lessons from one of the footmen and she asked him what he knew. That night he took her to the library and read her letters going back some time. She realised Sir Charles was a good friend to Mr Pelligrew and had lent him money for the dredging – so of course Sir Charles would have been down by the river to talk to the dredger. She thought no more of it. Especially as everyone said Joshua Pelligrew was ruined and had taken his own life.'

'They were lies to cover his tracks. He almost fooled me, too.'

The clock struck seven, the candlelight casting shadows across the ceiling, lighting our pale faces. Mrs Pengelly spoke my very thought: 'Where's Mrs Pumfrey's brother now?'

'He's a carpenter. He got an apprenticeship and works for the cooper behind the Ferry Inn. He's John Pumfrey.' He glanced at Mrs Munroe. 'She's *Mrs* Pumfrey out of respect.'

Mrs Pengelly straightened, her voice soft but firm. 'It's too stormy to do anything tonight, but tomorrow I suggest we pack our bags and go to Polcarrow. All of us – including Mrs Pumfrey and John Pumfrey. One of the guards can stay behind and look after the house. First thing tomorrow we'll get a message to Mrs Pumfrey and her brother.' She reached for my hand. 'I'll send an express to Matthew Reith and mark it urgent.'

Chapter Forty-nine

From the outside Polcarrow looked grey and austere. Built from stone after the Spanish Armada – the Polcarrow baronetcy awarded for gallantry and services to the Queen – it crouched like a fortress above the town, its crenelated balustrade more like a castle than a house. Four turrets stood at each end, the windows arched, the mullions carved into intricate patterns. Inside, however, the house radiated warmth and love.

Fifteen years ago, I had sat on this very chair taking tea with Alice Polcarrow, Sir James's stepmother. We had watched her son Francis playing by the fire. He was four, the same age as Rose's second daughter was now. Back then, I had thought it a rather cold room but new drapes added colour and the portraits of the Polcarrows' smiling children filled the room with love. Tall Chinese vases stood either side of the vast stone fireplace, the flowers placed around the room bringing in the scent of the garden. Three large windows opened on to the terrace, the sky still dark, the lavender in the urns blowing in the wind.

Mrs Pengelly sat next to me on the chaise longue. I had spent the morning explaining everything to Rose – everything except Cécile Lefèvre's involvement in a spy network. I would keep that secret to myself. Rose stood by the fireplace and even in the dull light her cream gown seemed to shine. Sam had gone to fetch John Pumfrey; Oliver had returned to the Hall to deliver news of a 'terrible family tragedy' to Mrs Pumfrey. Both had quickly packed their bags.

They were with us now, Mrs Pumfrey sitting straight-backed and pale-faced, balancing on the edge of her chair. Her brother sat next to her, a bearded man in a brown corduroy jacket and breeches, his huge hands squeezing his hat.

Rose Polcarrow listened intently, smiling to put them at their ease. 'I believe you understand the seriousness of this accusation against Sir Charles? The description you give of the man in the wood fits the man we know as Sulio Denville. He's been wanted for seven years – he was a ship's master and we believed he had long since sailed. Thanks to Nathaniel Kemp we know he's still working for Sir Charles and now calls himself by another name. It is he who we believed drowned Joshua Pelligrew.'

Sulio Denville. Not Phillip Randall. Sulio Denville was the man who had held Joshua beneath the water. Sulio Denville's huge bulk a match for even the strongest swimmer.

Rose was still speaking. 'Mrs Pumfrey, I know you don't think highly of Nathaniel Kemp, but he isn't dead. He's been running from Sir Charles ever since his dismissal. His family sent rumours of his death — even the papers it was printed in — but he's been in hiding all over the country trying to keep ahead of Sulio Denville.'

My admiration for Rose Polcarrow was growing by the minute. She was strong, grasping everything so quickly. Understanding everything. Tall, assured, her beauty nothing in comparison to her intelligence. She rang the bell pull and a man in red livery entered.

'Henderson, could you ask for a hamper to be packed? I imagine Mr Reith will want to take Mr Pumfrey and Mrs Pumfrey straight to Truro. I believe he won't stay but will want to make the most of the light.' She smiled at the petrified brother and sister. 'No one will blame you for not coming forward. Sir Charles's web of lies was designed to put everyone off. He's more devious than we gave him credit for – that's why you must be taken to a place of safety.'

Mrs Pumfrey had been glancing at me since she arrived and I knew she recognised me. Not only as Mrs Barnard, but as Madeleine Pelligrew. I cleared my throat. 'I know what you read in the library, Mrs Pumfrey, because I read it myself when I was pretending to clean the books. I, too, nearly believed his lies.'

Henderson stood at the door. 'He's here, m'lady. Just drawing up outside.'

Rose Polcarrow's iridescent silk shimmered as she swung round. We heard the front door open and footsteps rush across the marble floor. Matthew Reith hurried into the room. Mrs Pumfrey curtsied, John bowed, and Matthew stared back at their terrified faces. 'I came as quickly as I could.' He bowed, acknowledging us all. 'I've borrowed my father's coach. The road's still passable but this wind's wreaking havoc.'

Standing next to Rose, he clasped his hands behind his back. For such a hurried journey, his clothes were barely creased. His shrewd eyes darted from one to the other, his mouth tightening. 'I understand your concern but it behoves me to place you out of danger. From what Mrs Pengelly told me in her letter, your description certainly fits the description of Sulio Denville – and the dates are irrefutable. I can assure you, neither of you would be here today if they had seen you that night. They'll stop at nothing – both then and now.'

'Is Sarah Nicholls safe?'

'Yes, Eva. She has my men with her. When Sulio Denville makes contact she'll agree to meet him. They'll set a trap and arrest him. It's vital he doesn't suspect – I don't want Sulio Denville taking off again. Not now we're so close.'

'You've enough to arrest Sir Charles for ordering Joshua Pelligrew's murder?'

He nodded, no sign of a smile. 'Originally, the plan was to persuade Sulio Denville to turn King's evidence, but from what I've heard today – and the evidence I've corroborated from the diaries – we've enough to arrest Sir Charles. There have been other cases. I've had men looking into his accounts for several years now. This isn't his first case of fraudulent practice. Two other *friends* of Sir Charles found themselves facing the same bankruptcy after dealings with him, and the same unfortunate end. One was run over by a coach; the other "threw" himself in the Thames. Sir Charles believes he's untouchable, but no one's above the law.'

413

Mrs Pumfrey reached for her handkerchief. Her voice was strong, despite her fear. 'I've brought what Oliver asked for . . . it's in my bag. It's Sarah Nicholls' housekeeping book from back then, and the page is still there. It's not been torn out. All the jewellery's listed as Oliver said it would be. They won't know it's missing – there's at least five books since.' Her eyes held mine. 'I'm so sorry . . . I should've come forward.'

I shook my head. 'There was no one to come forward to – no one was free from Sir Charles's power. He would have silenced you, just like he silenced me.'

Matthew swung round. 'A list of Mrs Pelligrew's jewels?' He allowed himself a brief smile, a rise of his eyebrow. 'I have to say you're quite remarkable.' Mrs Pengelly returned his smile and his eyes darted to the window. 'I'll need to borrow some horses if I may, Rose? I'll bring them back when we come for the ball. I hope this rain doesn't set in.'

The bed had four elaborately carved posts with a canopy above, its heavy damask curtains tied with gold tassels. Rain beat against the window, the candle casting shadows across the beamed ceiling. 'It's like a castle,' Rowan whispered. 'Honest . . . I can't believe how many rooms there are. All those corridors and there's three kitchens . . . one fer meat, one fer baking, and one fer scrubbing and preparing vege- tables. There's three pantries, and two sculleries . . . and *five* ovens. There's a butler's pantry and the housekeeper has a whole set of rooms, and ye know what?'

'What?' I whispered, tucking her up under the thick eiderdown quilt.

'They *love* Mrs Munroe. They want her to stay. She knows the head cook from when they were children. Cook said, *Good job ye've come to help . . . there's none make pastry like ye . . .* And Mrs Munroe just sniffed like she does and said, *Best let me take a look at what ye've got planned fer the ball.* And they was – sorry, they were – together fer such a long time. And Mrs Munroe said, *I'll need my own office an' I'll do the pastry . . . nothin' else.* And Cook kissed her cheek. And all the maids cheered and clapped and Mrs Munroe said, *Well, best get on with it, then . . . nothin' makes itself.* But they just kept smiling and clapping and I could see tears in her eyes. Honest, and Sam just stood smiling like he was so proud of his sister.'

I bent to kiss her cheek. 'And I'm so proud of you. But it's late . . . you need to sleep.'

Shutting her eyes, she whispered, 'Lady Polcarrow says her girls get up to all sorts of mischief without their father . . . she says she'd be grateful if I play with them as much as I like. She's that kind.'

Lady Pendarvis had sent her servant with a letter, and as Rowan's breathing deepened, I drew it from next to my heart, holding it to my lips, rereading it through watery eyes.

Bodmin Gaol
July 3rd, 1800

My Dearest Madeleine,
Thank you, a thousand times, for your letter and painting.
I have placed it against the narrow slit of the window and I

can feel the wind on my face. It brings with it the scent of the flowers and when I look at it I feel you by my side.

Never blame yourself for my action. I would do it again in an instant if I thought you were in danger. Your sweet words bring me a whirlwind of happiness. That you feel such love for me is a dream I never thought possible. I have never loved before; never known the sweet agony of wanting to see someone every moment of every waking hour. The yearning I feel for you is visceral, painful, yet so sweet it fills my heart with joy.

But the truth must be faced. It is likely that I will be found guilty. I went against my solemn promise — ships and rowing boats are forbidden — and there is very little to say in my defence. I believe they will not hang me, but will imprison me. If that happens, I will bear it with fortitude. I will never, ever, regret my action. That you have formed a regard for me is enough to sustain me, and my deep love for you is all I need to see me through any imprisonment.

Your devoted friend,
Pierre

I held it to my lips. My darling, you do not know how highly you are esteemed. How everyone has rallied to your defence. How Opie and Billy are coming.

Removing my turban, I caught a glimpse of my fine blonde hair finally regrowing — soft, like a layer of velvet. My cheeks were plumper, my skin no longer raw. I had eyebrows, and no sign of sores on my lips. Mrs Pumfrey must have recognised me from my portrait in the dining room in Pendenning Hall and I stared back in the mirror, at the face of my past: Madeleine de Bourg, fourteen years older; stronger, wiser, getting better by the day. My mind was clearer, I could concentrate for longer, I was no longer scared of the sky, rarely dizzy, and my mouth had lost its tautness. But best of all were my eyes.

I would never change places with the woman in the portrait. The love in my eyes shone stronger than hers — fiercer, and more intense. *A thousand times* stronger. I put the letter to my lips. *Opie and Billy are coming. Stay strong, darling Pierre.*

Chapter Fifty

Polcarrow, Fosse
Monday 14th July 1800, 11 a.m.

L ess than a week to go until the fete for the opening of the
mine. I stared out of my window. The preparations
were well under way: the sheep taken from the pasture, the
building of the pavilion taking shape. A steady stream of men
were heaving equipment across the grass, Sir James's steward
pointing to where he wanted everything to go. Sam had his
sleeves rolled up, laying down a heavy plank, and at last the
rain had stopped, the sky turning an azure blue. Opening the
casement, I breathed in the smell of damp grass, the scent of
roses drifting up from the terrace.

To the north, the river snaked through its heavily wooded
banks, bright and glistening, bending out of sight. In line with
the church tower, I could see the slate roofs huddling down
to the harbour, the ships pulling up their sails in readiness
to leave, yet my heart remained heavy. Though I smiled and
talked with what I hoped sounded like enthusiasm for the
preparations, I could not but dread the busy fete and ball. My

thoughts remained with Pierre, filling my every waking hour. And Rowan? What of my dearest Rowan?

Happy squeals caught my attention, a dog barking, and I looked down to the terrace. Rowan was holding hands with the two eldest girls, the nursery maid carried the baby, and Lady Polcarrow held her youngest daughter's hand. She picked her up, chasing after the spaniel, all of them smiling, running as fast as they could, and I leaned further out, seeing what they had seen. Sir James's carriage was coming up the drive.

Please let there be good news. Please, please, let Pierre not be imprisoned. Two weeks of jumping at the sound of wheels. Of hoping and praying. I wanted to run down the stairs, but I knew to hold back.

Over an hour, and I could wait no longer. I walked swiftly down the elaborately carved staircase and across the vast hall with its black-and-white marble floor. The smiling portrait of Rose Polcarrow filled the hall with beauty, and I stopped as laughter rang from the drawing room. The door was open and tears stung my eyes. I had heard much of Sir James's adoration for his girls, and I watched all three of them smothering him with kisses. Mrs Pengelly opened the vast French window and the girls followed her out, smiling back at their adored father.

Sir James slid his arm around his wife and seemed to have no intention of removing it. The footman announced me and Sir James smiled his greeting. 'Mrs Barnard, this is a pleasure. You're very welcome – we have you to thank for bringing

Eva to us, and Mrs Munroe . . . and I believe Sam is proving invaluable. All very welcome additions for my wife's preparations.' His intensely blue eyes held mine. He was tall, slightly severe, with short dark hair and chiselled features. His jacket stretched across his broad shoulders, his clothes of the finest material. He looked elegant yet not overdressed, his silk cravat held in place with an enamel pin. A powerful man with no cruelty in his face. A man clearly in love with his wife.

I curtsied deeply. 'No, it is I who must thank you . . . for everything.'

'Rose has told me who you are and why you're here, and it's my pleasure to serve you. As long as you need us, my house is at your disposal.' His eyes filled with compassion. 'I'm afraid I bring no letter. Pierre's in Falmouth – he's being kept in Pendennis Castle. The conditions are harsh and he's allowed no access to paper for letters. But he speaks of his hope, of his love, of his gratitude to you and everyone in the town. Considering his three weeks of imprisonment, he remains well, even buoyant. The fact so many people were prepared to speak on his behalf has lifted his spirits. He feels humbled, though I did tell him it was *his* kindness that inspired such a response.'

I breathed deeply. 'Do you think the evidence will help?'

He had depth to his eyes, wisdom and kindness. 'I believe so. These cases can drag on for months but I'm fairly sure his is to be heard within the week. I've collated everything we have in his favour and there's a lot there, including a character reference from the naval officer who first accepted his parole – Captain Frederick Carew. I've left Pierre's defence to him.

Sir Alex can't defend Pierre but Captain Carew will. He's on leave in Falmouth and was more than willing to take on his case. He's taken it to the highest tier.'

His smile brought the tears I had been so desperate to avoid. I gripped my hands. 'I can't thank you enough.'

'Billy and Opie haven't been granted permission to see him but he knows Opie is to give evidence. Billy's written to Pierre – I must warn you, *all* Pierre's letters will be read out in court. Including yours.'

'I'm not to be a witness?'

He shook his head. 'No . . . may I call you Madeleine?' I nodded and his voice softened. 'Your letters speak volumes, Madeleine, your statement's very clear, and I believe we must remain hopeful that Pierre is returned to Bodmin on parole.' He waited for me to dry my eyes. 'I hear the net is closing around Sir Charles. I've spent *seven* years fighting him in the courts. I know him to be dangerous and evil and I'm very glad to have you safe behind these walls – not in some inn in Falmouth.'

Rose smiled up at her husband. 'Madeleine came with four nightwatchmen. They left this morning. It seems they were diverted from Sir Charles's warehouse and I believe he's had to halve the price of his salt.'

Sir James threw back his head, his deep laughter making me smile. 'Excellent.' They stood watching Eva chase her grandchildren around the terrace. 'Can we finally persuade her to stay permanently, do you think?'

'I hope so.' Rose reached for his lips. 'Did the girls tell you they all want kittens?'

He seemed surprised. 'Kittens? Oh, don't tell me ... of course! Mr Pitt's come too.' He smiled, shaking his head. 'I presume that hugely fat, ugly, one-eared, soppy, ridiculously spoiled tomcat has taken up residence in the kitchen?'

Her lips brushed his. 'Yes. Dear Mr Pitt. He seems very well settled. But not just in the kitchen – I'm afraid he's taken rather a fancy to your side of the bed.'

Chapter Fifty-one

The musicians stopped playing and loud cheers erupted. Sir James stepped forward. Flags flapped around him on the podium, the canopy keeping the sun off the dignitaries standing alongside him. Ribbons fluttered on the women's bonnets, the men smiling, exchanging glances. Sir James's voice was strong, carrying across the crowd gathered on his lawns. 'This is the man we have to thank. My excellent engineer, Mr William Cotterell.'

He gestured William forward, his hand remaining on his shoulder. 'Without Mr Cotterell's engineering advances, Wheal Elizabeth would have had to remain closed. The copper is there – and always has been – but with the duty imposed on the coal, and the *patent* holding us back, mining it proved unprofitable. My father and his sponsors had to take the only sensible decision to close. I believe it broke my father's heart when the last men put down their tools and Wheal Elizabeth ceased production.'

Murmurs followed his words, the older men nodding in

agreement. Waiting awhile, Sir James Polcarrow continued. 'Even now, coal grows more expensive by the day. Yet with his alterations and additions – with Mr Cotterell's skilful adaptation of the old engine – I believe we have every chance that Wheal Elizabeth can compete *successfully* in the market again. William's new engine will use *less* coal to pump up the water. And less coal means greater profit. I give you William Cotterell – one of Cornwall's finest engineers. Indeed, the finest.'

He waited for the cheers to subside, his face growing serious. 'I've said this before, and I must say it again – there'll not be the same profit made now as in our grandfathers' day, nor in our fathers' day, but I believe we have every chance of competing profitably with other mines, and of producing good quality copper that the stannary will approve.'

Cheers and whistles carried on the wind, the sky a perfect blue. No clouds, just the sea breeze blowing the feathers and ribbons, fluttering the flagpole with its stream of bunting. Everyone was in their Sunday best, children playing hoopla, toddlers running from their mothers. Eva Pengelly linked her arm through mine. 'Doesn't Elowyn look proud? Wait . . . yes, there she goes.'

Young Elizabeth Polcarrow, her grandmother's and the mine's namesake, walked joyfully up the podium steps clutching a large bouquet in her hands. Stopping in front of Elowyn, she curtsied deeply, turning to smile at her parents. Elowyn stepped forward to receive her flowers. Wiping away a tear, she thanked Elizabeth with a returning curtsy. The clapping stopped and taking his daughter's hand, Sir James continued.

'I cannot guarantee the returns our forebears received, but

I believe we have work enough for thirty families.' He turned to the dignitaries, among them Thomas Scantlebury. 'I give my heartfelt thanks to these forward-looking men. These investors in our future. . . the adventurers who have made this possible.' Nodding to each in turn, he raised his hands and the crowd applauded the smiling men in their colourful silk cravats and tall hats.

I turned to see someone working her way through the gathered crowd. At first I saw only the tall feathers in her headdress, but then I saw her hawk-like features. Only she was smiling. Not just a smile, Lady Pendarvis was holding out a letter and looking straight at me. Within minutes she was beside me.

'The best news. . .' She was barely breathless despite her hurry. 'Pierre is *not* to be imprisoned. He is to return as *prisoner en parole*. But he is no longer allowed to be agent for Sir Alex. He must remain in Bodmin – he's not to come to Fosse or go elsewhere. Just Bodmin. . . but he is *not* to face imprisonment. Oh, my dear. . . don't cry.' She wiped her own tears. 'If you cry, I will.'

I could not help it. My shoulders were heaving, my handkerchief pressed against my face. I could hardly breathe for my sobbing. Eva Pengelly took the letter. '*The evidence in his favour. . . his own demeanour, his obvious honour and good standing . . .*' I was smiling, laughing, crying at the same time. She continued reading, but I hardly heard her. '*Given the circumstances. . . the actions of a brave and selfless man. . . Applaud his chivalry . . . born out of gallantry . . . shouted loudly before he picked up the oars. Not the actions of a man trying to escape.*'

Rowan was with Rose's youngest girls. Sir James must have finished speaking as the crowd was clapping again, his two youngest daughters clambering up the steps to be with him. She must have seen me crying as she came rushing over, tears spilling down her face.

'No . . . he's free . . . he's allowed back on parole.' I clutched her to me, my heart searing with pain. 'Pierre's coming back to us.'

A hush descended as Rose Polcarrow stood beside her husband on the podium. Two ceramic jugs were placed on a table in front of them and she smiled at Sir James. His hand lingered over one of the jugs. 'It now gives us great pleasure to draw the names of the King and Queen of the fete. After we crown them we must all do their bidding. Are you ready?'

The cheer was almost deafening. Mrs Munroe and Tamsin turned round and Rowan pulled me forward. '*Every* unwed maid and unwed man. Look. Sam's there an' all.' People parted to let us through, and I linked arms with Mrs Munroe and Tamsin. Dressed in her beautiful gown, she glanced at Oliver, who was standing next to Sam.

'Captain Pierre's to be freed,' Rowan shouted across the crowd.

Sam and Oliver embraced, all of us smiling, throwing back our heads, laughing, and the burning in my heart grew fiercer. Next to me, Mrs Munroe wiped her eyes. 'Lord love him. That dear man.'

'Our Queen of the Fete is . . .' Rose Polcarrow's hand hovered above her jug. Dipping it in, she held up a slip of paper. '. . . Morwenna Cooper.'

A young woman beside me clutched her chest. The cheering subsided and Sir James pulled a name from his jug. 'And our King of the Fete is Joseph Williams.'

I remembered him. He had been one of the first men to come forward to give evidence for Pierre. Sam and Oliver patted him on the back, others immediately kneeling in mock reverence. Morwenna Cooper seemed slightly overwhelmed, but Joseph Williams looked born for the role. Bowing to Morwenna, he took her hand, kissing it amid loud whoops and whistles. Two thrones had been elaborately decorated with flowers, and walking up the wooden steps, they sat regally as Sir James placed the crowns of flowers on their heads. Bowing deeply, Sir James stepped away and Joseph Williams, boat builder, stood with the ribboned orb in his hands. 'It is our command ye enjoy yerselves.'

He waited for the whoops and whistles, the hats thrown in the air to be caught and returned to their owners, and banged his orb for silence. 'There's to be dancin'... competitions ... greased pigs fer ye to catch... and a strongman to pit yer strength against. There's cakes to eat, games to play... trinkets to buy an' there's a hog roasting in the pit. But before we declare this fete open, there's something ye must know. Captain Pierre's *not* to be punished fer his bravery.' He smiled back at the cheering crowd and took Morwenna's hand. 'Now my queen will start the proceedings.'

Morwenna stepped forward, wearing the crown of every girl's dream. 'Let this fete be open.'

'Well,' Mrs Munroe shouted above the cheering, 'ye'll not get a chance again, neither of you! Not if Captain Pierre and

Oliver have their way. But I will. One of these days, I'm goin'
to be queen for the day.'

Behind us, someone shouted, 'But ye're queen already,
Mrs Munroe – Queen of Pastries!'

Not wanting to dance, I slipped away, seeking the shade
of the cedar tree. A bench had been constructed round its
trunk and I sat watching the couples spin and weave, ducking in pairs beneath the floral arch. The carnival jugglers
had left, so, too, the men on stilts, the knife-throwers and
the strongman. The oiled pig had been caught, the prizes
awarded.

'Not dancing, Mrs Barnard?' Jack Ferries bowed. Like me,
his eyes remained on the dancing. 'I think my guards would
have liked to have stayed here permanently.'

'We're very grateful for your help. You've heard no more
from the person who employed you?'

A shake of his head. 'No further instructions.' He drew out
his fob watch. 'But as it happens, we're meeting Matthew
Reith in an hour. Up at the Hall. I believe the constable's also
meeting us there. It's been a pleasure, Mrs Barnard.'

I clutched my hand against my mouth, almost dizzy with
delight. Charles Cavendish was to be arrested. That must
mean Sulio Denville had been apprehended. The breeze was
soft against my cheeks. Rowan saw me and came tearing over,
her hands clutching her bonnet, her blue ribbons flying. Her
cheeks were flushed, her eyes full of mischief.

'Oliver's just *kissed* Tamsin. Right in front of *everyone*. Under the rose arch... The King pulled him forward for Dare, Kiss or Promise... an' he chose Kiss!'

'And how did the King know to ask him?' I whispered.

She giggled, shrugging her shoulders, her palms held upwards. Immediately she swung round. 'Look... look! They've come...' I turned to see Billy and Pierre walking up the long drive. Opie was between them. He looked shy, obviously scared, holding Pierre's hand.

'Captain Pierre... Billy... Opie.' Rowan started down the long drive, her bonnet bouncing against her back, her arms outspread. Pierre reached out and swung her round, Billy did likewise, and I watched her take Opie's hand and reach back for Pierre's. Tears stung my eyes, my heart burning so fiercely I could not breathe. Two months ago I would have laughed at the absurdity of crying with happiness, yet I could not stop smiling back at them as they hurried towards me.

Their love had saved me, their goodness and kindness ousting the hatred and mistrust: Rowan had saved me from sliding into insanity, Opie's love for Pierre had saved me from Marcel Rablais. And Pierre. Pierre. The burning grew fiercer, the ache so deep it ripped my heart.

Billy knew to direct Rowan and Opie towards the cakes. Pierre stood beside me and sudden shyness made my face burn. His shirt was newly washed and pressed. He stood tall, upright, the brass buttons on his uniform glinting in the sun. He seemed as nervous as I was, his soft voice echoing my thoughts. 'Opie has quite captured my heart.'

He held out his arm, leading me back to the bench. His cheeks looked thinner, his complexion paler, slight shadows beneath his eyes. 'We thought you were to return to Bodmin...'

'I'm allowed here until Tuesday – to collect my things – and I want to thank everyone.' His voice was hoarse. 'Everyone's been so generous in their support. It's... quite overwhelming. Mainly... I have to return a certain *lost* piece to Lady Pendarvis's clock! I didn't have time to put it back before I left.'

His smile ripped my heart. 'She told us you can't be Sir Alex's agent for the prisoners any more. That you won't be able to leave Bodmin.'

He seemed hesitant, shy, unable to look at me. 'Any further violation of my parole will bring instant imprisonment. I'll miss my journeys with Sir Alex, but Bodmin offers me plenty.' He took a deep breath. 'Thomas Getty, a renowned watchmaker, has offered me an apprenticeship – unpaid. I've been working with him for quite a while and I think I'll take up his offer.'

'But that's what you've always wanted...'

There was a sadness in him, a flash of pain in his eyes. He reached for my hand. 'Madeleine, dearest Madeleine. I have longed for this. Longed for the chance to hold your hand, to tell you how much I love you. But time in gaol sharpens the wits – it sharpens reality. It focuses the mind. I am in no position to offer you anything like the life you deserve – the security I want to give you, the comfort of a fine home. I live on one shilling and sixpence a day in simple lodgings because they are all I can afford.' His grip tightened, his furrow deepening. 'I have nothing to offer you. My trinkets can fetch a good price, but in the cold light of day . . . *the cold light of day* . . . I cannot expect you to live on a prisoner's allowance.'

My heart was thumping so loudly I thought he must hear. The pain was unbearable. 'I've lived without love or hope for fourteen years. I've lived in plenty and I've lived in great hardship and I know the only important thing is to live with love. That's what I've always longed for. I'd rather live on one shilling and sixpence a day with you in your prisoner's lodgings than in any great Hall with untold wealth. But . . . I can't.'

He kept hold of my hand, putting it to his lips. 'I understand. Of course, I understand.'

'Not because I don't want to but because I cannot. Pierre, don't you see it would put you in too much danger? I've tried to conceal who I am but people know – Sir Charles knows, and his housekeeper recognised me. I can't hide my birth or my connections. If you marry an émigrée they'll know your true leanings. The moment you return to France you'll be stripped of all honour. You'll be imprisoned, maybe even guillotined, just like every other naval captain who refuses to swear alliance to the regime. It would be like signing your death warrant.'

His cry tore my heart. 'My family's lost to me, our lands and estate are lost to me . . . the France I served is lost to me. When this war ends, I have no desire to return to the France of today. I'm tired of living a lie.' He crushed my hand to his lips.

'Pierre, you must understand I intend to take Sir Charles Cavendish to court. And when I've done that, I intend to write a treatise on the injustices of locking women in madhouses

– everything I've been subjected to must be laid bare. People have to know the power of the physician's pen and what happens to women who get in the way of powerful men. They'll label me mad – they'll call me insane – and the mud will stick. I can't have you living under such public scrutiny.'

His eyes burned mine, scorching my heart. 'And I would help you write this treatise.'

Across the lawns the flags were fluttering, the smell of roasting pork filling the air, a crowd gathering round the fire pit to watch the spit turned by a giant wheel. 'There's something else . . . there are my grandmother's jewels to consider. Sir Charles kept them but they were never his to keep. Matthew Reith can prove they weren't part of my dowry. Father made that very clear. If they become mine, I intend to sell them.'

He shook his head. 'Madeleine . . . they are your only link to your family – like my watch, the memories are too precious.'

'They're *currency*, Pierre. Currency I intend to use. Just like every other émigré selling their jewels to live. It's as if my family knew I would need them one day. I'll keep one piece only. And one piece I intend to give to you, so you can use the jewels in your watches. The rest I will sell.'

A firm shake of his head. 'Sell your jewels for your own comfort and future, but not on my account. I'll not profit from them.'

'Pierre . . . one piece. The necklace. Please. I'd like you to make me a watch using some of my grandmother's jewels. That's all I need to remember the past because it's the future that's important. The past is gone, our life is never going to be what it was – it's how it's going to be that matters.'

I could see his pain, his honour compromised. His chivalry, his longing to provide for his wife and family snatched from him. He pressed my palm to his burning lips and I had no notion that love could feel so fierce, so powerful, so completely overwhelming. Never had I known such certainty. I had been set free to become the woman I was meant to be. 'I want you to buy a shop and start your business. Please don't let *the cold light of day*, or your notion of honour, prevent you from accepting my gift. You gave me a seagull so I could take flight, and I want to give you a necklace so you, too, can take flight. I need your promise, Pierre.'

He could not speak but pressed my fingers to his lips. 'Promise me, you'll use my grandmother's necklace? Make me a watch everyone will admire and want one the same?'

'Madeleine, if you only knew how much you've already changed my life . . .'

Happy laughter came ringing across the lawn and we looked up. Between them, Rowan and Opie were carrying a beautifully wrapped box. They held it out. 'We've chosen the very best. Mrs Pengelly said we could have *two* each.' Rowan beamed down at Opie.

A gold ribbon was wrapped round the box and I pulled the bow, opening the lid. 'Frangipane! How lovely. It's my favourite.'

Opie held the box as I took a piece and offered it to Pierre. 'That iced bun . . . No, maybe the tart.' Pierre shrugged. 'I can't decide. You choose first. Here, let me have the ribbon.'

433

He pulled it between his fingers, stretching it out, reaching over my head to tie it in a small bow. His voice was tender, his look sending shivers through me. 'One day I'm going to make Madeleine a beautiful watch to hang on a gold chain, like this. It's going to be the finest watch in the world. With jewels that shine... and we will remember today. For ever. Shall I do that?'

Rowan nodded, tears in her eyes. 'It's the happiest day of my life,' she said, her hand flying across her mouth.

'Mine, too,' whispered Opie, his large brown eyes gazing from one of us to the other.

And mine. I could not speak. Nor could I eat, but I watched them licking their fingers, trying to work out which cake was the tastiest. Opie could not decide, so Pierre thought they must try them all again. Holding their hands, he smiled back at me and I watched them skipping beside him, my heart bursting with love. Holding the ribbon to my lips, I kissed it softly.

Shadows were forming across the lawns, the sun dipping behind the cliffs. Across the river the houses of Porthruan glowed in the evening sun. Word had got round that Pierre was back and a large group started forming round him. Thomas Scantlebury, the first of many, was waiting to congratulate him. In fact, it seemed all fifty-nine signatories wanted to welcome him back, and I watched the man I loved realise for the first time how much he was esteemed.

Chapter Fifty-two

The Polcarrow Ball

'Mama looks so beautiful,' whispered Elizabeth.

The last of the guests were gathering in the hall below, Sir James and Rose welcoming them in turn. Pierre stood next to them, smiling and bowing, glancing up at us with raised eyebrows. Eva Pengelly knelt beside her eldest grand-daughter, Rowan and Opie on either side of me. Dressed in their best clothes they had laid velvet cushions for us to kneel on, and dressed in our finest gowns, we peeped between the banisters beside them.

Rowan's eyes were like saucers. 'I've never seen so many candles lit at once . . . and such beautiful clothes. Look, there's Elowyn and William, and Billy. Don't they look wonderful?'

Opie had eyes only for Pierre. Rose had agreed Opie could stay the night in our bed so Rowan could look after him. Part of me wanted to join Pierre, but part of me was happy gazing down at the man we all adored. He seemed to know so many of the guests, receiving everyone as graciously as if he was giving the ball himself.

'There's Reverend Bloomsdale,' whispered Eva Pengelly with a sideways glance at Rowan. 'I like his gold waistcoat!' Rowan smiled back, and I caught a strange sense of conspiracy. A number of men in naval uniform joined Reverend Bloomsdale, a small group of woman greeting each other with warm embraces. Their silk gowns caught the light, the jewels in their hair glistening, and I caught my breath. It was as if the sun had come out again.

Celia Cavendish was in the centre of the group – a tilt to her chin, a certain arrogance, an air of confidence. Her words were clearly witty as those around her were laughing. A man resplendent in naval uniform, the gold brocade of his jacket matching the gold beading on her gown, handed her a glass of punch and raised his own in salute.

'Captain Edward Pendarvis cuts rather a dashing figure,' whispered Eva.

'Very dashing. Very . . .' Something drew me to him. Not his handsome features, nor the gold braid on his uniform. Not the way he held himself, not his straight back, fluid movements, nor the slightly arrogant lift of his chin, but something strangely familiar.

'Will they start dancin' soon?' whispered Opie.

Eva smiled. 'Not long now. Madeleine, my dear, I'll see the children to bed. Go and enjoy yourself. Let them see you two together.' As if he had heard her, Pierre glanced up and smiled. 'Go on, my love . . . He's waiting for you.'

Halfway down the stairs, Celia Pendarvis swung round to greet me and my heart thumped. I felt winded, as if struck by a physical blow. She was smiling, waiting to be introduced, and Pierre stepped forward. 'Mrs Pendarvis, may I introduce Mrs Barnard?' Curtsying, I stared back into her laughing eyes.

'I wondered who it was peeping at us through the banisters. How lovely to see you again. Are you enjoying your stay here in Fosse?'

She was not how I expected her. She seemed frivolous, turning away, ready not to give me a second glance. She stood smiling at her husband, her brown curls bouncing as she tossed her head. He held up his glass, his long fingers grasping the stem, both of them seemingly disinterested. I felt immediate disappointment, a sense of deflation. It was hard to grasp my thoughts but it was as if I expected some bond of sisterhood. I had felt so drawn to her yet she had looked straight through me, and I stared after them, my heart hammering.

Swags of greenery decorated the drawing room, vases of flowers, the candelabras fully lit. Dancing was to be on the marble floor in the hall, supper served in the dining room. Already people were drifting out on to the terrace. Pierre drew me into the moonlight and I breathed in the scent of lavender. 'What is it?' he whispered.

'Pierre, you know the portrait of Celia Pendarvis in the hall of Admiral House? The earrings in that painting are my earrings – the ones from my *parure*.' He blanched, suddenly understanding the value of my set. 'They're the exact sapphire blue of her dress – yet she's wearing simple diamonds.'

'Perhaps she doesn't have them with her?'

I shook my head. 'She has the perfect earrings but she isn't wearing them. Yet she chose to wear them for her portrait.'

Pierre seemed mystified about matching earrings. 'You think she's not wearing them because she knows who you are?'

'How well do you know her?'

'Quite well. I've met Celia Pendarvis many times, but not Captain Pendarvis. He's often away – when he's not on board ship he spends a lot of time up at the Admiralty.'

The dancing was about to start, the musicians taking their places, and I shook my head. 'She can't know who I am. Lady Pendarvis doesn't know. We're still keeping it secret. It's not that she's *not* wearing them – Mrs Pengelly says she never wears them – it's more . . .' I could hardly get my head around it. 'Why did she wear them for her portrait if she hates her father so much? She must have had plenty of other earrings to choose from. Or it is just a coincidence she has an identical pair!'

The music started and couples began taking their places. Celia and Edward Pendarvis were next to Rose and Sir James, William was leading Elowyn. The gold on the uniforms flashed, the silk gowns swirling elegantly. Lady Pendarvis, Reverend Bloomsdale and Billy were in deep discussion.

'A coincidence – your earrings being so similar?'

'Why did you say it like that? What are you thinking?'

'That it is no more a coincidence than me meeting you unexpectedly on the coach. I have never told you this, but meeting you was my sole intent. I hurried to that coach . . . I made the excuse of needing to return Sir Alex's chronometer but in reality, I had been all but summoned. I needed to be assured of your welfare.'

'You were summoned? By who?'

'An unsigned letter arrived – a mere note, containing a ticket for the Fosse coach. It looked to be written in haste and wasn't signed. I forget the exact words but it urged me to *look to the welfare of a French lady as in need of my help as any other of the prisoners I take care of*. I thought it was from the landlady of the inn. We often pass the time of day and she knows me well. But now I'm not so sure. I see it as just the first in a string of coincidences.'

'Like Mrs Munroe being the only person in Fosse who could recognise me? And Mrs Pengelly knowing Alice Reith, my only friend?'

My heart froze, a sudden certainty. Those laughing eyes in Celia Pendarvis's portrait were saying something. Portraits were painted to be seen – clothes, jewellery, position, wealth. To be hung on the wall for everyone to admire. Celia Cavendish wore my earrings because she *wanted* them seen. She was showing everyone she had them in case anyone came looking for them.

I stood watching the room. The dancing had ended, Pierre greeted by an endless stream of friends. People were spilling out on to the terrace, Celia and Edward holding up their glasses to Rose and Sir James, and I thought I might faint. There, right in front of me, hidden in plain sight, were the familiar long fingers I had watched with such disgust. 'Pierre, look! Edward Pendarvis... can you see his hands? I always notice hands.'

In the moonlight Edward Pendarvis's fine tapering fingers held his glass to his lips. He saw us looking and a flicker crossed his eyes. 'Men can grow beards and wear their hair long,' I whispered. 'They can pretend to be drunk...dribble and spit...use foul language, but fingers are hard to disguise – even filthy ones with dirty, badly bitten nails. Especially in summer when you can't wear gloves.'

Pierre seemed puzzled. He drew a deep breath. 'Good Lord, I think you're right – it's his hands. Thomas Pearce... with us from the very start.'

'He was watching the madhouse, he followed us, boarded the same coach. He must have been waiting for Marcel Rablais.'

'He's one of Madame Lefèvre's men?'

'He attacked me outside Coombe House. Why just there?'

'Because he knew you'd be taken in by Mrs Pengelly.'

I nodded. 'And she would call upon the only friend I had – Alice Reith, whose husband just happens to be the best attorney in Cornwall. Pierre...he's watching us. He knows we've guessed.'

'It doesn't make sense.'

'It does, Pierre, but it's not just him – it's Celia Pendarvis, too. She's spent the last seven years looking for Billy's sister. She even sent men to Ireland. She won't give up until she finds who she's looking for. What if it's she who has been searching for me? Oh my goodness...he's coming over.'

Edward Pendarvis, dashing, handsome, adored only son of Sir Alex and Lady Pendarvis, held out his arm to Celia, and started walking across the terrace towards us. His voice was educated, refined, his eyes sharp. 'Would you care to join us in the rose garden.' It was not a question but a command.

Pierre's hand tightened. 'We certainly would.'

The scent of roses hung in the air, the moon streaming through the arbours, bathing the flowers in silver light. The sundial glinted, Edward Pendarvis's voice a whisper. 'What I'm about to tell you must remain between us. Understood?' We nodded and he drew slightly closer. 'When the war broke out, my cousins were in danger and I helped them flee. As you know, I'm half French and speak the language fluently. Between us, we set up an agency to free others in hiding – those fleeing for their lives. My cousins became scouts, then spies, sending back any information they could. We grew in numbers and were soon recruited by the government in London. This April, one of our agents' lodgings in Truro was searched. Nothing was found, but it was clear someone was on to us. We're part of a network of spies collecting information from all over Europe. We have agents in Ireland, across France to Italy and Switzerland. This war will be won on intelligence, every bit as much as by the might of our navy and armies.'

Celia Pendarvis stood by her husband, tall, imposing, far from frivolous. 'I've been searching for you, Madeleine, for almost seven years. When the man I employed found you, he watched you through the tiny gap in your pigpen. His opinion was that you were severely *affected*... that you showed clear signs of madness... and we thought only to get you to a place of safety. On the same day we heard our premises in Guernsey had been searched we had confirmation a French spy was active in our area.'

'A coincidence? One you thought you could use?'

'Exactly so. Finding you gave us an idea. We set a trap. We

sent a letter to an address in Guernsey that we knew would soon be searched. We signed it from *Marcel Rablais* and said you'd been found and that you were soon to be freed. And we addressed it to the one name we knew would bring the Republican spies on our trail out into the open.'

I stared into her unwavering eyes. 'You are Cécile Lefèvre?'

'There is no Cécile Lefèvre. But her name alone was like offering meat to a starving dog.'

Apart from his hands, a man less like Thomas Pearce could not be imagined. 'Once we'd sent the letter, I stayed on the moor to watch the madhouse. The name Marcel Rablais was fabricated yet it took barely two weeks for a man calling himself Marcel Rablais to turn up. We had no idea what he would do, but we suspected he would see you for himself, then wait and watch. We'd sent a letter to the proprietor with the address of the linhay hoping to lure him there. We needed to know who his contacts were, and how he gets to and from France.'

Pierre looked furious. 'Rather callous, if I may say. You had Madeleine's life in your hands!'

'I understand. And yes, it was underhand. I agree we were using her, which is why we kept as close a watch as we could.'

'And why you sent for me. That note was from you, I take it?'

'It was. We knew this man would search the address we gave him. He changed his name to Barnard because he believed the real Marcel Rablais might be on his trail.'

'Which is why he hid, and why he didn't stay in the inn.'

'Yes, Mrs Pelligrew. Believe us, our intention was only to

flush him out and see you safely out of the madhouse. We had a comfortable home prepared for you, with servants to look after you.' His smile was rueful, a shrug of his elegant gold braid. 'But we did *not* account for your clear state of mind – nor for Pierre falling so deeply in love with you. Our plans were in immediate jeopardy. I saw at once you were not to be hurried off to some place of safety so, instead, we had to make sure Eva Pengelly took you in.'

'Where the cook would recognise me and I'd be told my only friend was happily married to the one man in Cornwall who could help me the most.'

The moonlight caught Celia's earrings, the brilliance of her smile. 'Nor did we realise that you would *understand* everything quite so completely. It was almost intuitive, like you could read our minds. Dangerous for us, as it's proved.'

'Did you expect me to be forced on to the ship?'

Edward Pendarvis shook his head. 'Not at all. They kept that from me. I was horrified when they forced you aboard. I was going to jump with you, although I knew you could swim and Celia was watching from *L'Aigrette*. She would have dived in to save you. *L'Aigrette* was waiting to follow – Jago about to join the ship. I saw Pierre rowing out and I had to decide – jump with you, leave you for Celia, or hope Pierre was a good rower. Fortunately, that proved to be the case.' His voice was soft, a tinge of a Cornish accent.

'Jago is one of you?'

A brief nod. 'Now we're discovered we'll have to disband. We've remained undetected for *seven years*, yet just now, I saw you'd seen through my disguise. We wanted you on that coach,

Pierre, so I had to take the chance. We've never met and I thought it safe, and we thought Madeleine would be in no fit state to notice.'

'It was your hands. You have fine, tapering fingers. I first noticed the likeness in your portrait in your mother's hall, something I recognised but couldn't place. A clue... like the earrings you were wearing in your portrait, Celia, but you didn't wear tonight. Two small clues that suddenly made sense.'

She flashed her smile. It was strange how compelling her looks were. Not classically beautiful, but something far more thrilling. Intelligent, far-sighted. A woman who would lure her father's guards away. 'A French set of jewels my father said he *stumbled* across. I was given the earrings for my eighteenth birthday. I loved them and used to wear them all the time. It was several years before I understood where they'd come from.' Her eyes were bright in the moonlight, sharply focused. 'Mother has the necklace and rings, my sister Charity has the brooch and my youngest sisters were given the hair clasps.'

'The colour of your dress, yet you didn't wear them because you never speak to your father. I know what he subjected you to – how you knew where to look for me.'

'You are quite astonishing, Madeleine. How you know so much is uncanny. But you're right. My father subjected me to the same forced abduction. Maddison's Madhouse was to be my new home, but I was more fortunate than you. I escaped... and when my father returned to London, Ella let me into the house and I searched it from top to bottom. I felt compelled to find out all about you. Yet all the evidence showed you had returned to your family after a *short illness*. I read his letters and followed Father's false trail. Everything clearly stated you'd been discharged and had remarried, but then I studied that portrait of you. I could just make out the shoulder brooch on your shawl and I called for a ladder so I could study it more closely.'

'You recognised my jewellery?'

'Yes. Straight away I realised you must be held somewhere and Father had kept your jewellery, dividing it among us like the spoils of war. I knew you couldn't have gone home – not willingly. Nor had you been discharged, because if you had, you'd have come back to Pendenning to claim your jewels.'

'So you wore my earrings in your portrait – to prove you had them. Two portraits with women wearing jewels from the same set. How very clever.'

Another flash of her radiant smile. 'It's been a long search, Madeleine, and I can't tell you how thrilled I am to see you so unaffected. I know what you've suffered, and I admire you so much. Please believe me that our intention was only to see you housed in a comfortable home, not catapult you into such danger.'

'Yet I will repay your kindness by seeing your father in court. The evidence is overwhelming . . . he'll stand trial for duplicitous lending, conspiracy to defraud and ordering the murder of Joshua Pelligrew.'

Her voice hardened. 'Among other murders. Too many have suffered at his hands. When we left Admiral House tonight, we heard he'd been arrested – which is why Matthew isn't here.'

'They've arrested Sulio Denville as well. He murdered my husband. Not Phillip Randall.'

A look of disgust crossed Celia's face. She shook her head. 'Randall was equally guilty – the man was evil.'

Edward twisted a rose free and handed it to his wife. 'We kept Marcel Rablais waiting . . . no one came to the linhay. He needed money and so we kept him dangling. I fabricated the diamond story to ensure I went with them.'

'They weren't real diamonds, and there was no woman murdered?'

'Indeed, Madeleine. All fabricated. Just access to a printing press to print a few posters.'

'How very useful.'

A flash of his smile. 'It is, Pierre. People believe what they read, even if you tear it up in front of them. Marcel needed money and another pair of hands to sail the ship. I told them I would pay on arrival but I believe they intended to kill us both. Certainly they'd have killed me and taken the diamonds. Only once we were in the harbour, I pretended to fall overboard, and swam safely away. I was acting drunk and they presumed I'd drowned, but I stayed to watch the ship – to see who came and went.'

'You planted *false* codes to throw them off the scent and now you know who they are?'

'Yes, Pierre. We do. We've put names to the faces of people we believed we could trust. And it's proved invaluable. It's proved we can no longer work the way we've been working. We must think of other methods to get our information through. Our old systems are too obvious, and too dangerous for our men. So, in a way, it's for the best.' He flashed his dashing smile once more. 'Disband before they catch us. Always the best policy.'

A breeze blew across the sea, rustling the leaves. High on the cliff, the moon flooded the linhay and Pierre slipped his arm through mine. He was silent for a moment, as if turning something over in his mind. When he spoke, his voice held energy, a new vibrancy. 'Well, you know what they say: one door closes and another opens. Did you know I'm to be an apprentice watchmaker? I'm already in touch with several watchmakers all over Europe. In fact, we correspond on a regular basis.'

Edward's eyes sharpened, a sudden stiffness to his shoulders. 'Go on...'

'We send each other a steady stream of instructions – diagrams, whole pages of intricate drawings with very detailed directions. And if some of these instructions just happened to contain coded words, would that help?'

Edward Pendarvis blew out his breath, a slight shake of his head. 'Ingenious. A group of like-minded watchmakers sharing their work? Pierre, I salute you. It's utterly ingenious.' Glancing at Celia, he caught her nod of approval. 'What an evening this has turned out to be.'

A rueful smile. 'You'd trust a Republican officer in the French navy?'

Edward Pendarvis nodded, his face serious. 'We investigated you when you became agent for my father. My mother asked her brothers, and many in London could furnish the details of what had happened to you – and who you really

447

were. But you've always kept your cards close to your chest — never a hint that you weren't a committed Republican officer. We had to take a chance, and I'm glad we did. Getting you on to that coach was incredibly fortuitous.'

Pierre put my fingers to his lips. 'Fortuitous? Maybe, but I would call it fate — the inevitable drawing together of two souls destined to meet.' He glanced towards the house. 'Maybe we should continue this conversation some other time?'

A group was spilling from the terrace: Lady Pendarvis, Sir Alex, Sir James and Rose, all laughing and pointing in our direction. 'I've found them . . . Here they are.' Rose Polcarrow stood smiling back at us as Reverend Bloomsdale stepped forward.

'For the sake of my sanity . . . for just one moment's peace so I can enjoy the ball, my answer is *yes*. All day, it's been utterly relentless. Yes, yes . . . to everyone else who wants to ask. *Yes*. Not tomorrow, because the bishop must be asked, but Tuesday. Shall we say eleven o'clock, on Tuesday? Will that finally put an end to everyone asking? Mrs Pengelly?' He swung round, his white hair and gold waistcoat shining in the moonlight. 'First, Mrs Pengelly and Rowan, then the King of the Fete *commanded* it. Then Lady Polcarrow, then Lady Pendarvis, then Elowyn . . . Mrs Reith . . . Mrs Munroe . . . and just about everyone who gave you a witness statement. Everyone determined I should have no peace until I agree. So the answer is *yes*.'

I must have looked strangely blank as he shook his head. 'A licence, my dear. For you to marry Captain Pierre here, among your friends, before he goes back to Bodmin?'

Tears filled my eyes, a sudden rush of giddiness. 'But . . . it's not that simple . . .'

'I think it might be . . .' Pierre was looking at me like he did in my dreams. Loving, mischievous, his eyes burning. Falling to one knee, he held my hand to his lips. 'Madeleine, dearest, darling Madeleine. I love you more than life itself. I will honour you, cherish you, love you until my dying breath. Will you take a humble watchmaker to be your husband? Will you do me the very great honour of becoming my wife?'

I could hardly speak for the burning in my heart. For my tears. For the immense happiness I could not have believed possible. 'Yes, Pierre . . . I will . . . a thousand times, I will.' Amid the clapping I felt myself lifted in strong arms, Pierre holding me tightly, swirling me round. We came to a dizzy standstill and his arms closed round me.

Eva Pengelly smiled at Rose. 'Lady Polcarrow wants to host your wedding breakfast here. And Mrs Munroe has the menu all planned.'

Moonlight flooded their sea of smiling faces. Lady Pendarvis held out her hands, Sir Alex rushing forward to congratulate us. Everyone filled with joy, congratulating us and wishing us well. Reverend Bloomsdale glanced up at the two beaming faces looking down from their arched casement. 'I'm not being precipitous, am I? Not misunderstanding your wishes? I presume you're wanting to adopt Opie and Rowan as your children?'

We spoke as one, not needing to confer. 'Yes, absolutely yes, if we can? They've grown so dear to us. They seem already . . . that is . . . we couldn't part with them. Not now.'

'Then I shall send word to Opie's aunt. I see no reason why not.'

'But we need to ask Billy. Where's Billy? And Elowyn, too.'

'I'm here . . .' Billy stepped forward, his hands held against his chest. 'From the depths of my heart all I can say is my sister's a lucky girl. I can think of no two people I would rather entrust her to . . . And for my part, I consider it an honour to be joining your family.'

They returned to the lights and music, the laughter echoing through the open windows. Pierre drew me to him, and we stood staring out across the moonlit rooftops, down to the ships in the harbour and out to the silver sea. 'I meant what I said about two souls destined to meet. I shall always be grateful for that scribbled note, yet when I saw you on that coach I knew it was fate that had brought us together. I had been sent to help you. Your suffering seemed so cruel. I've been living a half-life, Madeleine. Going to sea for my father, serving my country. Going through the motions of life, but not living it. Yet when I saw you on that coach, it was as if my soul awoke. I thought only of your welfare. I began living for the first time. Like emerging from sleep and waking to a whole new world. A glorious new world.'

His arms were strong, holding me as if they would never let me go, and I leaned against his broad chest. My watchmaker and spy. My one true love. Emerging from my incarceration to a whole new world. To a glorious new life.

His voice was soft, no more than a whisper. 'I don't come to you entirely empty-handed, my darling . . . I have a wedding present for you. Something very precious to us both. It has no roof and is tumbling down. It's open to the sky and filled with beetles and butterflies. It's full of ox-eye daisies, scarlet poppies... lupins and the scent of thyme and honeysuckle. The wind howls through it... the rain lashes it. The sheep shelter in it. It's all I have – apart from you and Rowan and Opie.'

'The linhay is yours? You *own* the linhay?'

The breeze blew against his cheeks, ruffling his hair. 'Two years ago I made a doll's house for a very sick girl – and furnished it with everything she asked for. She loved that doll's house and played with it right up until she died in her father's arms. A year ago, her father joined me in the linhay. He said he wanted to repay me for my kindness and I shook my head. I told him I wanted nothing except the peace and beauty found in the linhay – the sight and smell of sea, the view, the flowers. Six months ago, he negotiated its lease and bought it on my behalf. An attorney wrote out the contract and I found myself holding the deeds of a tumbled-down linhay and the quarter-acre field surrounding it.

'That day, when I turned and saw you standing behind me, I was imagining you there. Imagining it was our home. That we'd replaced the roof and rebuilt the walls. That our bedroom overlooked the sea.'

'We shall rebuild it,' I whispered. 'I saw it in a dream. The breeze was blowing the curtain, the sea stretching for miles around us. I saw a vase of ox-eye daisies... and you were ... kissing me.'

'Was I?' His laugh sent tingles racing through me, his lips brushing my forehead. 'Like this?'

'No,' I whispered. 'Not like that.'

'Like this, then?' His lips lingered over mine and I shook my head. 'Oh dear . . . maybe more like this?' I shook my head again, thrilling at his touch. 'I see . . . perhaps a little more like this?'

His kiss took hold and I could not answer. But yes, my darling Pierre . . . exactly . . . and completely wonderfully . . . just . . . like . . . that.

Snippets cut from The Courier
and pasted into Eva Pengelly's diary

14th August. Coombe House, River Street, is to be let. Interested parties please apply to:

    Mr J. Danvers of Danvers & Danvers, Quay Street.

8th September. The marriage took place today in St Fimbarrus Church between Tamsin Fry of Coombe House and Oliver Jenkins of 22, High Street, Fosse.

    Officiated by Reverend Bloomsdale.

12th September. Coombe House has been let to Mr and Mrs Morcum Calstock. Mr Calstock is an Architect and will be putting up his plate to conduct business from these premises.

14th September. A headstone has been commissioned for Mr Opie Burrows, late of this Parish. The dedication service will take place on Sunday 28th.

9th November. News from the Bodmin Assizes. Sir Charles Cavendish has been found guilty of duplicitous lending, conspiracy to defraud, and ordering the murder of Joshua Pelligrew. He has been sentenced to fourteen years' deportation to Botany Bay.

Sulio Denville, convicted murderer, was sentenced to hang. However, his sentence was commuted to fourteen years' deportation after turning King's Evidence against Sir Charles. Both will be sent to a prison hulk in London to await transfer to Botany Bay; both men are to have their property and land forfeited to the crown.

1st December. An application has been submitted to make safe the walls of the disused linhay on Cliff Road. Further applications to re-roof the building will follow.

14th December. A rich seam of copper has been found in Wheal Elizabeth. Sir James and his committee are delighted, calling it a truly magnificent find.

21st December. Engineer William Cotterell and his wife Elowyn announce the arrival of their son, James William. The baptism is to take place on Christmas Eve.

And just so you know. Mr Pitt was immediately evicted from Sir James's side of the bed and, when not scowling at the new kittens, divides his time between Mrs Munroe in the kitchen, Sam in the butler's pantry and Eva Pengelly in the East Wing of Polcarrow House, where Madeleine de la Croix, Rowan and Opie are frequent and cherished visitors.

Acknowledgements

The Cornish Captive is my sixth book and follows the story in *The Captain's Girl*. Although I have waited until now to tell Madeleine's story I am delighted that she has finally found her voice. I had enormous fun researching 'madhouses' and the shocking treatment the poor inmates received, and I'd like thank Rowan Musser and all the archivists in Kresen Kernow for their enthusiastic help in my research.

I am honoured to have such a supportive and talented team alongside me: thank you to my editor Susannah Hamilton at Atlantic Books whose sure pen has, once again, crafted my manuscript into the book it is. Thank you to Sarah Hodgson, Poppy Mostyn-Owen, Hanna Kenne, Sophie Walker and Kate Straker, among so many, and to my copy-editor, Alison Tulett for her eagle eyes.

As always, I would like to thank Teresa Chris, my agent, for her unstinting support, her expertise, and her unwavering enthusiasm for my books. So, too, I would like to thank my

455

husband, Damian, for his endless encouragement, his patience, and, quite possibly, the best coffee in the world.

The history and research behind my books can be found on my website – nicolapryce.co.uk. Or please join me on my FaceBook Page: Nicola Pryce-Author, where I would be delighted to hear from you.

Thank you for choosing to read *The Cornish Captive*.